Bones of Rebellion

The Generations of Noah Series:

Blood of Adam – the story of Japheth and Denah

Bones of Rebellion – the story of Ham and Naomi

Breath of Knowledge – the story of Shem and Eran

Bones of Rebellion

Rachel S. Neal

A Novel

Generations of Noah

Book II

withallmyheART

Printed in the United States

To Rebecca and Debbie,

my sisters, my friends

and

To Ralph and Sara,

for loving me as your own

"Come, let's build a tower that reaches

to the heavens..."

~Genesis 11:4~

If we deliberately keep on sinning after

we have received the knowledge of truth, no

sacrifices for sin remain, only a fearful

expectation of judgment...

~Hebrews 10:26, 27~

Historical Timeline*

4004 BC: Adam is formed

2948 BC: Noah is born

2348 BC: The Flood

2242 BC: The earth is divided by language

* Dates estimated

Chapter One

A single scream ricocheted off the rocky streambed, muting the playful banter among the women and children. Naomi sucked in a breath and turned to the source of the cry, instinctively clutching a handful of sodden linens over her heart.

Mara, the frightened young mother, stood on the bank with one hand over her mouth and the other pointing to the stream. Naomi jerked her eyes from the shore and scanned the waters for a child venturing too deep or struggling to stand against a tugging current. She saw nothing. Nothing but Mara's boy, safely perched on a stone, hurling pebbles at the opposite bank.

The dozen or so other women stood still, like Naomi, arms laden with dripping laundry, eyes scanning the waters for the unseen danger. Even the youngest children stopped their play amid the mossy stones. The stream gurgled around their legs, with only the plink, plink, plink of the boy's pebbles interrupting its cadence. Confused expressions waited for an explanation.

Naomi didn't have one. "What is it Mara? What's wrong?"

Mara's hand slid over her chin and caught on her throat. "Look," she said. She pointed at her boy, still firmly in place on the rock.

"He's alright, Mara," Naomi said. "He's safe."

Mara pushed her head side to side, as if the air itself was fighting against her. Her eyes remained fixed on her son. "No," she said. "No. Look." She barely had the breath to make the words audible.

Naomi turned back to the boy. He chucked small stones into the water, his little arm winding up and flinging them as far as he could. Naomi watched one hit a rock and bounce onto the far shore.

The woods rustled just beyond the stone's landing.

Naomi's scalp prickled as shadows shifted, then converged, thrusting through the foliage into the light.

A dragon. The mother pointed not at her boy, but at the great lizard capturing her little one's attention.

"Go 'way," the boy yelled, aiming another stone in the dragon's direction.

Naomi's heart hammered inside her chest. The intruder was a juvenile, its earthy toned hide still bearing verdant splotches of camouflage. On hind legs, it stood only a head taller than she, but this was one of the great lizard-dragons, the feared ones. Still an inexperienced hunter, its dangling front legs already had the power to restrain prey long enough for spiked rows of teeth to take hold. There was another reason her heart pounded against her ribs, seeking escape, however. The dragon was too young to be on his own.

The great beast sniffed the air and whipped its tail along the bank, flattening the underbrush. Dark eyes probed the line of women where they stood frozen, defenseless. "God of the heavens," Naomi prayed. "Help us."

A child whimpered, stirring a reaction from the mothers. They turned to Naomi. She pointed to a place on the grass near the tree line and forced a reassuring nod. "Yes," she said. "Go." Tremors traversed her spine. Naomi pressed her heels into the creek bed to keep her knees from unhinging. They had all practiced this drill. It did nothing to remove the fear.

One by one the mothers gathered their children and stepped out of the water, scarcely rippling the current. They knelt in a circle, hip to hip, locking their arms across the shoulders of the women beside them. The children hunkered down inside the protective ring, babies in the arms of older siblings.

Naomi couldn't drop to her knees with the others, not yet, not until the boy was tucked inside the circle, too. His chubby legs wobbled on the rock, his arms stretched towards his mother. Mara's legs were rooted to the earth in fear.

Naomi breathed in and out through her teeth, summoning resolve before stepping toward the boy. Toward the dragon. It snorted and whipped its head around to face her. Naomi gasped, then spoke gently, as if to one of the children. "Go away. Leave us in peace. We mean you no harm."

She took a step. Then another.

The dragon cocked its head and huffed. Naomi willed her legs to move. When she reached the rock, the boy clasped his arms around her neck, legs around her waist. She wrapped him tightly against her chest, pressing his frightened heart against her own. Holding her breath, she backed away from the dragon.

The beast watched them for a moment, then dipped his head and slopped water from the stream.

Only a few more steps.

The mossy stones near the bank caught her off guard. Her foot slipped. The boy wailed as she jerked herself upright, his cries startling the dragon. It reared back and stomped the earth before retreating into the dense foliage.

Mara splashed into the stream. Naomi shoved the crying child into her arms and pushed them up the bank. She scrambled to reach the top herself when abruptly the boy's crying stopped and there was silence. Dreadful silence. Naomi turned from the child's fixed stare, back to the far shore.

The great lizard's mother.

The she-dragon raised her head and bellowed. The whiny hiss engulfed Naomi's senses and dissolved her joints. She crumpled, sealing her head in her arms, willing her body to disappear among the stones, a vain attempt to outwit a beast whose baby had been threatened. The mother wouldn't be fooled, she knew.

And mothers always defend their children.

Naomi compressed her limbs, tightening her body into one mass, her breath skimming the water in jagged ripples. "God, help me," she prayed. "God help me."

When the splashing stopped, Naomi peered between her arms. Three dagger tipped toes caged her on either side and she was no longer in the light of the sun. The dragon hovered, sniffing the scent along her spine, sucking her hair into its nostrils. Foul breath sent a new wave of shivers through her body that Naomi tried to control but couldn't. Anticipation clung to dread. She clenched her eyes and waited.

The dragon nudged her with its snout.

Then again, harder, the force tipping her over into the water. She screamed for the God of the heavens.

The dragon reared back, jaws wide, releasing a penetrating wail of conquest.

Naomi sucked down her last breath as the teeth descended.

Death didn't come.

Instead, the dragon jerked its head away from her and violently shook it back and forth. The smooth shaft of an arrow protruded from its snout. In moments, it wasn't the only arrow, but one of many that whizzed over Naomi's head and pierced the beast's hide. The shrill hiss became anguished as barbs of defeat ripped through flesh.

Naomi followed the arrows' path back to a man armed with a bow. He fired in rapid succession while striding toward the stream, determination propelling him forward.

The archer was Nimrod, her grandson.

He stopped on the bank and faced the dragon. Naomi started to rise but he shook his head. "No, stay there. Don't move." The calm tone of his voice didn't lessen the ferocity of his gaze.

Her limbs ached to unfurl and run to his side, to gather him in her arms and lead him from danger. She didn't, lifting only her head to watch. And to pray. Nimrod was no longer one of her little ones, one whom she needed to protect. He was a man. He was her protector now.

With the last arrow aloft, Nimrod dropped the bow, withdrew a spear from the quiver, and stepped into the stream.

The dragon whined in pain, in anger, in fear. Poison from the arrows mingled with her blood, confusing her equilibrium. She staggered as Nimrod danced around her, until his weapon found her heart, draining her life with one last hiss of defeat. The clear water cascading into her prostrate body retreated downstream, thick and murky red.

Naomi tried to stand and found limbs unable to bear her weight. Nimrod strode to her side and lifted her from the water, hugging her into his warm chest before placing her on the grass. Mara dropped down beside her with the boy in her arms. His face had no color, but he was alive. Mara was alive. All of them, alive.

"Thanks be to our protector," Mara said. "Thanks be to your Nimrod."

Naomi grasped her arm. "And to God," she reminded. "Thanks be to our God."

Tears burned in Naomi's eyes and she swallowed hard to

control the flow as she relaxed into the grass and peered into the heavens. Her life had been spared, once again. Over one hundred years ago she had escaped death, surviving as the breath of life on earth was extinguished beneath the waters of judgment. She had been saved from God's great flood. So had a pair of young dragons.

She didn't fear them then, on the ark of her father-in-law Noah. Beasts of all kinds existed in harmony, the remnant sleeping in peace with no tumult of kind against kind.

It didn't last, not once they left the confines of the vessel. The creatures were awakened from their passivity. Fear and danger resumed their purchase on a land scrubbed free of all life. It was kill or be killed now.

The she-dragon was simply protecting her baby. Naomi had been doing the same thing since stepping from the ark, seeking survival of her children, survival of mankind. Beasts of the earth defended their little ones. So did the ones created in God's image. Ham, her husband, would destroy any life threatening his own offspring.

So would she.

Protect. Preserve. Defend. Destroy.

It's the way things were now.

▲

"Are you hurt?" Cush, Naomi's firstborn son, dismounted his horse with a thump. He dropped his arm over her shoulders and gave her a squeeze before wiping a mud streak from her chin. He smelled like fresh sage and cooking fires, like the security of home.

"No. God was gracious. All of us had a good scare, though. You heard about Abed's son?"

Cush's eyes found Mara, her head on her husband's shoulder,

the boy cradled between them. He nodded. "Uncle Shem's kin. Abed lays bricks at the tower. That's his firstborn."

"Yes, and he's a brave little man, trying to protect us. Abed is raising him well. He deserves the honor his son has placed in his lap today. I hope the boy recovers enough to enjoy it, too."

Cush let a smile creep up his cheeks. "You don't have to remind me to divert praises Nimrod's direction, Mother. He'll get his share of glory for weeks to come, I'm sure." He turned toward the clump of women and children surrounding his firstborn.

Naomi slid her hand into Cush's. "He saved my life, that son of yours. Your mother would be in the belly of the dragon if he hadn't arrived so quickly."

Nimrod stood with his hands on his hips, a child dangling from each sculpted arm. Wet black ringlets curled around his face, a face scrubbed clean of the dragon's blood. His smile was easy and he laughed at the young ones vying for his attention. It wasn't the first time her grandson stood amidst an appreciative throng, lapping up adulation like a cat at the cow's udder.

Cush squeezed her hand then turned his attention to the men gathered in the streambed. Many of them heard the scream of the young mother and the cry of the dragon rattling the treetops. They came with Nimrod from the tar pit nearby, standing back while her grandson took action. Now they wielded their weapons fearlessly, hacking the dragon into chunks so she could be removed from the water supply. The joints would be disconnected to keep the bones intact but the bulk of the meat and organs needed to be removed first. The poisoned flesh wasn't edible. It would be offered as a sacrifice to the God of their fathers.

"Cush is here!" The men spotted her son on the bank and stopped their labors to cheer in one loud voice. Naomi's eyes immediately found Nimrod.

Her grandson's broad smile flickered, a flame caught in the draft. His dark eyes narrowed as he watched praise fall on a man who was making stew while he risked his own life blood. Then as quickly as his joy faltered, it stabilized, his features resuming a pleased expression.

Fathers share the honor of a son's triumph. It was customary. A child raised well was his father's doing. He was a reflection of the man who gave him life. Firstborns, especially, were regarded as the measure of the family character and bore the weight of maintaining respectability. Fathers reported the successes of their offspring as they sat around the fire pits and smoked, and as they toiled in the fields or ambled through the markets. Business deals and marriage arrangements were made and broken on the reputation of a man's boy. A practice Nimrod despised.

Cush and Nimrod walked separate paths. Her son, calm and mild, struggled to raise a boy driven with fire and ambition. Fearless and strong, Nimrod struggled to respect a father who preferred a cooking pot over a fine hewed bow.

Naomi sighed. This wasn't new in her family, fathers and firstborn sons viewing the world from opposite shores, sharing little common ground beyond the ties of bloodline. Cush's temperament stood at odds with the other two, a spring breeze between the two storms, as if Ham's seed skipped a generation to replicate itself in his grandson.

Cush delighted in the tradition that raised the hackles on his son. He graciously stood among the men, soaking up their words. "You raised a fine son, Cush," they said, kissing him on the cheek and slapping his back, careful not to soil his clean tunic with the dragon remains covering their own.

Her son smiled deeply. "Yes, indeed. Nimrod makes his father proud again. He served us honorably today."

Nimrod turned his back to his father, the children receiving his full attention. Anyone looking at him would assume he was content in spirit. Naomi knew better. She saw through the mask disguising his frustration. It was a familiar one, one he used to cover his disappointments and irritations. Few understood his real emotions. She did, of course. A grandmother knows such things, and she knew he suppressed anger towards his father and the men intent on garnishing Cush's head with praise. Tradition tainted the glory of Nimrod's valor.

Naomi feared the resentment lurking beneath his congenial demeanor. She feared his heart found fulfillment in his own success, leaving little room for the ways and words of his God. 'He will rebel' was the name Cush gave his firstborn when the infant refused to take his mother's milk for his first day of life. She feared her beloved grandson would grow into his name.

Chapter Two

Ham drove his knife through the scaly hide, severing tendons and ligaments until most of the meat separated from the bone. He tossed the flesh onto a table of stones with the other pieces and rolled the chunk of tail bone through the grass toward the feet of his wife. Naomi glanced at the piece, then back at him. A smudge of dirt rose on her cheek as she smiled. Her tunic was a mosaic of lizard bits and a crimson smear traversed her forehead where she wiped hair from around her face.

Ham smiled back. The bride of his youth would have complained incessantly about the nature of this task. This Naomi, seasoned with time, didn't complain when her hands were soiled and her garments glistened with the slimy ooze. The struggle to survive hardened her over the years, strengthened her. Her priorities shifted and the petty jealousies of her past remained buried. He had always been proud of this wife that captured his eye so long ago. Never as much as now. Staring down the throat of a dragon in the morning, stripping its remains by evening. He had been wise giving her his promise of faithfulness.

"Will you dump the buckets, please, Ham?" The pail at Naomi's feet was full again, filled with the tiny remnants of beast that she painstakingly peeled off the bones for the sacrifice. His daughters-in-law filled buckets, too, and a hill of stripped skeleton parts grew behind them. Ham grabbed the full buckets and heaved the contents onto the altar. The blackened stones were covered in the dragon's stringy remains.

The altar sat in the middle of a grassy field, with the mighty Euphrates flowing to the sea on one end, the rising tower to God on the other. Ham resumed his position near Naomi and scanned all directions, observing the people of Noah coming together, three lines of offspring, intermingling, one cohesive clan. It was difficult to imagine there were only eight of them once. He and his brothers, Shem and Japheth, their wives, and his parents were alone preserved when the earth was covered in the flood waters. Now there were far more than a thousand people in the fertile plain of Shinar. Fertile, not only in producing crops. His wife tended as many delivering mothers as he to expectant livestock.

"Word spread quickly, it appears. Look at them, Naomi. Dropping everything to come hear about the dragon. It'll be a good crowd."

"A good scare will do that. It's unfortunate it takes me almost being eaten alive to draw such numbers to a sacrifice."

Ham caught her eyes. "They know how you speak, wife. From your heart. As you retell your adventure, there won't be a sound in this field. They come for that, too. They come to hear and feel the passion."

Naomi shook her head. "I want them to come to honor God, to appreciate what he has done, to worship him above all else."

"God gave us Nimrod. He deserves a little honor, too, don't you think?"

His wife's eyes misted as she nodded. "Yes, of course. He saved my life." She smiled at him, her familiar constrained smile that snuck out when she was so proud she could hardly contain herself from dancing and carrying on. The smile, if she allowed it to grow, would swallow her face and tears would flow, too. She kept it contained now, though, as the people arrived. "And Abed, too."

Ham's gaze rested on Abed. The young father beamed, his pride pulling his spine straight and his lips into a toothy grin. The young father had reason to be proud of course, his firstborn already bringing him honor at such a young age.

A twinge of frustration accompanied the thought. Ham's own firstborn would not have demonstrated such bravery. It was rarely Cush rising to a place of honor. Ham shared in the glory of his own firstborn on only a few occasions and they were forced affairs, not outright glorious celebrations as the one he prepared for now. Still, he had little room for disappointment. There were all those years Before, before the flood, when Naomi's womb was closed. He wondered then if he would even have a son. He couldn't see that it was God himself who kept his wife empty. Innocence was meant to be born in a land stripped of sin.

His brother Japheth's firstborn came soon after the ark wedged itself into among the rocky boulders of the land they named Ararat. Seeing the squalling babe in Japheth's arms opened Ham's eyes. God spared their lives for a reason. Life would continue. The consuming wrath of God ended with the promise of new life, of a future. Of sons. It was a new beginning.

This first child was only weeks older than Cush. Shem's son came a month later and just like that, the eight were eleven. Babies had been arriving ever since.

A familiar laugh drew Ham's attention to Japheth, standing with his wife Denah, amid the circle that held the chattering Cush.

"I wish Noah and Jael were here." Naomi said. "Eran and Shem, too."

Ham agreed. Shem and his parents chose to remain removed

from the bulk of their descendants. They lived too far from Shinar to even hear about the dragon slaying in time to attend the festivities. At times like this, he wanted them all to be in close proximity. He wanted to share the triumphs of his offspring. He wanted his father to witness the good that lived in the seed of Ham. But perhaps it was better this way. Noah and Shem would find fault with the sacrifice. They had rigid rules. Always the rules and always the reminders of the way this or that should be done. And tonight's sacrifice would not go strictly by their plan.

A strong hand grasped his shoulder and Ham turned to Nimrod. He felt his shoulders rise and wondered if his own face revealed as much pride as Abed's. His grandson smelled of lye soap and wore a fresh linen tunic. All the hair was shaved from his face leaving a smooth sheen with no nicks. Even with shaving tools his grandson wielded his mastery. A bright smile reflected Ham's own emotions. "Are you sure you don't want my help, Grandfather?" Nimrod asked.

"Of course I'm sure. You did the dangerous part. We'll do the messy part. Go mingle, enjoy yourself."

Nimrod hesitated, surveying the clumps of people in the field. His forehead crinkled.

"What bothers you, Nimrod?" Ham set his work down and stood beside his grandson.

Nimrod crossed his arms over his chest. "Where is everyone? I expected a greater turnout. It is a sacrifice after all."

Ham looked out over the crowd. He figured there were at least three hundred people. "It was short notice, Son. I'm pleased with the numbers. There are plenty of people here to honor you."

Nimrod's eyebrows raised and the corner of his lip turned up. "God, you mean. The sacrifice is to honor God, right?"

Ham shot a glance over his shoulder at Naomi. Fortunately her attention was elsewhere. He exhaled loudly. Nimrod laughed.

"Of course, Nimrod," Ham said. "Plenty of people to honor God."

Nimrod relaxed his arms, draping one over Ham's shoulders. "It's important to gather together. One people. One purpose. That's how we're strong. A wall of many bricks, not just a scattering of stones."

"One people. One God. Yes, it's good. You have to have reasonable expectations, though, Son. There are still men in the fields. More will come as the light fades."

Nimrod turned to stare at the structure at the far end of the field. "I wish the tower was finished. When the torches on top are burning, the whole plain will know it's time to gather. There will be no excuse. We'll really have grand sacrifices, then."

His grandson's ambition surpassed all expectations Ham could have dreamed for an heir in his lineage. Nimrod had taken it upon himself to lay out plans for a real city to replace the haphazard layout of fields and shops, tents and pastures that dotted the plain. It was a simple grid design that made the city accessible and functional. For a man that never walked a city street, Nimrod had a unique vision for organization. He probed Ham's memories of cities, and those of the rest of the Eight who lived Before, then took the information and made it his own, even foreseeing ways to control the growth so the people of Noah would remain forever linked.

The tower was a later addition to his plans. It would oversee the landscape, reaching into the heavens. It was a gate, he said. A gate for man to approach God and for God to come to his people. Sweat from nearly every household mixed with the mortar, now both city and tower were nearing completion.

Not everyone supported Nimrod's dreams, of course. Noah had the loudest voice of disapproval. He wanted to wait for God to speak, to provide the plans, like he did for the ark, if the tower was to his liking. God didn't speak, though. And once Nimrod drew the plans himself, he followed through with the construction. It was the first time Ham could recall Noah's opinion being overshadowed. It was painful to see his father humbled that way, and part of him wanted to side with Noah. He didn't. Nimrod's ideas were good. Leadership must always wax and wane. It was time for his father to see beyond his own connection with God and see others rise. If his parents lived in Shinar, they would understand. They would see the benefit, no, the necessity, of maintaining control of the religious practices. They would see how the system would unite everyone under God so that there was but one God. Couldn't his father remember the world before the flood? Couldn't he remember all the gods and all the hatred, the deaths, the fear, the sin? Did he want the new earth to go that way again?

"Yes, Nimrod," Ham said. "Your tower will be good for the people of Noah."

▲

Naomi leaned back on her arms and watched her husband and grandson as they spoke privately. With their backs to her, Nimrod could be Ham's twin. Almost. His black locks didn't have the gray highlights of his grandfather, or the assortment of scars from years of controlling the land. In build and dress, however, and even in manner of stance they resembled one another. Both stood with legs spread, bulky arms crossed over broad chests. Both had daggers holstered on belts that circled narrow waists. Hide boots rather than sandals. Thick, woven linen garments without any fussy work. Two strong, working men, always ready. Ready to hunt, to protect, to defend. In contrast, Nimrod was now spotless while her husband still wore the messy remains. Her love for these men was endless.

"Smile any wider and these flies will take up residence."

Naomi broke from her thoughts and turned to her sister-in-law. "Denah! I'm so glad you came. And by the looks of you, I'm getting a little more assistance?"

Her sister-in-law wore an old stained garment. "Yes, and to see for myself that you're alright." She smothered Naomi in a tight hug before sitting on a stone beside her and picking up a chunk of bone to clean.

A loud cheer crossed the field as Cush guided his mount through the crowd towards Nimrod and Ham. Denah nodded toward the three generations, the two as lean as the other was plump. "You should be proud. You've raised a fine family."

Reassurance from Denah temporarily eased the doubts dwelling in Naomi's mind. The discord within her family made her question it at times, whether they really were fine and good and pleasing to their God. So did the sins among them. There were grievances among her offspring that raised fear in her heart.

How much would God tolerate? Where was the line, that when crossed, brought judgment upon them again? Honoring the ways of Noah and his fathers was more than tradition. One obeyed God to stay alive.

"Yes," she responded. "They are good men." The land was fertile. The women were fertile. Surely these were signs that they were in God's favor.

But God didn't speak anymore.

Not to Noah. Not to anyone.

▲

The kindling wood was in place around the dragon's remains,

and a torch stood ready. Japheth obviously struggled with the proposed change in formalities. Ham could read it in his pinched expression. His brother was never eager to veer away from tradition. Ham let him mull it over for a bit before speaking again. "I really want Nimrod to do this," he said. "He risked his life for those women and children. He deserves to say the words of sacrificial blessing."

Japheth planted his hands on his hips and shook his head. "Brother, you're the patriarch. It's your responsibility. I'll say the blessing if you won't, but your kin made the kill, I think you ought to step up."

Ham tapped his lips with his finger and exhaled. "If it's my responsibility to own, then it's mine to give away. I want my grandson to have this honor. He earned it. If not for him, this would be Naomi's funeral. Come on, Japheth. There's no harm."

Japheth looked out over the crowd. His lips were pressed together in a line and Ham knew this battle challenged his brother to the depths. He also knew his brother wept openly when he heard of Naomi's rescue. He hoped gratitude towards Nimrod would prevail over a little breach in routine.

"Alright, Ham. I won't stand in his way. I don't think this is right, though. Father-"

"- isn't here, Japheth. It's alright." Ham grinned and punched his brother on the shoulder before trotting toward Nimrod, then leading him to the front of the altar. Japheth was right, of course. If Noah was here, he wouldn't allow Nimrod to act as priest. Only Noah and his sons and their sons were permitted. The next generation didn't have approval. Not yet anyhow. It would happen eventually. His other brother led most of the sacrifices, when he came to town for council meetings. But Shem wasn't here today, and neither was their father.

Ham grinned to himself. He never intentionally pulled rank on his oldest brother. He didn't have to. Japheth knew his place in the family line-up. Although Japheth was Noah's firstborn, he forfeited the leadership rights years ago and had been placed at the bottom. Shem was the leader, after Noah, then Ham. If he wanted his valiant grandson to say the blessing then it would be so. He would hear about it later, of course, after it was over. It was Nimrod's moment now.

Nimrod took position in front of the altar, the torch in his right hand. The restless motions of the crowd dropped off and a hush covered the field. No one had ever taught Nimrod the words of the blessing that Ham knew of and for a moment his pulse quickened. He didn't want to embarrass his family. His grandson's countenance was serene as he tipped his chin towards the heavens, however, and Ham relaxed. Nimrod surely knew the words well enough.

The torch sent a dancing flame into the evening sky as Nimrod straightened his arm and began. "We acknowledge you, O God, God of creation, God of our ancestors." His voice was strong, echoing in reverence. The hair on Ham's arms tingled.

Nimrod continued. "We seek your mercy and your favor, and deliverance from your hand of righteousness."

Ham saw Naomi flinch from the corner of his eye. 'Your hand of righteous judgment' was the correct phrase.

"Accept this offering, and bestow a covering of compassion upon the remnant of your creation, on those who seek your ways. May my voice be heard throughout the land as we extol thee before the generations, and the generations to come."

Ham grimaced inwardly at the next slip. He kept his face straight, daring not look at his brother or his wife. 'May THY voice be heard,' he said to himself.

"We offer this sacrifice," Nimrod finished, clearly and earnestly.

Ham looked away from Nimrod to the faces in the first few rows. If anyone caught the omission and the mistake, no one seemed to mind. Almost no one. Naomi's hand covered her lips, and her eyes traveled between him and Nimrod with a look of uncertainty. Denah's eyes were squeezed shut, a frown dominating her face. Ham didn't search for his brother's expression.

Nimrod turned to the altar with the torch held to the sky, toward his God. His head tilted back as if to watch God open the heavens and descend. Ham couldn't help but look to the skies himself. There was a depth to the moment he couldn't explain. Even with the words not quite right, the repetitious nature of the sacrifice suddenly felt new. An aura of worship accompanied the soulful expressions emerging from Nimrod's lips.

Slowly his grandson lowered his head, then the torch. He ignited the remains of the dragon and watched the flames lick up the slain beast. His slain beast. Nimrod's eyes were bright, twinkling with the light of the burning sacrifice.

Ham joined the thundering applause that chased the whirling smoke to the heavens.

Chapter Three

Morning dew saturated Naomi's bare feet. She intentionally strayed from the stone path to allow the coolness of the grass to prickle her toes. It was reminiscent of the way things were Before. Before the flood, when misty vapors seeped through the soil every night to quench the earth and refresh the streams. Water didn't come from the sky like it did now. It was predictable, scheduled with the rise and fall of the sun, and always, just enough. Never did a man have to witness his crops withering onto soil that cracked in its own parched skin or rot away in fields of mud.

The new earth displayed the volatile nature that man had refused to control within himself. They gradually learned to read the signs. Colors in the sky, fragrance on the wind, even the behavior of beasts and birds foretold the conditions to come. And by monitoring the placement of the stars, they knew when to expect the heavy rains and knew when the arid winds would prevail. For a time, they feared the seasons. Now they understood the changes and the times of planting and harvesting rotated routinely with creation itself guiding the process.

Noah's heirs banded as they learned the rhythm of the elements in those early years, then as they moved away from the high places in search of pastures and warmth, and now as they built their dwelling in the plain between the rivers. Unity, purpose, and labor itself gave man little time to feud. The violence permeating society before the flood was gone. No more man against man, kin against kin, city against city.

Soon the core of the city would be established. Then what? The land, stripped bare, had been a daily reminder of God's displeasure, and the consequences. Time had softened those edges. The forests grew, fields were cultivated, civilization rose in layers of earthen brick. The sharp evidence of judgment was dull, the deluge no longer cutting through man's conscience.

"God, in your wisdom, let your presence be known," she prayed. "Don't allow us to forget."

Naomi slipped her sandals on as she neared the fire pit. A steamy brew of dragon bones churned in a great pot. The softened pieces would be refined with flint tools before they hardened again. Already her sons had been at work and shards of shaved bone covered the area like a rug.

Three of her four sons were there, their own grandchildren beside them, practicing the skills of their ancestors. She could see Ham in some way in each of them, and not just physically. There was the attention to small details, the focused squint with concentration, the perseverance to make something perfect. Except for the green eyes among them, her own lineage wasn't so obvious. But this was a blessing.

Canaan, her youngest smiled when he caught sight of her. "Bowl of soup, Mother?" He offered a bucket with bones floating in murky liquid.

Naomi laughed and shook her head. Her husband's three dogs yipped and clamored beneath the offering, tails wagging. "They can have my share," she said, nudging a dog out of her way to see the bone Canaan worked.

Ham taught the boys how to carve intricate designs into their handles without sacrificing strength and function of the resulting tools. Canaan's work featured horses with braided manes coiling around the hilt to create a thumb rest. "Beautiful," she said, eyeing his work, then that of the others. Even the youngest child demonstrated the emerging skills of fine craftsmanship that poured through Ham's seed. "You'll get a fine bit of trade for all these pieces."

Her husband's creative side surpassed that of his brothers. He could figure out new uses for familiar items and better ways to produce them and ways to make items stronger or smoother or safer or simply more beautiful. The hours spent in his workshop were never wasted, and he made sure his sons followed his example. Most of them anyway. As usual, one was missing.

"Where's Cush?" she asked.

"Fetching us something to eat. Father sent him. We'll cover his portion."

Naomi crossed her arms over her chest. "You do him a great favor. He should work some of those bones when he gets back."

Canaan shrugged. "If there's more to do, we won't stop him."

A shrill whistle shifted her attention. It came from Ham's workshop and stopped the dogs in their tracks. They jerked their heads toward the source and tensed, ears and eyes on alert. With the second set of three clipped whistle beats, the dogs barreled toward the workshop, leaving all hopes for a boney treat behind.

Naomi shook her head. Ham treated his dogs like children and they in turn adored him, prancing in delight at the sight of their master at the workshop door. He was in the habit of providing their food now, so the things didn't even have to hunt to survive. They knew they'd be cared for, whether they labored at his feet all day or slept in the cool shade. Naomi sighed. He raised his firstborn the same way.

▲

Ham wrestled the dogs and allowed them to tug on his hem. They were near lifeless pups when he found them. Now they were strong adults, loyal, with gentle spirits, making it impossible for him to set them off on their own. He couldn't stand the thought of them getting attacked by other beasts. Naomi was tolerant of them at best, so he shooed them off as she approached.

"I didn't realize I trained my wife to respond to the whistle," he said. "That was my next goal and here it is already accomplished."

Naomi wrapped her arms around his waist. His own arms pulled her in tight and he kissed the top of her head.

"Train me to that whistle contraption? Don't you wish that were possible," she said, then jabbed him in the ribs with her thumbs. He retaliated by scooping her up into his arms and carrying her into the shop despite protests drenched in giggles.

He loved Naomi's laughter. It was what attracted him to her in the first place, years ago in the city. She had a deep, from the gut laugh. It was genuine. He picked it out from the cacophony of sounds in the market then followed it until he found her. Casually, of course. He never let on that he just happened to be at the perfumers shop or the weavers stall just as she passed by.

"Put me down, you brute." Her eyes glared with false indignation, the emerald green flashing with merriment.

"There's no bed. I guess the bricks with have to suffice."

Naomi swatted his face and wriggled to her feet. "Ham! That's not why I came."

"No? A pleasure to see you all the same, my wife."

"I want to talk about yesterday," she said, picking wood slivers from his tunic.

"It's been over a year since a beast that large came near the city. I don't think you need to be afraid. You handled the situation perfectly. I do wish I could have been there to see Nimrod wield his weapons, though. Even on our hunts, we rarely see anything that large."

Naomi twisted her lips and looked at him with amusement. "What do you mean, 'there to see'? You would not have been on the sidelines as the others were, Ham. Your grandson is you all over again."

Ham nodded and laughed. "Yes, that's true. I would have enjoyed a good fight."

"She was protecting her baby. She had to be killed, but still…"

Ham ran his hand over his wife's wild mane of curls. She respected mothers of all the created kinds, and if she could assist with the birthing of every baby in Shinar, he knew she would. "Better the beast than the little boy, though. Or you."

"I know, and I'm not frightened to go back to the river, really. It's last night I want to discuss."

"It was quite the celebration. I'm glad so many came, maybe six or seven hundred of us by the looks of it."

"I was surprised that you allowed Nimrod to speak the words of blessing."

Ham pushed aside a spark of irritation. "I know. I could read it on your face. I felt that he deserved the honor. He made the kill. He saved the lives. I could tell it meant a lot to him."

Naomi nodded. "It did, I'm sure. Your father wouldn't be pleased, though."

"No, nor Shem. But they weren't there and no harm came because I allowed it. God was honored and that's what matters."

Naomi twirled a curl through her fingers. "It came naturally to

Nimrod, didn't it? He was confident with the task. He took on the role of a leader without hesitation."

"He will be a leader in Shinar someday. He already is, really. I don't know anyone who could rally the people to build a tower like he's done. I'm glad to know my son's son doesn't shy from taking the reins."

"Does he want it too much, Ham? I worry he won't be content to wait until his fathers are all gone to take his place as a leader. At the river, after the kill, when Cush arrived, his face was full of fury at his father's standing. Just for a moment. He hid it well. He wanted all the praises for himself, though. I could see it in his eyes."

"All men do, Naomi. It's only natural for a man to want all the glory for his successes. Fathers share the credit and share the blame. That's how it is. Nimrod knows it, and he'll be alright. He'll enjoy it as his own sons get older."

His wife's sense of right and wrong followed a much tighter line since the flood. She worried herself over little matters, expecting their children to imitate a standard of behavior he could not even live up to.

"Will you speak with your father about it? I'd like his approval and then be sure Nimrod knows the correct words?"

"I'll talk to them both. Nimrod and I will go scouting for tar pits in a few days and we'll have time to discuss it."

"Is Cush going, too?"

"No. He has no sense for finding the pits."

"He'd like to be asked, I'm sure. Even if he chooses not to go with you."

Ham tousled Naomi's hair and hugged her again. "Alright, I'll ask. If nothing else, he cooks up a good pot of stew."

Chapter Four

Ham stepped back from the dust puffing around his horse as it snorted and danced, anticipating a good long ride. He felt it, too. It had been a few months since time allowed him to venture beyond familiar lands. Finding additional stores of tar was important, though perhaps not as critical as he made it sound when he planned the excursion. There was a restlessness he yearned to satisfy more than anything, a need to get beyond the city and fields and pastures.

Nimrod and Cush stood at the door of the stable, loading the last of the supplies. Cush's poor horse grunted as a kettle was lashed to the saddle. Ham laughed and shook his head at his firstborn. Cush preferred the comforts of home, to be sure. He rarely ventured into the outer regions in search of herbs and such. It must have been a good ten or fifteen years since his last real expedition, coming home in a sour mood, his bags of mushrooms and berries barely half filled. Now he gathered cooking ingredients within a day's ride or relied on the produce of his own land. Sleeping under the stars didn't suit him any longer.

It was for the better perhaps. Cush no longer made the long, solitary journey back to the ark either. He was gone for weeks then, camping out in the splintered hull to seek God, he said. As the ice descended and covered the ark, his trips ceased. If he had found God on those trips, the divine presence did not bring his son lasting peace. He returned home jubilant, then it waned, and an air of melancholy set in. Ham was not sorry the journeys ended. For many reasons.

Cush surprised him with a lack of complaints regarding this outing. He seemed keen on exploring a new region, intent on finding new herbs to pound and grind and add to his recipes. His boy could cook, Ham had to give him that. Cush had an instinctive way with spices that turned any grisly meat into a tasty feast. He was useless as a scout but they would dine well as they traveled.

Nimrod and Cush mounted their horses and Ham led the way from the family landsite toward the eastern horizon, facing the rising sun as it climbed through a red tinted veil. The clip-clop of hooves was accented by rhythmic clinking of cooking elements. Morning fires were already burning among the rows of brick homes and the smell of bread clung to the air. Ham inhaled deeply. There was peace accompanying the aroma. The simple routine life guaranteed their survival. Occasional threats from beasts or foul weather were temporary distractions that could not defeat them with the proper interventions. Rarely was there significant upheaval in the life he and the others developed here.

Ham acknowledged the greetings of the men and women they passed. Such a difference from Before. People knew him then because he was the son of a crazy man. They acknowledged him now as one of the Eight, one of the Fathers of the Triune Council. He was respected. His opinion mattered. Even though his father had been right about the flood, those days had been difficult, filled with ridicule as the ark was constructed. Years of hope wrapped in a cloak of doubt. For all the struggles in this post-flood land, he wouldn't return to that way of life, if given a chance. Life was too good now.

Beyond the last home, they crossed the Euphrates River, then allowed the horses to pick up their pace on the path toward the distant Tigris River, the twin of the mighty Euphrates. Noah named the great rivers after the ones that coursed around the sacred garden of First Man. The paradise of Eden was gone now, lying somewhere beneath the silt and rubble the flood waters left behind, but his father wanted reminders of what was, and what was lost. Ham had his own names for them – Brakha, the Blessing, and Arar, the Curse, for the rivers surged and pummeled whatever lay in their path this time of the year, yet without them there would be no life giving flow to feed the crops through the dry season.

His horse crested a rise and Ham slowed the creature beneath him to a halt. He scanned the landscape stretching out before him. The flood waters were good to this plain, depositing their riches as they receded. The earth nestled between the Tigris and Euphrates swallowed seeds and pushed healthy crops back in their place. Fertile fields intersected wooded hills, supporting the animal populations that thrived and multiplied. Life was abundant in all its many forms. It was never too hot, never so cold they could not survive. It was home. Shinar, the land between the rivers, was his Eden.

Fierce mountains of stone hovered beyond the Tigris, jutting from the ground then disappearing in the heavens under crowns of frozen rain. The air itself had teeth on those mountains and the snow brought an ache to his bones. Life was sucked from the earth beneath the frigid white blankets that fell, for days, then months. The snow was necessary they soon realized. It supplied the rivers, but he never regretted moving from their heights.

To the west of the city, beyond the Euphrates, the land was altogether different. Away from the rivers, the land was sparse and dry with only the occasional spring to provide water. If there had been mountains of stone, they were disintegrating into mounds of sand. Ham had no idea how far the sands stretched or what lay on the other side. Someday, he would explore it.

The patchwork of fields and pastures before him covered the land in golds, greens, and rich earthy hues, all woven together by a network of canals. His canals. Yes, his brother Shem spent countless hours before their God, seeking the wisdom to control the rivers and it was Japheth's ideas that maximized their function, but it was his plan. He tamed the rivers so the soil produced a harvest and sustained their herds in safety. Even Noah gave his youngest son the honor of the accomplishment.

Ham craned his neck to monitor the sky. Change occurred quickly this time of year. The red tint to the sunrise spoke of foul weather and he wanted to be prepared. He would keep watch for a secure campsite along the way, hoping they would find a new tar pit first.

Nimrod reined in beside him. His grandson's dark eyes smiled as he surveyed the open land. "There's plenty of space, isn't there Grandfather?" he said.

"For what?"

"For us. For our children's children and their children after them. The sons of Noah can call this land home for endless generations."

Ham didn't respond. A barb rose to the surface of his mind. God told them to fill the earth. They were marrying and reproducing, yet only a few had ventured beyond the borders of the great rivers. It wasn't safe to be alone, and most of those that left returned in time. Even men seeking isolation in the caves and hills between the rivers eventually returned to their families. Men needed one another.

They would fill the earth, in time. This is what he told Naomi and any others who spoke of it. Their descendants would multiply and move beyond the boundaries of the rivers. What was he to do until then? No one wanted to leave the safety of the clans. Not yet.

Thinking of God reminded Ham of Naomi's request. "Nimrod, your grandmother asked me to speak with you about the sacrifice."

Nimrod leaned back and laughed. "I was wondering when it would come up. I could tell she wasn't pleased with your decision."

"She understands why I let you lead the ritual. She was right about the actual blessing, though. I should have made sure you knew the right words."

Nimrod shrugged. "I got most of them, didn't I?"

Ham chuckled. He took his family to Japheth's for sacrificial gatherings. Despite his older brother's loss of standing in the family rank, Ham was all too eager to let Japheth say the sacrificial blessing. He hadn't said it himself in several years. Recognizing errors was one thing. Reciting it without practice another. "Yes. You got more than I would have."

"No one seemed to notice."

"There were those that did, but they understood that it wasn't a planned event and you were unprepared."

Ham watched Nimrod's lips pinch together at the perceived insult. He let him brood a moment before another laugh escaped. "You and I can only excel at *most* everything, Son. We have to leave something for my brother's kin."

"What's so funny?" Cush joined them on the rise.

Ham turned to his firstborn and hesitated. The day started well and he didn't want to introduce discord. "We were talking about your mother's fears. Her concern that God was displeased with the sacrifice the other night."

Cush pointedly looked away from him. Ham knew he was hurt. He had never asked his firstborn to lead a sacrifice. But Cush had never slain a dragon. He turned back to them shortly and nodded. "It burned like the rest. God accepted it just fine."

▲

Sweat trickled down Ham's back as he followed fissures in the ground. An acrid smell rose on the heated air, stinging his nose as they neared the rift in the earth where tar oozed in a steamy pool. The dark sticky substance made perfect mortar for bricks, bricks he had been making since the early days on the plain. It held tight between the bricks in the summer season without cracking or dissolving in the wet cold of winter. It waterproofed the bricks as well. Although canals conquered the Euphrates in that respect, a little security against the rising river was a bonus. Ham hated floods more than the snow-filled heights of Ararat.

It was a good find, an easy to access pit less than a day's ride away. They would bring wagons and collect the tar later, store it in earthen jars for transport then reheat it on site for use. Nimrod handed Ham a piece of hide on which he carved a map to the site where they now stood. His attention was on the horizon and Ham turned to see what held his grandson's focus. A thin gray plume rose from the landscape, further on toward the Tigris. Even Cush stopped examining succulents in the rubble to look at the smoke. "Looks like campfire smoke," Cush said. "Or homestead."

His son was right. It wasn't the smoke of a fire started by lightning.

"Let's check on it, Grandfather. See who it is and why they're out here." Nimrod had his hands on his hips, squinting at the line of hazy air.

Ham scanned the sky again. For early summer it was warm in the sun but ominous clouds hovered on the horizon as the dawn skies had warned. It might be one of the last big rains of the season, or it might be a drizzle of no concern. One never knew this time of year. He had been surprised, and drenched, on other occasions. If they left now, they might escape its path, or at least be sheltered in caves they passed a short distance back.

"Father, there's rain in those clouds. We should head for shelter." Cush paced near his horse.

Nimrod started to disagree. Ham held up his hand to silence them both. There had been minimal bickering between them so far and he wouldn't put up with it now. He looked back to the smoke. "We've come this far," he said. "Let's see who of our kin has ventured beyond the perimeters of safety. We can deal with any storms that come."

Chapter Five

A tributary from the Tigris River supplied a grid of groomed fields. Ham recognized his channel design, including the gates that raised and lowered to control the flow and the banks that guarded against flooding. The soil had been turned and planted recently in the nearest squares of land, the oxen prints still visible in the furrows. This was no temporary home site.

Ham and his boys followed a well worn path through the fields toward the smoke plume, stopping behind a stand of palms that shielded them from view. The rectangular dwelling was constructed of mud bricks, one level only, with a small enclosed courtyard on the back side. The bricks forming the house and fence were irregular in size, the walls not perfectly plumb. It wasn't the work of one of his offspring, Ham knew.

Four people worked the soil behind a team of oxen in one of the fields. One man and a boy drove the beasts while another boy and a girl tossed seed in the furrows. A woman stood near the house with a baby wrapped tightly against her back. They rocked in rhythm as she wielded an axe against a chunk of wood. Two little children squatted by the stream with buckets, naked and wet as they dug through the rocks. A dog bounced back and forth between the woman and the children. Ham caught his breath. It was an entire family, firmly established beyond the reach of the community.

Nimrod shook his head. "I don't recognize them."

"Nor do I. They aren't of our line though, I'm sure." Ham prodded his horse to step toward the home, followed by Cush and his grandson. When the woman saw them, he stopped and got off the horse, handing the reins to Cush before walking toward her with his hands free. It was an old habit, from Before, showing he didn't approach with a drawn weapon.

The woman's look of surprise warmed into a smile and she greeted Ham with a light kiss on both cheeks while the dog circled his legs and sniffed his tunic. "Visitors," she said. "What a welcome surprise. You're Ham, son of Noah, are you not?"

"I am. This is my firstborn, Cush and his son Nimrod." At the introduction both men dismounted and stepped forward to receive the kiss.

"I'm Iris, wife of Eli of the line of Shem. My husband is there in the field with my older children."

"Shem's kin. You're from my father's settlement, then. That's why I didn't recognize you," Ham said. "We followed your cooking smoke. I didn't know anyone lived out here. Shem has given his approval of this?" Ham knelt down and roughed up the dog's dense brown fur and was licked in the face in return.

"Yes, of course. He gave his blessing to my husband."

Nimrod placed his hand gently on the woman's shoulder. "Don't you fear the danger? I killed a great lizard just recently and we've heard of men that wander these parts. Men under no man's rule. There's no one here to protect you."

The woman met his direct gaze and patted his hand. "We're aware of the dangers. It hasn't been an easy situation, yet this is what Eli prefers. He's willing to face the trials."

"And you? And your boys?" Nimrod ran a hand over the baby's

head then looked toward the field, squinting at the rest of Iris's family. "And your daughter?"

Iris kept her eyes on Nimrod as she spoke. "It's kind of you to be concerned, Nimrod. Perhaps it wasn't my choice to be so far from my sister kin, but I'm content here, with Eli. The children haven't been in need. We've managed well thus far. The land is good to us."

"But-" Nimrod tried to continue but Ham caught his arm and stopped his words. If Nimrod wanted to convince this family to live in the safety of the community, he needed to speak with Eli. Stirring fearful discontent in the woman would not bring about the results he desired. Besides, if Shem gave the man permission to take this land then there was no reason for them not to be here, whether or not anyone else approved.

"I'll gather my family, if you have the time to sit for awhile. They'll take pleasure in hearing news from the city." Ham nodded and Iris headed toward the fields. She went only a few steps before stopping abruptly and turning back around, her eyes traveling appreciatively over Nimrod. She smiled and wagged a finger at him. "Yes, it's fortunate we have honored guests among us."

Cush dug his elbow in Nimrod's side as Iris scurried to fetch her husband and older children. "She likes you, Son. But don't be getting any crazy ideas. You have a woman already."

Nimrod jumped away and laughed. "Thank the heavens."

Ham rolled his eyes. His grandson had an eye for beautiful women, his own wife a dark eyed, smooth skinned beauty. Iris had the weathered skin and dirt crusted nails of a woman with little leisure time and no reason to add paint to her face.

He turned his attention to the two little children sitting by a deep bend in the stream, staring as if they'd never seen strangers. "What are you boys collecting so diligently?"

One of the boys held out a grubby hand. Ham knelt down to examine the rock he presented, prepared to feign interest. The stone took his wind.

"You can hold it," the boy said, placing the stone in Ham's palm. It was the size of an olive, with edges ground smooth. The saturated color was unmistakable.

It was gold.

Ham rinsed the stone in the stream then held it up so sunlight bounced off the tiny hills and valleys. "Do you have others like this?" he asked, forcing a calm to his voice that he didn't feel.

The boys pushed their buckets towards Ham's feet. The younger child had a bucket of flat, smooth stones, not a one of which glimmered gold. The older child's held nuggets like the one in his hand. Ham felt his heart rate quicken in his chest. "Where did all these come from?"

"They wash down the stream and me and Beni pick 'em out of the water." The younger boy pointed proudly at the smooth stones. "Those ones are for skippin.' Them others don't skip good. They're for looking at. Pretty aren't they?"

Ham nodded. "Yes, they are. What do you do with them, besides look at them?"

The boys glanced at each other and shrugged. "Just collect 'em."

The choice nuggets released a desire in Ham that caught him off guard. Gold he'd collected around Shinar would hardly cover the bottom of the boy's bucket. He used bits of it to demonstrate the smelting process to his offspring so the craft wouldn't be lost, but had never shown them how to form anything of great size. With this treasure...

No. Not treasure. No one understood the amazing qualities of these rocks that captured the rays of the sun. Gold had no value in this post-flood world. It was far too soft for any sort of functional use. No one realized it didn't tarnish or rust, or that it could be reformed over and over without loss of purity. It could be poured into molds or hammered into thin sheets. It could be spun into threads and sewn into garments. Gold transformed the mundane into marvelous, the every day into exquisite.

Not that he had been allowed to own anything made of the precious nuggets. His mother wouldn't permit it. It was the element of the Evil One, Jael said. Temples to false gods were layered in gold, their priest and priestesses adorned in the same substance, as chains around their throats and wrists and ankles. Her sons would not dress as the sinful ones, would not worship the rock of greed. Ham had no doubt his parents would rejoice if gold was lost forever under the flood waters, unknown and forgotten.

Ham could not forget. He had a small stash hidden away. It was a link to life Before that he couldn't seem to break.

Nimrod and Cush stood silently beside him, watching his face with amusement. The little boys, too, studied his face. They had no idea what they pulled from the stream.

Ham handed the nugget back to Beni. "No," he said, though no one had asked him anything.

"You want one?" The boy held it out to him again.

Nimrod and Cush eyed the nugget, leaving the answer plain in Ham's mind. "No," he said again, "You keep them." He turned his focus to the skipping stones, admiring one of them in the sunlight and inspecting it as if it were as golden as the other. After a show of fussing over the buckets, he made himself turn away from the little boys and their treasure. He could not allow his own boys access to the gold.

▲

Ham sipped fresh goat's milk and nibbled on crusty flatbread with Eli's family. The older boys were hungry for news of their friends and family, asking an endless stream of questions. Most lived in Noah's village and Ham had little information to share. He had not been there in a long time. Fortunately Nimrod knew nearly all of Shem's kin in the city. They were faithful to the tower construction, so he filled in bits and pieces of information.

Cush relished the opportunity to brag of his son's dragon kill then described the tower on its climb to the sky. The young men looked at Nimrod with the awe that Ham had seen many times when he was with his grandson. Their daughter, too, looked at him with awe but hers was of a different sort. When she glanced at Nimrod, a crimson hue blended into her sun browned cheeks.

Eliamah had the thin frame of her mother, the same wiry hair wrapped into tight coils, the same pale lips, only hers didn't speak except a word or two at a time, and only when he asked her a direct question. She kept vigilant watch of her hands as they twisted in her lap, looking up only when she laughed. Her eyes flickered on Nimrod when she did, only for a brief moment before finding her hands again, or her mother's reassuring nod.

Iris changed the flow of conversation as the pace of chatter slowed. "Ham," she said. "As we're a distance from other families, I have a concern for my daughter." The pink stain intensified on the girl's face. "I don't want her to marry one of her brothers. We wish to offer Eliamah to your grandson."

Ham choked on a bite of bread. "To Nimrod?"

"Yes," Eli said. "He seems to be a fine man and our daughter is old enough to tend her own home. She can't stay here forever to grow old. She needs a husband. Take her with you and make her welcome in the house of Ham."

Ham looked at Nimrod. His grandson stared at the girl with an expression that did not need defining. She wasn't the sort to turn his head, even if she were cleaned up and perfumed. Ham forcefully cleared his throat and broke Nimrod's mortified trance. Cush found words to fill the dreadful silence. "That's generous Eli."

"She works very hard and she's obedient. You can see her mother brings sons to life easily and she'll be the same, I'm sure. And I can guarantee she's unblemished."

Ham chose his words carefully. "Your offer is indeed generous," he said. "But Nimrod has a wife already."

"It wouldn't surprise me if he had several," Iris said. "Can he not take one more? Can't he take Eliamah and protect her from the dangers of our dwelling place?"

Cush and Nimrod froze at the woman's words. Ham shook his head, for once grateful that his father's conservative mindset held fast over the years. "Noah would never allow the taking of a second wife, Iris."

"It isn't the way of our ancestors, though, is it?" Eli spoke calmly but there was an edge to his voice. "Before the great flood, our people took as many wives as necessary for their happiness and to fill their homes. Our father Shem has told us of the way it used to be. Perhaps there was reason in the taking of more than one wife. Certainly, we don't disapprove the practice. It's for our daughter's benefit and surely Nimrod desires more sons at his feet."

Nimrod sat rigidly, his mouth clamped shut, eyes wide and fixed on Ham. Cush leaned back on his elbow, sporting a broad grin as his eyes traveled from face to face. The weight of the moment fell on Ham. He took a long sip of milk as he considered Eli's request, surprised his brother would even mention the forbidden act. It was one that got buried with the flood. Shem would never tolerate its return. He imposed a strict line of obedience among his children and any sort of rebellious thinking brought discipline. Harsh discipline. Exile, perhaps. It made sense, now. Eli was banished from the land of his fathers. He didn't live in these unknown lands for sheer desire of isolation.

"I'm sorry, Eli. I can't disobey my father and the God who sets the rules on man's heart. I can't marry her to Nimrod. I can, however, take her to the city and find her a suitable husband. This I can do for you. She can live in my home until the arrangements are made. Naomi will treat her as a daughter of her own."

Nimrod exhaled audibly followed by his father's amused chuckle. Ham gave them both the eye of disapproval. He didn't intend to offend this family of Shem.

Eli had his attention on Iris. She considered the offer then shook her head. "You can, son of Noah. You can choose a different road than your father has directed. But you won't. I can see that you won't." She glared at Ham before shifting the harsh eyes to Nimrod. His grandson excused himself, choosing to wrestle with the dog rather than linger in her resentment.

Iris wrapped her arm around Eliamah's bony shoulders. The girl's head remained bent, eyes seeking no one. "It's unfortunate you find my daughter unsuitable. She'll stay here where she's wanted."

Ham tried to steer the conversation to safe terrain. He asked about the crops and how they faired the winters. Eli was the only one willing to speak and his words were clipped. Ham was suddenly impatient and stood to leave.

Cush pointed toward the darkening sky. "The rains are coming in. Do you have room for us to stay until morning?"

Eli crossed his arms over his chest. He shook his head as his eyes fixed on the blanket forming above them. "No, son of Ham. There's no room for you here." His voice was cold. It was no wonder Shem wanted this family excised from their midst.

Ham roughed up the dog once more before he and his boys mounted their horses and headed back towards caves they spotted earlier in the day. The dog was the only one whose attitude toward them remained unchanged. Even the little boys adopted the unwelcoming stance of their father.

Ham grunted his displeasure. The lack of respect from Eli's household was unnerving. He was not one to be shunned. Disrespect toward society's leaders bred rebellion. It was obvious this family chose a path of independence rather than adhere to the customs of Noah's descendants. Ham didn't like it. They were just one family, now, far removed from the rest. One day the children would be married off, and the dissention they learned from Eli would adhere to their thoughts. The attitudes would perseverate. What was Ham to do? Nothing. There was nothing to be done. He kept his horse at a brisk trot, allowing Nimrod to lag behind with Cush.

Society would decay without proper leadership. A strong hand at the reins guaranteed order and order meant viability. Rules, set and followed, prevented chaos and destruction from within.

He and his brothers made all the critical decisions for the people of the earth, and Noah's presence, seen or unseen, held sway over the rules they enforced. It would not always be so. What would happen when Noah was dead? When Ham and his brothers were gone? Cush couldn't hold the people as one. Neither could the firstborn sons of his brothers, in his opinion. One leader was needed. One man, wise, compassionate, fair, hardworking and devoted to his God. There was only one choice in Ham's mind. The destined ruler of the land of Shinar was Nimrod. Mankind needed him.

Ham stopped beneath a tree and waited for his boys. The wind stirred up debris and he wrapped a scarf over his nose and mouth. Dirt wasn't the only unpleasant taste on his lips. He hoped the sour dealings with Iris and Eli would diminish with a good sleep. Ham urged his ride forward as the others came near, eager to make a nest for the night. He shivered, although he wasn't really cold. The foreboding air swirling around Eli's home nipped his skin like the storm that brewed.

Chapter Six

The jar crashed to the floor, sending pot shards in all directions. Naomi drew in a slow breath to calm herself. It was just thunder. For only a few hours the heavens would rumble and the rain fall. It wouldn't last. By morning the sky would be clear and the sun would soak up whatever moisture the earth refused.

Naomi stooped to gather the broken pieces, chiding herself. After all these years, a little rainstorm still set her nerves on an anxious ledge. God promised he wouldn't flood the entire earth again. That was a comfort, of course, but it didn't relieve the tightness in her chest when the blue of the heavens turned fierce.

She made great effort not to show fear to her four sons and seven daughters when they were young. As the clouds grew black, she wrapped them up in her arms and told them once again about the flood that came because men rejected the One God, and also of the promise that it wouldn't happen again. They learned to watch for the rainbow and find comfort in its presence. There would be no rainbow on this dark night. Nothing to stave the old fears from creeping back.

With the children, fear of storms grew less as they aged. Naomi found her own anxieties increasing. With the first rumble she felt unease settling in her mind. Tonight it was especially heavy, a gnawing sense of foreboding making her jump at the slightest sound. It was just thunder, she told herself again.

She wrapped the broken bits in a rag, then peered through a window, looking eastward, beyond the Euphrates. A sliver of road was visible when the skies were clear. It was cloaked in darkness now. She looked anyway, hoping to see some sign of her men. On occasion Ham found tar easily and was home by sunset. Other times he was gone for days. The rain itself wouldn't send him home, but Cush was with him and he hated the inclement weather as much as she did. There was still a chance she wouldn't have to slip into the cold bed alone.

The hot day was gone, turned over to the uncomfortable chill of the wet sky. Naomi wrapped herself in a warm cloak and picked up the mending basket. They were all alone in the main house now, she and Ham. It was this time of night when she felt the children's absence most keenly, when the only steps pattering about belonged to herself and husband. Their boys built homes for themselves as they began to have sons. When it wasn't raining, she could hear their laughter across the courtyard. It wasn't like she lived far away, and any of her daughters-in-law would welcome her into their fold, even at this late hour. Naomi didn't want to be a nuisance, however, and didn't want them to see her fear.

Running her hand over her abdomen, she felt the sag of skin that held her babies years ago. It was good those days were past. She didn't mourn the transition from a life-giver as Denah and Eran had. The days of bringing babies into the world were stressful, more than anyone truly understood. Her concerns rose from a deep place within, haunts she shared with no one. And never would. Thankfully, each new generation of babies reduced her fears. But there would always be a lingering seed.

A sharp rap echoed through the household. "Naomi?"

The tension in her shoulders dissipated. Naomi hurried to the door where Denah waited. Her sister-in-law's hair clung to her face in soggy waves. She clutched sandals to her chest beneath a thin woven wrap that drooped under the weight of the moisture it retained. Its laden hem sent a steady stream of rainwater into a puddle around her feet. Her bare feet.

Naomi stopped short from wrapping Denah in a hug. "Look at you!"

Denah grinned and shook her head, spraying Naomi with the droplets. "It's raining," she said.

Naomi helped her sister-in-law out of the drenched shawl and threw her a towel. Denah plopped onto a stool and proceeded to wipe red mud from between her toes. "What a storm. I didn't expect it to get here so quickly."

Naomi snuggled into her cloak. "A cold rain, too. And you're playing outside barefoot like one of my little grandbabies. Aren't your feet freezing?"

"They're new." Denah pointed at her sandals.

Naomi grinned. Reason enough. "And you came all the way over here to show them to me?"

Denah ran the clean end of the towel over her head. "Well, that was some loud thunder, and I knew Ham was going to be gone."

Naomi breathed a quiet sigh. She didn't deserve a friend like Denah, not after the despicable way she treated her when she was brought into Noah's home as the wife of Japheth. It was half of their lifetime ago, yet the sting of her own jealous behavior against her sister-in-law remained. Denah never deserved Naomi's animosity.

Naomi had felt inadequate in her presence. Denah was so accomplished. She knew about business and could create the prettiest fabrics from supplies she gathered herself. She was respected for her skill. She was useful. She had value. And her wardrobe was elegant. Marrying Ham should have meant an allowance for nice garments. She had been mistaken on that account. Noah's family didn't spend resources on items deemed unimportant and pretty clothes were not on that list. She intentionally destroyed some of the prettiest tunics that Denah colored with her own hand. If she couldn't have any she didn't want Denah to have them either. She had been so selfish.

The ark was a great healer. How could it not be? When all they had ever known was dissolved in the deluge of God's wrath, how could they not cling to one another and make amends? As the heavens poured the waters and the earth spit out fire and the ark was tossed for day and night, day and night, day and night and not even Noah knew what was happening to their world, how could they not become one in spirit, one in humility?

When the ark struck land and wedged itself securely in the rocks, when the waters receded and the new earth was visible, when the first rain came, then the first baby came, they had only knit a tighter cord of friendship. "Thank you for coming, Denah," she said. "I thought the rain might bring my men home but I guess they'll endure the elements for the night."

"And so will you, sister dear. But not here. There's work to be done. My great-granddaughter is about to burst with that baby of hers. Her mother caught me on the way over. She's asking for you."

Naomi jumped to her feet and snatched up her birthing supplies as Denah tied on her shoes. "It's just a drizzle now, Naomi," she said. "You won't get too wet."

Naomi tied a scarf over her head and opened the door for Denah. Rain didn't matter when a baby was on its way.

Chapter Seven

Ham quietly slid mud-caked boots from his feet and set them aside before easing onto the earthen bed and pulling a deer hide up to his chin. He hated sleeping shoeless in the wilds, but the wet leather would curdle his skin if he left the boots on, then cold feet would prevent him from finding sound sleep again, sleep that so far refused to be grasped. Shadows still danced across the cave walls, faded now, along with the fire, gradually merging with darkness. The crackle of smoldering twigs would soon be silent, leaving the even breathing of his boys and the droning rain to lull his mind.

That man Eli stepped into his thoughts again. He had the gall to bring up Before, as if he had been there, as if he really understood. The taking of multiple wives was one of many practices that Noah wanted forgotten. Seeds were planted in the minds of Shem's kin however, and now in his own.

He didn't show the decency to discuss his daughter's plight privately, either. It became an ugly situation. The poor thing was humiliated. Then Nimrod allowed his feelings regarding the girl to be evident on his face, which was inexcusable. Ham would let it slide though. What was done, was done, and fortunately Naomi hadn't been witness to it all, finding another issue to pick apart. And

Nimrod's momentary loss of control was nothing compared to their own firstborn's behavior.

Did she even know what Cush did? That he traded artifacts from the ark as a source of income? He proclaimed the saving power in a length of rope or a chunk of gopher wood, claiming God's protective hand would carry over to the owner of such relics. The trading was discreet but Ham had been informed. He was keeping watch, and needed to end the practice, especially knowing the last few items came from his own household shelves, never having seen the ark.

Adjusting his cloak into a more suitable pillow, Ham longed for the warmth of Naomi's arms. Tomorrow he would sleep in his own bed, hopefully free of all nagging thoughts of Eli and his family. He wished he had turned for home now, instead of going to that homestead.

Intentionally closing his eyes, Ham pursued sleep for the second time. Roasted rabbit dominated the smoke that lingered in the heavy air and he breathed in deeply. He could feel his senses relaxing. He wouldn't need to get up again and go for a ride. Sleep would not be long in coming this time.

The rustle of bedding bounced around the cave walls. Drowsiness kept his eyelids shut as one of the boys rose and stepped toward the mouth of the cave and the dreary rainfall. Checking on the horses or feeling the effects of the excess wine. It was no concern. Ham rolled onto his side. It was time for sleep to put the day of mixed blessings behind him.

▲

The newborn wailed as Denah washed his tiny body with a salt and barley juice concoction. Naomi stopped for the first time since entering the home and taking charge of the birthing, taking a deep breath, thanking God for his safe arrival. She had worried greatly over this one. His young mother grew very large, quickly. Naomi had seen too many of her own family, from Before, carrying their young as this mother did and it had not ended well. This mother was from Japheth's line, but her own blood mixed with the child's through his father's side. It was a close enough relation to foster Naomi's anxieties.

This baby came earlier than she anticipated, and was small considering the girth his mother carried. Naomi inspected every bit of his body and could find no flaw, however. He was dark in skin tone like his father and already had a sprouting of hair. His lungs had obviously developed fully and he exercised them as Denah wrapped him snuggly in a wool wrap.

The child's family began filtering inside and Denah handed the boy to his father. The man had three girls already and now his firstborn at last. He whooped in delight and proudly showed him to the others. Naomi turned back to the exhausted mother with clean linen towels. The woman's eyes were large and she grabbed Naomi's hand and squeezed. "Why is there still pressure?" she asked. "Pains like before, like I need to push?"

The room grew silent. The haven of life had already been expelled and placed in a wooden box to be buried later. There was only one reason for the mother to feel a need to push again. Naomi placed her hand on the mother's abdomen. A ripple of motion brushed against her palm. She felt the color drain away from her face, then forced a calm smile. "There's another one," she said. "Another baby."

The mother cried out in a rush of pain. Denah shooed the men and children back out of the room. They had no time to get the mother from the soft pallet to the birthing chair as the second baby came out nearly of her own accord. A girl this time.

Naomi stroked the infant's spine until she let out a cry of life, then placed her on the mother's belly. The mother kept her hands clasped together rather than take hold of the infant. Naomi wiped a cloth over her forehead. "Don't be frightened. You have another daughter," she said.

The mother glanced at her newborn then back to Naomi. "Is she alright?"

"She's smaller than her brother, but she appears healthy." The women in the room were quiet. Too quiet. Naomi made sure they could see as she stretched out each of the infant's limbs and examined her eyes and ears. "Yes, she's a beautiful little girl."

The room filled with family again. There was no laughter this time, and the children clung to the adults in silence.

Naomi smiled at the father. "Your firstborn son has a sister," she said.

The father handed his son to a relative and walked closer, peeking at the tiny girl. He shuddered and stepped back. "She's cursed," he said.

"No, she's fair skinned, that's all. She'll be the color of her mother. God has favored you with two children today." Naomi could read the disbelief in the father's eyes.

Denah held the baby as Naomi separated the mother cord, then cleaned the infant with a new salt mix, and bundled her like her brother. The father watched, arms folded over his chest. "It isn't natural for there to be two in one womb," he said. "One dark, one light. The beasts of the land have offspring in that manner. Not man. My son is small because that one has taken the strength that should be his. She's his curse."

Naomi drew in a slow controlled breath. "She's your daughter, a gift from God to be treasured along with your other daughters and your new son."

Denah held out the tiny girl to the father. His arms remained locked over his heart. The mother lay on the mat with her eyes squeezed shut, hands clasped under her chin, not reaching for her newborn. None of the women in the room moved to take the child. Her fate rested in the father's hands. Hands that refused to accept the new bundle of life. Naomi's heart screamed for the infant girl.

"One child is for me," he said, "and the other for God, then. If God gave me two, I will give him one back."

Naomi drew her spine straight and caught hold of his gaze. She was of the Eight. If there was ever a time to pull rank, it was now. "You will not kill this child. You will not leave her outside to die. She is to be raised as the others."

The father's eyes did not break Naomi's stare. After a moment they softened and he nodded. "Very well. But she will not share what belongs to my son. She has taken enough already." The father turned to a young woman with tear lines striping her cheeks, a baby on her hip. "Will you take the second child as your own?"

The infant girl's aunt rushed forward and took the bundle to her breast. Naomi exhaled and turned to the mother once again. The woman's eyes were still pinched shut, a steady flow of tears breaking through and drenching her pillow.

▲

Naomi linked her arm through Denah's. Her sister-in-law's eyes were red and puffy against the pale strip of drizzly dawn. They were exhausted. "Frightened by his own child," Naomi said. "If we hadn't been there, that little girl would have disappeared and no one outside the family would have ever known she existed."

"I'm glad you were there. They're a good family, really. They'll respect what you said."

"You would have stood up for her, if I hadn't."

"Yes, but when it comes to babies, it's you they want to hear from. You have favor with all our mothers, you've helped so many."

Naomi didn't respond. It was good to have a skill to offer. Her reason wasn't as noble as Denah thought, though. It was that tattered remnant of her past, refusing to dissolve in the waters of judgment. The beast that followed her onto the ark and burrowed into her soul.

Denah allowed exasperation to coat her words. "Why would it even cross someone's mind that a newborn child was a curse? Where does that thinking even come from?"

Naomi peered up at the brightening sky. "Do you fear God's wrath? Do you fear he will come down on us again?"

The bones of rebellion were evident. In her family, in the families of Shem and of Japheth. Despite their teachings of the beginnings and the ways of the Creator, ears were closing, eyes shutting out the truth.

Denah pulled her in close, saying nothing. Both lost their entire blood family once. Naomi could not bear for it to happen again.

Chapter Eight

Cool clay oozed through Ham's fingers as he packed it into the rectangular mold. He pushed the wet substance into each corner, tapped the wooden frame to settle the air pockets, then ran a trowel across the surface to make it level, and to be sure the aggregate was buried within. The last step was to push a stamp into its top to create a grid pattern. The valleys formed by the stamp were for the tarry mortar mix that sealed adjoining bricks together. This brick would never join with another, however. It wouldn't even be placed in the sun to bake properly. Ham put it on the floor of the shop with the other couple dozen he made that morning.

These newest bricks wouldn't firm up enough to bear any structural weight. He knew it, and didn't care. Forming bricks that morning wasn't all about the finished work. Sometimes he just needed the clammy feel of fresh clay on his hands, needed the familiarity and the mindless repetition.

With the last of the clay used up, he grabbed a stick and scraped the bulk of the sticky mess off his hands and into a bucket. He didn't once regret moving to Shinar and settling on a career of brick making and building. He liked to experiment with the moist earth, finding the right combination of ingredients to yield resilient bricks. Simple straw was still the best additive and even with that, he made hundreds of bricks with varying amounts to find the best recipe.

It was a necessity at first, mastering the available elements to provide protection. The ark was home for only a short while. The rocky mountain of stone where they landed was unsuitable to farm and then came that first dreadful winter. He could not have foreseen that rain would grow so cold it froze as white flakes, gathering as a thin blanket at first, then piling up until everything was beneath a dense covering.

He and his family bundled all they could and followed the beasts down the mountain to more hospitable terrain. But the trees were gone. The uprooted timber was mostly rotted and though there were sprouts of new growth all around, there were no trees to cut and build any form of dwelling. They lived in the caves of the lower hills of Ararat several years before moving on. The primitive home they eventually constructed of sun baked clay still stood, still housed his parents as it had for a hundred years. Ham's bricks were solid even then.

He was compelled to form more bricks this morning. The busy work of his hands didn't distract his thoughts from Eli's homestead, though. In fact, he could focus on little else.

▲

Naomi peered inside her husband's shop. She had barely seen him since he returned the other day from the tar expedition. Ham stood with his back to her, looking over neat rows of newly formed bricks. The earthy aroma was heavy in the room, a scent as familiar in their household as the baking bread. How many thousands of those had her husband and sons formed over the years? Now they hired others to do most of the actual brick making, while they focused on construction, but she knew Ham still needed mud on his own hands once in a while.

The dogs stood when she entered, tails wagging to the same beat. "Am I interrupting a moment of creative ingenuity?"

Ham spun around. His eyes were wide. "Oh! Naomi," he said.

"I didn't mean to startle you," she said.

Ham glanced quickly at his bricks then back at his wife. "It's alright. I was just finishing." His hands were still coated with a film of dried clay and Naomi smiled. She didn't mind the wet clay on her hands. Dry clay was intolerable, sucking the very moisture from her skin and crackling beneath her nails. Her husband didn't mind the annoying layer of earth on his calloused hands, at least until food was presented.

"I brought you a sweet roll."

Ham walked to a basin and began washing off the grit. It wasn't like him to startle so easily. He was struggling with something. His mind was plagued since he and the boys returned. It was a successful venture. They found a good new source of tar, yet there was an odd air surrounding them that she couldn't identify. She supposed it had to do with the people they found living out there.

Naomi handed Ham the honey drenched roll and told him about the birth of the twins. "I'm afraid for us," she said. "We're straying from God."

Ham wiped his lips on his sleeve. "They were frightened because there were two babies, two different colored ones at that. It is rather unusual. You did the right thing, making sure the girl child lived." Ham picked up a half whittled stick and examined it closely.

"If I wasn't there, though, or Denah. I think they would have found reason to let her die. The father's thoughts were of cursing, not blessing. He saw evil first. It didn't occur to him to seek God's position on the matter. Ham, what if our offspring turn away from the One God? What if it happens again?"

"You fear another flood?"

"No. Not that. God promised. He could punish us in other ways though. He could close wombs again, or stop the rains all together. Or, I don't know. I don't want us to test him."

"You can't prevent men from thinking like men, Naomi. Fear over the number of babies in a birthing isn't standing against God. You're making too much of it."

"No one even thought to seek God, or thank him. We can't let it be as Before, Ham. We can't let God find us unfaithful."

Ham sorted through a box and pulled out a desired tool without responding.

"Ham? Are you even listening to me?" Naomi felt the sting of tears welling up.

Ham sighed and faced her, pinching the bridge of his nose. "What do you want me to do? I can't control the actions of every man in Shinar."

Naomi noticed the dark lines beneath his eyes. "No, I suppose you can't."

Ham directed his attention to his carving while she stood and waited for him to take her in his arms and reassure her as he always did. He was right. He couldn't control all humanity. But they had to try, to set the example for the others. They had to be the guiding force for their own kin. Naomi squeezed her eyes to stop the flow of tears. She hoped it wasn't too late.

Strong arms wrapped around her shoulders and pulled her in tightly. Ham kissed the top of her head. The familiar endearment was effective. Naomi let out a sigh. Burrowed into her husband's chest she felt her tensions ease. Ham was a strong leader. She could trust his ways.

The dogs jumped to their feet and barked at the door. Cush bolted into the shop, red faced and panting. "Father, there's trouble.

Come quickly."

Ham took Cush by the shoulders and stopped him from leaving. "What trouble? What's happened?"

Cush drew in a deep breath. "A man, a man was murdered. They're blaming my son."

"Which son? Who? Tell me!"

"Nimrod."

Chapter Nine

Murder. The word alone brought churning to Naomi's gut. There had to be another explanation. It had to be a mistake.

A small crowd hovered at the base of the stairs leading up the face of Nimrod's tower. Ham disappeared among them, creating a path by pushing bodies aside. Naomi slowed to catch her breath and waited for Cush to catch up. Sweat soaked her son's tunic and dripped off his brow. He stopped at the back of the gathering beside her.

Low rumblings increased as several men caught sight of Ham and immediately began demanding an explanation.

Nimrod stood on the stairs surrounded by a few dozen men. His wall of protection was composed of laborers, dusty and clothed in simple working tunics. The tools of their trade were piled nearby, trowels and buckets, mostly. A few had belts wrapped around their waists holding picks and knives but none of them held a real weapon in his hand.

Ham and Nimrod talked on the steps with animated motions but she couldn't catch their words above the hum. Both turned and stared when Nimrod pointed to something off to the side, then resumed their conversation. After several minutes Ham turned to the crowd and acknowledged them by raising his arms, asking for their silence. "Please," he said. "Please. Let me hear the accusations for myself."

The people parted to make way for a woman to climb the steps.

"Iris?" Ham said at the same instant the woman's name left Cush's lips.

Iris stood before Ham and drilled a finger in his chest. "It was you, you and your kin that killed my Eli."

Ham stepped back away from the accusing finger and shook his head. "What are you talking about? Eli was very much alive when we left your home."

"You came back for him. My boy saw it. That one took my Eli's life." The woman pointed at Nimrod.

The crowd gasped, then grew silent as the weight of the charge fully penetrated their minds. They had not been immune from the sting of death: the boy who fell from a cliff while hunting with his father, the women who drowned in the Euphrates, the father of nine attacked by a boar. These were unforeseen deaths, untimely deaths. The street brawls now and again left a man injured, never dead. No one had intentionally taken the life of another. Until now, the children of Noah's children had not faced the charge of murder.

Cush took Naomi's hand and squeezed. "Iris and Eli are the ones we told you about, living near the Tigris. The man was alive when we left, Mother. There's no truth to her words."

Naomi looked up at her grandson, surprised there was no anger on his face. Nimrod's hands were clasped in front of his chest, his head shaking side to side with eyes locked on Iris. "This is not so," he said, then raised his voice to the crowd. "The accusation is not true. I did not lay a hand on her husband. I promise before all of you that I am not responsible for the man Eli's death."

Iris squinted at Nimrod then spit on his feet. "Your life for his."

Naomi felt her knees buckle at the woman's words. Cush caught her and pulled her close. He too was shaking. She searched the crowd for Japheth and Denah. They wouldn't allow the situation to turn dark and Ham needed the support of his brother.

Her husband's face had grown pale and she could see him scanning the crowd as well, searching for Japheth, an assured voice of reason. The faces looking back were waiting for him, and him alone to speak. It was up to Ham to control the flow of emotions and determine a sequence of events. He put a hand on another man's shoulder to steady himself. Her husband could be rash when challenged and Naomi prayed for God to clear his mind. When he lifted his face she could see that he made a decision. He took in a deep breath and addressed those gathered below. "This is a matter for the Triune Council," he said. "We can't settle this matter here."

The crowd murmured in approval. Ordinarily the patriarch of a family decided the punishment for his offspring but this dispute crossed the lines of family lineage, and the horrific accusation was not yet founded. Taking the matter to the Triune Council was wise. Ham managed the situation well. Naomi let out a welled up breath.

"Then what shall I do with Eli?" Iris stood on the step and addressed those gathered near. "It was a day to get here already. He must be placed in a grave."

Naomi didn't realize the woman brought her husband's body into the city and she strained to look over the heads to see where it was. A cart near the tower was surrounded by people. A young woman and two young boys sat on the seat and two young men stood in the back. The sorrow on their faces made it evident they were the children of the dead man.

Eli's body was already returning to the dust of the earth if he traveled all day in the cart. Naomi needed to see for herself how the man died, before his body was under the stones of the earth. An animal attack or fall would be evident with a simple inspection. Even if he accidentally ate poisonous berries, there might still be the telltale signs of discoloration at his lips. Eli's body had to be inspected, and it needed to happen soon. The Council members had to know for themselves how the man died. The accusation of murder, at the hand of her grandson, wasn't tenable, despite what the woman claimed.

"He can be buried on my field," a grandson of Shem called out.

Ham shook his head. "He can't be buried on lands that we allow to flood with overflow in the spring. Eli may get washed away."

"We should offer him to God, then," the man said. "Put him on the altar."

Naomi grasped Cush for support. There were places all around the city where the mound of stones wouldn't wash away or be disturbed. Even on her own land. She looked around the crowd, waiting for protests against the man's suggestion. No one spoke out against the idea.

Ham didn't respond either, his hand moving automatically to rub his chin as he thought. Naomi caught her breath. No. He can be buried elsewhere. A man can not be burned as a sacrifice unto God. No, Ham. No.

Ham did not read her thoughts. He looked at Iris as if to gauge her response. The woman didn't appear appalled and Naomi could hold her tongue no longer. "No! It isn't the way of God. A man cannot be the sacrifice!"

"Has he said so, Naomi?" The man who offered his field asked. "If the best of our herds is pleasing, then why wouldn't a man in God's image be even more so? This man Eli was a good husband and father. Why shouldn't he be honored before God?"

Naomi put one hand over her heart and linked her other arm

through Cush's elbow, unsure of her own strength. Ham kept his mouth closed. No one spoke up as they waited for her response. "It, it just isn't the way. Remember Cain," was all she could think to say. As soon as the comment fell from her lips, she knew it held no meaning.

The man chuckled and grinned, knowing he won the battle. "God demands blood on the altar. Cain's offering was of the field, it didn't contain blood. If God isn't pleased, I suppose Eli won't burn any more than Cain's offering did."

Naomi looked to Ham. He shrugged, then looked at Iris.

Iris nodded affirmatively. "I wish to offer my husband to God."

Ham avoided Naomi's eyes and stared at the cart containing Eli's body for a moment. He was the patriarch among them. His word would stand on this matter. "Let the widow make her offering," he said.

▲

Naomi made her way to the cart where the body of Eli was lying on a doe hide, a length of thin linen draped over his still form. A stale urine odor hovered around him and she could see the tint of death on his skin, even through the shroud.

The young woman on the cart bench held a little boy on her lap, rocking him as he sobbed. She was very plain and Naomi realized this was the one offered to Nimrod. The girl paid little attention to the people peeking into the cart as they passed. She nodded and smiled a bit at the ones who expressed condolences but otherwise focused on her littlest brothers. She had a kind smile and soft words for them. Dried tears streaked her cheeks. The girl looked up at Naomi when she didn't move away from the cart. "Are you kin?" she asked.

Naomi shook her head. "No." She hesitated before explaining her interest, that she was the accused man's grandmother. "How did your father die?" she asked instead.

The girl looked down at her father for a moment before nodding to the older boys. They knelt down in the cart and peeled the drape from his body. Eli was on his back with his arms at his side. Except for the urine stain, his tunic was clean. The boys rolled their father to his side. Naomi swallowed the sick feeling rising in her throat and clutched the side of the cart. Dark blood clotted the back of the man's head, matting his hair into a stiff sheet. His tunic was stained, the smeared blood adhering fabric to skin nearly to his waist. Naomi ran her eyes over his limbs. She saw no injuries other than the one that obviously led to his death. The cavity on the back of Eli's skull would kill any man.

The boys returned their father to his back. There were no abrasions on his arms or legs, no indication that he struggled with man or beast. His hands didn't appear to be injured, either. They were like Noah's, calloused with a rim of dirt embedded beneath his nails. She was glad her father-in-law wasn't here to witness the horrific accusations against his great-grandson, or see the brutal signs on the dead man's head.

Naomi turned away as the boys pulled the shroud over their father's lifeless form. Ham and now Japheth were both there, standing behind her. She could tell from their expressions they had seen the wound as well.

Two of Shem's grandsons approached the cart with Iris walking between them. "We'll take him now," one said.

Naomi took Iris's hands and pressed them together between her own. "My grandson could not have done this. I don't know what happened to your husband, but I know Nimrod is innocent."

Iris pulled her hands free and put them on her hips. "You know nothing. You weren't there." Iris took her son's hand and swung herself up into the cart on the bench beside Eliamah. Naomi turned to the girl. Her watery eyes held Naomi's until the cart jolted forward. They were sorrowful eyes, not angry. They were eyes that knew more than her lips were allowed to speak.

The crowd made room for the cart to turn, then followed in its wake. Naomi spun toward Japheth and grabbed the front of his tunic. "Do you understand what she intends to do with him? Are you allowing this?"

Ham exhaled loudly and cursed under his breath. Japheth glanced at Ham then back at Naomi, running his fingers repeatedly through his curly hair. "My brother has decided. What's done is done." His hands stopped their restless motion and dropped to her shoulders. "We have to stand behind his decision." Japheth's lips quivered as he spoke.

"But-"

Ham took her arm and gently pulled her from Japheth. "We have far more to worry about than this man's remains, Naomi. Let the widow be appeased and do what she wishes."

Naomi pressed her lips together, turning to follow behind the cart with the solemn crowd. Cush wisely escorted Nimrod away from the gathering, toward home. No one questioned his leaving and she couldn't believe anyone took the accusation against him as truth. Nimrod would stand before the Triune with an explanation and it would all be sorted out. An accusation of murder didn't mean one actually occurred. How Eli received the blow to his head was surely not what it appeared.

Murder. Naomi wiped away the tears burning in her eyes. Once sin was set in motion, it continued. One man killed, then another in retaliation. Then another, and another. Families would fight against each other, brothers against brothers. One man's death would escalate and put them all at odds, all on sides. The fear of God would not stop the hatred once it started.

They had to find the truth, not only to protect her own heart. Not only to protect Nimrod. For the sake of all mankind beneath the watchful eyes of heaven, they had to find the roots of this sin and destroy them before the hand of God intervened.

Chapter Ten

Iris wouldn't allow Eli's body to rest on the animal remnants, even though the charred altar was cleaned of the blackened bits of the last sacrifice. Shem's descendants shouldered the responsibility of making the adjustment, gathering heaps of dry wood from among the trees to cover the stones, creating a clean barrier between Eli and the ashes. Shawls were donated, too, to line the sticks but the man was not wrapped in them. He lay on top with nothing but the drape of blue sky.

Naomi tried again to talk Iris out of the plan, to no avail. The woman insisted that Eli would be honored in this manner, reminding Naomi that Ham approved the actions. Naomi had no say above his and the crowd that gathered seemed intent to allow the man to be offered to God.

The unfolding events could still be averted. If enough men would rise in protest and insist the man be buried properly, the sacrifice could be stopped. But no one stepped forward to question the proceedings.

Naomi watched silently. "What does it matter if he returns to the earth slowly in the ground or quickly on the altar?" That was the question she was asked numerous times. She tried to explain that it wasn't the handling of Eli's remains she opposed; it was the offering of man as a sacrifice. There was a weight on her heart at the thought, and she knew it would not please God.

The field filled rapidly with people as news spread. Waves of new-comers worked their way to the front to see Eli at rest on his cushioned bed. Most had never seen the lifeless shell of a man. The brave ones touched his waxy skin with a tentative hand, recoiling at the coolness. Few spoke and most had a wide-eyed look of disbelief etched on their faces. One woman brought a small jar that she showed to Iris before sprinkling the contents over Eli. The aromatic spice filled the air and Naomi recognized the heady mixture of myrrh and frankincense. The same mixture was used in their previous burials, rubbed onto the skin before the deceased was wrapped in cloth and entombed beneath the memorial stones. It was the smell of sorrow.

Iris climbed onto the stony altar by her husband's feet. She rubbed the spices over his dusky pink soles and up his shins. Periodically she stopped and kissed the feet that led her away from her kin and into the unknowns to the place of his death and her grief. It was a simple gesture of devotion amid the chaos that had to be swarming inside her mind. The woman's man was gone, and all that she knew would change. Her boys would take possession of the land and they were barely old enough to steer the oxen. Her life would increase in difficulty on top of the heartache and loneliness.

Eli's children stood nearby in a line, quietly absorbing the activity. Their father's death and deliverance back to the earth had become a spectacle and Naomi's heart ached for them. The crowd didn't bother the children, averting their eyes from the mourning expressions and whispering among themselves. The girl didn't look at anyone except her siblings. Naomi longed to have a moment alone with her, to console her away from the mob, and to question her about the accusations. This was not the time.

When the preparations were complete, the crowd gathered in a solemn mass. Naomi scanned the faces over and over, relieved that Ham wasn't present. Japheth didn't attend either, and no one stepped forward to take leadership. Naomi's heart quickened. Maybe the men of God realized it was wrong to make this sacrifice. Perhaps no one would lift the torch and Eli could be buried properly after all.

A low rumbling stirred among the crowd then softened again as a man made his way to Iris. It was Shem's kin, the man who offered his land for the burial. The man who suggested the defiant affront to God. He held a torch.

Iris nodded and the man stepped in front of the altar, lifting the torch to the heavens. He didn't speak. His lips were pursed and he twisted them as he stood. Had God sealed his lips? Naomi clasped her hands over her heart, hoping it was so and at the same time looking to the sky for signs of God's displeasure. Surly he would strike this man to the earth.

Finally the man exhaled and lowered the torch. He looked at Iris, then at the crowd. The words he spoke weren't the words of the sacrifice unto God. He didn't say anything except to stumble over the line, "We honor this man, Eli." Then he set the torch to the timber.

Naomi could take no more and ran from the field through the empty streets, her mind swirling. She would not have been surprised to see the dark clouds of storm on the horizon, descending from the heavens to destroy mankind again. But the sky was clear and blue. Whatever his intentions, Shem's kin didn't say the damning words. He was wise. Eli's body was sent back to the earth in a dramatic fashion and that was all.

This time.

It had to end. Naomi fell to her knees in a stand of trees, covering her face with her hands in the dark shadows. Ashamed of her people. Frightened for her offspring. First Man Adam spoke of the judgment by water and of the judgment by fire. She witnessed the one. She did not wish to see the other.

There was still time. Surely men could see that now. They could see how far from the ways of God they had wandered. Murder and the unorthodox sacrifice had to remind them of the God who demanded their allegiance. There was still time to steer their ways towards the God of the heavens.

Naomi collapsed in the leaves and allowed herself to sob. How far they had fallen.

Again.

▲

A red stain crept up Shem's neck and colored his face as Ham and Japheth described the events of the previous days. His brother had been sent for immediately, a full day's journey for the messenger to get there, another one coming back. He came with his wife, Eran and half a dozen others. Noah and Jael were not among them.

Their wives sat quietly, hands gripped together in solidarity, listening as he and his brothers spoke. Cush was there, too, as was Japheth's firstborn, Gomer, and Shem's Elam. They all sat on the floor, on soft pallets, as Noah instructed when he formed the Council. Sit and discuss like family, he told them.

The meeting place stood in the center of town originally, when there were only sons and a few grandsons of Noah. It was a simple brick structure, one large open room where the family could gather together for meals and celebrations. It could not contain all the descendants now and had become the home of the Triune Council. The six men present made the bricks surrounding them and the tiles overhead that repelled the summer rays and the winter rain. Each labored to level the land and raise the walls so no one had claim over another to the site. Each of Noah's boys had blood and sweat mixed into the mortar. It belonged to all.

Shem exhaled loudly and started to rise before gaining control of his emotions and sitting back down in the circle. His hand instinctively clasped the black stone dangling from his neck. He clung to it when he needed strength or self-control, as if he was gripping the very hand of God.

"You allowed Eli to be offered as a *sacrifice*?"

Ham groaned but controlled the words on his tongue. He could have predicted that the serious accusations against Nimrod would take second place to the perceived defilement upon the altar of God. "What was I to do? I kept the crowd under control by honoring the widow's wishes. No harm was done."

"And you allowed this, Japheth. You approved?"

"The decision was made by the time I arrived. I couldn't have stopped anyone at that point."

"Then which of you spoke the words of blessing?" Shem forced a calm expression of words from his tight lips.

Ham and Japheth shook their heads. "We didn't attend the funeral," Ham said.

"I was there." Naomi said. "It was your kin that offered the torch, but he didn't speak the words unto God. He didn't offer the man as a sacrifice. He wisely held his tongue."

The room grew quiet and Shem's expression softened. His eyes glistened as he locked his gaze on Naomi. "And no one spoke up against it? No one feared the outcome?"

"No, Shem. The men were silent. No one protested."

Shem wiped his eyes on his sleeve. "I don't know what God has to say about burning a man once his soul is gone, but can this Council agree that those formed in the image of God must never be offered as a sacrifice unto him? God told our ancestors what was clean and presentable. The body of man was not included. We must follow the ways he has prescribed."

Japheth nodded in agreement, as did Elam and Gomer. Cush, as usual, waited for Ham's response and he would vote similarly. Half the time Ham doubted his firstborn even knew what the Council was deciding. He thought the two of them were more like-minded than he gave Cush credit for, until he realized his son barely paid attention and voted like his father every time. He was a puppet in the Triune. At least his son chose to vote with him and not against.

"Ham? Your vote?" Shem didn't need to know his, or Cush's, vote. It was four to two as it stood. And agreeing indicated he had made a poor decision. The gravity of this decision among the people required a united face, however. He nodded his assent and heard his wife let out a pent up sigh. No one asked Cush's opinion, he noticed.

Japheth ran his fingers through his hair and cleared his throat. "About Eli's death, then. Shem, what is the situation with that family?"

"Eli kept his home near mine, until four or five years ago. He was the cause of regular dissension, questioning every practice, every decision of his father and grandfather, and me. I didn't ask him to leave us, but I didn't stop him when he wanted to live alone, by his own rules. He filled the others with all sorts of lies about the past. He took the bits he knew and made his own history. I was glad when he left. I thought the reality of living on his own would bring him back to a right understanding."

Ham nodded and looked at Cush who smiled a bit. Even in the short time they were with Eli, he brought dissension among them.

"His widow claims he was killed intentionally. Murdered." Japheth spat the word out.

Ham drew in a sharp breath. This was the first time the Council had to even consider the possibility that a life was taken from another. An adult life anyway. Naomi suspected that newborns were allowed to die at times. There was no evidence, no way to prove her suspicions, and no parent tossing out blame onto another, so it was never a matter for the Council. This was different. A man was killed and the accusing finger was pointed at his grandson. "The man was very much alive when we left his home."

"Someone killed him. Or it was an accident. We have to find the truth." Shem said. "And, we must remember what God has said, and stand firm in the necessary discipline."

Ham's mind filled with an image engraved forever in sharp detail. The rocky out-cropping surrounded by jagged points of land in all directions. The stiff wind piercing his clothing as he stacked stones to make an altar. The frightened cries of the antelope that his father led by a rope around its neck, suddenly afraid away from the security of the ark. The sharp stabs of pain as he knelt on the hard, uneven land. The smell of wet wood that took the flame. The glory of the bow in the sky.

And the voice of his God.

"Whoever sheds human blood, by man shall his blood be shed."

A life for a life.

Nimrod's life.

Naomi leaned on Denah's shoulder, swallowing hard to control her emotions. They, and Eran were pale, eyes red and swollen. Ham closed his eyes and remained silent, as did his brothers and their firstborns. He sucked his own emotions down to a place of control. He could not let go of the pain yet. The day was just beginning.

Chapter Eleven

Iris positioned herself on a cushion and accepted a cup of hot water mixed with aromatic leaves and spices. Her children sat beside her, facing the interior of the circle where bowls of food held their attention. None of them took anything. They sat quietly, glancing at each other before turning back to the food, not even whispering. Naomi tried to catch the eyes of the little ones to give a reassuring smile but they didn't look up at the adults around them.

The six men of the Triune sat in the circle, too. Naomi sat behind her husband and son where she could see over their shoulders. She identified members of all three lines of Noah in the room, forming rings around the Council. All were required to sit, even those nearest the doors. They sat in family groups, she noticed. Kin with kin on the father's side. Sisters greeted one another with a simple nod from across the room as they sat with their husband's family. There was a tense air hovering above them all.

Nimrod sat next to Cush. He was clean shaven, still smelling of soap. He was up early, before the sun rays of dawn. Naomi saw him riding towards the barn as she was getting up. His horse was frothy with sweat after a hard ride. Nimrod seemed calm and controlled. Just like he did now. He sat cross-legged on a mat and held a cup of tea, though he wasn't actually drinking it. He just rolled the warm cup in his hands. He looked at his accusers from time to time, without any hint of malice. Naomi was pleased. Her grandson stood falsely accused before all men yet he maintained dignity and honored his fathers.

Naomi rose slightly to her knees and caught Iris's eye. "Please eat," she said. "And the children, too."

Eager faces turned to the mother who nodded in approval. The older boys filled their bowls with the variety of treats while Eliamah assisted the younger ones. The girl's own dish remained empty, as did Iris's. The Council members made a show of eating, as was expected, nibbling on breads and fruit to pass the time while the children gobbled the meal. It was the custom to eat first, before the business began, but none of the adults were hungry. They were all anxious to begin and end the issue at hand.

Iris wore a simple garment with her hair pulled back away from her face. Prominent cheek bones sat beneath a set of intense eyes. Her back was straight as she looked around the room. The woman was strong of body and mind and will, Naomi decided. She didn't appear the least bit intimidated before the Council. Many men renounced their accusations before the meal ended, unable to stand before the sons of Noah and proclaim lies as truth. Others were unable to look the patriarchs in the eye as they repeated their version of the events in question. Some fiddled with their belts or their hair or they blinked a lot. Naomi noticed these details. Guilt spoke loudly without words. So far, there was no guilt to be read on Iris.

Ham initiated the trial. "The accusation against Nimrod is that of murder, willful taking of the man Eli's life. Iris, please tell us what happened."

Iris looked briefly at Ham, then Shem, then fixed her attention on Japheth. She was considered in the line of Shem because of her marriage to Eli but Iris was the great-granddaughter of Denah and

Japheth. "Five days ago, these men came to our place." She pointed at Ham, Cush and Nimrod. "They were looking for tar pits and saw our chimney smoke. We fed them and talked about our people and the crops. Then they left. Or so we believed."

Naomi watched her husband nod slightly. No one spoke so Iris continued. "They came back in the night. They killed the dog and killed my Eli."

The room gasped as one then hushed immediately. Iris squared her shoulders and looked directly at Japheth. Ham flinched at her words and glanced at Nimrod before fixing his eyes on Iris.

Japheth took a deep breath. "Back up, Iris. They left. Then what? What did you see? What did you hear?"

Iris took a sip of tea as she looked at her children. All of them, even the baby in the girl's arms were focused on their mother's words. "They left our place. We finished our chores, and went to bed. I woke up early and Eli wasn't there. He wasn't in the house." Iris stared at her hands.

"And?" Shem gently prodded.

Iris exhaled and turned her glistening eyes to Shem. "And, I wasn't worried then. Thought he was relieving himself or something, some little chore before he ate. But he didn't come back, so I went looking for him. He was by the stream. Dead."

"You didn't hear anything? See anyone?"

Iris shook her head. "No, and not them either, except this one." Iris pointed at her older children first, then at the boy beside her. She ran her hand over his head. The other boys nodded with the same tight lipped expression, affirming her statement. The girl dropped her head and focused on the baby.

"So you didn't see Nimrod?" Ham asked.

Iris turned to Nimrod. "No, not me. He was already gone when I found Eli. But my boy here did. Beni saw that man outside his window." Her bony finger pointed at the accused.

Again, a uniform gasp, followed by silence. Japheth bent forward to speak to the boy at his level. Beni fidgeted with a grape stem and looked between Japheth and his mother. "It's alright, son" he said. "Just tell me the truth."

Iris put her hand over the boy's to still them. He slipped one out, rubbing the back under his nose before he spoke. "I was in bed and I heard something so I got up and looked out and there was that man." Beni pointed at Nimrod with his eyes then jerked them away.

"What was he doing?" Japheth asked.

The boy turned to his mother who nodded for him to continue. "I guess he was looking for my rocks."

Naomi saw the increased tension in her husband's posture.

"What rocks?" Japheth asked.

"The pretty ones me and my brother get from the water."

Ham's jaw line tightened.

"Did you see your father?"

The boy shook his head no.

"Did you hear your father? Did you hear any fighting? Any yelling?"

"No."

"Then what happened? Then what did you do?"

The boy shrugged. "I went to mother." He buried his head in his mother's lap.

Iris stroked his back. "He went to sleep beside me. That's where he was when I got up." Iris looked up and her expression hardened. "I think Eli heard noise and went outside to see about it, and got himself killed. Got hit on the head."

Nimrod was shaking his head back and forth. Cush stared through a bowl of fruit, running his hand over his chin. Ham's eyes were wide and his jaw locked tight.

"But no one witnessed it that way for certain," Japheth said. "Tell us about Eli."

"Like I said, we found him with his blood drained out already, from the hole on the back of his head. You saw it. You know that was no accident. We put him in the cart and came here straight away. The rest you know."

Naomi watched Eliamah rock the baby. She hoped the Council would ask the girl what she saw, what she believed. She was tender of nature and Naomi felt sure she would answer honestly when pressed. But no one paid her any attention. Her calm, plain demeanor faded into the floor.

Japheth turned to Ham and Cush and allowed them to speak of the evening in question. Eli was alive when they left. They spent the night in a cave and went home the next morning. Both claimed their own innocence, that they did not kill Eli.

Nimrod's version of the day was no different from theirs. He talked about the meal the family provided and about their discussions. The girl stiffened and looked up at Nimrod at this point and Nimrod smiled at her gently. The girl blushed and looked down, for a moment, then her eyes were on his again. Nimrod hesitated as he watched her, then continued without mention of her parent's offer. The girl relaxed noticeably as Nimrod avoided humiliating her publicly.

Eran reached over and squeezed Naomi's hand, aware of the strength in Nimrod's soul allowing him to protect this girl in spite of the charges from her family. His kindness didn't alter the hostile expression on Iris's face, however.

Shem straightened his shoulders and spoke slowly. "Nimrod, did you harm Eli in any way, killing him by accident or intention?"

Nimrod shook his head. "I did not."

Iris hissed under her breath. "He lies."

Shem held up his hand to the low rumble building in the room. "We have heard the accusations and the witness. Is there any other evidence?"

The room was silent.

Naomi held her tongue. Her mind whirled in frantic circles, searching for the missing bits that would connect the facts and make the picture whole. The proceedings had not cleared Nimrod as she anticipated. He had been at the home and there was nothing discussed to prove he wasn't guilty. There was really only the testimony of the little boy, but someone killed Eli. She wanted to stand and scream. Her grandson had his faults. He was not a killer.

Chapter Twelve

The dragon skull glistened in the sun where it sat on a large stone, stripped of its life giving blood and fleshly covering. Nimrod sat nearby. Only the three sons of Noah and their firstborns remained in the Council room. Everyone else was asked to leave so the men could discuss and rehash the evidence. They would vote and decide her grandson's fate.

Nimrod whittled a chunk of wood with furious motions, sending slivers into the air like tiny arrows, covering the dragon anew. Naomi watched him as she walked up the path with a basket of food. Her strong, brave grandson had never been faced with an obstacle he couldn't learn to conquer. He mastered the beasts by practicing his skills with the bow and the slingshot and the bolo, over and over, until he could catch a hare on the run without harming it or slay a dragon many times his size. He mastered the will of men with his charm and gentle persuasion. He mastered his circumstances with planning and calculation.

He had no control over the decision of the Triune Council.

"I brought some food, Nimrod," Naomi said as she sat beside him.

"My last meal, Grandmother?"

"Don't say such things. The Council is just. If you are innocent, that truth will reveal itself."

"If? If I am innocent?"

Naomi looked deeply into his eyes while cupping his face in her hands. "I know you didn't kill that man, Nimrod. I know."

"And the Council? You heard the words of the woman against me. I don't know how to prove that I am unjustly accused."

"The words of a little boy don't carry much weight. And the Council knows you, your character. They know you aren't the man Iris has portrayed."

"But they can't show favoritism, can they? The Council must make a decision based on the evidence. And Uncle Shem. He won't support my acquittal."

"Shem doesn't decide alone. He'll ask God for wisdom, as will the others."

Nimrod hurled his carving against a tree. "I don't believe God will support me either."

"Why would you think that?"

"Because I stand accused. Why would I be in this position if God was in my favor? Perhaps I'm not one that God chooses to show attention. His eyes are closed to me."

Naomi bit down on her lip and squeezed Nimrod's hand. "He is always seeing. You know that. I don't know why this is happening to you, but it isn't because God isn't watching."

"He shows his favoritism, though. He picks some to bless, some to destroy. He wiped out your entire family, Grandmother. Was your own mother so evil? Your sisters? He destroyed men who sought truth from other gods. Was that fair?"

Naomi stood abruptly. Her heart thumped in her chest. She took in a deep breath and let it out slowly, allowing her mind to gain a controlled stance before she responded. Nimrod's accusations raised her defensive guard. He was questioning God's decisions, questioning if God was just. He always looked for answers to the ways of man, the reason for the sacrifice, the reason God is thanked for the harvest and the rains and the babies filling each man's home. Nimrod wasn't satisfied with the answers he had been given. He doubted God.

So had she.

Not when the door of the ark was set in place by unseen hands, when she was sealed into the vessel and the sky turned black in a fury against the earth. God's sovereign power was of no question. It was later, as the ark shifted on the saturated hillside, then lifted off the land, carried on water that came from the heaven and the earth in an explosion that she felt the sting of doubt. Not in God's power, but in his mercy. As the very earth disappeared and she realized everyone had perished beneath the churning flow, she cried out in her heart for his answers.

Her entire family drowned.

Noah sent her to the city to tell them about the beasts that were gathering, about the impending flood. They didn't believe her. Her mother laughed and said she was sorry she ever allowed Naomi to marry into the disturbed household of Noah and Jael. She would have been better off not marrying at all. Animals came to the ark because of the food stores Noah was hoarding and because his sons were trapping them and keeping them imprisoned on the ark. There was no flood. There was no judgment. Naomi was as crazy as the rest of Noah's family.

None of them came to the ark.

They had the chance to be saved and this is what Noah reminded her as the days turned into months. God knew the hearts of men and men knew the ways of God, but chose to act in defiance. God had not been unjust. Man had been rebellious.

Nimrod was feeling the doubts now, too. Standing face to face with his own mortality, he was terrified. He needed the arm of justice to lean on.

"God will judge. We must trust him to provide for your protection."

Nimrod said nothing.

"Tell me about the girl, Nimrod. Tell me about Eliamah."

Nimrod looked up in surprise and didn't try to suppress a sneer and a gruff laugh. "The daughter? What is there to tell? They expected me to just take her and marry her. You saw her. Even if I did take another wife, it wouldn't be that one."

Naomi felt her defenses rising again, this time for the plain girl with the sad eyes. "She seems compassionate. There is a good woman inside her, I think. One that might tell the truth if given the opportunity."

"But she won't speak, will she? I even smiled at her. I could have shamed her mercilessly in the meeting, but I didn't. Still she didn't speak. Iris has control of that thing's tongue."

Naomi wrapped her arm around Nimrod's stiff shoulders and squeezed her eyes shut, feeling his presence in her arms and memorizing each detail. He leaned his head against her shoulder.

"Don't expect another ark of salvation, Grandmother. God doesn't always protect the innocent. I must save myself somehow."

Chapter Thirteen

Ham filled his lungs then plunged his head into the barrel of cool water, keeping it there as long as he could before his chest threatened to burst open. He shook the water from his hair and tied the wet locks behind his head with a cord before going back into the room where the Council was gathering again. The short break wasn't long enough. It was sufficient time to clear everyone out except the six men. Sufficient time to stretch and heat more water for tea. Sufficient to hug Naomi and listen to her concerns. It was not enough time to fully clear his head and think the matter through. Not enough time to come up with the sound reasoning he wanted as they discussed his grandson's fate.

Determining the disciplinary action against his offspring was nothing new. When there were issues crossing clan lines, more likely than not, one of his own was involved. He tried to be fair, as did the others on the Council, but he was certainly more lenient than his brothers. He was more forgiving in general. They were, after all, one family, the children of Noah. Mistakes would be made.

The last time the Council met they decided the punishment of a young man accused of slinking through the streets at night, looking into windows. After the first five women testified, it was obvious he was guilty. Shem wanted both of the man's eyes put out. Ham disagreed. He would be unable to work then, at least at full potential, and he did have a young wife of his own to support. No lasting damage was done, he said. Nothing was stolen, no one was hurt. Both eyes was too high a price to pay. He suggested the man be under a curfew for a year, allowed outside after dark only if accompanied by others. In the end they decided to take one of the man's eyes as his punishment, with the promise the other would be taken if he broke the curfew or continued his practice. It was a steep price.

The man adhered to their rules, as far as Ham knew. He didn't leave his home at night. He also refused to attend the sacrifices. His wife was forbidden to attend as well. Had the harsh punishment made the situation worse?

Nimrod's accused crime was much more severe than that of the young man. Ham dreaded the discussion to come.

The others were already waiting. Ham sat down with them in the circle.

Shem initiated the proceedings. "All of you had a chance to see Eli before he was burned. From what you tell me, are we all agreed that he died from a wound on the back of his head?"

"Yes," Japheth said. "It appears he was struck from behind. He may have fallen and cracked his head open, but this seems unlikely. I won't say it's an impossible scenario, but I say the blow was intentional."

"Ham? What do you think?"

Ham hesitated. An accident cleared Nimrod of sin. He couldn't support the theory though. He'd seen too many similar injuries in the time before the flood. This was no simple fall. His brothers knew it. "Eli was a fit young man. I see no reason for him to fall backward with that much force yet sustain no other injuries. His hands weren't damaged. If he tripped in the night, he would land face first anyhow."

"Iris said he was near the stream," Cush said. "They cleared that land of large stones for the most part. It was primarily dirt. The river rocks were no larger than my fist and were smooth. Even if he did fall backward, I can't see how the stones would break his skull like that."

Shem's son Elam held up his hand. "Aunt Naomi slipped on stones. In the stream, the day of the dragon kill. It isn't impossible to imagine. I know it's not likely but I don't think we should eliminate the possibility."

"Eli was found near the water though, not in it."

Shem looked at the five men. "Eli was murdered, in my opinion. Can we agree this is the most likely scenario, and keep our minds open to the possibility we have missed facts that would lead us otherwise?"

Ham reluctantly nodded, as did the others.

Shem continued. "We have one child as a witness."

"He's just a little boy. We can't take his word." Ham kept his voice low and even.

"Not that little," Japheth said. "Old enough to give an account for what he saw."

"Or what he thinks he saw." Shem leaned back on his arms and closed his eyes as if visualizing the scene. "He's either speaking the truth, and he saw someone outside the home in the night, or his mother told him to tell a lie."

"If she were going to have one of the children lie, wouldn't she choose one of the older ones? Little ones will show the falsehood if pressured. I think the boy saw someone. Someone, not necessarily Nimrod. I can't even tell Ham and him apart from a distance."

Ham slammed his fist on the floor. "You are accusing me now, Japheth?"

Japheth shook his head. "No, no, no. Of course not. I'm just saying, I believe the boy is telling the truth about seeing someone. But who knows who he saw in the darkness of night? Maybe one of his own brothers."

Ham could feel blood heating his face. He knew this discussion would turn all directions yet he wished for once his brothers would just side with him. For once, couldn't they believe it wasn't his offspring in the wrong.

"We have to face the fact that Nimrod was nearby the night Eli died," Shem spoke softly with his eyes fixed on Ham.

"Father and I were in the area too," Cush said. "We slept in the same cave."

"But you haven't been accused. Iris seems sure it was Nimrod. What was his mood, after you left Eli and Iris?"

Cush shrugged. "Same as ours. We had a good laugh over the situation, all three of us. The wine helped." He smiled at Ham.

"And Eli? He didn't offer you a place to stay for the night."

"He was angry," Ham said. "Because of the girl."

Japheth ran a hand through his hair. "They were all upset about that, right? Angry enough to blame Nimrod for another man's crime? Angry enough to kill Eli themselves to blame Nimrod?"

Ham shook his head. "No. No, they were obviously a tight family. They weren't pleased about the situation with the girl but it was me who said Nimrod couldn't take her. If anyone was set up to take blame, they would have chosen me."

Cush nodded. "I can't believe it was any of them. There must have been a traveler. Someone else was in the area."

Members from all three clans took off exploring the land from time to time. Many left with the intent to survive on their own. Few were gone more than a year. Most returned to the safety and abundance of Shinar, full of adventurous tales. Those that didn't return were presumed dead – eaten by bears, frozen in the descending rivers of ice, poisoned from eating the berries of an inviting bush. The land near the Tigris was lush and any number of travelers could have camped near Eli's homestead and gone unnoticed.

Shem's head was down and he rested his chin on his tented fingertips. Ham watched his brother, knowing the spinning thoughts were weaving opinions in his mind. His brother thought matters out to the last detail. "What Shem? he asked. "What are you thinking?"

Shem paused before speaking. "It's possible there was someone else there that night, that it's all coincidence. However, the evidence, as it is, still points to Nimrod. I'm sorry, Ham. I don't see how we can prove otherwise."

Ham exhaled in exasperation. "You've decided his guilt already?"

"No. I don't want it to be Nimrod. But it is someone, someone killed Eli and he must be punished as God has determined. We have to set an example before the people."

"Life for life, you mean."

Shem nodded without speaking. Japheth sat with his eyes closed. "We don't have sufficient proof that Nimrod is guilty or that he's innocent," he said. "But Shem is right. We can't allow Eli's death to go unpunished."

"It's my son's life at stake," Cush said. "His death isn't mere punishment for a crime. We can't take his life on such feeble evidence."

Ham nodded. "I know he's my grandson, but if he were yours Shem, I would feel the same. We can't take a man's life without real proof of his guilt."

"Japheth?" Shem was calling an informal vote.

"We must punish for this crime. But we have to be certain. I suggest each of us take an accounting of our kin. See who is here, who is traveling. Who was out of the city at the time of Eli's death."

"I agree with Uncle Japheth," Elam said. "It's too much to decide based on what we have heard so far. We need to explore further."

"Gomer?"

"The matter is heavy on everyone's mind right now. I'm reluctant to wait too long for justice."

"I agree. Swift action is required." Shem spoke quietly while Ham's defenses clamored to the surface. Shem wasn't vengeful. He knew that. His brother had never sought another person's pain for any reason other than payment for sin. He was not now lightly asking for Nimrod's life. He followed what he believed was the correct course. His brother wasn't always right, however.

"We've stated a number of opinions. I say we take a preliminary vote and see where we stand." Shem said. The circle nodded in assent. Ham's gut churned.

"With the available evidence, is Nimrod guilty or not guilty?" Shem allowed the words to hover on the heavy air for a few moments before continuing. "Ham?"

"Not guilty."

"Cush?"

"Not guilty."

"Japheth?"

Japheth swallowed hard then looked directly into Ham's eyes. "Guilty," he said.

"Gomer?"

"Guilty."

"Elam?"

"Not guilty."

"And my vote is guilty," Shem said.

Japheth's head snapped up and he smacked his hand on his thigh. "Undecided. Three to three. We have no consensus. By our own rules, we must take the matter up with Father."

Shem nodded. "It will be a day to send word and a day for him to get back. So we meet three, maybe four days from now. Or, we can go there. Bring the discussion to him for further instruction. I'd rather go than sit on this."

A chill snaked down Ham's spine. He would rather not wait either. He just didn't relish the thought of going back to his father's home. Noah would be in charge, in control in his element. Ham wasn't sure that was in Nimrod's favor.

The other members of the Council agreed, go rather than stay. Ham nodded reluctantly.

The room exhaled as one. The matter would be taken to Noah for discussion. He would cast the seventh vote when they voted officially. Ham got up quickly. Nimrod was spared, at least another few days.

"Tomorrow, then, at sunrise, we'll leave. Will you take Nimrod with us?" Shem asked.

Ham bit down on his tongue, understanding beyond his brothers words. "No. He stays. If he flees in our absence, he declares his own guilt."

With Cush on his heels, Ham left the meeting place, ignoring the myriad of questioning eyes that lined the streets. Let Shem and Japheth explain the decision. He needed to speak to Nimrod. His grandson would be home, he was sure, yet deep inside Ham hoped his beloved heir had already taken a horse and fled the fertile plain.

Chapter Fourteen

The procession of horses started up the well worn road towards Noah and Jael's vineyard. The sun was just peeking over the horizon and they would make it before night fall if they kept a steady pace. There would be no stopping to explore or hunt or bathe in a cool stream in the heat of the day on this trip.

Naomi, Denah and Eran rode with the Council, and that was good. They would see that peace was maintained along the way. The task had been easy so far. Except for the hooves striking the earth, Ham wouldn't know anyone followed behind him. No one spoke.

His decision not to bring Nimrod was logistical. If he came, Iris and her brood would need to be present as well, and the journey would be unbearably tense. He could see now it wouldn't have mattered who accompanied the Council. All lips were sealed.

He was glad for the silence. He couldn't guarantee any words coming from his mouth would be civil. Both his brothers voted against Nimrod. It was like Before. If there were two against one among them in their years before the flood, he was the man that stood alone. He knew better than to expect their loyalty over their honest judgment, yet it stung clear through to his soul to hear them utter the word "guilty."

The road north was nothing more than packed dirt and cleared foliage, easy ground for the horses. The flat land would turn into rolling hills for many miles before they reached the small community where Shem and his parents lived. It was the first village the sons of Noah constructed and they intended to remain there originally. The discovery of the beautiful land between the rivers enticed them to pack and move again. Most of them, anyhow. His father refused to move to Shinar, the rich plain with endless skies. Shem chose to stay near Noah, although the bulk of his offspring moved on with Ham and Japheth's relatives. Really, Ham believed, it was Eran who feared moving onto the flat stretch of land. She preferred ground that rose higher than the flooding Euphrates, though she claimed they stayed for the sake of Noah and Jael.

Ham glanced over his shoulder at Shem and Eran, riding side by side on the familiar road. They made the journey once a month for the Council meetings, remaining in town until all the business was complete. There were days, Ham remembered, when there was nothing more to discuss then the status of the crops. As the years fell away so did the ease of governing. Shem and Eran stayed for seven or eight days at a time now and had to be summoned in between times for the unexpected cases. Perhaps they would see the wisdom of relocating before long. Noah wasn't likely to follow, he knew. The man who traversed the land to preach of the impending judgment of God rarely left his home now.

Dread began a slow rise up Ham's gut as his thoughts turned toward his father. His relationship with Noah was similar to the one Ham had with Cush. Cush was a disappointment to his father. Ham was a disappointment to his father.

It hadn't always been that way. Ham challenged Noah in his youth, keeping a controlled walk on the edge of discipline, stepping over from time to time but never so far as to shame the man that raised him. Later, after the flood, the two fell into discord and though they were able to speak to one another now, the wall had never been completely removed. Nor would it ever. It had been three years or so since Ham accompanied Naomi to his parent's home and he was conveniently away on expedition trips the few times Noah and Jael journeyed with Shem to town. Directing his horse up this road was an action made out of necessity.

▲

Naomi knew the burden in her husband's heart was magnified beyond her own. His shoulders sagged as he urged his horse along the road, keeping on the alert yet unfocused at the same time. His thoughts were not solely on Nimrod. Memories climbed to the forefront that he wanted to stow away and forget, memories of the incident with Noah.

It was many years ago, back when they traveled this road together with their sons: Cush, Egypt, Put and Canaan. Their seven daughters, too, in the back of the wagons, squabbling over which of their cousins would make the best husband. Japheth's brood was on the road behind them so all would be present at Noah's for the annual Day of the Covenant celebration. It was the only time everyone left the plain and traveled to the home of the patriarch. It was a time of feasting and dancing, of establishing marriage bonds among the oldest of their children. It was a time of remembering. Remembering the beginnings when Adam was formed, remembering their fathers that lived on the earth that was. Enoch's grand departure and Methuselah's wisdom were recalled. God speaking to Noah brought a hush to even the tiniest children, and each anticipated the day they would be old enough to climb the rugged terrain to see the great vessel for themselves.

It was a grand time in the house of Noah. Until that year.

After the incident, there were no more Day of the Covenant celebrations such as they had known. Only partial families made the journey, excuses abounding as responsibilities grew with the increase in children and the expanding of homes and crops and territories requiring protection from predators and floods. Ham didn't forbid his family from attending but he himself didn't return for eleven years, carrying his first grandchild in his arms as a means of reconciliation.

Naomi remembered the day clearly. She was baking with Jael when Ham ran into the house, laughing and calling for his brothers. The three men dashed away toward the vineyard and Jael herself laughed after them, her three little boys at play. They were tighter than ever, the boys, at that time.

Japheth and Shem came back alone. Not running. Not laughing. They assured Jael everything was alright but their faces were drawn tight. Ham retuned much later and was in a sour mood. He avoided his brothers completely and made plans for his family to leave the following day.

Naomi drew the story from him in the middle of the night as they both lay awake. He told her how he found his father in a tent near the vineyard, completely unrobed and lying on a mat. At first Ham was frightened and he ran to Noah. Then he noticed the empty wineskins and smelled the fermented drink on his father's lips. He was drunk.

Noah, the man of God, the man of rules, had broken one of his own standards. He allowed himself a pleasure to an exorbitant extent. He put aside the regulation and followed his own desire.

Ham was delighted. If his father could bend the standards, why couldn't he? Why not all of them? Who was Noah now to chastise any one of them for behaviors deemed inappropriate? He no longer held the standard. Ham brought his brothers as witnesses, expecting them to rejoice in a new found freedom, rejoice in the broken chains of guilt and admonition. They did not. They were angry with Ham. They covered their father and left Ham without an ally.

Noah was waiting in the morning. Ham couldn't look at him as the family gathered. The conversations were stilted. Noah never tried to justify his own behavior and Ham didn't address his own disrespect. They should have made amends then, right away, instead of suppressing their hurts. Instead, Noah blessed Shem and Japheth. And Noah cursed her son Canaan. He didn't curse Ham, as a curse on his own son was really a curse to himself. Instead of cursing his youngest, Noah cursed Ham's youngest.

It was a horrible incident. Canaan would never forgive his grandfather, she knew. And Ham still rode the waves of his own folly, tossed from guilt to anger, anger to guilt. She couldn't recall when her husband had last seen Noah but it was two or three years now at least.

So what would Noah decide regarding Nimrod?

▲

Jael's hair smelled of the cooking fire and helped ease Ham's tension as he was crushed in her embrace. She smelled of home, of family, of the united kinship they had all once breathed. He hugged his father, too and felt a brief melting of anger. They had yet to be alone and that was alright. There were other issues that needed to be seen to first, like where they would all sleep and what they could round up to eat. Jael wasn't the least bit distressed by the sudden influx of mouths to feed. Ham could see it in her eyes and hear it in her voice as she greeted and directed and organized the troop. They were her chicks seeking shelter beneath her wings.

The house and surrounding land were little changed since he

was last there to visit, little changed since he lived there. The small valley sat below peaks of rocky terrain, green and fragrant with life. The spring carving a path through the gardens rumbled on its way down the mountain toward the plains below. Familiar sounds, familiar smells. Ham took his time leading the horses to the pasture, letting his senses soak in his past.

Their homestead stood as solid as the day it was constructed. It was nothing like the fine home he grew up in before the flood. This one was a simple rectangle, one story, composed of stones and clay bricks. The roof was flat at first, providing a gathering space, but it had to be reconfigured. It held the water that fell from the sky, then leaked and collapsed in places. They had to tear it out and build peaked supports so the rain rolled off the house, not inside. They didn't build a protective wall around the perimeter. There was no one left alive to protect themselves from.

The Council planned to meet as soon as the women had a meal prepared. There would be no delay in the business to enjoy each other's company. The sky was already fading toward the indigo shade of night when Ham returned to the home and helped Jael clear a space for them to sit together. Naomi squeezed his hand and offered a reassuring smile before she sat down. He could read the fear in her eyes.

Noah eased down onto a cushion and Ham winced at the grinding in his knees. His father was over seven hundred years now. His brown curls were outlined in gray, yet his mind was still sharp and his limbs still strong. A deep tan settled into his skin from the hours upon hours he tended his fields and vineyards. The only time the color faded was on the ark, a striking loss of color Ham noticed the day they all stepped onto the deck for the first time in weeks and saw each other in the sunlight.

His father listened as the case was presented. It was unchanged from the previous discussion. Ham forced himself to look at his father as he spoke. He had no reason to hide from anything he said. The parts he presented were the truth. No one asked about the events after he and the boys went to sleep in the cave. Ham chose not to bring anything more into the discussion. It only complicated the matter.

"You saw the injury up close?" Noah asked Naomi.

Naomi nodded. "Yes, I wanted to see for myself, to substantiate the claims. The man Eli received a blow to the back of his skull, as Iris said. He may have fallen onto a rock, but…"

"It's not likely, is it? Was there a weapon found?"

"No," Shem said. "There was no evidence of that sort mentioned."

Noah sat quietly for a long time. Ham felt the nerves in his mind tingle, especially when he glanced up and found his father's gaze fixed on him.

"And the accusation lies on Nimrod because the boy saw him, correct?"

"Yes, Father," Shem said. "The family placed no blame on anyone else."

Ham didn't return Noah's stare, feeling a finger of blame pointing his direction. He tossed an uneaten piece of cheese into a bowl. Naomi's clammy hand took hold of his and he willed his shoulders to relax. "It looks bad for Nimrod, I know. But there is only the testimony of a child, looking out in the dark of night."

"Yes," Noah said. He looked up at the ceiling as he continued. "I hoped to be in the ground with my fathers before this day arrived. Our ways have strayed again from those of our God. We shouldn't be having this discussion." Noah brought his head down and looked around the circle. "But we must. My decision is this," he said.

Naomi's grip intensified. Ham squeezed back and sucked in his breath.

"We must punish for this crime. We can't let the matter be unresolved. It must be dealt with decisively as God has decreed. A life for a life."

Naomi groaned and leaned against him. Ham kept his lips held tightly, his limbs set to bolt from the room.

"However," Noah said. "I'm not convinced Nimrod is responsible. It isn't our tradition to delay punishment but we must give Nimrod a chance to prove his innocence. I give him until the next full moon. Then he must stand before us and his accusers again. If he cannot prove himself, he will be found guilty of the charge against him. He will be stoned."

Chapter Fifteen

pproaching footsteps took Ham's focus from the horses just long enough to feel the nip of equine teeth on his arm. He stepped away as his father entered the shallow cave where the beasts were eager for food before the journey home.

"I intended to have the horses ready before you awoke," Noah said. "You're up early."

"Yes. I don't want to delay. Nimrod will be anxious to hear of your decision."

"Our decision. The Council is one in my eyes, once a decision is made."

His father put his hands on his low back and arched his spine in a series of cracks before taking a pitch fork and tossing feed to the animals. His movements were slow and deliberate this morning, each joint synchronized with the others so no one set of bones took on too much of the effort. His hands maintained a firm grasp of the tool but Ham noticed he didn't lift a significant load of hay with each rotation. The vitality of Noah's youth was declining. Ham started to take the tool from him to finish the job then stopped himself. If he took that job, Noah would find another. Nothing would stop him from working except the memorial stones that would cover him in death, and even then, Noah might climb his way back into the light of the living.

God chose wisely when asking Noah to build the tremendous ark. The man never stopped. He was like his grandfather, Methuselah, in that respect. There was always a task to attend, a chore to complete, a reason to get the soil of the earth under one's nails. He had no measure of laziness within his bones. Ham believed he was like Noah in that respect, and he wondered if his father recognized it.

Ham watched Noah pitch hay around the stomping hooves. "Yes, our decision," he said.

Noah glanced up at him. "Iris, too. She'll be waiting the outcome. Everyone will. Everyone."

There were dark puffs of skin under his father's eyes and the wiry gray curls that fell near his temples were especially unruly. Ham heard someone up in the night, saw the flicker of the lantern in the vineyard. His father probably talked to his God the entire night.

"Then we shouldn't delay our return." There would be no stoning when they got back to Shinar. He had his father to thank for the decision. Noah could have voiced an opinion, proclaiming Nimrod's innocence, but that was too much to hope for. He could have pronounced a sentence of death, and didn't.

Noah put the rake aside and dumped a bucket of spring water into the trough. "It's good to see you, Son. I wish it weren't because of the matter at hand. It was too much to think I might go to be with my fathers without the weight of such a great sin to deal with."

Ham had no response for his father. He curried the ebony coat of his mare with a steady hand and didn't look up. His offspring brought Noah grief. He knew that all too well.

"Japheth told me about the sacrifice, Ham."

Ham stopped brushing and took in a slow breath to control his emotions. Which one? The one where he allowed Nimrod to say the blessing or the incident with Eli. "I see." He wasn't going to make excuses for either one.

Noah stood for a moment watching him, then picked up a brush and began his own circular rhythm on a brindled coat. Ham could see the down-turned corners of his father's mouth and the silence magnified the distance between them. He was surprised Noah didn't continue the conversation, didn't reiterate the ways of God, didn't tell him how to raise his children or do this or not do that. For once his father let matters be as they were. For once he didn't have the last word, forcing a promise of renewed effort. Ham should have enjoyed the silent tongue of his father. But the heavy air only served to weigh his heart with condemnation once again.

▲

Jael leisurely stirred the big pot of hummus. Naomi knew Ham was eager to leave. Thankfully he was kind enough to let them dally a bit, for his mother's sake. She sat with Eran and Denah, enjoying tea and biscuits still warm from the griddle. Her husband was already out of the house by the time she got up. He was up a good deal of the night, too. Restless. Eager to move on even in the dead of night.

"Who else, then," Jael said. "Who else could have been in the vicinity?"

Her mother-in-law hardly aged, Naomi noticed. There was more silver woven through her long braid, and more tiny lines etched into her skin, but she still had the energy of a much younger woman. Her shoulders stood straight and confident. And although her eyes could still see into the heart of those around her, Jael's actions spoke of compassion more than judgment now. In this, she had mellowed over the years.

Naomi feared her in the early days as Ham's bride. Her mother-in-law was a woman of expectations and her standards were hard to meet. At least for her, and later for Denah. Eran alone flowed into place as the woman's shadow. Of course, Eran would not speak her own opinion in those days. She absorbed Jael's personality to some extent, becoming what Jael wanted while leaving her own self hidden away. Eran was stronger now, but she would never have the confidence of her mother-in-law, no matter how she tried.

"I know of several men who were hunting at the time," Denah said. "Japheth will speak with them. He'll contact all our kin and sift through what's being said. If he suspects one of our own, he'll bring it to the Council's attention. As heart wrenching as that would be, Japheth will seek just punishment for the guilty man."

Denah looked at Naomi as she spoke. No one needed to say that it would be difficult to find any evidence to clear Nimrod. Naomi knew the grace period might just be a delay of the inevitable. And Nimrod found guilty meant all of them would be required to participate in his execution.

Jael stopped stirring. "I think you need to pay Iris a visit, Naomi. You and Denah. Speak with her and the girl, Eliamah. Iris is a widow after all and you should bring the family provisions. Perhaps, now, there will be more for them to share. Woman to woman."

"She's not an unreasonable person," Eran said. "Iris is stubborn, and opinionated, but she's kind, and was good to her children when she lived here. It was Eli, filling his family with myths about God. It was he that Shem struggled with, trying to stop the spread of the rebellious attitudes. Iris is not so disagreeable. At least she didn't use to be."

Naomi nodded in agreement. "I'll do that. I want to see for myself anyway, see where Eli died. Maybe speak to the boy outside his mother's control. Perhaps I can find answers, answers that clear my grandson's name."

The three women with her didn't respond and looked away at her last words. "You believe he's guilty, don't you?" she said.

Jael put down her spoon and pulled Naomi into her arms. "I don't know, Naomi. One of my offspring has committed a grievous sin. My heart is torn no matter who pays the price for Eli's life. I don't want it to be Nimrod. I don't want it to be anyone."

"I've asked our God to guide us in truth. " Eran said. "He will provide the answer."

Naomi swallowed hard and willed the burn of tears to cease. God alone could help her. No one was certain of Nimrod's innocence. No one, not even her own husband, she feared. She alone knew. Proving it would require wisdom far beyond her own.

Chapter Sixteen

Nimrod's tower reminded Ham of a beehive. There was a constant busyness hovering over its surface, undulating in a myriad of directions at once, and it was difficult to see the work being completed until the bees were driven away, or went home for the night. Then the seemingly random motions became apparent. Layer by layer the structure grew, taller, wider, more opulent. There were six of them stacked on top of one another, each one smaller than the one beneath it so that shape was pyramidal. The grand central staircase connected them all, leading to the pinnacle, the seventh and last layer, which would be the temple to God, the place of the sacrifice.

As he got closer, the drone of labor grew steadily more obvious: the screeching of heavily laden carts as they ascended the ramps connecting the layers on each side, the thunking of bricks heaved into position, the chinking of chisels carving patterns into stony surfaces. The sounds were carried on a blanket of dust that rose in the day and settled as the evening came to send the workmen home.

Ham stopped to observe his grandson's glory. The scene drew his mind back, back to when the ark was rising from the cleared land in his backyard. The rhythm of the hammers was forever embedded in his memory. Pow pow. Pow pow. Pow pow. Day after day after day. The smell of fresh timber, too, took his thoughts to the great vessel, as did nearly every squeak, cry or grunt that an animal could produce. The tower held a key difference, however. It wasn't a symbol of eccentricity, a flagrant badge of humiliation. Friends didn't desert him because of it. The tower of Nimrod was revered. From its onset, people willingly gave of themselves to see to its birthing. No one mocked him now.

The town already knew the outcome of the meeting with Noah, despite the early hour. The Council told a few people on their way home and that was all it took. There was an air of relief surrounding the city. The decision was delayed, at least for a time. It gave everyone a chance to expel the stress and resume their lives.

No one was anxious to initiate punishment for the unthinkable sin. No one was eager to put a man to the stones. Once the practice began, it would not be long before it was commonplace.

The tower would be connecting ground for all. Under its shadow the people would unite as one people. Disagreements would melt in the heat of celebration. Conformity would dominate the platforms on their rise higher and higher toward the place of God's dwelling. Joy would permeate the skies, chasing the smoky trail of the sacrificial animal, burning for God's pleasure. It was good, this tower of Nimrod's.

Ham climbed the steps one by one past the first three tiers. They were perfect squares, as were all the levels, oriented to maintain alignment with the North Star. Within their walls, packed earth created a stable base for the upper tiers. Only the perimeter of these levels had rooms, to be used as storage. Outside the rooms lay an expanse of tiled flooring anticipating the assembly of worshippers.

The fourth level held a complex of rooms inside its tiled patio. Nimrod intended to house men in the temple there, to oversee the tower activities. When he called them priests, Naomi's anger exploded. It wasn't God's design she had said. Like every issue, Ham talked her through it, showing her how godly men were essential to maintain the correct procedures. They had to have men trained to assist, men trained to follow the ways of God.

Ham stopped on the fifth level and tried to ignore a prickle of discomfort. Doorways on each side led to an open interior with a vaulted ceiling. He paused under one marble door before stepping inside to the cool shade. Celestial bodies were in the process of being carved into the interior support columns and the floor was a mosaic of stars on a field of deep indigo blue. It was reminiscent of the ornate temples of Before, where he dared to cross the threshold from time to time. There were no images of false gods peering down at him, of course, but the similarity was unnerving all the same.

Nimrod probed Japheth's mind when designing this level. Not that his brother knew it at the time. Nimrod came full of questions about the cosmos and no one liked to talk of the stars more than his brother. Out of those discussions came the idea for the small window on the wall facing east. On the first day of the year, the rising sun aligned with the window, sending a shaft of light into the interior. It pierced the room and pointed directly to a stone carving of the sun in the room's center. The effect was brilliant.

God created the sun, Nimrod explained to them, his grandmother especially. It was surely pleasing to God to recognize its importance in their lives.

"I still don't feel comfortable in here."

Ham turned to find Japheth in the celestial room. His brother rarely came to the tower. Shem had never even set foot on the first step as far as he knew. Neither had his father. "It has your inspiration all over it, Brother," Ham said.

Japheth nodded. "I know. Still, there's that gnawing sense that this is an affront to God. You feel it, too, don't you, Ham?"

"No," he lied. "I believe God will be pleased when we worship as one from this location. We honor the world he created with this artistry. That's all. If it's for God it should be majestic, shouldn't it? Shouldn't we give our best?"

Japheth stood with his hands on his hips and looked around at the freshly frescoed walls. "It feels too much like the old temples," he said.

Ham looked at his brother in surprise. "And how would you know what a temple felt like?"

Japheth laughed. "I let that out without thinking." He shrugged. "I looked in several of them out of curiosity, long before I was married. I didn't understand the appeal. Too much incense, too much dramatic atmosphere. Too many women with sinful intent. And too much praise for idols made of gold."

Ham flinched at the mention of the beautiful stone and turned his back to the sun statue. "Your grandson Kittim expressed interest in devoting himself to the work here," Ham said. "Full time, as a priest."

Japheth didn't respond. His expression wasn't what Ham expected, not one of pleasure at the notion.

Ham continued. "They are rightfully yours, Japheth. The priesthood duties. My grandson built this tower, and he'll lead our people in one way or another, but the priesthood belongs to you and your boys. You are the eldest."

Japheth crossed his arms over his chest. "I lost that right another life ago. The flood didn't change my status in the house of Noah. Shem carries the leadership. You know I won't usurp his position."

"A position he disdains. He won't accept his responsibilities here, Japheth. His boys won't either. His son Arphaxad openly speaks of tearing the tower down, in fact. Shem won't allow himself or any of his kin to wear the role of leadership. Our dear brother can't even bring himself to live among us."

"It's still Shem's responsibility, whether he likes it or not."

"If you don't participate in the sacrifices here, we have to find others who are willing."

"Like Nimrod?"

Ham ran his finger along a smooth table top and tried to keep the resentment from his voice. "It's seems a logical choice, if it doesn't keep him away from other duties. The tower is his dream, after all. Of course, his future is uncertain now, isn't it?"

Japheth exhaled forcefully and ran his fingers through his dark curls. "Brother, I can't be partial with matters of the Triune Council. I have to speak without bias. You know that. You know how difficult the matter is. I want Nimrod to be proved innocent. I want your grief to be dissolved."

"How will it happen, Japheth? There is no other evidence. At the next meeting we'll be where we are now unless our father casts a favorable vote and we both know that won't occur. Nimrod's only chance lies with you or Gomer. Not Shem. He won't change his vote and he may convince Elam to change his to guilty before we all meet again."

"It's not a favorable situation. I'll do what I can among my own kin but I'm not optimistic I'll uncover anything."

"And you won't change your vote."

"No, my brother. If there is no more evidence, I see no other direction."

Ham turned and stalked across the star studded sky, leaving his brother alone. Who were they to judge another man anyway? Because they were the oldest, they survived the flood? He enjoyed the power until now. Maybe it was time to heed God's old command and move on, take his family and cross the Tigris into the unknown lands where they could begin again. Where Nimrod would be safe, alive.

He wouldn't do it. Ham skipped steps as he ran down the incline. As tempting as it sounded, he would never give it all up, all that he had built for himself in the last hundred years. He hated to admit it, but even for Nimrod he would not leave the plain of Shinar.

Chapter Seventeen

The sun was warm enough to send Naomi into the shade to watch her husband with his dogs. She followed them to a place along the Euphrates where the water pooled in a little cove, knee deep at most, a refuge for the fishes living among the reeds. He brought a basket for his catch but had no net. She noticed it propped against house after Ham left and that's why she followed. Now she could see that her husband had not made an error. He knew exactly what he needed. He had full control. And he needed full control, of something.

There was weariness in Ham's eyes, stemming from restless nights, restless days, a restless mind. His focus on projects was spent quickly and the strain on his heart kept his stomach from digesting meals properly. There was little he could do for their grandson. Ham's frustration wove a blanket of tension that enveloped the entire family. Even Cush kept his distance.

The three dogs sat at their master's feet, tails thumping on the bank in anticipation. Ham lifted the whistle and blew a series of beats. His animals flurried into the water, charging into the downstream end of the cove. Another whistle pattern and the dogs turned and headed back toward the shore, this time noses to the surface of the water. Each ducked his head under long enough to snare a fish before splashing onto land and dropping the writhing catch at Ham's feet.

Naomi laughed and clapped, catching her husband's attention. He waved, then sent the dogs back for another round of fetching. They repeated the drill, dashed back and stood proudly before Ham, lavishing in his praises. Naomi would swear they were smiling.

Ham gathered the catch in his basket then sent the dogs to play. He sat down beside her.

"Why don't they eat the fish?" she asked.

"They know they'll get the heads later if they demonstrate control now," he said, then pointed to the net as her feet. "I have a better system than the net, I believe."

Naomi slipped her arm around his waist and pulled herself close to his side. He smelled like the carp collected in his basket. Ham patted her shoulder for a moment then put his hand back in his lap. She wanted him to wrap her up in his arms, fishy stench and all. He didn't realize how she drew strength from his touch. She needed the reassurance. She wished her own arms could cinch Ham against her heart and provide him with the same comfort, like they used to.

His thoughts dwelt elsewhere today. They had since Iris came to town with her accusations. And even before that, once Naomi thought about it. There had been a fragile connection between them since he, Cush, and Nimrod returned from the expedition that took them to the home of Iris and Eli. She brushed off her husband's lack of warmth as fatigue then, but now it made her wonder.

Naomi withdrew her arm. Ham stood and whistled for the dogs. There would be no kissing in the shadows. He was ready to move on. "Ham, I'd like to visit Iris," she said.

Ham turned abruptly and stared at her as if just realizing she was present. "Why?"

"I want to see for myself. I want to see where Eli died and see if there might be something she missed in her sorrow. And she is widowed. I need to bring her supplies."

Ham rubbed his chin. "I can see no benefit, Naomi. She's Japheth's kin. Denah can see to the woman's needs."

"Denah will go, too. Just for the day. We can leave early and be home by nightfall."

"You and Denah? I don't know if I like that idea."

Naomi placed a hand on her husband's face. "Because of the vote? Are you holding that against your brother?"

Ham walked away from her touch and stood facing the river.

"Of all times, Ham, I want to show our people that we are one. We are still one family, the house of Noah. The line of Ham meeting the needs of the widows of Japheth, the children of Shem. Denah and I together, not divided. Eran would go too, if she were here."

"I don't like the idea. It isn't safe."

The dragon incident was unusual. The beasts of the land didn't attack without provocation. They feared man. She traveled with Denah to Noah's community from time to time and had never being threatened by anything, or anyone. There were risks, yes. The benefits far out-weighed them in her mind. "I know how to use a knife and a bow. So does Denah. We can take some of the boys along with us, if it makes you more comfortable."

Her husband roughed up the dogs and allowed them to lick his face before sending them back to the water. He exhaled and shook his head. "I don't see why you need to go."

Ham never questioned her request to travel. She crossed her arms over her chest. "Are you afraid of what I might discover?"

Ham turned to her. "What are you asking?"

"I know my grandson didn't kill that man. That's all I know. I feel you've been keeping something from me."

"You think I did it? Are you accusing me?"

"No, of course not. Not Cush either. But you've kept me at arm's length since you returned. Ham-"

"Naomi, enough. Go if you must. Go see Iris. I have nothing to hide."

Ham walked away, the three staccato beats on the whistle calling the dogs back to his side. She hadn't meant to irritate him. He had enough to contend with. But she had to see all the pieces. It was the only way to find the right answers. It was the only way to find the truth.

▲

Naomi and Denah led the horses the last stretch to the remote homestead of Iris and Eli. They brought two additional mounts to carry provisions and all four beasts were anxious to be free of their burdens. Naomi wouldn't let them approach the stream just yet. They stood on the edge of the property and surveyed the area.

Iris was in the field with the baby strapped to her back. Both older boys and the younger ones were with her, coaxing the oxen team to move forward with the plow. The shrill commands had little effect. Her words were supplemented by threats from the boys who flicked switches into the hides of the immobile team. Denah sighed. "That is a man's job," she said. "The oxen know their master's hand isn't present."

"I don't see how they can manage alone. Perhaps they'll return to their kin soon, before the winter rains."

"Why don't you stay here while I speak to them. It may go easier."

Naomi nodded and held the reins. She would not allow the horses one sip of the water on Iris's land until she knew their presence, her presence, was accepted. It was an unfamiliar sensation.

She was one of the Eight, one of the mothers of the entire population on earth. She had the right to take the horses where she pleased, but she wouldn't. For the sake of harmony she would show respect for the woman who condemned her grandson.

Denah made her way to the field and stood with the family. They all looked toward Naomi when Denah pointed in her direction. She lifted her hand in a simple greeting. It was not reciprocated. A minute later Denah waved at her and pointed to the stream. Naomi led the horses to the bank and allowed them to quench their thirst. She stood near them and turned her focus onto the house. The girl, Eliamah, wasn't outside and Naomi looked for her in the shadows of their home. She hoped to catch her alone. There was no sign of her.

The children followed Denah and their mother from the fields and gathered near the horses. Each face had a layer of sweat mixed with dirt beneath unkempt hair. Naomi wanted to wrap each one in a tight squeeze, promising days of joy and plenty, telling them to go play and not worry about raising food or having enough strength to survive the winters. She didn't though, she couldn't promise them anything, so simply gave their mother as warm a smile as she could muster.

"Naomi wanted to be sure you were alright," Denah said. "She wanted to bring provisions."

Iris looked at the horses, then Naomi. She didn't smile but she dipped her chin a bit. "Thank you," she said.

Naomi exhaled and began unbuckling the straps on the horses. Iris cared about her children and wouldn't let them suffer needlessly. Providing for and protecting one's offspring was a point where they could meet.

"Would you like to help me?" Naomi asked the boys. They turned to Iris who gave permission with a single nod. The provisions were generous. She and Denah filled their arms with bagged grains and pots of olive oil, dried fruits and medicinal herbs. Denah added fabric for clothing into the supplies, mostly strong and functional pieces but two softer and more colorful ones as well. She held out a deep red one to Iris who took it and held it to her cheek for a moment, then stroked its smooth surface. The other one, a vibrant green, green the color of mossy river stones after the cold winter retreated, was meant for Eliamah.

"I thought your daughter might like this one," Denah said.

Iris took it but said nothing.

Denah caught Naomi's eye and raised her eyebrow.

"Where is Eliamah?" Naomi asked, forcing lightness to her voice.

The boys hesitated in their actions for a quick moment then continued without looking at anyone, their lips tightly closed. Iris dumped the load of cloth into the arms of one boy and shooed him toward the house. "She's hunting," Iris said. "She's not much help with the oxen."

Naomi bit down on her lip and felt the disappointment rise. Hunting? She couldn't visualize the girl with a weapon. To feed her family, of course, she would do what was necessary. Naomi saw her tenderness towards her siblings. She wouldn't let them go hungry if she could help it. "Well, I hope she likes that color." Naomi put a smile across her face. Iris kept her attention on the dried meats Denah loaded into her arms.

When the provisions were stored away, the family gathered around them. Iris didn't offer them food or the opportunity to rest in the home before their journey home. Naomi sucked in a breath before she spoke. "You know of the Council decision?"

Iris nodded. "Denah told me."

"Will you show me where your husband was found?"

Iris folded her arms over her chest. She squinted at Naomi.

"Why?"

"Please, Iris," Denah said. "It's her grandson. Please."

Iris walked along the bank of the stream, followed by her children. "Here," she said, pointing to a dry earthen patch. There were small pebbles and stones scattered around, nothing that Eli could have fallen on to break his skull. The dusty patch held nothing that gave Naomi a reason to question the accusations. "And you found no weapons? No tools or large stones?"

"No. He must have took it with him."

Iris's son pulled on her sleeve. "The dog," he whispered.

"That's right. We know how he killed the dog. Beni found the weapon that killed it."

The boy ran to the house then returned with a cloth. He unwrapped it and held it out on his open palms. The thin structure was the length of his hand, the width of a small stick. It was dark brown and rigid, coming to a point on both ends. "I don't know what that is," Naomi said, gingerly picking it up and holding it to the light. "A thorn of some sort? A sliver of bone?"

Denah took it from her hand and performed her own inspection. "The dog was stabbed with this?"

"You can talk," Iris told the boy.

"I found it in its gut," he said. "It didn't have any wounds on the outside so I looked on its insides and found that thing. That's what my father would've did."

"Dogs eat anything. He probably found that and swallowed it."

"I've never seen anything like it before." Iris said.

Denah examined the piece from all sides. "It may have come from the stream, from the river, clear back to the mountains. May I take it to my husband? He might know."

Iris snatched the item from her fingers and gave it back to the boy. "It's his. You can't have that. It's his."

Denah put a hand on Naomi's arm. "We best be going, so we get home before dark."

"One more question, please." Naomi knelt down to face the boy. "Where did you see the man the night your father died? Where were you?"

The boy pointed to the same earthy patch of land place where Eli had been found. "He was here. I was in there." He pointed toward a window facing the stream. He didn't hesitate and he looked her in the eye as he spoke. Naomi sighed and stood. The stream was shallow enough for a man to cross from the other side, from a place beyond this homestead, but there was no evidence. Nimrod had been here, and the boy truly believed he saw him later in the place where his father was slain.

Naomi held back her tears as they said their stilted farewells and mounted the horses. She and Denah provided supplies to the heirs of Noah, so the trip held merit. The greater purpose was left unfulfilled. She had no answers. She failed her grandson.

Chapter Eighteen

"Where do you think Eliamah was? Do you think she was really out hunting?" Naomi urged her horse and the pack animals over a narrow brook and up an embankment.

"No. I don't. It was all too strange the way the family reacted when you asked. I had the feeling Iris was lying."

"That's what I thought, too," Naomi said. "Wouldn't Iris send one of the boys for that duty? Or at least send two of them together. It didn't look to me like an extra boy made those oxen move any quicker. And the little children. I've never seen boys so quiet. They wouldn't say a word without her permission."

"That was more than sorrow written on their faces. They were scared to talk to us. Like we came with evil intent."

"Do you suppose she told them not to speak?"

Denah nodded. "Yes. Like when they came to town. Poor things. It isn't an easy time for them. I wish they were around families to ease their burden."

Naomi stopped along a ravine and consulted the map Nimrod drew for them. "The cave is just up ahead," she said. "It's early enough yet. Do you want to go up there and rest in the shade for a bit?"

"Why not?" Denah responded. "It's good to know where the

shelters are in these parts, in case we're ever here again."

Naomi turned up the hill to the cave where her husband spent the night. "I don't think the boy lied to me," she said. "About that odd bone and about seeing someone in the night. He could have seen a man. Could he identify anyone clearly from that distance? Perhaps someone else planted that thought in his mind, that it was Nimrod."

"That may be. I hate to say it Naomi, but he and Ham are built the same."

"I know. I also know my husband didn't take that man's life. Neither did Nimrod."

"What of Cush?"

Naomi laughed. "More likely a leviathon swimming upriver from the sea and attacking Eli than Cush wielding a weapon against him."

The cave was nestled into the hillside at the end of a gently sloping trail. It was a wide, open mouthed hollow that promised a cool interior. They tied up the animals and stepped inside, expecting empty space. "Oh," Denah said. "We're intruding." There were blankets heaped against a wall and a cooking pot beside the remnants of a fire. She knelt down and put her hand to the pot. "It's still warm," she said.

A shadow crossed the ground from the mouth of the cave. Naomi stood abruptly and turned. They were no longer alone. A man stood between them and the horses. "What are you doing here?"

Naomi felt her pulse quicken at the brusque tone. Beside her, Denah sucked in a mouthful of air and clutched her arms over her heart. She was pale, breathing quickly. Naomi put her arm around Denah's waist. Her sister-in-law had been captured by nephilim once, the warring descendants of the men from the sky. It was like this, in the woods, and they had surprised her. But she was alone then. Denah was not alone now.

Naomi planted her free hand on her hip. "Greetings to you. I am Naomi and this is Denah." It wasn't like Before and she would not be threatened. There had been no reason to fear men in the woods for decades and she wouldn't allow this one to put any measure of fear into her now.

"You aren't supposed to be here." The young man looked around the cave at the belongings. "This is mine." His plain tunic was stained and crumpled, his beard scraggly and chopped off at an uneven length, like he'd been in the woods for some time without the influence of a woman. His limbs were toned and strong, though, and he pulled a dagger from his belt as he spoke.

"We didn't intend to intrude and we didn't take anything. We were visiting the widow Iris, and stopped here to rest."

The man's eyebrows raised over a long hooked nose, emphasizing one eye that crossed toward the center while its mate peered straight ahead. Naomi tried not to stare. There was a vague familiarity in his features. "Widow?" He rolled the word on his tongue. "Oh. I remember. That means her man is dead. It's so. He's dead. He was killed."

"Yes. Eli was killed. Did you know him, and Iris?"

"It's so."

"How did you hear about Eli? About him being dead?"

The man ran his fingers up and down the knife. He spit on it, then rubbed it, polishing the blade. He thought about his words before he spoke. "I heard about it from my woman."

"What did your woman say? Does she know what happened?"

The man drew his shoulders back and held up his knife. "Why are you asking me this? I don't like it."

Naomi took a step forward. "It's important. Don't you think we should try to understand why Iris's man was killed? Wouldn't you want to know what happened to your woman if she were harmed somehow?"

His eyes opened wide. He let out a growl and clamped his hands over his ears. His red face screamed. "Stop it! Stop it! Stop it!"

The women stepped back. Naomi pushed him too hard, she realized, and now she was trembling. Denah, however, had a calm expression. She waited until the man stopped ranting before she smiled a little and spoke in voice coated in honey. "We're sorry. Please don't be upset. We mean you and your woman no harm."

Her soft words rinsed the anger from the man's face. He dropped his arms and returned to eyeing his weapon, rubbing his fingers over and over the surface.

"That's a beautiful knife," Denah said. "I can tell it's something real special."

The young man nodded vigorously. "It's special alright."

"Every man needs a special knife. One that fits just so in his hand."

He looked squarely at Denah with his good eye, the eye that went where he wanted to look. "Do you want to see it better?" He held the weapon out to her.

Denah took the instrument as if handling a newborn. She examined it closely and openly praised the craftsmanship before handing it to Naomi. The man's hard edge melted in the flow of compliments.

The knife wouldn't cut through a fig, its blade was so pitted. The worn flint came from the mouth of a behemoth, crudely carved into the handle. The bone itself was worn to a shiny finish with telltale yellowed stains that followed the mans grip. Even in its original state, the piece was of poor workmanship but Naomi took Denah's cues and added her own words of praise before handing it back. It wasn't a weapon to be feared.

"What's your name?" Denah asked.

The man pinched his lips shut and didn't respond.

"Where do you live?" Naomi stayed quiet and let her sister-in-law continue. "Where are your kin?"

"I live where I want. I got no kin 'cept my woman."

"What happened to your parents?"

He kicked at a stone embedded in the earth until it came loose, then sent it careening off the far wall. "I don't know about that. Maybe they're dead. Maybe not. It don't matter. I made my way out here, without them."

Denah looked at Naomi who nodded, encouraging her to continue. "How long ago? How long have you been out here, away from the city?"

"Since I was a boy. We was in the woods hunting, me and my father. Long time ago now."

Naomi suppressed a gasp as the boy's irregular face became clear, only much younger. She grasped Denah's arm, forcing a control to her voice. "Denah, remember when your grandson's boy was, was lost, during a hunting trip?"

Denah's hand flew to her lips as she too placed his features into context. They were told the boy had fallen off a steep ledge, that he died. "Oh, yes," Denah said and forced a smile to replace a look of shock. He didn't die after all. He had been living on his own for some fifteen years. "Samuel? You're Samuel, aren't you?"

Samuel's expression left no doubt of his identity. He confirmed with a nod.

"You're my kin. You're my great-grandson."

Samuel's jaw went slack as he stared at Denah. "Oh," he said.

Denah stepped close to him and ran her fingers on his face. "You were just a child then. Look at you. A man, all grown up. No wonder I didn't recognize you. We thought you were dead, Samuel."

The young man stepped away from Denah's touch. "I guess I'm not."

A shuffle in the back of the cave caught Naomi's ear and she peered into the darkness. Samuel looked the same direction for a moment before turning back to Denah. "You live by the river? Where the houses and shops are?"

"Yes. And your mother and father live there. They're still alive."

The shuffling returned. Samuel looked toward it, his lips twisting around each other.

"Samuel, is your woman here?" Naomi asked. "May we meet her?"

Samuel hesitated, then walked into the darkness, returning with a young woman. The girl's ankles were bound with a length of cord, so she could only shuffle along beside Samuel. Her wrists were tied together, too. She stopped when Samuel did and lifted her head. Samuel brushed the locks of hair from her face.

Eliamah.

▲

Naomi's surge of relief knowing the girl's whereabouts came with the same intensity as the horror over seeing her bound and disheveled. She grabbed Denah's hand for support, both attempting to appear nonplussed. Samuel's wide grin had returned as he displayed his prize. "This is my woman," he said. "I married her."

Naomi nodded politely. "We've met. This is the daughter of Iris and Eli."

Eliamah stood still, her head tipped down. Denah ran a soothing hand over the girl's arm. "Why is she tied up, Samuel?"

"I didn't want her to get away. I like her."

Denah smiled her best motherly smile. "Well, if she promised not to run off, you could untie her then, I suppose?"

Samuel looked uncertain then nodded slowly. "I could."

Denah ran her fingers gently thought the girls' hair like a comb, skipping over the worst snarled portions. "Will you not run off, then, Eliamah?"

Eliamah's eyes traveled between Naomi and Denah. They glistened with tears. She nodded in agreement.

Samuel pulled the binding cords apart with his bare hands. They weren't that tight, Naomi noticed. Eliamah could have wriggled out of them herself. Then what? She wasn't the sort to survive in the wilds on her own and it appeared she wasn't wanted in the home of Iris any longer. Eliamah chose to remain the man's prisoner. And wife.

"Well, a nice young couple we have." Naomi said. "We didn't know you were to be married Eliamah. We saw your mother. She forgot to mention it."

The girl lowered her head again and ran her hands over her crumpled tunic. "It wasn't long planned," she said.

Iris lied about her daughter's whereabouts. Did she know where her daughter was? Did she know about the strange young man living in the caves near their home, claiming her as his own?

"I believe a celebration is in order," Denah said. "We'll take you two with us, to my home. We'll make sure your marriage is honored among your kin."

Eliamah said nothing as she watched her husband's response.

Samuel shook his head vigorously. "No. No. We're alright here. I don't want to go there."

Denah put a hand on his shoulder. "Your family will rejoice that you are found, Samuel. My husband will want to see you. We'll help you settle in a home."

"No. No. We'll stay here." He put his hand back on the weapon.

"We can't force you, of course," Naomi said. "We thought you might think that was best, that's all. We want the best for you and your woman." She held the girl's gaze, trying to gauge her mind and let her know that they would help her. Samuel was strong in body, but she would fight if she had to. So would Denah. They would do it for Eliamah's sake. They would not abandon the girl, married to this man or not.

Eliamah lifted her lips in a slight smile and put a hand on Samuel's arm. She patted him as she spoke, soothing his tension. "We will stay, as he said." Her voice was controlled. There was no hint of fear.

Denah told them of the growing city and its abundance of food, of the safety it promised. She reminded them of their family, of the great celebration they would hold in their honor. Samuel could not be swayed. He crossed his arms over his chest and huffed as she spoke. He kicked at rocks imbedded in the cave floor with increasing force.

Naomi felt her heart sink. She and Denah couldn't force the two of them to leave. She should have taken a few of her sons along for this journey, after all. It was hard to talk sister to sister with them there, but now she regretted the decision.

Samuel had to be brought before the Council. Even if he didn't want to return to the city to live, he needed to be questioned. He needed to prove his own innocence or collapse in his own guilt. Whatever he knew of Eli's death deserved to have voice.

Eliamah would be left in Samuel's care. Guilty or not, she felt sure the two would disappear back into the wilderness where Samuel managed to survive for many years, alone. Naomi would lose her grasp on the truth that dwelled in Eliamah's heart. Samuel and

Eliamah were the key, she was certain, to securing Nimrod's innocence. It was likely that meant condemning themselves.

"No more talk." Samuel's face was red again. "You should leave now."

Inciting him to anger would not bode well for Eliamah. Denah put a hand on Naomi's shoulder and they left the cave. As she turned to leave, she caught a glimpse of the girl with tears streaming down her cheeks. Naomi stopped and caught her eye. Eliamah turned abruptly and ran into the dark void of the cave.

Chapter Nineteen

Naomi barely breathed as she told Ham the details of her day. They sat outside in the darkness after eating a light meal and seeing to the horses. He listened carefully. His wife was intuitive. She pursued answers, dredging out truth from dank bogs when she needed to prove something. Usually, her quests weren't in vain, and her initial instincts lined up with the facts. Especially about people. Fortunately, blood ties blurred her vision at times.

"And Denah said he reminded her of Beth. Remember Beth, Ham? Denah's little sister?"

"Yes. She was a simple little thing, sweet, always smiling."

"That's how Denah knew how to talk with Samuel. She remembered how Beth thrived on praise for the simple things she accomplished, and she was right. Samuel warmed up immediately. I wish she could've convinced him to come with us. I think the girl would have come, but he wasn't about to leave the safety of the woods. It's his home. I wonder if he remembers what happened, when he was young, if he blames his father for leaving him."

Ham was on the search party when the boy was lost. Young Samuel fell off the trail into a treacherous ravine. Ham rappelled down the steep slope in a cascade of loose rock, further than any of the others. His eyes never stopped peering into the crevices and along the ledges below. He couldn't see every last space of jagged ground, nor could he simply untie the ropes and search. The land wasn't stable enough for that. He wanted to, though. He wanted to find the boy and bring the man's firstborn back, alive. There was no boy to be found, however. Nor any remains of a battered, lifeless child.

He assumed a natural role as the head of the search party. He pushed the men hard, not conceding to defeat for several days. By nightfall the third day, he admitted the search was futile. The ravine would be difficult to scale for a healthy man, impossible for one with injuries. If the boy did survive, they would have seen some sign of him by now on the jagged terrain. None of the others were willing to say what they all believed. The boy was gone, back to the earth from which his flesh was formed. It was one time Ham wanted another man to rise up in leadership. None did. Ham was forced to terminate the search, forced to pronounce Sam's death.

And he was wrong.

Ham drummed his fingers on his knee. "We have to find him," he said. "We have to talk to him."

"Samuel's father? He'll be overjoyed that his son is alive."

"No, find Samuel. We have to find Samuel."

"Yes. I'm sure he knows who else is living in those parts, or who traveled through."

Ham turned and faced her. "Naomi, haven't you considered that he's the man we're after? That Samuel killed Eli?"

"I thought of that, of course. Then Denah compared him to Beth and now I don't know. He's simple. When you meet him, you'll see. He's rather sweet and innocent in his ways."

"He's physically able to strike a man though?"

"Yes, but-"

"And Eli's death was no surprise to him?"

"No, but-"

"And now he has the man's daughter tied up as a prize?"

"Ham! You can't decide his guilt. That isn't right. I know how it looks. It doesn't mean he did it."

"Maybe Iris asked him to kill Eli and the girl was his reward. Maybe the girl killed her father to be with Samuel. Maybe Eliamah and Samuel worked together."

Naomi stood abruptly and put her hands on her hips. He could tell he prickled her nerves. That was good. He wanted her to think openly. If no one else was guilty, it all came down on Nimrod again. "What happened to Eli?" he said. "What did you find when you went to his home?"

His wife sat down again, elbows on knees and fingers to temples "I have no answers. I just know in my heart it wasn't Nimrod. And I can't imagine Eliamah was involved. She's tender hearted. Iris obviously loved her husband. And Samuel, I just don't know. I wish I could sense his guilt. I couldn't Ham. He's still like the little boy who disappeared."

Ham let go of the breath he was holding. His wife wouldn't let condemning evidence slide by unseen, even if it pointed to her own grandson. Or son. Or husband. She would report the truth to secure favor in the eyes of her God. She found nothing. He could persuade her to look at the boy in the woods with different eyes as the time of Nimrod's grace period grew to a close.

A cold nose nestled in his hand. Ham scratched the furry head behind the ears.

"Oh, the dog." Naomi stood abruptly and ran into the house. She returned with a piece of bark. She showed him the sketch she scratched in its surface. Ham drew in a quick breath but said nothing.

"Iris said this killed the dog. One of the boys found it inside the animal's gut after it died. Do you know what it is?"

He knew exactly what she had drawn. "No," he said, without looking her in the eye. The drawing was of a springbone, a simple weapon carved from animal bone. It was boiled until it became flexible enough to fold the prongs in on themselves, then they were secured with a tether. The little bundle was then hidden within a piece of bait meat. The ingested bone would break free from the tether in the presence of the gut fluids, springing its barbed legs through the gut walls, killing the beast as it bled out.

Noah made springbones to fight beasts that raided his food stores in the night. Ham hadn't used them on the new earth. As animals left the ark and multiplied, they found their own places to thrive without invading the city. The larger ones anyway. Rabbits were a nuisance, and grasshoppers, but these weren't the kind of pests for springbones. He had taught his boys how to make the device, though, just like he taught them how to make knives and bows and slingshots. His grandsons, too. All his boys were shown how to make and use a springbone at one point in time. Cush and Nimrod weren't the only ones. If anyone kept one handy, though, it wasn't Cush. Only a hunter would think to keep one in his arsenal.

Naomi watched him closely. He shouldn't have said he didn't know what it was so quickly. Ham pretended to examine her drawing again before handing it back. "What was it made of?"

"I think it was bone."

Ham nodded. "Makes sense. If the dog ate a sliver of bone like that, no wonder it died." The springbone wasn't damning to Nimrod, but his grandson didn't need any more fuel for his pyre.

What if Denah made a similar etching? His brothers knew about springbones, of course. He stopped a curse word from slipping past his lips. He should've just said what it was. There were many men who knew about this type of weapon. Even that Samuel. Naomi was probably the only one to make a big deal of its presence around Eli's home, however. Except Denah, perhaps.

"Forget about the dog. A man died. That's our concern, not some beast," he said. "And Naomi, I want you to stay clear of Denah for awhile." Maybe both women would forget about the springbone if they didn't have one another to dwell on its significance.

Naomi's eyebrows arched high on her forehead. "Why?"

"Until this is all over," he said. "I don't want it to look as though the house of Ham is siding with the house of Japheth against our brother Shem."

"No one thinks that, Ham. If Eran were here, she'd be with us, as sisters. Shouldn't we show our unity by acting as one?"

He didn't want to seem unreasonable. "I'm not telling you not to see her at all, Naomi. Just not as much as you have lately. No traveling, or discussing this business with Eli and Iris. None of that sort of controversy. Don't make me look biased against my brother."

Naomi's emerald eyes glistened. He hated hurting her. He had to, for her own good, and the good of his family. She would understand in time. He could tell his wife was shivering even in the warm air but he turned and walked away. He couldn't kiss the top of her head and let his love pour over her body, soul and heart. He couldn't allow her touch to dissolve the wall he was building to safeguard all that he had worked for in the last hundred years. He wouldn't let it all be taken away.

Chapter Twenty

The traveler smelled of wilderness. Campfire smoke, crushed leaves, leathery hides, clothes that had been wet then dried then wet again without a real scrubbing in between. His presence in the Council chambers was evident by scent alone. His family, a wife and four boys, followed him into the room with the same scent, same rough hewn clothing, same weary expression.

A line of curious people followed them. Curious not only about the nature of the man's request to speak before the Council, but curious as to the family themselves. The man was her son Canaan's grandson, gone now for seven years. He was barely a man when he took a young wife and left for the land from which the mighty Euphrates erupted, the land where the earth took abrupt turns upward, creating mountains of stone. It was the land where the rain froze as it fell, where snowy blankets crept among the peaks and crevices, smothering the living spaces. Cold. Wet. Dreary.

Naomi shivered at the thought of living in such horrid conditions. Yet here was the traveler, alive and well, back from the land of icy rivers. When he didn't return after a year, then two, it was assumed the two perished in the inhospitable terrain.

Two weeks had passed since the Council met and heard the accusations of Iris. Two weeks remained until the full moon would draw them together to decide Nimrod's fate. The previous week there had been no significant issues presented. In the face of a man's death at the willful hand of another, the usual petty issues were pushed aside. Today she hoped for an easy distraction but the pinched expression on the face of the traveler's wife gave little hope for an uneventful day. Naomi settled in behind her husband to listen.

The traveler ate without reservation, grabbing handfuls of the fresh produce in front of him and stuffing it into his mouth while bits of it flew in every direction. He purred with the first bite of fresh bread oozing with honey, licking the sticky substance from each finger when he was finished. The woman and children ate as well, she with manners and they with hesitation. Many of the foods were obviously new to them. Fruit, even, was a thing to sniff and lick and taste gingerly.

The traveler was tall and lean. He was one Naomi worried over as he outgrew his parents at a young age. The growing stopped in due time, and now here he sat with boys of his own. They seemed small in comparison. Their skin was pale and dry and all four had reddish colored spots on their shin bones. Naomi recognized the spots. Her own children had them one winter, after a late spring freeze. They relied on meat for many months until the crops once again began to sprout from the earth and the trees forced a handful of fruit. These young boys needed the food of the land in their diet.

Shem was eager as she to hear details. "And the ice? Does it continue to grow?"

"It does," the man said. "This year the frozen river near us didn't melt completely, even in the late summer. It always melts for a time. Not this year. I had to bore through the surface to reach the fresh flow."

"It's progressing, then, the cold of the land?"

"It is colder each year. Our cave was in a green ravine once, but the last few years it's been difficult to raise sufficient food in the short time we see the earth. We rely on the mammoths for provision. Their meat keeps us strong. My oldest boy can bring one down on his own now." The man slapped the boy on his back and gave him a wide grin.

Aren't you lonely? Why do you stay in land that won't produce crops? What is to be gained by mastering the challenges of the northern world? Naomi had many questions she wanted to ask. She would have to wait. The men governed the council and this discussion would be in the circle only.

When there was no food larger than a crumb left on the mat in front of them, the conversation changed its course. "So," Japheth asked, "What brings you before the Council today?"

The man looked at his wife. She kept his gaze for a moment then turned away. "It's my wife," he said. "She's thin skinned. She hates the life I've given her."

"Please continue," Shem said. "How does this involve the Council?"

"She's always cold, always filling my head with complaints about our situation, always unhappy. I chose unwisely when I married her. She isn't made for the adventurous life I've chosen. I don't want her to stay with me any longer. I want to leave her here, where the sun will warm her cold spirit since she refuses to warm mine."

The Council drew a collective breath and let it out slowly. Abandoning one's wife was not in the ways of their God. The man was responsible for the woman he wed.

Shem turned to the woman. "What is your position?"

The woman straightened her spine and gripped her hands together. "There isn't enough food for my children. Even the animals have the sense to move away from the snow. He is stubborn and refuses to move our family. He's correct when he says I'm not made for the unbearable cold. I hate it. I wish to stay here, with my children."

The traveler shook his head. "Not the children," he said. "They will be with me. Just her. It's just her I want to leave among you."

"God expects you to care for your wife, and you to remain with your husband," Shem said to each of them.

"We want the same outcome," he said. "It's in both our interests to see this happen. It isn't me against her. I wish her no harm. I could have left her to freeze or let her be mauled by a tiger. You would never even know. I'm here as an honorable man."

"She has given you four sons. You would leave her here and raise them yourself?"

"No," the traveler said. "I intend to take another in her place. I'll find a heartier wife to warm my bed and bring me sons."

Naomi hands flew to her lips, stifling a cry. The man wanted to exchange his wife, the mother of his children, for another. She looked at the woman, expecting horror to be written on her pale face. There wasn't. The woman nodded in agreement.

The three firstborn sons of the Council were wide-eyed at the suggestion. Shem and Japheth looked grim. This was not new in the heart of man. It was done regularly Before. Men sent wives away and obtained new ones. If their fathers didn't take them back and provide for them, the husband maintained responsibility for his abandoned wife's needs. There was an alternative if he didn't want to provide for the woman — he could accuse her of adultery and slash her throat. They did not want to travel that road again.

Naomi couldn't see her husband's expression but by the slump of his shoulders she knew he was deep in thought. All of the men of the Council were. She wished to see aversion written in their eyes. There wasn't.

Denah had her face in her hands, and Eran sat in stunned silence with her eyes to the ceiling. She knew their thoughts without question.

▲

Ham could feel Naomi's horror at the idea that the traveler be permitted to take a new wife. He heard her gasp and felt her tension wrap around his body. But the traveler's woman wasn't being abandoned. She wanted to stay behind. Of course the children would remain with their father, that was never in doubt. She was making a clear choice of widowhood, without her own offspring. She was the one abandoning the family, in his opinion. If her kin chose to provide for her, he saw no reason the traveler shouldn't find a woman more suitable. He said it himself. He could have killed his wife and taken a new wife without question. He was making an honorable gesture.

Ham avoided Naomi's eyes as everyone was asked to leave the Council chamber. Everyone, their wives included. It was his idea and he knew he would face Naomi's wrath for the suggestion. Their wives had no say in the vote. They didn't need to be in attendance.

Japheth and Shem were in agreement that the man could not take a second wife. There was to be one wife, whether he liked his chosen woman later or not. Their sons agreed. Now it was Ham's turn to speak. Technically the matter was decided with the majority opinion but he wanted his say. Japheth and Shem didn't always know what was best for the people. He predicted a negative consequence if they decided against the couple and they didn't need another tumultuous issue on their heads. Let the man and woman have their request and be done with it all. He voted in favor of the man's request. It would be a 4 to 2 vote.

But it wasn't. Cush took an opinion opposite his. It was a 5 to 1 decision. Ham felt the familiar irritation rise against his firstborn. He stuffed it away. It was about time Cush took a stand.

Ham didn't regret voicing his thoughts. He enjoyed the shock on his brother's faces when he spoke in favor of his great-grandson. There were occasions in the past when he joined his vote with theirs in order to present a unanimous face to all their offspring. Those times were past. His brothers voted against him when they voted against Nimrod. He saw no reason not to do likewise.

▲

Naomi pressed her hand to her lips to keep from screaming. She was hidden behind a water barrel, beneath a window in the Council chamber, listening to her husband speak. His words hammered into her heart. Ham defended a man's right to abandon his woman and take another in her place.

Chapter Twenty-One

The young woman was anxious for her child to arrive. Naomi was anxious, too, ready for the birthing to proceed, though for different reasons than the woman on the mat. The squeezing in her chest had nothing to do with the baby on its way. It was the tension in the household, thick and ripe with unrest, that made her uncomfortable. And it was Naomi herself that caused it.

She was doing her best to ignore it, focusing her skills and energy on the mother, trying to keep a positive perspective and loving demeanor. The mothers and aunts and sisters hovered in the shadows, conversing among themselves, maintaining distance both physical and emotional. They were of Shem's descent. They didn't welcome her into their home as a sister.

It wasn't like she burst into their home of her own accord. She was summoned by the girl's mother. Her daughter was small boned and the family feared a difficult delivery. They wanted Naomi's expertise at the birthing. That was all. She was there as a hired hand, expected to perform her duties, ensure the well being of mother and child, then go away. No one said anything of the sort to her face. They didn't have to. Naomi knew what was on their hearts. They didn't trust the grandmother of Nimrod. They withheld respect for the bloodline responsible for a grievous sin against God and their own kin.

Naomi soaked a rag in a basin of warm water and gently wiped the mother's brow. She volunteered her time to assist with these birthings. She never asked for payment. Never. Baked goods and pieces of fabric, baskets of fresh produce and small game were delivered to her home by most of the grateful fathers anyhow. The gifts were always appreciated, they were never demanded. Naomi felt her heart stiffen as she thought about it.

It was said the blessings of God flowed through the Eight, his protected ones. The homes welcoming her presence were blessed themselves. There were none of these blessings flowing among them today. For the first time in her life, Naomi wanted to walk away and let the tight mouthed women deal with the delivery themselves.

The mother moaned and her sweaty hand latched onto Naomi's wrist. Naomi looked into her fearful face and knew she couldn't leave, despite the brood looming against the far wall.

"Is it time?" The women stepped closer. Several had arms crossed over their chests.

Naomi stood and faced them. 'I'm not your enemy,' she wanted to scream. 'We are one under God in the house of Noah.' But she didn't say those words, just, "Yes. The baby has decided to come at last."

It was an uncomplicated delivery, the newborn a healthy, squalling boy. The father held him proudly while Naomi tended to the exhausted mother. When she finished she sucked in a deep breath and approached the father. It was her custom to pray a blessing of gratitude over each little life that God brought to this people. She had been ignored since the birth and no one offered to assist with the follow-up care and cleaning. But she would not simply evaporate into the night without thanking their God.

The father's forehead was a furrowed field of animosity as she held out her arms for the bathed and swaddled boy. Reluctantly he laid the infant in her arms. Naomi lifted the bundle to the heavens. "God our Creator, I thank you for this child. May his ways be your ways, his heart, your heart. Clothe him in your cloak of protection and let not his hand slip from yours." Naomi lowered him and kissed his forehead, then lifted him up again. There were more words in her head that she felt compelled to speak. "And may his trust in you be his salvation, his perseverance, his reward."

The father took his child as if Naomi had uttered a cursing. "On the day of his naming I will recall your presence in this house," he said. "My boy will be named 'Job.'

Afflicted. The father would give his firstborn the name as an insult to the midwife who slapped the breath of life into his lungs.

▲

Ham used a long handled broom to brush debris off the stone altar. Last year's leaves matted the surface and he found field mice in a burrowed crevice. Naomi gathered kindling nearby, watching as her husband scrubbed the surface and cleansed it with water. She hadn't noticed how neglected it had become.

When was the last time they held a sacrifice here? It was over a year ago she figured, when Japheth took his newest great-grandchildren to visit Noah. It was their tradition, she, Ham, and most of their children, to go to Japheth's home for the sacrifice each seventh day. Shem came too, when he was in town. It was good for them to be together, to honor God, to immerse themselves in the richness of their familial bonds. Ham never offered to hold the ritual on their land, though. He took his turn in supplying the beast but preferred the use of his brother's altar.

Naomi tossed a bundle of twigs on the stones and turned back to gather more. She wouldn't be surprised if the steer refused to burn. How could they expect God to accept a beast offered from hearts of anger? Despite her pleas, Ham refused to go to his brother's home today. Her words fell on closed ears. He didn't want to hold any responsibility. He didn't care to maintain unity. Avoiding the gathering with Japheth would only drive wedges of discord in the homes of their offspring. Ham couldn't see the ripple of contention that would follow. It was a grave mistake.

Ham's refusal fueled Naomi's anger. Shunned at the birthing, then later at the market, the stab of her brother's kin against her own heart was raw. Biased minds needed to see the Council as brothers, sons of Noah and the living God. Ham was making the situation worse. Resentment swelled inside her. Resentment for her husband. He who felt a man should be allowed to toss a wife aside when he tired of her.

And who was she to appear before God with such discord in her soul?

Cush wasn't in a place of peace either. He surprised her by keeping an even perspective, despite the accusations against his son. Until recently. The news of Samuel living in the woods near Eli's home stung his heart. He was hostile toward any mention of the man. She feared he was like his father for once, accusing a man because there was no other explanation to satisfy their ears. Her soft spoken, easy firstborn was riddled with anxiety that took a fiery course. He stood alone with his arms crossed, head down, and her mothering instincts took hold. "Forgive his vengeful thoughts, O God. And mine."

All her sons gathered for the unusual homebound ritual. Their children and their children's children milled around the altar in a hum of energy. The little ones asked why they wouldn't spend the time at their cousin's house and Ham told them he and their Uncle Japheth decided to have sacrifices separately now. Naomi held her tongue. As far as she knew, Denah and Japheth weren't aware of this decision.

Ham and the boys chucked the animal onto the kindling. She put on the face of a contented matriarch, waiting for Ham to say the blessing so she could escape his presence. Her husband dawdled, in no hurry to complete the preparations. He reorganized the wood and adjusted the same kindling that he just moved moments before. Periodically he glanced around at his offspring then back to his minor adjustments. Naomi took inventory of the faces. Nimrod, she realized, wasn't present. Ham was waiting for his grandson. She exhaled another prayer of forgiveness at her impatience. If anyone needed to seek the favor of God, it was Nimrod. There was only a week until the full moon.

Ham finally took the torch and stood before the altar, raising the flame towards the cloudless sky. Naomi tried to focus her mind on the mighty God of creation, the God of Adam who saved her from destruction. She tried to push the tangled thoughts from her head to see God clearly. It was impossible. Altars of resentment blocked her view of heaven.

Ham made no attempt to recite the words of their beginnings, the history of light and of plants and of Adam. He stumbled through the sacrificial blessing. A blessing, at least. The words were wrong. He didn't know them anymore. Naomi walked away, ignoring the eyes that followed her. She didn't wait to see if the beast would burn, didn't wait to see if God would send a firebolt to destroy them all.

Chapter Twenty-two

The riderless horse wasn't interested in following the trail. It smelled the stream and wanted to veer toward refreshment. Ham pulled it back into formation. The search party needed to reach the cave as soon as possible and it was too soon for another stop.

Sweat trickled into Ham's eyes. He retied the cloth over his head to soak up the burning drips. His brothers were feeling the heat as well, red in face and speaking little. Of course, the nature of the man-hunt didn't exactly invite good humor or hearty discourse. All three of them were weighted with their own concerns. All three had their own opinions and reasons to track down this Samuel who lived in the wilds. Three strong men, three strong wills.

Even the discussion as to who was to go today fell beneath a shadow of disagreement. Shem wanted the entire Council to find the man and to question him where he lived rather than drag him back into Shinar. Japheth thought he should go alone to find Sam, as a relative looking after the well-being of his offspring. He would bring the man into the Council, he said. But not as one already condemned. Ham thought it made the most sense to form a search party from all their kin to retrieve him, a dozen men or so, in case Sam was no longer at the cave and they were required to extend the search.

In the end it was agreed the three would go alone and if they couldn't find the man in a day or two, they would return and organize a larger contingent. Ham brought the extra horse with extra provisions strapped to its back. He fully intended to lead it home with a rider. He packed a length of rope to bind the man and secure him to the horse if necessary.

They maintained a brisk pace and Ham was relieved they didn't have Cush along. His son struggled to prepare even a simple meal the past days, he was so high strung. One minute he slammed his fist into a wall, speaking of the justice they could administer in the woods. Then his face was in his hands, blubbering over poor Nimrod's fate. He was flying emotionally to the extremes and even Naomi had her fill on a few occasions, splashing his face with cold water and demanding he find an even temperament before they all went mad. It was good Cush was not with them. He had become unpredictable. Justice in the woods would solve nothing.

Cush wasn't the only one to receive a cold slap from Naomi of late. She still held a grudge about yesterday's sacrifice. Why was going to Japheth's of such importance? He thought she'd be pleased when he said the family would resume the practice on their own altar. She wasn't, though no one else seemed to care. Of course, Nimrod didn't arrive until later, after the beast was a cooling pile of ash. She wasn't happy about it. Actually, Ham wasn't pleased by his grandson's late arrival, either. He wanted Nimrod to say the words of the blessing. It seemed better to allow his grandson to say it with a few errors than to speak the words himself. With errors. Ham hated to admit he couldn't pull the words from his mind with precision anymore. His wife's expression said more than any of her stinging words.

The air in their home was unpleasant. Naomi didn't even rise to make him breakfast that morning. She should have been happy he was going out to fetch the man that appeared to be guilty of killing Eli. She wasn't, that he could tell. Did she want Nimrod to found guilty? Ham was glad to be out of her sphere of fire, regardless of the mission.

"Tell me about Samuel, Japheth." Shem said. "What do you remember of him?"

Ham pulled his mount up beside his brothers, grateful for a distraction. Japheth took a long drink of water from a skin before he spoke. "He's my grandson Jabal's boy, born twenty, twenty-five years ago. The firstborn. Pretty quiet. I do remember he had funny eyes. They didn't track together. He was pleasant enough when they came for the sacrifices. His father seemed embarrassed by him, though, since he wasn't worth his weight in any of the games the boys played. I don't recall the boy being mistreated however."

"We were told he died. I remember how upset Eran was when she heard."

"Yes," Japheth continued. "That's what we thought. Sam and Jabal were hunting, and the boy slipped over the edge of a ravine. His father couldn't find him, so came back to find help. I assumed he was dead as soon as I saw the place where he fell. I would never imagine he was still alive."

"We looked for him," Ham said. "Three days. We found nothing. It was too dangerous to descend all the way down the ravine and it didn't matter. We knew he was dead. We knew it."

Japheth nodded. "It was steep. I don't see how that boy survived an accident like that."

"If there was an accident." Ham said. He watched his brother's eyes narrow.

"You think, what? My grandson lied? He pushed his son off the edge?" Japheth jerked his eyes from Ham and focused straight ahead as he spoke.

Ham chuckled in surprise. "I wasn't implying that. I'm suggesting that our search party didn't fail. I don't believe that boy ever went over the edge of the ravine. You saw it. No one could survive that kind of fall. Perhaps the tale told by Jabal wasn't the full truth. Perhaps he found his son a new home, in the woods, where he wouldn't be an embarrassment any longer."

The silence returned. Ham didn't intend to dampen the mood further. He could not, however, sit there and hold his thoughts. It wasn't just his line of offspring that broke the rules and his brothers needed to be reminded of that. Japheth's people weren't beyond the veils of guilt and blame. There was darkness in all the sons of Noah.

"We'll find out soon enough." Shem said. "The cave is near here, I believe."

Ham nodded and steered his horse in front of the others as they approached the turnoff. He smiled to himself. It was nice to have a member of someone else's line be under suspicion for a change.

▲

Sunlight poured into the mouth of the cavern, drenching the young couple sitting huddled together near the back wall. Ham stepped into the entrance with his hands on his hips. His shadow fell over them like a verdict of shame and they clutched one another in fear. "Samuel, son of Jabal of the line of Japheth?"

Samuel looked up and nodded with one tip of his chin. The girl with him stared at the ground.

"Stand up then. You're coming with us."

Japheth put a hand to Ham's chest. "Brother, I'll handle it," he said.

Ham glared at his older brother for a moment before stepping back and giving the floor to Japheth. A little sweet talking wouldn't make a difference. They had the young man cornered and even with a weapon he was no match for them. He was theirs.

Japheth sat down on the earth before the couple and explained who he was. Samuel's shoulders relaxed as he listened, eyeing Japheth with curiosity the entire time. The girl listened as well but her eyes flicked up to Ham's several times before she turned them away again. She remembered him, of course. He was the one who rejected Eli's offer. If she was holding a grudge, she didn't reveal it in her expression.

"Your family, your brothers and sisters, are anxious to see you." His brother slathered honey on the situation.

"I'm not of the city any longer," Samuel said. "I have no family there anymore." The young man straightened his shoulders and looked at Japheth now without fear. He was fit and had the strength to put up a fight. His methods of taking a man to the ground would be crude, no doubt. Especially with the funny way his eyes worked. He would be an easy conquest if it came to that.

"You remember your father, though? And your mother?"

"I remember. It was them who didn't come to find me after I was left in the cave." Samuel crossed his arms over his chest and leaned back against the cave wall.

"Left in the cave?"

"It weren't no accident. I wasn't so stupid as they thought. I know it was on purpose. That's why I didn't go home. They could have found me if they wanted to, if I was really just lost. And I wasn't lost. I knew how to get back home. The path only goes one way or the other. I didn't go back, though. Why would I?"

Japheth tented his fingertips at his chin. "Your father just left you all alone in the woods, in this cave, on purpose?"

"Not this cave. A different one. And not him. The man he was mad at. The man he made take me away."

"Who was it Samuel? Who left you in the cave?"

Samuel lagged his head side to side. "I don't know. I don't remember."

Ham stepped in behind his brother. "Can't we have this family chat on the way back?"

"No," Samuel said. "I'm not going back. I won't see them again."

Shem knelt down beside Japheth. "This is a serious matter Samuel. It's about the man Eli."

"That was her father." Samuel pointed at the girl. She nodded. "He was killed by someone. It wasn't me. You're asking me that, aren't you? And I'm telling you, I didn't hurt him. He gave me food when I worked his fields. I was good at driving his team. Wasn't I?"

The girl patted his arm and nodded in agreement. Shem took in a slow breath. "I understand this is difficult, but if you don't come, we have to believe that you did it, that you hurt Eli."

Samuel whipped his head to and fro. "No, I told you. It ain't so."

Japheth took the young man's hands and looked him in the eye. "We need you to come with us, Samuel. It's the only way we can hear your side of this. It's the way of Noah and Noah's God. You have no choice."

"Noah? That's what he wants? For me to go to the city?" Samuel's eyes were wide. Ham applauded his brother in his mind. He found the key. All little boys revered the old man, the man of the ark with his long winded stories. This Samuel had never grown up enough to realize the man he idolized was as ordinary, and fallible, as any of the men of earth. That was a good thing. To the boy, Noah was to be obeyed without question.

Samuel turned to the girl. "I have to go, then. Do you see?"

"Eliamah may go with us," Shem said.

The girl's head snapped up and she took on a look of defiance. "I will stay," she said.

"We'll take you to your mother's then," Shem said.

"You will not. I'll stay here."

Shem started to argue but Ham had been standing there long enough. "She isn't being questioned by the Council. Let her do as she pleases."

Samuel took his wife's hands in his as they all stood. "She's strong, this one. She can stay and wait for me. She won't run off. She promised." Sam grinned at his wife and she patted his cheek.

Ham pulled the length of cord from around his waist. "We need your weapon," he said.

Japheth snatched the rope from his hands and hurled it across the cave. "He comes willingly. We don't need that."

Samuel withdrew a knife from his belt and handed it to Shem. His brother immediately put it in Eliamah's hand. "She should hold on to this," he said. "To protect herself."

The girl took the weapon and followed them out of the cave into the glare of the overhead sun. "Wait," she said and ran back inside. She returned with a length of green fabric. "Kneel down, Sam."

The boy dropped to his knees and allowed his wife to fashion a turban from the fabric. She was careful to cover the back of his head, where a bald patch surrounded a raised ridge, an old scar, never properly sutured. From the fall in the ravine? If he had fallen, and hit his head, it explained why he didn't call out to the search party. He would've been passed out. He could have come around later, though, and got himself to safety. If he ever was in that ravine.

"Keep this on, now," the girl told Sam. "Even if it's hot. It'll keep that scar from getting burned. Hear me?"

The boy nodded and rose, favoring one leg. He was an assortment of injuries.

Ham waited as Shem untied the provisions on the fourth mount and put them in the cave. They wouldn't need them on this expedition. Once the boy and his brothers were mounted, he got onto his own horse. The girl grabbed his reins before he could move. She looked deep into his eyes. For a brief moment she reminded him of his mother, whose piercing eyes read his most hidden thoughts. Ham shifted uncomfortably.

"He's innocent," the girl hissed.

▲

Four horses and four men. Naomi let out an exasperated groan. They didn't bring Eliamah. She meant to remind Ham that morning, but she was awake most of the night, fuming about the sacrifice, then crying because her own husband couldn't fulfill the ceremonial requirements. Then she overslept. Her husband was gone before she awoke.

Naomi ran down the street behind the search party. She fell in place behind them until they stopped at the home of Japheth's eldest daughter, married to Shem's third son. Samuel would be housed with them until he could be interviewed by the Council. Naomi caught her breath and examined the young man as he dismounted. He was all in one piece, not bloody or battered, not bound or prevented from running by a weapon at his throat. Not hauled about as one already condemned.

The pretty fabric wrapped on Samuel's head caught her eye as he stepped toward the home. It was the mossy green fabric Denah gave to Iris, intended for Eliamah. Naomi clapped her hands together. Iris and her daughter maintained contact. There was still a bond. With her husband in Shinar, Eliamah would surely seek refuge in the home of her mother. Naomi suddenly had urgent plans for the next day.

Chapter Twenty-three

The mother and her boys were all in the field beyond the home. Naomi stayed out of their sight, pulling off the scarf protecting her skin from the bright sun and drinking water from a goat skin tied to the horse. She had no plan really, no formula to break down the walls of communication between herself and Iris. Woman to woman she wanted to find the truth. She hoped the bonds of sisterhood would connect them enough to clear the haze of accusations and see what really happened to poor Eli.

She hadn't asked Ham's permission to see Iris, just packed a load of supplies and told him she was going and would be home by dark. He grunted something and started to walk out the door when he stopped. "Is Denah going?" he asked.

"No. You told me not to spend time with her, remember?"

"You're going alone, then?"

"Yes." She hadn't asked anyone to go with her. She wanted to see Iris and Eliamah by herself. Maybe then, unthreatened, one of them would talk.

"Be careful," he said. He didn't kiss her. Naomi stood for a long moment until the empty feeling was replaced by the urgency of her mission. It had to be today, before Noah arrived and the Council gathered to question Samuel. There would be no equally divided decisions made with all seven men present.

Naomi turned her eyes to the blue expanse overhead. "God who saved me, help me to see the truth," she prayed.

With a deep breath Naomi tied the horse to a tree and led the pack mule out into the open. Iris and the boys froze in place. Naomi waved and pointed at the mule. Iris gave instructions to the boys who turned back to the weeds they were hoeing, still with eyes on the visitor. Iris shifted the babe tied to her back around to her hip and approached. "Why are you here?" Her eyes scanned the property for signs of others.

"I came alone, Iris. I brought a few more supplies. I hoped we could talk."

Iris scowled but did not order her off the land. Naomi waited.

"Alright then. You can bring those inside." Iris turned to the house.

Naomi followed the woman into the home, to the cooking area near the door. She set the bag she carried onto the floor and did a quick scan. Eliamah wasn't there. She let out a sigh.

"What? Not the elegance you're accustomed to?"

"Oh, no. No, not that. I hoped your daughter would be here. That's all."

Iris pinched her lips together and didn't respond as she put the baby down on a pallet and unpacked packets of lentils. Naomi retrieved the remaining bags and helped, her eyes examining the home more closely. It was a simple rectangular plan. One low table in the middle of the main room was surrounded by flattened cushions, none with the brightness of being new. All of the possessions had seen the wear of daily use, it seemed. Even the cooking pots bore the dents and dings of many years. She would have to remember to bring Cush's extra ones next time she came. He wouldn't miss what this family would treasure.

The sparse room was sectioned off on one end by stacked stone walls, allowing a separate sleeping area and space for storage. Naomi could see at least a half dozen pallets, stacked on one side, the hide blankets and reed mats rolled up together like flat bread rolled with hummus. A small window faced the stream. It wasn't high on the wall. Iris's boy could have seen out easily if he stood beside it. He could have seen someone that night.

A single pair of worn sandals sat by the door. Naomi pushed back the sting of tears threatening to find their way out. Iris would probably leave them there, and everything else that spoke of her husband. The things that made Eli Eli, would be preserved.

Naomi understood their importance. She had nothing to remind her of her own family. There were times on the ark when she cried, aching for the family that was gone, aching for something tangible to hold to say this person was real. Her mother's bracelet, shaped like a serpent coiling around her wrist, her father's pipe that smelled of sweet herbs, her brother's favorite mug carved from a tree burl. She had nothing but memories in her head and even those were gradually fading. Sometimes she had to question if her life Before was real at all.

Her husband took her in his arms those times, when he found her dissolving in tears while sitting in a pen with the sheep or on the deck overlooking the endless watery grave. That's when he started kissing the top of her head and telling her how he was covering her with his love. His comfort, protection, promise of forever flowed over her head and penetrated her heart. In those moments Naomi knew everything would be alright.

He rubbed her aching feet then, too. The ark was in chaos for the first weeks, until they established a regular routine of care and cleaning. She and the others traversed the vessel over and over again. Did anyone gather the eggs? Were the uncaged birds fed? Has the lamp oil been replenished? Whose turn is it to feed the humans? Endless chores, endless laps. When she finally collapsed at the end of the day, Ham was there. He warmed a bowl of water for her to soak her feet then rubbed them with eucalyptus oils. It was a time of talking and listening. Of sharing. Of being one together.

An ache in her soul rose with the image of Ham. She would do the same as Iris if anything happened to him. She wouldn't allow anything of his to be given away. His knives, his tools, his whistles. His essence lived in the artifacts that he touched, that he loved. Even those dogs of his, she would find a place in her heart to tolerate them for his sake. It was a valley of turmoil she and Ham traveled right now, but they would get through it. They always had before.

Iris had no more chances to find joy in her husband's eyes.

Naomi wiped a renegade tear then walked to the table, bending to inhale the fragrance of wild roses in a clay pot.

"My Eli used to bring me those," Iris said. "Now my boy does it."

"I'm sorry he's gone. I know you're hurting. I wish there was something I could do." Naomi faced Iris. The woman's eyes were misty. She tipped her head in acknowledgement then turned away. Her husband was never coming back. Finding his killer was her only way to serve him now, to ensure justice. Iris needed a trial and a condemnation as a balm to her own ripped open soul.

Naomi gathered the empty bags. Nothing would be gained by forcing Iris to speak again of what happened. She told what she knew. There was nothing new to be learned by making her repeat it again and again and again.

▲

The cave was empty. Naomi touched her hand to the fire ring.

It was cold. Eliamah was gone.

Chapter Twenty-four

The newborn's cry pierced the warm evening air, echoing off homes and surrounding Naomi with the haunting wail. It was a healthy sounding cry. But it didn't stop.

Why was this infant wailing without the comforting breast of his mother?

Naomi's heart raced along with her feet. Denah sent word through a neighbor girl that she was needed as soon as she returned from delivering goods to the widow. The matter was urgent.

Both mother and father of this child were from her own offspring. Naomi monitored the young mother as the developing child within her grew. It was something she did out of habit almost, noting her complexion and the brightness to her eyes. She looked for indications of infection and illness, and how the baby was positioned. There were no indications of complications with this mother at first. Then it became obvious the baby was soon to outgrow his confines. At seven months in the womb, he was already the size of a nine month old.

Naomi prayed that the mother calculated incorrectly, that she was further along than she realized. She prepared the family for the possibility of more than one baby, just in case the rare occurrence should happen again. Thankfully this family didn't believe in a cursing of that nature. If twins arrived, both would share the love. Naomi clung to the hope that this was the case, that there were two thriving in the large abdomen. Not one. Not one of unusual size.

But she heard only one cry in the night.

Denah met her at the door and stepped outside inside of letting her into the home of the newborn. "I'm so glad you're here, "Denah said. "It's been difficult."

"Are there two babies?"

"No. I thought there might be but there is only one, and he, he isn't normal Naomi."

Naomi wiped her sweaty brow with the back of her hand and forced herself to take deep breaths to slow her heart. "How, how is he not normal?"

"It's his skin that's odd, and the family is upset. They aren't sure what's wrong. They don't speak of the baby as a cursing but you can hear, no one wants to touch him."

Naomi squeezed her eyes tightly shut and leaned on the doorframe.

Denah took her shoulders. "Naomi? You went pale. Are you alright?"

Naomi forced her eyes open and nodded. "Yes. Let's see to this."

The newborn's mother lay on the mat weeping softly. She had already been cleaned and her ripped tissues dressed with salve and bandages. One look into her dark rimmed eyes and Naomi could see that the painful delivery was secondary to the fear that her infant was abnormal. "See to the baby, please," she whispered. "Tell me he'll be alright."

Naomi gathered her resolve and stepped up to the basket where the baby emitted his mournful cry. He was clean and swaddled. Her first glance was not the horrific sight she anticipated. The infant was the length of any newborn. Naomi let out a sigh and unwrapped the long binding strips.

"Hush, little one," she said as she examined him more closely. A thick patch of soft hair covered his head and matched his tiny eyelashes. A set of deep brown eyes seemed especially large on his small face. Open and bright, they sat above a little nose and the pink rimmed cavern of his mouth. His skin was deep red and wrinkled, like he'd been too long in a tub of water, but there were ten fingers and ten toes sprouting from two arms and two legs. Skinny and long, every part of his body was present.

Naomi bound the baby in his coverings and held him to her chest, rocking him back and forth. This was a seven month old baby, she was positive. He hadn't developed like a nine month one, except in length. She had delivered early babies before, their skin appearing like this one's, only they were so small they slipped from the womb and had arms that could fit through a finger ring.

She had been present, as a girl, when an early baby of this size was snatched up by a relative and taken away. The baby died, she was told.

"Naomi?' Denah said.

Naomi realized the room was silent except for the baby, whimpering now, exhausting himself with the effort to find comfort. It was her call. She could pronounce the infant diseased and suggest allowing him to die. Denah might question the decision. No one else would and the matter would be resolved. No one would find out what was really wrong with the baby. This one, at least. The young couple would bear other children and what then? She couldn't annihilate all their offspring.

The infant half closed his eyes then let his eyelids fall closed. It wasn't his fault his blood was tainted.

Naomi handed the baby to the father who looked at her with

wide eyes. "Your son will be just fine," she said with more assurance than she felt. "His skin is fragile now and he'll lose that hair, but it will grow back and his skin will even out. He'll be a fine young man. He'll be tall and strong."

Tall and strong.

And evil? The child had nephilim blood.

Her nephilim blood.

▲

Naomi found the darkness of the wooded area desirable. She needed to be alone, hidden from eyes that wouldn't understand. She emptied her stomach and cried until she was exhausted like the baby she just held. It wasn't his fault.

It wasn't Naomi's fault either. She wasn't permitted to choose her lineage any more than the infant. But she knew she had it. She knew the despicable blood could flow through her and be revealed in her descendants. She knew. No one else did. She did not reveal the family secret to Ham.

Ham hated the nephilim. Everyone did. At least everyone that lived Before. No one knew about them anymore. They were gone, all dead, all drowned in the deluge that removed evil from the earth. That's what the Eight thought. Seven of them anyhow. Naomi knew she carried evil inside her veins, she knew she carried evil onto the ark and now it would infect the new earth.

The nephilim were descendants of the men from the sky, it was said. Long before her birth, these men from above rebelled against their Creator. They abandoned their heavenly dwelling and came to earth to live as sons of Adam. Daughters of Eve were used for their pleasure and the nephilim offspring were born. The nephil children were powerful, strong and tall in stature, filled with prideful hearts.

They took what they wanted with no loyalty except to their own lustful desires.

Before they were reviled and hunted, the nephilim gained the respect of men. They were as gods themselves and that's how they wanted to be known, feared and revered. They destroyed predators and fought battles in exchange for glory. The daughters of men were given as homage. Naomi's great-grandmother was a nephil prize.

To an outsider, Naomi's family was cursed by God, or one of the gods, or all of the gods. Many of the infants born to them died at birth. The mothers, too, seemed to die in childbirth more often than in other families. It was true that the mothers died. Sometimes the babies were forced to rip their way out and there was too much blood loss to save the woman. But the babies didn't die like that. They were alive when her aunts took them away. The aunts returned later. Alone.

Naomi was terrified when her own children were born. Terrified they would reveal their ancestry. Terrified they would reveal her secret. Somehow none of her children carried the traits of the nephilim, at least not obviously. Her youngest, Canaan, gave her worry. His boys were taller than all their cousins. But they were nice boys, not seething in evil and discontent. None of her grandchildren seemed tainted in that way. The evil blood had thinned out, she hoped. Still, all births among her own people brought fear to her very core. That's why she had to be there. She had to see and know for herself there would be no nephilim offspring.

Tonight, the first was born. What was she to do? She couldn't allow his life to be taken. If anyone had asked her before what she intended to do, she would have said she would allow the baby to die, but looking into his face she knew she couldn't do so. She couldn't take a life to save her own. She couldn't stand before her God and commit the very grievous sin that her grandson was accused of performing.

At least now she knew her own heart. She wouldn't commit the sins of her mothers. The baby wasn't all that much too big, anyhow. Perhaps he wouldn't be so different from the other children. If he were kind, and gentle, perhaps it would be alright. No one needed to know.

▲

"What are you doing out here in the dark?" Naomi sat beneath a tree with her legs tucked up beneath her, head on her knees. "The dogs keep barking." Ham stood with his hands on his hips. He wasn't in the mood to be scolded for some error in his ways. If his wife was crying because of something he did or said or didn't do or didn't say, he would leave her alone in her misery. He couldn't, wouldn't, listen to her complaints against him tonight. His father was at the house and there would be the same old discussions between them at some point. One condemning voice at a time.

Naomi shifted in the grass and stood, approaching him with her arms out. Ham stepped into the embrace and relaxed as she put her head on his chest. He brushed his fingers down her soft loose curls.

"It's been a trying day," she said.

"You saw the widow?"

"Yes. I brought the supplies. We spoke, a little."

"Why did you go, really?"

Naomi picked at a thread on his tunic. "I hoped there was something more. Something missed, something to clear Nimrod's name."

Ham felt his tension rise and fought to keep it from his words. "And? What did you discover that everyone else missed?"

Naomi stopped picking and looked up at him. "Are you angry

that I search for answers, Ham?"

"No. I just think you're wasting your time on a quest with an obvious outcome. We have our man already."

"Samuel, you mean. You think he's guilty."

What he thought didn't matter. What the Council needed to believe was what mattered. "I see no alternative answer for what happened. So what did you discover?"

"I found nothing new at their home. I wanted Eliamah to be there. I believe she knows what really happened. But she wasn't at the home, or in the cave."

Good, Ham thought. The Council didn't need another opinion to muddy their thinking. She was just a girl and would say what her mother told her say. That was obvious. His wife clung to her as if she would save Nimrod with some confession. Naomi clung to false hope. That meek girl would not be the answer.

"About Samuel, though," Naomi said. "I don't believe he hurt anyone. It looks bad, because he's a strange man, without ties, but he's just simple and I can't believe he would intentionally harm anyone."

"You said he had the girl tied up in the cave."

"Because he liked her and didn't want her to run off. The bonds weren't tight. She could have escaped easily. He isn't used to people and how to treat them."

"You defend him? If he didn't attack Eli and Nimrod is innocent, what do you think happened?"

"I don't know, Ham. Maybe Samuel was protecting Eliamah and he killed Eli by accident. Maybe Eliamah was protecting Sam and something happened. I don't know."

"Tomorrow we'll find out, Naomi. Let the Council worry about Samuel." Ham pulled away from his wife and started toward the house.

"Ham," she said. "There was a baby born." Naomi bit down on her lip and looked away.

"And?" he said.

His wife shook her head. "Nothing. I just wanted you to know where I was this evening."

"I heard," he said. "My father is here. Don't be long." Ham left Naomi in the shadows and headed for home. The Council decided to delay the interview with Samuel until the day after tomorrow, after a day of dealing with the throngs come to see Noah. Ham wanted a good night's rest. There was much to be decided in the next few days and mental fatigue would only hinder his thinking. He had to stay alert, had to be ready with answers and reasoning.

He intended to initiate a new rule for the Triune as well. No women in the meetings. Unless they were directly involved, they took up space that should be given to the men, the ones responsible for societal unity. Eran, Denah and Naomi had always maintained a silent presence, not a neutral one. Their expressions declared their bias openly and he wasn't the only man to be pinched and have opinions communicated through his wife's touch. It was time to set them aside and allow the Council to proceed without the unvoiced words of those who had no vote.

Ham began running through a list of reasons for the decision in his head. He really didn't know what his brothers would think. He expected opposition, as always. If nothing else, he would set the precedent and tell Naomi to leave. He didn't want her sighs of disapproval and condemning glances to sway opinions in the room. More importantly, she wasn't accepting the good fortune of finding this man Samuel, and he didn't want her around when matters of such importance were laid bare for inspection.

Chapter Twenty-five

It was all Naomi could do to mash the walnut seeds beneath the pestle gently rather than pummel them against the stone. It was early. She didn't want to disturb Noah, Shem, and Eran just yet with a cacophony of kitchen noise. They needed a good sleep before the chaos of the day began. Naomi couldn't afford the luxury of extra bed time today and claimed the calm before the sunrise all to herself. The home would be a beehive of visitors before long, coming to see the patriarch. She had food to prepare, in ample quantities.

Noah had a following of admirers since the first set of grandbabies were born on the grounded ark. They tangled tiny fingers in his beard and chewed on the coiled strands while Noah held them close and spoke his blessings. As children they fought for his knee, then his ear, then his approval. His words were kind, full of compassion, an endless flow of affirmation. Naomi understood the draw. She craved his presence, too. The channel between him and God flowed freely and she never felt more safe than by Noah's side, engulfed in the power of his presence. He was a sanctuary, a refuge.

Before the flood, her father-in-law was virtually shunned. He was mocked and called unrepeatable names, causing such dissention in the market that he was banned from public speaking. He proved himself a prophet, of course. All his words were true. The flood, the judgment of God, the destruction of everything came just as Noah warned, over and over. The throng gathering today would hang on his every word, not hurl insults. Naomi couldn't help but wonder if the scenario would change if Noah once again spoke with the fury of impending destruction. Would any more listen than Before?

Naomi sighed as she scraped the walnut paste into a bowl and grabbed another handful to grind. Most would come today out of respect. There would also be those who merely wanted to see what a man over 700 years of age looked like.

"I can't read that expression of yours, Naomi."

Naomi turned to Noah's easy smile. "Good morning. I was just thinking about how old you are."

Her father-in-law let a deep laugh escape, working hard to keep the volume under control. He scanned the table of dishes in various stages of preparation. "You need lots of food to satisfy the masses as they gawk at the ancient relic on display, I see."

Naomi clapped her hand over her mouth. "Oh, I didn't mean it that way! But you do bring in the crowds. It's good they respect you."

Noah dipped his little finger into the walnut paste and gave it a taste. "And it's good they are curious about an old man. Questions bring remembering of the days past."

Naomi ripped off the end of a warm barley loaf so he could eat from the bowl properly.

Her father-in-law didn't hesitate and scooped the mix onto the bread before sitting cross-legged beside her on the floor rather than on the stools near the cooking fire. He used the low table to ease himself down, his knees groaning in protest as he descended. He settled onto the cushion and planted his elbows on the table, nibbling on the bread. "It will be a busy day. A good one. I enjoy the smiles of all my children's children."

"I know. And there will be many fathers bringing the newest babies for you to bless, I'm sure." Naomi caught her tongue as she finished. Surely the nephil tainted one would not be presented.

Noah nodded slowly. "Yes. I'll see the mercy of God over and over today in the lives of my offspring. Perhaps even the little fellow born yesterday."

Naomi could feel his eyes on her so she stared intently at the grinding stone. "Perhaps," she said. This was not the direction she wanted the conversation to follow.

Noah nodded and turned back to the bowl of paste. "Tell me about him, Naomi. Denah said he came early. Is he alright?"

"I believe he's fine. He wasn't too early, and everything seemed as it should. His skin was red and wrinkly, but it will mature. He's fine, I'm sure."

"Your own kin, this boy. A blessing to the line of Ham."

Naomi forced a smile. "Yes. A fine boy for the family."

"But?"

Noah waited for her to look at him, catching her eyes and holding them. Naomi felt the tears well up. She had fought to keep him from knowing her ugly family secret for so many, years. He couldn't know. He would regret her marriage to his son. He would despise her.

Noah let silence pass between them before wrapping his hand around her wrist. "And this boy was large for his age wasn't he, Daughter?"

Naomi sucked in a deep breath and nodded.

"And his mother?"

"It was a difficult birth but she will heal from her wounds."

Noah squeezed her hand then patted it. He chewed on the bread before he spoke. "Your great-grandmother nearly died from wounds at the birth of her sons, three times. Your grandmother was not difficult, I understand."

Naomi felt her heart quicken in her chest. "My great-grandmother had no sons. Just daughters."

"That's what you were told. You, and everyone. It isn't the truth. Your great-uncles were killed, Naomi. Like so many of your relatives."

The pestle slipped from her fingers, rolling off the table onto the floor. "Killed?" It was feeble not to ask why they were killed. She couldn't. She didn't have to.

Noah gave the reason anyway, undraping the grave clothes of her past with tender fingers. "Destroyed out of contempt. And to keep anyone from realizing whose blood ran through the family veins."

Noah's eyes did not reflect horror. There was no condemnation etched in his expression.

"You know."

"Old relics see many things. I've been around a long time, Naomi."

"You've always known? You knew what filth is within me and still gave me to your son?" Her mind was spinning through the muck. "Didn't you fear for his children? Did Ham displease you so much you would risk the shame in your own grandchildren?"

Noah cupped her chin in his hands. "It's because I love Ham that you were chosen. He asked for you and it was a good decision. I've never regretted your marriage to him. The sins of your ancestors were not your sins, Naomi. I wouldn't despise you under my roof because your great-grandmother was given to a nephil. Nor would your children be a disgrace if they carried the traits."

Naomi turned away. "If. If they carried the traits. What if the traits aren't obvious? What if my children carry the evil?"

Noah was silent until she turned back towards him. "Which of your children, Naomi," he said. "Who do you fear carries evil?"

"Cush." Her firstborn's name barely made it past her lips. She had never spoken of the nature of his heart. Not to Ham, who needed no more reasons to be at odds with his child. Not to Denah, even. Not to anyone who might connect evil with her past.

Noah's eyebrows lifted for a moment. "You are aware of your firstborn's activities, then. Of his deceit."

He knew of that, too? "He took items from the ark in the early days, when we all used to go to celebrate the covenant. And later, too, I believe, when he went back there alone. I thought he treasured them, and wanted reminders. I didn't know he was selling them until I saw an oil lamp in the market that I knew Ham made. It hung on a post near the pigs. The merchant saw me staring and tried to lie about it. It was gone by the time I found Ham and took him there, and the merchant said I was mistaken, that it he had nothing like what I described."

"I stopped him from taking things from the ark, and from my home."

"Yet he continues to profit. He takes items from his own home, now. And mine, claiming them to be ark relics. He tells the merchants they contain God's power of protection. It's shameful."

Noah stood with a boost from the table and eased into a standing position, arching his back in a stretch before resettling on a stool. Naomi followed.

"What does Ham say of Cush's behavior?"

Naomi exhaled. "He doesn't know. There are already so many fights between them. I couldn't."

"He knows, Naomi."

"Ham knows his firstborn is a thief? A liar?"

"He knows. We discussed Cush's deviant intentions many years ago. I hoped my son would find the strength to discipline his child."

Naomi said nothing. She assumed Ham didn't know. But he did, and had done nothing.

The tears that lingered evaporated and she could feel anger rising in her gut. He was responsible for the behavior of his sons. Their actions were a reflection on him. How could he have been so lax?

"Cush isn't evil because of your ancestry, Naomi," Noah said. "You carry the nephil blood yet you didn't allow that baby to be killed yesterday. You chose what is right in the eyes of God. Cush is disobedient in the eyes of God by his own choosing. He profits from his deceit by his own hand. It should have been stopped, and Ham will no doubt regret not doing so, but even your husband is not to blame for the sin in Cush's heart. He chose his own way."

"But if Ham would have stopped him-"

"Or you. Or both of you, united as one. As it should be."

Naomi rested her elbows on her knees and put her chin in her hands. "We've never spoken of it, Noah. It seemed best not to divide them further."

"It's easier to look into the past to see which decisions were poor and which were good. It's difficult at the time. I know. I made many mistakes of my own in the raising of my boys. One thing I learned. You must always have trust between the two of you, you and Ham. Secrets will destroy your unity."

Naomi nodded, not fully opening her mind to absorb the notion. It was too much at once, too much to realize her sordid family lies weren't crammed into the dark corners of her mind where no one else had access. Ham's father knew of their existence. Her tainted blood. Cush's profiteering. Pain poked into her temples. Neither issue could she deal with now. It was Nimrod who needed their attention. Nimrod's life was the imminent concern. She rubbed her temples then shook her head, dismissing any other worries. "I can't think about that now." She stood abruptly. "There's something I want to show you." Naomi retrieved a simple sketch from a shelf. "Do you recognize this? Eli's boy had it, said it was used to kill his dog."

"That's a springbone." Noah saw the question in her eyes and continued. "It's like a tiny spear sharpened on both ends, carved from bone. The ends are softened in a hot bath then folded to the center and secured with thin string. You put it into a piece of bait and a predator will swallow it. In an animal gut, the string dissolves and the legs fly out and puncture the insides. The boy found it in his dog?"

"Yes."

Noah rubbed his chin. "Hmm," he said.

Naomi watched him closely. "Who knows about these? Who would know how to make a weapon like this?"

"I taught all three boys how to make those."

Another lie from her husband. Naomi suppressed her irritation with a simple reply. "I see," she said.

"Knowing my boys, their sons and grandsons know, too. It doesn't make a case for or against Nimrod. Eli himself may have carved it."

Naomi stuffed the drawing back on a shelf.

Noah stood and gave her a firm hug before turning for the door. Then he stopped and faced her again. "You need to tell Ham about your past, Naomi. It's time he knew."

Naomi watched her father-in-law leave and put the pestle in motion again, this time with no regard to the pounding rhythm. He was right, of course.

▲

The sun was already on the horizon by the time his father left the kitchen. Ham hated when his wife and father had time alone, at least in these later years. It used to be good. Naomi used to leave the man's presence more accepting, less judgmental. Somehow the irks and quirks of marriage were put in perspective. Ham reaped the benefit of their discussions at one time. Not any more. Now the two conspired, and it meant he was in trouble for yet another grievance. Naomi would walk away empowered with the wisdom of God through the words of Noah and would hound him until he listened to her every bit of informed opinion. The forthcoming advice would not be in his favor. It never was anymore.

Chapter Twenty-six

The twelve legs were in continuous motion, weaving in and out of his own and nearly knocking him to the ground. Ham knelt down and flipped one dog to her back, vigorously rubbing her belly. The other two stepped all over the first one and covered Ham with slobbery licks and persistent paws until they received the coveted attention as well. His dogs were always happy to see him, always grateful for attention. They never bombarded him with guilt.

It was still early yet the air held onto yesterday's warmth. Ham shed his coat before drawing the bucket from the depths of the well. Three wagging tongues waited for their turn to drink the cool water, too. The stream wasn't that far away but they wanted to follow their master's actions and slurp from the bucket, or perhaps they didn't want to leave him for a moment, even to find water. Ham ruffled their heads and chuckled. It was nice to be admired and appreciated, even if it was just his dogs.

He took a long refreshing drink before setting the vessel down and glancing toward the pale cloudless sky that promised to send heat uninhibited today. It was the kind of day he liked. He welcomed the feel of sweat running down his brow as he worked. It gave the chilling bite of river water and cooling evening air more depth, more value. It was a morning made for fishing followed by a day of shop work and an evening training the dogs. But none of that would happen. Before long his father's descendants would begin coming and going in a steady flow and it would be impossible to carve out time for himself.

Ham's stomach rumbled. He was hungry and there were tantalizing aromas wafting from the house. His father left the kitchen and headed into a pasture to walk and talk with his God a good hour ago. Naomi was still there, though, and he wasn't in the mood to deal with the repercussions of her conversation with Noah. He didn't want to seek food and find recrimination disguised as well meaning advice.

The dogs startled and turned as one toward the house. Ham followed their point and felt his shoulders stiffen. Naomi walked in his direction with a large pot settled on her hip. Ham sighed, already weary from the day ahead. It would be the first of many trips to the well. His wife wouldn't find rest until late in the night, supervising the flow of food and the cleaning of dishes. As the gifts to Noah were presented, she would see that they were stacked in like piles or if still alive, caged and penned appropriately. If a child were hurt, he would seek Naomi. If a woman felt faint, Naomi would see that she had a place to rest. All the events of the day would all fall under her domain. Ham's presence was expected and of course he would assist as asked, as would the rest of the family. But the success of the day was up to Naomi. It was good her mind would be occupied today with pastries and sanitation and the duties of a hostess.

The dogs resumed their jostling for position at the bucket. One of them nipped at Ham's leg and he realized too late that Naomi caught them drinking from the well bucket. He forgot to shoo them away when he saw her coming and already there was a frown on her face. So much for a day free from criticism.

"I didn't even realize you were out of bed." Naomi pushed beasts away with her leg. The dogs looked at him, begging wordlessly for support. He clapped his hands and sent them off before retrieving the bucket and swirling the remaining liquid to clean it out. He waited for her to make an issue of the vessel turned dog bowl, but she didn't. He looked squarely into her face and saw the tight lips, pinched forehead. Her mind was churning and he had time to walk away, before she let her thoughts loose. Instead, he took the vessel from her hands and set it down. He would hear her thoughts regardless. All he could control was the timing.

"What's wrong, Naomi?"

"I was talking with your father." Naomi leaned against the well, crossing her arms over her chest. "He said he taught you about the springbone."

Ham caught his breath. He should have realized Naomi would pursue the origins of the odd weapon. "Yes. I suppose he did."

"You told me you didn't know what it was. You lied to me."

Ham let the well bucket fall off the rim and watched it descend into the darkness then listened for the splash below. "You didn't need to know about it. What if I told you I knew how to make them? I've shown all the boys and most of the grandsons, too. I know how you think. Why would I give you reason to battle against your own blood? Why would I let you blame my own offspring of murder because of one dead dog?"

Naomi faced the well and began drawing up the bucket. Ham stood back and watched. "Your father taught your brothers, too. Anyone could have made that thing, Ham. You had no reason to lie, unless-"

"Unless what?"

Naomi dropped her hands and allowed the bucket to plummet again. She squeezed them together in front of her. "Unless you had something to hide."

Ham let the accusation hang between them while he controlled his tongue. "What are you insinuating? Just what do you suppose I'm hiding?" His voice sounded more controlled than he felt.

"Did you make that thing? It's a hunter's weapon, isn't it? Was it your springbone that killed that dog?"

"No."

Naomi gripped the rope again and drew out the bucket with little concern that she was sloshing it everywhere. "Cush doesn't carry weapons."

Ham listened to his own intake and exhalation of air as he watched his wife pour the little remaining water into her pitcher then toss the bucket back over the edge. She was pale as she leaned on to the rim, a sharp contrast to her thoughts, which he knew were leading to a dark conclusion. "So, you believe like the rest of my family then. You believe Nimrod killed that man."

Naomi looked up at him and he could see the tears gathering.

"My own brothers betray me. Now the boy's grandmother seeks his death. How can you do this Naomi? Do you care nothing for your sons?"

"Stop it, Ham. You know I believe in Nimrod's innocence."

Ham drew up the bucket and filled the pitcher. "And my father? Did you and he plan Nimrod's stoning this morning?"

Naomi's hand flew from her side and landed on his cheek with a loud smack. Her eyes simmered. "How could you?" Her voice was barely audible and Ham felt the sting of regret over his last words. He didn't really question her devotion to Nimrod. She was trying to find reason to prove his innocence. She just needed to stop. They had a man to take the blame. The matter didn't need to be pursued and confused by conflicting reports. It was time to leave it all alone and let the matter settle itself out in the Triune Council.

Ham rubbed his hand over the stinging cheek. "Your interference will not bring this matter to a close, Naomi. And tomorrow, don't plan on attending Council."

"What? I have to go and-"

"No, you don't have to go. You don't have a vote and I'm sick of your pathetic whimpers when you disapprove of my decisions. You dishonor me before the men of the city. This matter will be decided by those of us with a voice and if it were up to me, all you women would stay home."

If he wanted a shocked response, he got exactly what he desired. Naomi stood with her mouth open, tears flowing freely down her cheeks. Again, the pang of regret. But it would pass. Change was good and his brothers would agree. Japheth and Shem would see how nice it was to make decisions without a finger poking into their rib cages.

Ham snatched the water pitcher and strode toward the house. A motion near one of the barns caught the corner of his eye. He froze and focused his gaze on the brick building that housed the horses. Nothing stirred. Still, his hunter instincts were raised. Whatever he saw was too large, too slow to have been a dog and none of the livestock had the intelligence to disappear in the bushes. No sign of movement meant something was hiding. Something or someone. Someone didn't want to be seen from the house.

Ham waited motionlessly, ignoring the sound of crying coming from the well. On gentle feet he stepped closer to the house and stood in its shadow. He could see the bushes that ran close to the barn from there. His hands were poised to drop the vessel and grab hold of the knife in his belt. His heart was beating quickly, not in fear. In anticipation. He relished the thought of a good hunt right now. A good fight. A thorough display of strength and wit against a fierce opponent. He wanted to wrestle, to hit, to pummel something.

Of course, unless he was mistaken, there would be no beast to destroy, no intruder with ill-will to apprehend. It was probably just someone waiting to see Noah. Ham exhaled and felt a rush of disappointment. When this whole mess was over, he and Nimrod would take a long hunting and exploring expedition, beyond the Tigris even.

Nimrod. Ham returned his focus to the bushes that now rustled in a linear fashion as someone inched toward the door. This time his quickened heart rate reflected an unwelcomed thought. Nimrod might still choose to flee. He would declare his own guilt if he did so, seal his own fate for nothing. They had Samuel now.

Ham ducked behind one tree, then another, to gain a position where he could see the barn door. He pressed his spine into the rough surface and stood still. It was not at all like his grandson to flee from conflict. Nimrod embraced challenge. He conquered his opponents, be they the elements or terrible lizards or the charms of a pretty girl. But this one was different, Ham knew. Nimrod did too. He relied on the wisdom and compassion of his own kin to declare his innocence and he didn't know if they would. Nimrod didn't know if his family would lift their hands to pull him from the pit or lift the stones to kill him.

Perhaps he should flee. Ham felt the painful loss even as the thought crossed his mind. Nimrod would never be found if he chose to leave. His survival skills were impeccable.

The form moved into the shadow of the door. Ham would wait until it went inside before he followed. He wouldn't stop his grandson, though. He just couldn't allow him to leave without saying farewell, and perhaps giving him some idea as to which direction he was heading.

But the man who emerged from the cover of the foliage wasn't Nimrod.

It was Cush.

Chapter Twenty-seven

Cush led a horse from the barn on foot until he was well beyond the house, then he mounted and rode toward town. Ham kept to the shadows a good distance behind his firstborn. It was an easy tracking job. His son never looked to see if he had been followed.

Cush wasn't an early riser by nature. Why was he sneaking out? It was his horse. He had every right to take it for a ride. If he hadn't been so secretive, Ham would have assumed one of the women sent him on an errand. There was a lot of food to be prepared so it wasn't an unlikely scenario. Cush would be eager to impress visitors with his own tasty dishes and had every reason to leave the comforts of bed to obtain supplies. But he obviously didn't want to be seen.

Ham wanted to know why.

Cush went to a shop on a quiet street where only a few awnings were raised for the day's business. He tied off his horse and approached a man opening crates of merchandise, stacking them onto low tables. Ham stepped into the shadows across the street. He couldn't catch their words, however the hand gestures were loud enough to convey the nature of the conversation. Emotions were heightening in both men.

The shop was familiar. Naomi drug him there once, fuming.

She said the merchant was selling a lantern that Ham made, a lamp that had once been on the ark. He remembered the incident clearly. His wife recognized his mark, the way the handle had a little twist at the base before disappearing back into the clay. It was a simple design and anyone could have constructed it, yet Naomi was certain it was Ham's work. He believed her, but the lamp wasn't there when they returned. The merchant hid the vessel from him, he was certain.

He remembered the incident, and felt it gore into his gut. It had been the awakening of his eyes. In that moment, he glimpsed into a murky realm, one that bound his paternal pride in fetters. It was the day he realized his son, his own firstborn, was still selling relics from the ark.

Cush was just a boy when he first asked if he could take an item from the ship that spared mankind from annihilation. They were all there. Noah and Jael, his brothers and their families. Back when they made the arduous climb to the ark every year to sacrifice to God on the day of the covenant rainbow. Noah had been pleased with young Cush's request and gave him a piece of wood with tidy rows of carved lines. There were 371 notches to be exact, the number of days they lived on the ark. There was a star carved above the forty-first line, the day the rain stopped pouring from the heavens and the sun revealed itself, then the stars and moon later. Another star marked the day they saw land, another by the day the ark was stopped in place by the jagged peaks of earth that had been dislodged and strewn in massive rocky pyramids.

"Use the calendar as a reminder, Cush," Noah said. "Remember the God who hates evil. Remember the God who provides salvation."

On subsequent visits, Ham couldn't recall his son asking for reminders but the boy's coat would be lumpy on the return trip. When Cush was older, he made the long journey alone, a sojourn to the ark, where he lived for weeks. Noah told Ham that Cush was taking items and even pieces of the wooden structure itself on these visits and Ham meant to take the matter up with him. The conversation never came about. It wasn't like Cush ever showed him the items he took. And Ham didn't want to accuse him of theft. What was the harm? After all, Ham made a good portion of those items himself. Why shouldn't they belong to his firstborn? Ham didn't realize then what became of the items.

The slabs of slick ice cascading over the top of the mountain finally engulfed the ark and the relic taking should have resolved itself. It didn't. Cush took items from Noah and Jael's home, according to his father. This he addressed with his son. Cush denied the accusation and Ham let it pass. He couldn't prove it. It didn't seem to be such a great important matter. So his son wanted the reminders? Noah insisted the memories of God's judgment be preserved, repeated and told over and over so it would not be forgotten. Didn't reminders from the ark itself serve that purpose?

If only that was the reason. Wanting the objects for himself and selling them for personal gain were different matters.

Cush was making a profit from the ark, rather than from the real work of his two hands. What relics he sold now, Ham could only guess. All he knew was they weren't genuine anymore. His son, his firstborn, was a cheat. The label wasn't reserved just for Cush however. If it were discovered and made public, Ham would bear the shame as well.

Ham held back his anger as Cush retrieved a bundle from his coat and gave it to the merchant. He had seen enough.

▲

"What are you doing, Cush?" Ham relished the look of

surprise, then fear, then forced calm that spread over his son's face as he stepped from the shadows.

"Just some business, here, with Jabal."

Ham turned his attention to the merchant and felt a startle of recognition that he hadn't expected. The hooked nose. He had seen that nose all too recently. On Samuel. He drew in a sharp breath and cursed. This was the man the search party followed into the forested territory, to the ravine, to rescue the boy. Jabal was Sam's father.

Ham turned from Cush and Jabal and ran a hand through his hair. They thought the man lost his firstborn. The search party didn't return to try again. The city mourned his loss, their loss. But he didn't die. The boy survived. Guilt penetrated Ham's conscience. He pronounced the boy's death. He ended the search.

The two men stood silently, watching him. "Your son lives," Ham said.

Jabal jerked his eyes away and nodded slowly. "So I've been told." He didn't smile and kept his focus fixed on the merchandise on the table in front of him.

Ham wasn't surprised at the man's reaction. He would be angry, too, had it been his own child. Of course, he wouldn't have stopped the search until it was confirmed that his flesh and blood was dead. He wouldn't have gone home to the comforting arms of his wife until he knew beyond all doubt. But all men weren't like that. Jabal trusted Ham's wisdom, so the search ended. Jabal believed there was no hope in finding his boy. No one did.

But how? How could anyone survive that fall? They couldn't.

Jabal had to have known his son wasn't in that ravine.

Ham clenched his hands into fists then forced them open again, making himself push the past away to deal with the issue at hand.

Cush stood quietly with his hands gripping the bundle, his eyes flicking onto Ham's face then back to Jabal's. His discomfort was dripping like the sweat on his brow.

The Triune Council would discuss Samuel's involvement in Eli's death tomorrow. Ham didn't want to guess his son's intentions at the merchant's shop. The purchase of votes was repugnant. If Jabal summoned Cush in order to purchase favor, Ham would have both men cast away from the community. Without provisions.

He took in a breath to prevent himself for reacting based on nothing but intuition. It didn't make sense. Surely his firstborn wouldn't turn against Nimrod for a quick and easy profit. Even for him, that was low.

"Jabal's son will stand before the Triune tomorrow," Ham said. "Your interactions at this early hour look suspicious."

Cush fiddled with the bundle and pressed it under his arm. "Yes, you're right. But there's much to prepare for the day's company."

Jabal turned and spoke to Cush as if he had just arrived, as if there had been no heat filled argument between them moments earlier. "And what is it you need?"

Cush scanned the man's wares and finally pointed to a large fired clay platter. "That one," he said.

Jabal handed the item to Cush, who made great show of examining it for imperfections. "This is fine, then. I'll take it."

"And for what trade?"

Cush hesitated then set the bundle on the table. The deer skin was wrapped with cording that he carefully untied to reveal the contents. Ham held his breath. If it were at all related to the ark, he would show little mercy to his firstborn.

The hide held only a selection of knives. They were new, flint blades set into bone carved from the dragon's remains. The fine workmanship was that of Ham's son Canaan. Just one of the exquisite items could purchase most of Jabal's inventory, not just one unremarkable plate.

The merchant's eyebrows raised as he inspected the items. Cush carefully avoided Ham's gaze. When Jabal decided on his payment, Cush quickly wrapped the other knives and pushed the bundle into his coat. He grabbed the platter and gave the merchant a slight bow. "Thank you for opening early for me this morning, Jabal," Cush said.

Jabal smiled broadly as he daintily rubbed a fingertip over the carved features. "Come anytime to trade, son of Ham. Anytime."

Ham made a sharp pivot toward his horse, away from Jabal and away from Cush. His stomach threatened to erupt and he was glad he had had not eaten. He wasn't sure what he witnessed, what he stopped from occurring.

One thing he felt to his core. His firstborn was a disgrace.

Chapter Twenty-eight

The bricks were still emitting the cool of the night, sending a chill down Naomi's spine as she leaned against the well and watched her husband walk away. She clasped her hand over her heart and held it there. She had smacked Ham across the face in her fury. Never had she done that before. Never had she felt the desire, the need, to do so. He accused her of conspiring with Noah to allow Nimrod's execution. The thought brought the sting of tears to her eyes. How could he? The trickle of tears led to sobbing. She didn't try to stop the torrent. It took too much effort to be composed and the strength she needed was used up.

How did her simple existence turn into this mess in such a short time? "God in the heavens, help me," she whispered, wrapping her arms around her knees and pulling herself into a hug. There was no one nearby to extend comfort and the deep longing for her father surfaced.

She craved the warmth of his arms. And not just the warmth, but the security, the assurance that all would be well, that he would see to it, fix whatever mishap she caused. He was a good father. Was. He laughed at Noah and his One God. He ridiculed and ignored the warning. So he drowned like the rest.

Noah was a second father. He was reassuring, too, and there

was a sense of safety near the man who talked with God. But he knew. He knew the secret she kept hidden all these years, the secret she wanted to keep hidden still. Noah wasn't likely to tell anyone, not if he hadn't already. Not even his own son. But it wouldn't be the same in her father-in-law's presence now. The unspoken issue would fill the air between them in blankets of tension.

And Ham. Her beloved. She had never had reason to doubt his words. He lied to her about the springbone and now that she knew, she couldn't help but wonder what else lay hidden in his mind that he wouldn't allow her to see. He knew more than he spoke, she felt certain. How far would he go to save Nimrod? How many lies or hidden truths? She didn't want to believe Ham was capable of deceit. Didn't he fear God? How could he have forgotten the power of judgment?

A piercing stab penetrated her thoughts. She was not without fault. No matter how far she tried to stuff her past into fathomless pits, it crawled back to the surface. Every time a baby was born. With every hint of evil that appeared among the children and their children's children. Every time she nicked herself with a knife and saw the ooze of blood spilling from within, she was reminded. She withheld information about her family that would have damned her in society, or at least in Ham's eyes.

Naomi sucked in a ragged breath and let it out slowly. That was long ago. She was young and didn't know the truth of Ham's God yet.

Ham would never have married her, had he known. He would have certainly rejected her, without a second glance, and Naomi wasn't about to let it happen. Ham hated the nephilim and now she knew he wasn't opposed to a man leaving one wife to take another. After all these years and all they had suffered together and celebrated together, she realized she didn't know what Ham might do if he found out. Noah was right, of course. She needed to purge the secret from its vault. She would. Someday.

Naomi forced her mind from herself to tomorrow's Council. She wouldn't be attending. Her husband spoke in anger yet it didn't seem to be a thought that came from nowhere. He had been thinking on the matter already. Still, there was a chance he would relent in the morning. Unless he didn't want her there for a reason.

What reason? Naomi sorted her thoughts. The springbone? It seemed irrelevant and important at the same time. It was logical to assume someone killed the dog before attacking Eli, but it wasn't necessarily so. Why kill the animal slowly? If the dog was protecting his owner, it could have been killed instantly as he was.

Somehow the dog's death seemed out of place with the rest of the story, and perhaps it was. Perhaps there was no connection to the man's death. Eli himself could have formed the weapon that the dog devoured. It could have washed down the stream, even. There was no way to know for certain. The questions it raised in her mind were meant to remain there, it seemed. Ham made sure of that.

▲

Ham's horse was gone and so was Cush's, Naomi noted when she entered the barn. She let out a sigh of disgust. It appeared they left her to manage the feeding of all the visitors to come, escaping to follow their own interests rather than show hospitality. She had an errand of her own to run, one mission, then she would return and fulfill her responsibilities. She had to see Samuel.

Denah's grand-daughter opened the door and allowed Naomi inside. The entire household appeared to be stirring already. Tired expressions greeted her warmly. Had any of them slept? Housing the potential murderer must have been unnerving and she wondered how many slept with weapons tucked beneath their pillows.

Samuel sat on the floor with his legs out to the side and bent at the knee to form a ring. A large rabbit sat in the enclosure and nibbled on greens from his hand. His crooked smile was already in place when he acknowledged Naomi's presence. "Look here, Naomi. This rabbit is tame. I never thought to try and tame one before. I just ate 'em. Come feel how soft he is."

Naomi glanced at the women of the home. They were smiling like mothers watching their infants discover their toes for the first time. There was no fear, no apprehension. Naomi relaxed her shoulders. Just a short time under this roof and they knew Sam was innocent. Naomi could read it in their eyes. The patriarch, her nephew, busied himself at the fire pit but Naomi knew he kept a watchful eye on the man charged to his custody. Hopefully it was a protective eye.

The fur was silky and slid through her fingers like water.

"Eliamah would like this," he said. "I intend to tame her one of her own."

"That would be nice, Sam," Naomi said. "I know she would appreciate it. How would you catch it, do you think?"

"Just a regular trap. A cage with food inside. I wouldn't want to hurt it."

"How do you catch the animals you eat?"

"I shoot 'em with a bow or trap some in nets. There's lots of ways."

Samuel talked freely so Naomi just asked what she wanted to know. "Sam, do you know how to kill an animal by feeding it a weapon?"

His expression confirmed what she presumed. Samuel didn't know about springbones. He laughed. "I never thought about that. I'd have to catch it first. Seems backwards."

Naomi smiled at Sam who tenderly stroked the soft fur and told her about the foods that rabbits eat, what time of the year certain ones were born, where to find them in the woods, and how to catch them.

"How did you learn about traps?"

"Eli taught me mostly. Some I knew from before I went to live alone."

"Eli was good to you then? He helped you?"

Samuel nodded. "I'm sad that he's dead. I liked him."

Her niece's gaze shifted to the corner of the room, sharing a look with her husband. Not of suspicion, but of compassion.

"Your father thought you were dead all these years. He looked for you, you know. My husband went with a team of men to find you. They really tried."

"I know."

"How did you get out of the ravine?"

Samuel shrugged. "I don't remember a ravine. If I was in one, I don't know how I got out, unless it was that man that got me out."

Naomi glanced around the room, seeing only questioning expressions. "What man, Samuel?"

"The man that carried me and found me a cave to stay in."

"You were hunting with your father when you fell down a deep ravine. Then a man, not your father, carried you into a cave?"

Samuel looked up and sighed like he was explaining a simple process to a distracted toddler. "I was hunting with father. I remember that. Then I remember watching the rocks swinging past my eyes. It was me hanging over a man's shoulder and I was looking at the ground. It made me sick and I gagged all down the man's legs but he kept walking 'til there was a cave and he put me inside where it was dark. Then he left. My head was hurting real bad. That's why I didn't follow him. I was sick."

"Did the man say anything to you?"

"Said he was sorry. That's all. He didn't come back."

Samuel turned his focus to a loaf of bread that was scenting the room as it baked. The rabbit forgotten for the moment, his mind raced to the next experience and he began asking a cousin about how he could make his own bread when he went back to the woods. Samuel was hungry to learn. He wasn't as slow of mind as she thought when she first met him in the cave.

Naomi stood and approached her niece, keeping her voice low. "How was the reunion with his parents?"

The woman shook her head. "They haven't come. Samuel is the firstborn, and they haven't bothered to come see him."

She didn't need to say more. The father was ashamed of the accusations against his boy. After losing him once, now he was ashamed to claim him back.

But Sam was innocent. Of that, Naomi was sure. He didn't lie and steal and cheat. He didn't kill anyone.

A sickening feeling settled in her gut. She couldn't muster the same conviction of innocence for her own offspring any more.

▲

Eran grabbed Naomi's hand and led her away from the gathering of people encircling Noah. She smelled like paprika. Her sister-in-law's long hair was hidden beneath a gauzy length of fabric and she wore the plain simple tunics she had always worn. Her face was pale except for the dark shadows beneath her eyes. She gripped Naomi's hand tightly.

"I was worried about you. No one knew where you were."

"I had an errand to run. I'm sorry. There's so much to do and-"

"It's alright, Naomi. Denah has her daughters and yours

organized in the house. They have all the food under control. No one will go hungry here today."

Naomi scanned the crowd. Ham stood to one side, and with him were Cush and Nimrod. Naomi let out a relieved sigh. They were here as they needed to be, not off hunting or fishing and leaving her to represent the household. Her men needed to stand with dignity and face the men who arrived. There is no shame where there is no guilt. There is no need to hide if there is nothing to hide from.

Nimrod was clearly uncomfortable. His arms were crossed over his chest and his feet were planted in place. He didn't turn his eyes toward the gathering or invite interactions with the crowd. He, Ham and Cush stood alone. They spoke to one another and even that was in brief bursts. Mostly they stood, a wall of unspoken isolation. There would be no throng of children seeking Nimrod's favor today.

Naomi hoped he wouldn't be shunned entirely. He had not been found guilty. Still, the scent of suspicion swirled on the air of possibility, and people kept their distance.

Shem sat beside Noah on a patch of grass, and Japheth was nearby. As angry as she was with her husband, the scene made her heart ache. If there was to be a division between the boys, it was still Ham that was cleaved. It was Ham's choice to stand to the side, of course. He drew the dividing line himself sometimes. But today, she knew he needed the support of his brothers, and his father. This wasn't the time for old hurts to fester. It was a time to unite, a time to heal.

Naomi reaffirmed her grip with Eran's hand. "I'm not sure how I can stand anymore, Eran. I don't know what will happen. I'm not sure I know what's true anymore."

"You will stand firm by the strength of your God, Naomi. Moment by moment. Truth will be sorted out. You can't hold the weight of it yourself. God will judge. You know this. He will be the judge in his way, his time."

Naomi wrapped her arm around Eran's tiny waist and pulled her close. "I'm ready for it to be over."

Eran didn't respond. The pounding of feet running stilled her voice, and everyone else's. The runner stopped at the edge of the gathering, breathing heavily for a moment before he could speak.

"He's gone. Samuel. Gone."

Chapter Twenty-nine

Ham was at the man's side in only a few long strides. He took both shoulders in his hands and looked into the man's face. "Samuel's gone? He ran away?"

The man nodded. "He was around earlier this morning, then his uncle said he just vanished. They're looking for him."

"Is he on foot? Are the horses all accounted for?"

"Yes, he's on foot we think. Nothing is missing. Just Sam."

Ham pressed his lips together to prevent any hint of a smile appearing. A man that runs has something to hide. Samuel essentially affirmed his guilt by refusing to appear before the Council. He glanced at Nimrod. His grandson's eyes were wide and the corner of his lip was struggling to stay down. If relief was tangible, Nimrod was drenched in a sea of its sweet vapors.

Noah cleared his throat and spoke evenly, showing no delight or disappointment. "We mustn't be too hasty until we know for certain what has become of the boy." He could have made a stand that supported Nimrod. But he didn't.

Ham turned away from his father's eyes. He looked instead at Naomi. She looked horrified. Her hands covered her mouth and Eran was holding her erect. Why wasn't she relieved? She claimed over and over that Nimrod was innocent. Had that stupid springbone changed her mind? Naomi put her head on Eran's shoulder, looking away from his stare. He could tell she still believed in Samuel's innocence. The fact that the young man bolted was evidence against him. Couldn't she see that? This was a moment of triumph for Nimrod. What was wrong with his family?

▲

Japheth's son met Ham and the others as they rode into town. His charge had not yet been found. Men were still searching the hidden alleys and watching the roads that led from Shinar. There was no sign of him.

Ham shook his head. "It's good to watch the roads," he said, "but Sam is a man of the woods. He won't walk down the street. He'll follow the path of the deer."

"Unless she hid him," a woman said. She pointed at Naomi.

Ham faced his wife. She looked back at him and mouthed, "No."

"Why would you say that," Ham asked the woman. "Why would accuse my wife of such a thing?"

The woman put her hands on her hips and huffed. Her cheeks flushed crimson under the scrutiny. "Well, she was here this morning. I saw her. She was in that house where that Samuel was. Maybe she knows where he went is all I'm saying."

"Here this morning?" The question was to Naomi, who he left by the well in tears. With the food preparation, he was surprised she left the house. Surprised if it were true. Perturbed if it were true.

Naomi nodded. "I was. I spoke to Sam. I didn't hide him away somewhere."

"You spoke to him? Naomi-"

"Ham-"

"You helped him escape?" This from a voice standing somewhere behind them, among the men gathering to see what was happening.

Naomi turned and sought the owner of the voice. "No, I did not. He was most certainly here when I left." Ham could hear the change in her pitch. She felt threatened. He turned to his nephew to confirm her statement.

"He was here after she left. She didn't take him or hide him away," the man said.

Another man spoke above the crowd. "Did you tell him to run? Encourage him to get away? You tried to frame him so your kin would be freed."

"No! That is not at all true." Naomi looked ready to punch her accuser. She turned back to Ham. There was desperation in her eyes and she was seeking his rescue. He wasn't sure what to say. He wasn't sure the accusation was false, so he said nothing.

Naomi waited, watching his eyes. "Ham, I did nothing of the sort," she said when his lips remained closed.

Noah raised his arm to silence the murmurs. "What did he say, Naomi? When you spoke with Sam, did he say anything about leaving?"

"No. Nothing. He knows he's innocent so he doesn't fear the Triune. He talked about rabbits mostly."

Her statement brought a chuckle to the crowd. Ham was not amused. He felt the rise of anger climbing up his face. Sam wasn't a little child anymore, despite his lack of knowledge. He was a man capable of killing. Now he was gone. But it was the other part of her statement that now stuck like a thorn in his skin. His wife declared her belief in Sam's innocence. Publicly. She threw a spear into the heart of her own grandson's case. Ham felt his insides broil and crowd or not, he intended to escort her home in whatever fashion required, if that meant a gag and a rope, so be it.

Shem was quick to grasp his right arm and Japheth his left. Both of his brothers were strong. They didn't have the power they had back when they hauled giant timbers around the construction site, but they were strong enough to restrain their younger brother while he forced himself to gain control, and at least momentarily, set his anger aside. Ham exhaled and unclenched his muscles. His brothers withdrew their grip. They did not leave his side.

Ham snapped his eyes from Naomi and peered over the crowd, ready to speak, then realized their attention was elsewhere. Even Noah looked away from him, observing a commotion down the street. A handful of men pushed another man toward the onlookers, shouting taunts as they went. Ham studied the man they were delivering.

It was Sam.

▲

The venom spewing from her husband's eyes made Naomi wince. He was still angry about the conversation at the well and she fueled his flames by talking to Samuel. She was surprised, really, just how upset he was. Had she committed the sins of which she was accused, then yes, she could see his wrath. But she hadn't. He had to know that she wouldn't commit such acts to prevent justice or bring him shame. His face didn't reveal belief, however. Just fury.

He forced his attention away from her. She knew Ham, though. His issues would not be disposed of so easily and it would be unpleasant conversation until they could talk it through. She didn't look forward to the interaction, yet wouldn't hide from it. The sooner they got it out, the sooner they could move forward again. They always did. The times of displeasure would collapse beneath the weight of their commitment to each other. At least it always had before.

Eran and Denah stood beside her looking across the crowd, the same direction as Ham. Naomi focused on what was happening as the crowd divided and let two men enter the space. The older one was scowling as he led the younger one through the onlookers with a rope which bound the man's hands tightly in front of him. There was gash on the captive man's forehead, with a smear of blood dried on his face.

Samuel.

Side by side, there was no mistaking that Jabal was Sam's father. The same sharp down-turn of the nose, same angled line of the jaw, same eyebrows that came close enough to touch in the middle of a wide forehead. Sam had the one eye that didn't track straight and a short leg on one side, but they were kin for sure.

Their expressions were far different however. Jabal's lips were pressed into a tight line and the brows squinched together so that his forehead was furrowed like a freshly plowed field. Sam's brows were arched above his wide eyes and his tongue kept a constant sweep over his bottom lip. Naomi started toward him, to reassure him. Denah and Eran pulled her back. "Don't interfere, Naomi. Let Noah take charge."

Her father-in-law rested a hand on Jabal's shoulder. Jabal took in a quick breath when he recognized his forefather, the man who talked with God, the patriarch of all who lived. He bowed his head in acknowledgment for a moment before handing the lead rope to Noah with a sober face. "It's my shame to stand before you and present my, my son, tied like a beast. He intended to flee and I could not allow it. Justice must prevail."

Noah took the rope and faced Samuel. "You are Samuel, then," Noah said. "I am Noah, your grandfather's grandfather."

Samuel nodded enthusiastically. "I remember," he said. "I remember. You listened to God and were saved because you built the ark."

Noah offered a warm smile that put Naomi's own heart at ease. He wouldn't allow Samuel to be mistreated. "Why did you leave your uncle's home?" he said. "Where were you going?"

Sam frowned. "I wanted to see my mother, that's all. I wasn't running away." Sam nodded at his father. "He says I was, but I wasn't."

Jabal closed his eyes and groaned. "He told lies as a boy, before he ran off. He's telling one now, Father Noah. My delight in having my son returned has become my sorrow."

Before he ran off? Jabal himself took the boy hunting and reported that the boy fell. That was the story back then, anyhow. Naomi squeezed Denah's hand and they exchanged a knowing glance. Naomi started to speak, to ask why the story changed. Denah shook her head. "Hush," she said.

Noah caught Jabal's words, too. "I was under the impression young Samuel was lost in an accident when you took him hunting, Jabal. Is this not so?"

Jabal's jaw flinched to one side but he answered without hesitation. "I thought my firstborn was dead, lying broken in the ravine. But he wasn't dead, was he? Yet he didn't come home. He ran away from his mother, from his duties in the family."

Noah put a hand on Sam's shoulder. "Why didn't you return home, son?"

Samuel straightened his spine and looked his father in the eye. "He didn't want me home."

Jabal backed away and looked away from Sam. "He doesn't tell the truth. He is my shame."

Naomi watched Sam closely. His breathing was even. His voice was steady. His gaze with the one straight eye was uninterrupted. No hair on his body twitched the slightest bit as he spoke. He told the truth.

Noah looked between his two descendants. Two of the same blood, with different hearts. Her father-in-law had sadness etched into his face and she wondered if the feuding father and son reminded him of himself and Ham, or even of himself and Japheth, his own rebellious firstborn. No one interrupted his thoughts. After a few minutes he addressed Jabal. "Your son will remain with his uncle, as originally planned. Untie him."

Noah didn't thank Jabal for capturing Samuel, and he didn't ask Samuel twice about running away. Naomi felt pressure drain from her chest. Noah knew the boy wasn't trying to flee, trying to outrun his guilt.

Jabal started to protest then thought better of it. He did as he was told. Samuel rubbed his sore wrists.

"Son, you must remain here in this home. Don't leave until I come for you tomorrow. Do you understand?"

Sam nodded. "I do. I'll stay. I wasn't running off."

Noah patted Sam on the shoulder. "I know," he said.

Naomi smiled at the tenderness Noah showed the lost boy. Only the boy was a man now, with a wife. She turned towards Jabal and wondered if he even knew about Eliamah. Jabal's attention was no longer on his son, however. His eyes searched the crowd until they found who they were looking for, stopping on Cush.

Her son stood on the perimeter of the gathering. He caught Jabal's glance with a nod of acknowledgment before turning away. They knew each other, of course. Cush preferred the man's cooking implements over the others in town. Naomi didn't care what he sold. She refused to support the man's business. It was Jabal that had the oil lamp from the ark once, Jabal that lied about it. Later, she realized it was Cush who sold Jabal that lamp.

She didn't like their friendship. Jabal was a liar. And Cush... Naomi stopped her thoughts and allowed her sisters-in-law to draw her towards home. She intended to find a refuge. Alone. For the first time that she could recall, thinking of her own family brought more pain than joy.

Chapter Thirty

The cold water stimulated Ham's senses. Before the aching chill of the first bucket wore off, he drew another from the well and dumped it over his head. Despite yesterday's fatiguing chaos, his sleep had been spotty. Even after the drama with Sam, Noah's descendants continued to arrive with their offspring. And their gifts. There was enough grain to feed his parents for a few years, all bagged and stacked in the barn. At one time he, Shem and Japheth formed a line and tossed the bags in place together. He couldn't help but recall their same actions years ago, stocking the ark for all the people they intended to house while God purged the evil from earth.

They hadn't come, of course. His family alone ate of the stores while the ark floated and after it rested, and until they could bring in their first harvest.

No one came despite the warning from God. His father and grandfather and great-grandfather told people what God said, but it was mockery to the end. No one believed God would keep his promise.

It was easy now to look back and see how it was all in the One God's hands the entire time. He knew what each man's heart would choose. He knew he would save the Eight. Only the Eight. No more, no less. Even as the sky darkened and Japheth stood at the door of the vessel, alone, desperate. Even as he waited, watching, praying for Denah. Even then, God knew she would choose to believe. God waited with Japheth. Denah entered the ark as the first water fell from the tormented skies.

God knew about the animals, too. His family was prepared to house many beasts, but the sheer number that arrived was astounding. They came first in the night, led by an invisible hand. Then more came, and more. The birds, the beasts, even the bugs listened as their Creator called and because of it, were saved.

Mankind turned a deaf ear.

Yesterday, the men of earth heard it all again. For most of the afternoon and into the evening, his father sprinkled a dose of preaching into the words of blessing and chatter surrounding him in Ham's yard. Like the old days, except the external flame of his internal fire was diminished now. Noah's voice was softer, kinder. God's fervor, surging through his veins, was dispelled with all bitterness removed. The glisten to his eyes still spoke of the pleading from his soul, though. Remember, he kept repeating. Remember.

The chaos of the day gave Ham's temper a chance to cool. He was actually glad his responsibilities kept him from pinning Cush down for answers. It was a battle in his mind, the need to know what his son was up to with Jabal, and the need to not know, the need to let Cush's actions remain hidden. It wasn't a coincidence that Cush and Jabal had the suspicious interaction. It had to do with Samuel. It had to do with Nimrod, he was sure.

Would his firstborn barter in favor of Nimrod, or against? He wouldn't have placed a wager in either direction. It grieved him to even consider that Cush might be jealous enough of his own son to strike out against him.

Then Jabal turned on his own firstborn, dragging him in ropes.

Ham's thoughts went a different direction. Cush was trying to secure the freedom of his own firstborn. The knives were meant to purchase Jabal's loyalty, to purchase Samuel's disappearance, thus declaring the boy's guilt.

Ham's interference destroyed the opportunity to make the whole mess with Nimrod disappear.

The thought cut through his mind. The boy said he went of his own accord to see his mother, but there was no proof to back up his words. His own kin may have planted that notion, that he ought to go to the home of Jabal. It may have been arranged already, for the boy to fall into the hands of his father, assuming the price was right. Sam's own flesh and blood may have been willing to see that he missed his own trial. For a price.

The barter wasn't completely honored. What did one knife buy? Jabal bound the boy and returned him. It could have been less favorable. Jabal could have showed affection to his boy, swaying opinions by a lost-child-come-home routine. At least he didn't do that. The binding ropes alone seared an image in the minds of the crowd as to Samuel's nature.

What did Jabal have to gain by delivering Samuel back? He had to realize the boy would be found guilty and likely to be stoned to death. He would lose his firstborn all over again. Ham sighed and roughly donned a clean tunic. For justice? Not likely.

Ham interrupted the intended transaction too soon. Once he arrived, it was over. Neither Cush or Jabal would be openly deceitful in front of him. Both assumed he wouldn't allow impropriety, even on behalf of his close kin.

Had he realized what they were doing, would he have allowed the negotiation? If they had been open with him and explained their behavior, what would he have done?

Ham sighed and dumped one last cold bucket over his head, the stinging flow releasing a shiver and a sobering awareness. He would have stopped Cush. Not because he felt it was wrong. No, it wasn't justice that would make him prevent the barter. It was the vulnerability. Cush and Jabal would hold the key unlocking a corridor where Ham had no defenses. Even if they never acted on it, never allowed the negotiation to be aired, the knowledge gave them power. Cush wasn't man enough to wield the weapon, if he even recognized it in his grasp. But who knew of this man Jabal and what he might attempt. Maybe not now, but someday. It wasn't a chance Ham could take. He would live under no man's control.

It didn't matter now, anyhow. Samuel was back and would have his say in the Council. Ham couldn't imagine any words from his lips holding true. By evening, Nimrod's innocence wouldn't be in question.

▲

Naomi watched her father-in-law from the window as he made another pass. He prayed as he circled around the house, and had been since the sun first peeked over the landscape. He was alone with his God, as she knew he would be. It was wishful thinking on her part, that he walked side by side with his son in the early dawn of day. Ham's side of the bed was cold, and she thought maybe, just maybe, the two sought answers together. But Ham didn't follow in Noah's steps.

She and her husband hadn't spoken in almost a full day, other than passing comments required to keep the day running smoothly. She could tell his anger toward her had diminished over the course of the day, thankfully. They had not yet addressed the issue of Samuel, or of the Council meeting today.

Naomi drew the teeth of the ivory comb through the ends of

her hair, pulling through the snarls as they interrupted the rhythm. Ham hadn't revoked his decision regarding her presence among the Council members, at least not that knew. She intended to be prepared, dressed and ready with the others. In Noah's presence, perhaps her husband would let his command fall to the side.

Today of all days, she needed to be present. Samuel's words could be misconstrued. He didn't have a sophisticated mind to defend himself. He was brighter than he appeared but he had no practice in making logical connections or convincing arguments. He would speak openly. His own words might bring his condemnation if he wasn't careful. It wasn't her place to speak for him, of course, but she would if she thought he was misunderstood. At least Denah would be there, and Noah. They wouldn't allow the poor young man to be convicted by his ineffective communication. They would make sure he knew what was being asked. There was no end to Naomi's devotion to Nimrod but she didn't want Samuel to take blame that wasn't his.

A second man joined Noah, stepping beside in rhythm. Naomi caught her breath. Ham? No. Disappointment rose, then fell. It was Nimrod, and that was good, too. Noah could read a man. If anyone understood the truth about Eli's demise, it would be the man who spoke with God. If her beloved grandson's essence leaked any drop of blame of any sort, surely Noah would catch it in the wind.

Naomi craned out the window, following the pair. The weight of emotions pulled their shoulders down, their faces turned toward the earth they trod. When they stopped moving, they faced one another. Noah grasped Nimrod by both shoulders then pulled him into a tight embrace. Relief at his offspring's innocence?

Or sorrow, and farewell?

▲

Several dozen men convened at the base of the tower. None wore the clothing of labor, permitting the monument to stretch towards the heavens in stillness. The space would be hers to claim. Naomi tilted her head back as she approached, in awe of its beauty against the pale morning sky. The Council would meet without her. One glance into her husband's eyes and she knew. His decision stood firm.

"Naomi?" It was one of the workmen, Abed, the father of the boy she saved from the dragon. "Why are you here?"

Naomi patted his arm. Of course, he questioned why she wasn't at the meeting. She had no desire to explain, not to him or the other men now standing around her. "I won't be at the Council. I'll wait here." Her eyes went to the pinnacle. "I'll wait up there, near God."

Abed glanced at the others. "We're protecting the tower."

Naomi nodded and smiled at them. "That's kind of you," she said. She wanted to ask, 'from whom?' but held her tongue. They had no weapons and there were stairs on the other three sides of the tower as well, yet they appeared unmanned. They would be defeated in short order if an attack came. Still, their intentions were admirable, despite the lack of threat. It was a gesture to prove their allegiance to Nimrod. They would protect his creation since they could not protect the man from the accusations of Iris.

She lifted her foot to climb the steps but was stopped by Abed's hand on her arm. "We shouldn't allow you up there." His voice was full of uncertainty at first, then he gained his confidence. "In case you get hurt."

His words didn't fool her. He didn't want her to be on the tower. Naomi put her hands on his cheeks. "I'll be fine. And I won't touch anything, or steal anything."

A deep blush seeped onto Abed's face, warming her hands. "I

know," he said. He took a step back.

Naomi turned from the men and climbed the steps in the cool shadows of the western staircase, keenly aware of the eyes stepping with her. Her irritation was quickly pushed aside. They had no right to prevent her from being there, no matter how loyal their intentions, but it was nothing to waste emotion over. Too many other thoughts crowded their way into her mind vying for that right.

Up and up, past six levels, she stopped at the top and caught her wind. Standing there, alone, closer to God than anyone, she raised both arms and her face to the sky. "Master of the heavens, let the truth unfold," she prayed. "Let justice prevail." She spoke out loud, then stopped and looked around. There was a tingle up her spine, as if she were being watched, and not by the God to whom she called. A quick glace showed her that Abed wasn't there.

Naomi stepped around the short stacks of clay tiles forming colorful rows on one side of the space. Some were the size of a man's hand and others would fit inside a child's palm. Brilliant crimsons, violets and golden hues covered their surface. The completed floor mosaic would be an exquisite work of artistry. Resting below columns carved with intricate detail, the seventh layer would display a mastery of skill. How could God not be pleased?

A flickering movement drew her attention to the opposite edge of the tower. Naomi stopped in the stillness and squinted into the sunlight. She saw no one. "Hello?" She called out anyway. A flock of ravens fluttered at the noise and cried back at her before settling back onto a sun drenched ledge.

She watched a moment longer, taking the anxiety with her to the low wall lining the perimeter, where she could sit and look down at the meeting place. She couldn't expect her mind to be at ease, not while the Council was deciding the fate of Samuel.

The vote could go either way. Her husband was convinced

Samuel was guilty, but he was reasonable and could change his opinion if the evidence was presented. He was an honest man, really. He always had been. He lied about the springbone, but that was just to her, and in an angry moment. Would he lie before the Council? She didn't know the answer. A month ago she would have staked her life on Ham's integrity. She didn't know for certain now, not with Nimrod's life in his hands. Her husband had changed immensely in the short time since he journeyed with the boys to tar pits near the river.

Samuel didn't kill Eli. She was certain. If he were found innocent, the suspicion would fall on Nimrod. She forced herself, again, to consider the possibility of her own grandson's guilt. It simply didn't hold true. As hard as she tried to walk the path of an unbiased observer, there were no cairns that led to his guilt. There are things a grandmother knows, and as sure as she knew the sun would rise over the fields tomorrow, she knew that Nimrod did not kill Eli.

Samuel didn't have the heart of a murderer either. Nor did Ham, or even Cush. That left no one to carry the blame and suffer the consequences. Would the Council allow the vote to go that direction?

Losing Samuel was far different than losing Nimrod. He was already an outcast. He belonged to no one. His guilty verdict wouldn't cause enmity between Japheth's line and Shem's. And his death wouldn't be in vain. People would remember the man they stoned to pay for the crime he committed. Samuel would be a reminder of the penalty for sins against their God. His death would be far more reaching than his life.

Nimrod's conviction would carry far more weight. A beloved son in the line of Ham killing a son in the line of Shem would fuel divisions already mounting in response to Eli's death. There would never again be unity among the brothers, the sons of Noah. If he were freed, however, he would find favor again. He could restore what the previous month ripped apart. Nimrod's guilty verdict could destroy the men of earth, his innocence could save them.

Where did the truth lie? It wasn't justice to stone a man simply as payment if he had no hand in the incident.

The decision lay in the hands of the Council.

Naomi closed her eyes and thought over the events of the last month, trying to shake the personal bias. Someone killed Eli. Were her eyes blinded to the truth? Was her devotion to these men so strong she overlooked the obvious?

Even if she knew who to blame, would she speak out? Could she condemn her own blood to death?

A mother always protects her children.

Right? Naomi swallowed the dread rising up inside her.

No. Not always. Not in the face of truth. Truth had to be first, above all else no matter what that meant, or how fierce the ripping of her soul.

A thread of guilt wove into her thoughts. Truth. She needed to speak to Ham and the others when this was over, the nephil seed exposed. Protecting herself was living in a lie, too.

The rays warming her back suddenly disappeared. Naomi stiffened but didn't turn around until a long shadow crept up the wall beside her. She turned with a start, then gasped. It was Eliamah.

Chapter Thirty-one

Samuel's young wife stood motionless, a knife grasped between both hands, pointed at Naomi. A long scarf wrapped around her head, covering most of her face until the breeze pulled it back, exposing a weary, and wary, expression.

The thumping in Naomi's chest diminished. "Eliamah," Naomi said. "I'm glad to see you."

The girl shifted from foot to foot, finally lowering the knife, tucking it into her belt. "Why aren't you at Samuel's trial? I thought, I hoped..."

Naomi looked over the wall to the city below, to the groups of people milling about, never venturing too far from the meeting house so they could be first to know the outcome and start the flow of gossip. "I want to be there."

Eliamah nodded slowly. "You know he didn't kill my father. So the others kept you out."

Naomi suppressed a startled reaction. The girl was wise. "Samuel will be treated fairly. Noah will make sure of it." Noah would never accuse an innocent man. Neither would Shem or Japheth, That was three of the men, three of seven. "I have prayed to our God and asked him to reveal the truth to their eyes."

Eliamah inched toward her and Naomi patted the wall beside

her. "Why do you believe in Samuel's innocence?"

The girl sat, then swung her legs over the side so she dangled above the level below. "He isn't so simple minded as everyone thinks he is."

"I realize that. He's wise enough kill a man, then cover it up, but it isn't in his heart, is it? I feel as if I know him. When he says he's telling the truth, I believe him. Perhaps there's no sense to it. His innocence damns my own grandson."

Eliamah twisted the end of her scarf around her finger. "Samuel didn't kill Eli. Even if he hated my father, he wouldn't harm him, or his dog. That's why he created such fine traps and nets, so he could catch prey without harm. He wanted to kill them quickly, not allow them to suffer. He's tender like that. I was, when you found me in the cave, tied up, but he wasn't doing it to be mean. He was trying to protect me, like a, pet. Do you understand?"

"I do. I could see that."

"Men may have done Sam wrong, but he doesn't speak of revenge."

"Not Eli though, correct? Your father, he didn't harm Samuel, did he?"

"Father was good to him. He gave him work to do, to earn food and supplies, but he would have given it to Sam even without the work. He offered to let him sleep in the house even, like family. Samuel was the one who chose to come and go. But he was always welcome back."

"Do you know who wanted to hurt your father, then?"

Eliamah looked at her lap, twisting the scarf there until her finger was mottled. Abruptly she let it go and looked away from Naomi without answering.

Naomi sighed. "You said men did Samuel wrong. Who do you mean, if it wasn't your father?"

Eliamah inhaled a long deep breath and rubbed her temple.

"Are you referring to Jabal, his father?"

She turned to Naomi and nodded. "Samuel doesn't say much. I don't think his father cared for him, though. I think, I think he was ashamed of his firstborn. Samuel said he wasn't very good at the games with the other boys because of his leg and he has trouble with his eye, too. He says Jabal would beat him, trying to make him tough. Sometimes he would wake up in the shed and realize he had been there for days, and he wouldn't remember anything. His father hit him in the head those times, he thinks."

"Does he talk about the day he fell in the ravine? When he was out with Jabal?"

"It was the only time Sam can remember his father wanting to spend time with him and teach him something useful. Samuel remembers how excited he was. He remembers being on a horse and riding a long time and he remembers his father didn't say much to him at all. After that he remembers being carried over a man's shoulder and set down in a dark cave. It wasn't his father that carried him. He sat there for days and days waiting for Jabal to find him. Jabal never came. No one did."

Eliamah turned her face to the sky and closed her eyes. "I heard about the accident from Shem and Eran when I was four or five, I guess. We heard about the search team. About the little boy who wasn't very coordinated and fell off a trail into a rocky pit and how no one could find his body for a proper burial. Eran was so sad for the boy's mother, that she wouldn't have remembering stones to sit and grieve by. We were all so sad."

"But Samuel did survive. And someone found him, but didn't bring him back to the city. Didn't tell anyone, either. I don't understand that part."

Eliamah looked her in the eye. "He remembers getting so

hungry, he finally left the cave. All he could find to eat at first were leaves and worms. He remembers piling tree limbs on top of himself for warmth and being afraid to sleep and miss when his father came. He remembers marking a trail as he ventured further and further from the cave, calling to his mother. He remembers where to find all the watering holes that he ever came across and where the berry bushes are and when they are ripe. He remembers plenty."

Naomi felt nausea rising from her gut, waiting for the girl to continue.

"He doesn't remember any ravine. He doesn't remember any fall, or any injuries except a painful knot on the back of his head. Not even scrapes on his hands."

Naomi gripped the wall. "He was never in the ravine, was he? He didn't fall to his death. Maybe he didn't fall at all."

Eliamah looked at the sky again. "I think Jabal hit him on the head and left him. Maybe he hoped Sam would fall. Maybe he wanted to push him, then didn't. I don't know. He wasn't in that gorge though. He would've been hurt real bad, if he'd lived. I don't know who found him after that. Or why he left him. Even if Sam didn't want to go back, he was just a boy. Why would he get left there?"

Both women watched a pair of eagles soar above them, allowing the silence to surround their thoughts. Samuel could have returned to civilization. He didn't. He protected his family name. Whether he meant to or not, he protected the man who deserted him. Or men. Samuel's statement that he didn't come back because he wasn't wanted was the simple truth. Jabal's son, alive, wasn't part of the plan. Jabal tied him and led him to be sentenced and stoned, intentionally.

Eliamah placed the knife she carried in Naomi's palm. "Samuel's knife. He didn't make it himself, though he likes to pretend he did. The man that put him in the cave gave it to him."

Naomi ran her fingers over the smoothed bone carving. She had seen it in the cave when she first encountered Samuel. It didn't matter at the time where the weapon originated. It was just an old knife. Now she looked at it with new eyes. The scaly remnants of a behemoth wrapped around the handle, worn flint protruding from its open mouth. Simple. Familiar. Too familiar. It was a base design her husband recreated many times over, adding variety in intricate details before taking them to market. Just holding it in her hand brought a chill of uncertainty and she quickly put it down before it slipped from her clammy fingers.

Anyone could have purchased this knife or imitated Ham's design for themselves. Even Jabal. The carving wasn't a fine, finished piece at all. Naomi could feel her heart thumping in her chest all the same.

"What is it, Naomi?" The girl's eyes were wide.

Naomi forced herself to exhale, forced herself to rein in the tears that threatened to rear back and run rampant. She put the knife back in Eliamah's hand and closed her own over the top. "You need to hurry back down. Go to the meeting. Tell them what you told me. Tell them, tell them everything."

Eliamah drew back and shook her head. "No. I can't."

Naomi gripped the girl's arm. "I know you won't talk of your father's death. But you can help Sam. He needs you to help him tell what happened when he was a boy, what you think happened. The Council needs to know what kind a man Jabal is. And what kind of man your husband is."

Eliamah stared at the knife, turning it over and over in her hands. "He isn't really my husband. I mean, we said the vow, but we don't…"

Naomi watched the color rise up her throat. "I understand. Was it your mother's idea for you to marry him, then?"

Eliamah hesitated, then nodded.

One less mouth to feed or to keep her away from anyone seeking the truth about Eli's death? "Sam's your friend. You care for him. You want to protect him or you wouldn't be here."

Eliamah said nothing. Naomi put her arms around the girl's shoulders, pulling her into a squeeze. "Too much injustice has passed in our families. We must at least try to make matters right before God. If you know that your Samuel is innocent, go speak words that might help him find favor with the Council."

The girl stood and wrapped the scarf back around her face. She turned to the stairs then stopped. "If he is spared the stoning, what will become of your grandson?"

"I don't know, Eliamah. It's up to God to judge my family now."

▲

Shem's kin clustered on the right side of the room. Japheth's sat on the left side and his own filled the floor space between them. Ham stood in the door and took a quick assessment of the people in attendance. He couldn't help but notice the separation in the meeting hall. It was understandable, of course, the loyalty to one's closest relations in times of upheaval. It was just so pronounced today, the tension settling among them like fences. He could see where the family lines were drawn by the stiffened postures of the men on either side of the divisions.

Other distinctions among the three groups caught his eye, too. Distinctions beyond blood lines, distinctions he never noticed when they mingled as one. Many women of Shem's kin had scarves over their heads, indoors, where they didn't need protection from the sun.

Japheth's side had the greatest proportion of men with hairless faces, choosing to take a sharp edge to their chins on a daily basis. His own people still maintained their beards, braided and embellished with beads carved from the antlers and teeth of the beasts they ate for dinner. He hadn't noticed it before now, how very few men in Shem or Japheth's lineage wore the beaded braid. Their unity was cracking. Their sons' sons were peeling away from the core.

Ham worked his way among the lines of family and sat down in the Triune circle with his father and brothers and their firstborn sons. Samuel was among them, too, as was Iris. Nimrod sat near Cush, but not in the circle. He wasn't on trial today.

The room was quiet and Ham realized all eyes were on him. "Where's Naomi?" Noah asked.

"She won't be attending," he said, intentionally looking into his father's eyes then smiling slightly before looking away. There was a brief uncomfortable silence before Noah cleared his throat and invited the circle to eat the communal meal set before them.

Eran and Denah both stared at him for a moment longer before looking to one another with a question on their faces. His brothers turned to the food. They understood. Both had witnessed Naomi's inappropriate behavior yesterday, declaring her opinion of Samuel's innocence before the crowd.

A loud slurping drew his attention to Samuel, who was thoroughly enjoying a wedge of grapefruit. When that was gone, he chose a piece of salt-cured meat, sliced into a thin sheet and wrapped around goat cheese. He held it gingerly between his fingers and looked at it from every angle. He sniffed it and touched his tongue tentatively into the creamy center before stuffing the rest in his mouth. Cheese nestled into the corners of his smile. Ham turned away after the boy poked his little finger into a bowl of curry then put the finger in his mouth before Iris could remind him how to dip with a piece of flatbread.

The boy's uncivilized manners didn't seem offensive to the others. Samuel was like a stray cat with a blinded eye and one leg missing. He drew the sympathies of those around him, not the contempt. Even Noah had an amused expression as he watched Samuel sniff a fig filled pastry.

Ham shifted his position and focused on a hot mug of tea. He didn't want them to have compassion for this outsider simply because he licked almond paste from his fingers. This was a trial, in essence. No formal charge had been made against the boy. Not yet anyhow. It was up to Sam to prove he didn't kill the man Eli, and when he couldn't, a formal trial would follow and his own life would be the penalty. How could he eat, knowing what the day held? How could he not have a stomach full of knots already?

His own gut wouldn't allow food this morning. Cush wasn't eating either. His firstborn sat quietly with his head down. He hadn't spoken a word. Samuel's fate would directly affect Nimrod's and Cush seemed terrified of the outcome. There was no confidence in his demeanor. Cush had obviously hoped to avoid this Council altogether by having Samuel run away.

Ham lifted his eyes to Japheth's side of the gathering, beyond Samuel. Jabal wasn't sitting behind his son, in a position of support. He was among family, a few rows behind the Council, arms crossed and scowling. Samuel's mother wasn't even in the room.

Noah took a long drink of his steeped tea leaves and addressed Samuel as the bowls were emptied. "You understand what this meeting is about, Samuel?"

He nodded. "Eli was killed and you're trying to find out who did it."

"Yes. And there's a possibility it was you, Samuel. That's what we need to resolve today. What you tell us is very important. You must speak the truth."

"I know. I am speaking the truth. I didn't kill Eli. I was in my cave that night, the one up river from the one I was took from."

Ham held his tongue. He hated the way his father was treating the boy so gingerly. It made the boy seem fragile.

"Tell us about Eli and his family. How do you know them?"

"Well, I have Eliamah for my woman. That makes me kin with Iris here."

"What about before Eli died?"

"Eli taught me how to grow food and make nets to catch fish better. I helped him drive the animals in his fields and he gave me food and other provisions. I liked Eli. I'm sad that he's dead. He was my friend."

Noah nodded and seemed content with Samuel's answers. Shem continued the questioning, looking at Iris. "Is this how it was, Iris?"

The woman nodded. "Samuel here didn't hurt my Eli. He wouldn't. We gave him supplies in trade for his help in the fields."

"Did they fight?"

"I don't recall them ever raising their voices at each other. Never saw either one raise a fist."

"Why didn't you and Eli allow him into your home, Iris. Was there something about Samuel that made you afraid?"

"Afraid of Samuel?" Iris smiled at the young man across from her. "We weren't afraid of him. He wanted the life he had, in the caves, in the woods."

"Why Samuel?" Japheth asked. "Why did you stay alone in the woods?"

Ham raised his hand palm out to his older brother to get the questions back in line with the accused crime, but Iris spoke first. "He isn't here to explain why he didn't go back to his father, now is he? Living the way he does isn't an offense to Noah's God that I know of. He can live in the caves if he wants to. It doesn't make him full of evil to do so."

Iris was on her knees and her eyes were pinched as she defended the boy. Noah gave her an easy smile and motioned for her to be seated again. Samuel turned back and forth between Japheth and Noah, not sure if he was to respond. "No one wanted me back," he blurted. "I stayed where I was because I knew if I went home, I'd disappear again."

From the corner of his eye Ham saw Cush stiffen and suck in a deep breath. His head was up now and he fixed a stare on Samuel. The expression surprised him. It looked like fear. Across the room a fiery tinge crept up Jabal's face. He was trying to stand but the men nearby held him in place.

There was obviously no bond between father and son so Ham decided to take a risk and talk to Jabal. "I can see you disagree with your boy's words, Jabal," Ham said. "Generally we know the men brought before us. We've seen their actions and their lifestyle. It says much about a man. Your boy here, we know very little of his nature. I know he has been absent from his mother's arms for many years, but you know him best. What can you tell us about him?"

Jabal clenched his arms over his chest and peered at his son. "He is my shame."

Samuel flinched at the words and turned his eyes to the floor. His father continued. "He never respected me or the ways of our fathers, the ways of Noah. He's always told tales that were not true. And..."

"And what, Jabal?"

The corner of Jabal's mouth twitched to one side. "And as you can see, his mind is tetched. I don't know what he's capable of doing."

Samuel's head lifted and he turned slowly to the man placing him on the altar. Ham waited, hoping for a violent outburst. One that proved he was capable of unleashing his control and letting it loose on another. It didn't happen. The boy restrained his emotions. There was no anger, he just nodded his head back and forth before returning his eyes to the floor.

The room went still. The man betrayed his own blood. He could have said he had no idea what kind of character his boy had after all the years away from home. That would neither support or condemn Samuel, and would protect his own name as well. He chose instead to throw a cloak of shame upon himself by denouncing the boy. It was more than Ham could have hoped for, yet he was galled at the open display of disloyalty. Samuel was his firstborn, after all.

The room took on a significantly different atmosphere. He could sense the cords of unity knitting together across bloodlines again. The residual animosity towards Sam, towards the boy who needed to be accused of killing Eli, was slipping away. Ham could feel his own tension rising. He gained Jabal's condemnation of his own firstborn but it resulted in pity for the man he wanted stoned.

Noah took his time collecting his thoughts. Ham waited for the momentum to return to the meeting. The questioning needed to continue, needed to expose Samuel's lack of a proper alibi. No one spoke and Ham had nothing to say himself at the moment. He didn't want to make the situation worse.

Noah finally exhaled, then took a thin sheet of hide from his coat and held it out for Samuel. The boy didn't take it. His gaze was turned away from Noah. Ham followed the line of his scrutiny. The boy looked at Cush with a fierce intensity. Cush put his face down again.

"Samuel?" Noah restored attention to the drawing he held. Samuel took the hide and examined it. "Can you tell me what this is?"

Ham stretched his spine so he could see over the edge of the item in question. It was the sketch of a springbone. He let out an irritated groan, then covered it with a cough as Noah glanced his direction.

Samuel turned the drawing all different directions before shaking his head. "This is what was in the dog's gut. I never seen one before Beni took it out." Samuel pointed to Iris's boy, sitting behind her.

Shem called the boy forward, to sit beside his mother. "Is Samuel the man you saw outside your window, the night your father died?"

The boy's eyes opened wide at the question and he turned to his mother. Iris squeezed his hand. "Say what you know. Say the truth."

The boy looked at Samuel and shook his head. "It wasn't Samuel that I saw. I would've known if it was him."

"It was night. It was dark. How can you be sure?"

The boy stared at Samuel for a long moment, his eyes squinting and looking him over. He finished with a shrug. "I don't know. It wasn't him, though."

A low murmur trickled through the room and Noah held up his arm to restore the silence before addressing the Council again. "Are there other concerns to address?"

His brothers asked a few more questions, revealing nothing. Ham was the last one to speak. "No one saw you kill Eli, Samuel. But no one knows that you didn't either. You live in the area. You know the property. Why should we believe that you are innocent? How do we know you aren't lying to us?"

Ham tried to keep the venom from his voice. It leaked into his words anyhow and Samuel drew back from him as he spoke. He didn't look away from Ham's direct gaze, however. His voice was barely a whisper when he spoke but there was no other sound in the room so his answer carried into the crowd and fell on all ears. "It's a sin to lie, Ham. It offends God."

Blood steamed in Ham's veins. He drew in a breath and held it, unable to determine what words would come forth if he dare let it escape.

Noah stood and asked for any last witnesses, anyone to speak for or against the man. No one came forward, so he dismissed the crowd. "The Council will meet now," he said. "We'll send word when we're finished."

As one, the three groups rose and left the meeting hall. Iris took Samuel's arm and led him to the door. Abruptly the boy stopped and turned back. His eyes widened and he pointed at Cush. "I remember you, now," he said.

Cush spun on his heels and squared his shoulders. His face was white. Ham felt as if he should intervene but he didn't know what to say. He didn't know what the boy meant.

"You traded with Father," Samuel said. "Don't you remember? You brought him all those-"

"We can reminisce later," Ham said, stepping between the accused and his firstborn. He waited until Iris led the boy away.

Cush was breathing hard. He said nothing and refused to meet Ham's glare.

Noah caught Ham's eyes. He frowned and sighed heavily. Ham braced himself for the questioning.

Noah didn't speak. He shook his head and turned away, too.

Ham excused himself to clear his head. He didn't like the air overshadowing the proceedings, a tempest of his own failure.

Chapter Thirty-two

Ham shook his head in disbelief at Shem's analysis. "What do you mean you feel sorry for him? What about Eli? Just because there's a rift between Samuel and his father doesn't make the boy innocent of taking the life of another man."

"Nor does it confirm his guilt." Shem didn't raise his voice to match Ham's level. His brother's hand was pressed against his chest, the black stone from Eden enclosed in his fist. Its buckskin wrap was long disintegrated, the dark teardrop displayed on Shem's chest openly now, as if he had stepped up to the role it signified.

Ham suppressed a smirk. Other than possessing the Blood of Adam stone, Shem displayed little leadership potential. He chose to live in isolation, and so near to Noah that Shem had no real power. Their father still reigned in the small village. In Shinar, there were people who didn't even recognize his brother when he passed by on the street. It was unfortunate Ham would never own the stone. He didn't crave the spiritual leadership for himself, or for his own firstborn. It was for Nimrod he wanted the stone, and the title. Nimrod, wearing the old relic of their forefathers, acting as the spiritual guide, would unite them all.

If Shem and Japheth allowed him to live.

Shem clutched the stone as if he could draw guidance from it, as if the words of God would sink through his flesh if he worried his thumb across its surface enough times. He wouldn't be intimidated by any of them, especially when it came to issues of sin. Shem was a thinker and no familial loyalty would sway him from the truth as he saw it. Trying to get his brother to see correctly was the issue.

"You would give him your favor over Nimrod?"

"Now wait, Brothers," Japheth said. "That isn't what we're here to determine, whether Samuel or Nimrod is to be found guilty of Eli's murder. We are only concerned with Samuel. Is there sufficient reason to formally accuse Samuel of the crime? That's the question before us."

Ham threw down a chunk of bread and leaned toward Japheth. "Really, Japheth? I don't see it that way. We have two men accused, formally or not, of one crime. Unless they were co-conspirators, one is guilty and one is innocent. Will you also choose this long lost boy over my grandson?"

"Just because both are accused doesn't make either one guilty." Noah spoke with a tone that reminded Ham of the distant past, when he and his brothers were fighting. It had the same effect now as then and all three of them stopped and held their tongues until they could speak without the frustration so apparent.

"That's what I was trying to say," Shem said. "We can't accuse Samuel to free Nimrod. We can't free Samuel to blame Nimrod."

But that's what would occur. His brothers tried to word it so sweetly but did any of them really believe Samuel and Nimrod might both be cleared of the accusation? Put them side by side before the Council. Nimrod clearly had the character of a brave, hardworking man. He was respected. He saved the children of their children by risking his own life. He designed the tower and organized the man-power to see it rise above the plain, toward the heavens and the place of the One God. Many people agreed with Ham that Nimrod was destined to be their leader when Noah and his sons were no longer walking among them. Many people.

And Samuel? A disgrace to his father. A vagrant living alone in the wilds by his own choosing. He didn't have the mind to make any sort of productive contribution to the men of earth. His own mother stayed clear of his trial. What were any of them to lose by pointing the finger at him?

"Are we ready to take a vote then?" Noah was on his feet stretching his legs before easing down to the floor again. There were crevices on his face that seemed deeper than Ham remembered, ones that connected as they coursed over his face then merged with hair that was fading in color. He wouldn't be with them forever. Ham and his brothers wouldn't be either. There had to be a plan in place to provide leadership. Sound leadership. Of all their sons, only his son's son, Nimrod, stood out.

The future of all men on the earth was at stake here. Couldn't his brothers see that? Were they so anxious to see one of their own offspring rise in command that they would execute the one meant to rule?

"We will state then, whether we believe there is sufficient evidence to accuse Samuel, son of Jabal, of killing Eli," Noah said. "State guilty or not guilty."

Shem started the vote. "Not guilty."

"Not guilty," Elam concurred.

Then Japheth. "I see no evidence, Ham. My vote is 'not guilty.'"

Gomer, his firstborn paused for a long moment before he spoke. "Other than living how he did, and where he did, there is no piece of evidence for me to say he wronged Eli. Not guilty."

Ham exhaled loudly. That was four of the seven against him.

"I agree with Gomer," Noah said. "Not guilty."

Noah was trying to catch Ham's eyes but he refused to look

back. The Council didn't even require his father's vote. There would be no tie in this decision. Ham steered his gaze toward Shem, then Japheth. Both of them turned away from what he hoped was an expression revealing the animosity churning in his soul.

Ham straightened his spine and intentionally minced his words. "He is guilty."

The Council acknowledged his vote silently. Ham shifted his weight and prepared to stand, to escape the family willing to shove a sword through his heart.

Cush cleared his throat.

Ham stopped moving and turned to his first born. Cush glanced at Noah before looking away, toward the wall. "Not guilty," he said.

▲

The accumulation of people outside the building indicated the meeting was complete, and no one but the Council remained. Their opinions as to Samuel's fate would fall one way or the other. Naomi prayed again for God to intervene, to show the men truth. And for integrity to steer their actions.

She turned away and sat on the ground with her back to the wall, with no desire to join the throng below. If enough doubt was raised, Samuel would be formally charged by the Council. They could decide right then and there to hold his formal trial, declare his guilt. And stone him. She would be expected to cast stones with the others. They would take the life of an innocent man. Naomi scrunched down even further. Let them come find her, if that's what the day held. She would not make it easy.

Naomi's garments were sticking to her skin by the time Eran and Denah discovered her refuge. "Abed told us you were here."

Eran said. Her face was the color of beet juice, sweat beading on her forehead. "Let's talk where it's cooler."

"Tell me first. I have to know." Naomi gave Eran an arm for support while finding Denah's eyes. Her sister-in law's expression provided the answer she sought. She let out a pent up breath. Eran and Denah both smiled.

The sixth level provided shelter from the intensity of the sun, the tiles still cool beneath them as they sat on the floor. "Not guilty? Tell me everything," Naomi said. "Was it unanimous?"

"The vote was clear," Eran began. "There wasn't sufficient reason to charge Samuel for killing Eli. Other than knowing the family and living nearby, there was no evidence. Iris cast no blame at all in his direction and her boy denies it was Samuel outside that night. And, well, it was obvious Samuel isn't full of evil."

"Eliamah's support was beneficial then? Did she speak about Jabal?"

Denah shook her head. "Eliamah? She wasn't there, Naomi. No one spoke for him except Iris and her boy."

Naomi told her sisters-in-law about the conversation she held with Eliamah. "I think she's right. I don't believe Samuel ever fell into any ravine. That Jabal is a deceitful man."

"He spoke against his son in the meeting." Denah said. "Mocked his firstborn. It was terrible. I wanted to smother Samuel in a hug and kick Jabal out into the wilds to try his hand at isolation."

"Is he gone again? Did Samuel leave?"

"Noah asked him to stay for a few days. He wants to load up a wagon with supplies and give him a ride back to the cave, or where ever Sam chooses to go. But it will have to be after the next Council. I think he wants to protect him, too. In case someone decides Sam is guilty and seeks revenge. Here, he can be protected by those who know his heart."

Like Eliamah? She didn't attend the Council, but she was near Sam, Naomi was certain. She would see to his safety, as best she could, shielding him like she did her little brothers. And maybe the truth in her mind would fight for freedom yet.

"Tell me about the vote." Naomi tried to keep her voice steady, overriding the emotion making it crack. Her sisters-in-law each took a hand and squeezed comfort. "It wasn't unanimous. Ham cast a dissenting vote. He seemed sure of Samuel's guilt."

She knew already that would be the direction of her husband's decision. The words stung anyhow. He alone voted against an innocent young man. Alone? "Cush voted against his father?"

Denah nodded. "He did. He was distressed through the entire proceedings. I think he knew Samuel was innocent but claiming so put his own firstborn at risk. Your Cush chose admirably, Naomi."

Naomi leaned back on her elbows. "A man shouldn't be in the position to choose life and death for his own blood. I'm glad my Cush chose wisely, justly, even knowing what that may mean for his son. And Ham, he's desperate to secure Nimrod's life. He wants to believe in Samuel's guilt. It's the only answer he has to save his grandson."

Denah patted her knee. "Whatever the reasons, we saw justice for Samuel today."

Eran pulled the scarf from her head and allowed her long braid to fall free. Her eyes traveled around the room, seeing the carved columns and the vibrant mosaics for the first time. Her lips were turned down and Naomi could feel her disapproval. Shem and Eran didn't support the building of this tower. It wasn't under God's command to do so, they said. That was like the two of them, to prefer the simple, the unadorned, the plainness of life. Eran was most content in her garden, among aromatic herbs and the array of medicinal plants she raised. The addition of a colorful scarf to her attire wasn't characteristic.

"Are you growing more sensitive to the sun, Eran? I noticed you cover your head more often, even out of the sunshine. Even indoors sometimes."

Eran expelled a loud sigh. "Shem asked me to do so. For modesty in public, to keep my hair covered. He doesn't want me to unknowingly tempt another man and cause him to sin."

"And you don't resist? You don't think he's being too restrictive?"

Eran raised her eyebrows and shook her head from side to side. "I could ask the same of you, Naomi. Only two things would keep you from the Council, and you aren't dead, so it must have been the will of your husband."

Naomi nodded. "He forbade me to go."

"Why didn't Ham want you there?" Denah asked.

"He was angry. Angry that I keep trying to find answers. I think angry that I found Samuel to be so likable, too. As if I'm choosing him over my own grandson."

"It will pass. It always does with you two. This is a time of unnatural tension and there's bound to be disagreement. He'll seek the comfort of your arms again soon, I'm sure."

Naomi looked away and bit on her lip. He might, until she told him about her ancestry. Then he might choose to abandon her for another wife. He would detest the very sight of her.

Would Eran and Denah? These were her dearest friends. They held out their arms when there was no one else to lift her from the dark pits of life. Surely they would be her strength, even with the weight of this information, they would be a backbone to rely upon when her life wanted to crumble.

It was time to stop pretending her tainted blood was thinned out and the nephil traits gone. She knew otherwise. It affected all the sons of Noah. Denah and Eran deserved to know. This wasn't at all the place or the time she would have chosen, but the words tumbled out. "Ham may never want to see my face again. I have something I must tell him. When this is behind us and Nimrod is freed or put to his death, I have to tell him what he will not want to hear."

Denah and Eran remained silent. Naomi abruptly rose to her feet and began pacing. "The baby. You need to know about the baby."

Eran and Denah stood as well. "What baby?" Denah asked.

"The one born the other night. The one who was so wrinkled." Denah nodded so Naomi continued. "He wasn't a nine month baby. He was a seven month boy."

Denah described the newborn to Eran. "But his size, Naomi. If he went another two months he would have been-"

Naomi turned away from Denah's wide stare. "Naomi, what are you saying? Tell us. Why was this child so big already?"

"He carries nephilim blood. My nephilim blood."

Eran's hands flew to her mouth and she gasped one word. "No."

Denah closed her eyes and crossed her arms over her chest as color crept from her face. "How? Who?"

"My great-grandmother was given to a nephil."

Her sisters-in-law said nothing.

"It was said our family had a cursing of the gods, we lost so many newborns. But we weren't cursed. My cousins were killed to hide the fact we had the wretched blood among us."

Eran fell back against the wall, sliding down to the floor. She hugged her knees to her chest and put her forehead on them. "Noah will be grieved. If he had known..."

"He knows. He knew."

Eran's head snapped up. "And he allowed you to marry his son?

Allowed you in the ark?"

There was no mistaking the tone of her voice. Naomi felt the burn in her eyes. "Are you suggesting I shouldn't have been saved?"

"The evil among us, don't you think, don't you fear-"

"That it's all my fault? Of course I do. I live with the weight of my family past every day. Every expanding womb fills me with terror. But Noah says the dark hearts of men are not my doing, Eran. Each man chooses his own way of right and wrong. I thought you would understand that. I thought you would understand."

Eran turned her face away. Naomi looked at Denah, a woman with her own dark stain. She carried another man's child once, one taken away and buried before they entered the ark. God had not permitted a child born of adultery to father the new earth. And Denah herself was spared. She who walked in sin was favored still by the Creator. She understood grace. Could she remember? Would she draw from that well to quench Naomi's fears?

Denah stood in silence, eyes and lips locked tight.

Naomi didn't choose the blood in her veins. And she couldn't reveal that it was there, not if she ever wanted a husband. Not if she wanted to protect her family from shame. What should she have done?

It seemed right at the time, not to disclose this sordid detail to Ham. Besides, Noah knew. He could have stopped the marriage. He didn't tell his son, allowing Naomi to own the secret. Ham would blame him, too, once he found out.

Denah opened her eyes and relaxed her shoulders. "I don't despise you, Naomi. It is what it is. Your past, can't be undone. I won't allow it to alter our friendship."

Naomi collapsed into Denah's embrace, permitting herself to free the tears that had hovered all day. Her gut was in torment and the fatigue of bearing burdens was rapidly consuming her body as well as her heart. Her life was in so many torn little fragments, it was hard to know how to hold onto them all. Denah was there to keep her from falling apart. Denah would be the tar that kept everything in place. Denah would be her voice to God when she couldn't lift her head to seek him herself.

She turned at long last to beg Eran's forgiveness, so the three could stand united as before. No walls. No secrets.

But Eran was gone.

Chapter Thirty-three

"How can you still believe in your God's justice?" Nimrod stood by the creek, hurling stones at a tree trunk on the other side. Each one hit his intended target then bounced off into the brush. It reminded Naomi of the day he saved her from the dragon. She wanted to clutch him to her heart, as she had the child. She wanted to protect him from all that threatened to take him away. Forever. How much had changed since that day.

Nimrod's control was gone. His frustration tore into Naomi's heart. He couldn't fix his situation. Neither could she. He alone stood accused of the great sin now.

Naomi picked up a smooth stone to skittle across the surface of the water, then dropped it as soon as the cool surface registered in her mind. If her grandson was condemned, she was required cast stones. At him. She shuddered and stepped away from the bank, away from the rocks.

It wasn't a new practice, that of stoning a condemned man. It was one of the old methods for sending a guilty man to his death. Naomi had never witnessed it, and rarely was it was used in the years before the flood. At some point the practice grew too common and men resorted to new methods of execution. Beheadings were common, and hangings. None of these were approved by the One

God, however. According to Noah's fathers, he didn't permit anyone to receive a blow of death at the hand of another man. It was God's responsibility alone to judge and execute the punishment of death.

Then God spoke from the mount in Ararat, commanding life for life. It seemed so out of place at the time. The entire population of the earth was gone, save the eight who were spared. She would have never imagined the need to enact such punishment.

The practice of stoning was dredged from the abyss of time. It was Noah's choice, so there would be no one executioner, no single man to act as God's hand. He established the guidelines, years ago, at the first Triune Council: The condemned man's immediate family was responsible for digging the hole. Waist high in the earth, he would stand, hands at his side, while his children, his wife, his parents and siblings, filled the hole around him. It had to be packed tightly, so his arms were pinned, not allowing himself the self protection that only prolonged the agony. No one was exempt from the duty of casting stones. Not even the children. The Eight would lead them.

Facing the rising sun, the man's eyes would be blinded to the hands raised against him. His face wouldn't be covered, to protect them from his torment. They were meant to witness the brutality of it all, to see the light of judgment upon the man as his life was extinguished, to remember with horror the consequences of their sin.

This wasn't some nameless man, though. She would rather it be her in the pit then her own beloved one. How could she participate in his death?

Naomi realized Nimrod was watching her, waiting for a reply. His carved muscles were tensed, his eyebrows drawn to a point over his nose.

"He is God. How can he permit injustice?" Her voice wavered as she spoke.

Nimrod chuffed and turned back to his target. "Eli was at the wrong end of justice. Where was God to save him?"

Naomi didn't respond.

"Perhaps Eli forgot to make a sacrifice once. Perhaps he said the wrong words as he lit the consuming fire."

"I, I don't know Nimrod."

"I stand alone to face my accusers. There will be no God to intervene and speak on my behalf. Unless the guilty man steps forward, my fate is my own burden. I will continue to breathe or my breath will be extinguished by my own hand."

"Your family, Nimrod. They don't want to see you die. You must trust they will be fair."

Nimrod spun on his heel and faced her. Purple vessels snaked over his temples. "Fair? I wouldn't be standing here now having this discussion if there was anything fair to secure my faith. I'm not certain my own father believes I am wrongly accused. No, it isn't family I will rely on."

Naomi wrapped her hands around his arm. "It is God, then? Will you trust him?"

Nimrod pulled away from her touch. "God? No. No. He has left me."

Her grandson turned his back and strode away. Naomi watched until he disappeared around a bend in the creek. "You have to trust God, Nimrod. He is all you have left."

▲

Ham sat on a cushion at the low table with his father and firstborn son. There was no food on the table. There was no conversation rolling around from tongue to tongue. Noah called them together when they got home from the Council meeting. He would not begin without Naomi, he said, and so they sat, and waited. He had no idea where she was or where she had been during the meeting and it annoyed him now to wait for her. She was in town, perhaps, celebrating with that Samuel she so desperately felt the need to protect.

He hadn't seen Nimrod, either, but his horse and all his belongings seemed to be accounted for. Semiras, his wife, said he was out for a walk, out alone to sort through his thoughts. He was angry with the Council, she said.

Cush drummed his fingers on the smooth wood. Still anxious. Still restless and obviously eager to be any where but where he was. He was fidgety during Council, then afterward, after he spoke his vote, he bolted for the door. Noah stopped him, told him to go straight to Ham's home. Noah by contrast, barely flinched a muscle as they waited. He remained still and though his eyes were open, Ham knew he was talking to his God.

Naomi stopped short when she entered, obviously surprised to see them sitting there. "We've been waiting," he said.

"Oh," she said. She remained in the door. "There's food already prepared, if you were hungry."

"We need to speak," Noah said as he motioned for her to join them. "We weren't waiting for you to serve us, Naomi."

His wife crossed the room without shutting the door. She didn't sit next to him, choosing to sit by Cush, across from him instead. Her eyes glanced at the three of them in question.

Noah took a piece of cloth from his vest and placed it on the table. Ham didn't recognize it and Naomi was puzzled by it from the expression on her face. Cush stared at his hands. There was a line of sweat forming on his upper lip.

"This was a gift from one of my many offspring," Noah said. "Given to me by a little girl who said she wanted me to have it because she honors me and wants me to be safe."

The deep blue square of fabric was of a light wool with a pattern of embroidery on one edge. That was all. Noah was playing a game with them. He would make them ask questions rather than just speak his mind. "And how was this swatch supposed to protect you?" Ham asked rather than delay the inevitable continuation of the family discussion.

"It has protective abilities because it was on the ark."

Noah let them sit in silence. Naomi spoke up first. "No it wasn't. The pattern is one I made up, and taught the girls, but not that far back. Thirty, forty years ago perhaps."

"Yes," Noah said. "I recognize it. Denah gave a garment to Jael like this. If I were to look for that garment in her chest of belongings, I don't think I would find it there any longer, would I Cush?"

His firstborn snapped his head up, pursed his lips and said nothing. The loose flesh under his chin quivered as he moved and Ham felt repulsed at the sight. It was the flesh of a man who preferred indulgences over honest labor. It was the flesh of one pampered by his mother. Ham shifted his eyes to her. Naomi's hand covered her mouth and her eyes glistened. She didn't appear surprised at the words his father spoke.

He knew his son was a thief. She knew it, too. Ham clenched his hands together under the table.

"The cloth was purchased at Jabal's business." Noah's finger twirled the fabric on the table, his gaze remaining on Cush for a long moment before turning to Ham. "Apparently he's been trading items from the ark, items with this protective power, for many, many years." Noah's hand slammed down on the cloth as he leaned toward Ham. "You've allowed this deceitful practice to continue."

Ham returned his father's piercing gaze. He unclenched his

hands, putting them behind his head. "He's a man. He makes his own choices."

Noah shook his head. "Your son journeyed to the ark to seek God, to remember, he said. It was all a lie. He took from the ark until it was too ice covered to be reached. Then he took items from me, from his grandmother." Noah's shifted to Naomi. "Perhaps from his own mother."

Naomi kept her head down. She confirmed his father's words by refusing to look up, or to speak in Cush's defense. If there was any element of false accusation against her beloved boy, Naomi would be the first to speak her mind.

Noah sighed. "Samuel remembers you, Cush."

Cush jerked upright and caught his breath. He and Noah held a long stare before Cush looked away.

"He remembers that you traded with his father. He remembers the relics from the ark because he was fascinated by them."

"So you know," Cush spat out. "Everything on that vessel is gone except what I salvaged. You wanted people to remember. I gave them something to remember with, something tangible they could hold and look to. Something their children could see and ask where it came from. Why is this so evil?"

"Most of the items didn't really come from the ark, though did they, Cush? And you made a handsome profit, as did Jabal, by lying about the items. Whose idea was it to say the relics had the ability to protect their owner, then?"

"That was Jabal. He got twice the trade for them that way."

"And you saw no harm in this?"

Cush shrugged his shoulders.

"You stole. You lied. You participated in deceit to gain a profit."

Noah turned to Ham. "And you allowed the practice to

continue." Ham was ready to defend himself but his father held up his hand and he locked his own lips shut.

"I question now if there is another connection," Noah said. Again, a cryptic statement. At least to Ham. His wife's eyes were wide as her teeth clamped on her bottom lip. His son had a similar expression. It struck him for a moment how his firstborn still imitated his mother, adopting her own subtle expressive actions into his own repertoire. When Cush was still a boy, Ham resented it. A boy should imitate his father. Now side by side, mother and son shared more than a sickly pallor. They shared a common fear.

"What?" Ham demanded. "What connection? What else has my son done to pour shame upon me?" Ham rose to his feet as he spoke. As his eyes rose above Cush's head, he detected a hint of motion just outside the door. He didn't wait for an answer. He crossed the space in long strides and reached around the frame, grasping hair and drawing its owner inside.

Eliamah.

Chapter Thirty-four

Naomi gasped and jumped to her feet. She pushed Ham away from the girl and brushed the long black hair from her face, smoothing the pieces that her husband snarled in his fist. "Eliamah, are you alright?"

The girl nodded, scanning the room quickly. Her gaze rested on Noah, who was easing himself from the floor, giving her a welcomed smile. "You are welcome here," he said. "Forgive my son. He didn't mean to harm you."

Ham chuffed behind his breath and started for the door. His father stopped him. "We're not finished, Son," he said. Noah turned to catch Cush's eye as well. Her firstborn hadn't moved. He sat cross legged with his chin resting on his hands.

"I, I wasn't meaning to intrude," Eliamah said. She lifted her chin to face Naomi. "I didn't go to the meeting like you asked. I wanted to. I just couldn't." Her head was down again.

Naomi put a finger under the girl's chin and lifted it. "It's alright. Samuel was provided justice. He'll be glad to know you are here anyway, that you came to support him."

It was difficult to ignore the fire darting from her husband's eyes as she spoke. He stood with his arms crossed over his chest, feet spread, face tight. It was the stance he took on occasion when they were young, when she was harassed in the market and he stood as her defender, himself the barrier between good and evil. Today he protected only himself and it wasn't Eliamah he fought against. It was his own wife.

"He knows," Eliamah said. "My Samuel knows. He's here." She turned to the door and poked her head out. A moment later Samuel stood in the doorway beside her. "He waited in the bushes."

Samuel stepped in and took a glance at the people present. He shifted away from Ham and stood near Noah. "You asked us to come, to stay a bit, Father Noah. That's why me and her are here. We came because you said so."

Ham's arms flew into the air and he stepped toward Samuel. "You think you're staying under my roof?"

Samuel didn't hesitate to push Eliamah behind him and step toward Ham. His right hand gripped his knife. A heavy silence filled the room.

Ham was a head taller than Samuel and carried more muscle in his chest and arms. He was a skilled fighter and Naomi knew he could pummel his young opponent without breaking into a sweat. But he didn't. He laughed at Samuel, then stepped away.

"This man is not your enemy, Ham," Noah said. "He's a guest in your home, at my request. We'll treat him and his wife as such."

Ham threw himself back down at the table. Samuel and Eliamah turned to the door but Naomi caught Samuel's wrist, causing him to drop the knife. "Please don't leave," she said.

"We'll stay with the horses," Eliamah said. "We'd be more comfortable."

Not physically, Naomi thought. She deserved a real place to lay her head, with a soft pallet and no fear of creatures prowling in the darkness. She would be more comfortable in her mind, however. Ham was more terrifying than any creeping insect or scaled beast.

Noah retrieved the knife from the floor and held it out to Samuel. Eliamah intervened, stopping the transfer from hand to hand by grabbing Noah's wrist. Her eyes opened wide and she looked at Naomi.

Naomi nodded.

"That, that was given to Samuel," the girl said. She withdrew her hand and stepped back.

Noah held the weapon up, inspecting it more closely. "By whom?"

"The man who carried me to the cave," Samuel said.

Noah looked between them. He placed his hand on Samuel's shoulder and squeezed. "Please sit. Let's talk about that."

Cush scooted to allow them all room around the table. Naomi tried not to stare at her son. His face was devoid of color. His features were flat. In the few moments since Eliamah and Samuel arrived, he took on the appearance of a man already dead. Cush looked at no one around the table until Noah handed the knife to Ham. Then his eyes fixed on his father's face.

Ham rolled the knife around a few times in his hands and started to hand it back to Noah. Then he paused and brought the object in closer for inspection. His shoulders dropped and his eyes went wide as the object took on a new importance. He lifted his head, his expression sending daggers into his firstborn. Cush jerked his eyes away. Ham slammed the knife on the table.

Naomi sucked in a deep breath and closed her eyes.

"Tell us about the day you went hunting with your father, Samuel," Noah said. Her father-in-law's voice was a whisper.

Samuel repeated the story.

"Who saved you from the ravine? Do you know who it was?"

Samuel shook his head. "No. I don't remember that part."

Eliamah put her arm around her husband and drew him close

before she spoke. "He doesn't remember the fall. If he fell, like Jabal says."

"If. If he fell, Eliamah?" Noah asked.

"I don't think he fell down any ravine."

The silence was anything but dead. Naomi's own heart was pounding inside her chest and her mind whirled around the scene that was forming unbidden in her mind.

Noah turned to Cush. Her father-in-law struggled to keep his emotions under control. Naomi could see it in his lips as they twitched. There was anger lurking behind his calm demeanor, anger merging with grief and filling a great gulf of disappointment. For Eliamah's sake, and Samuel's, he spoke in an even rhythm. "Was he in that ravine, Cush? Did the boy fall like his father said?"

Her firstborn raised his head and locked eyes with Noah, then with Samuel. "No. He didn't fall."

Samuel's eyes traveled around the table. The grim expressions didn't answer his questions. "I didn't? What happened to me then? Why don't I remember?"

"You didn't fall, Samuel." Cush pushed his fingertips together and spoke into his tented hands, as if capturing the words in a safe place. "Your father told everyone that you had. He wanted your death to be a tragic accident."

"He wanted," Samuel paused. "My death."

"You were supposed to die. Your father-"

"He wanted to kill me? I knew he didn't want me. I knew he left me." Samuel put his head against Eliamah's shoulder. "Why didn't he, then? Why didn't he kill me? Why didn't he push me into the ravine?"

Cush swallowed hard then cleared his throat. "I, I was supposed to do it, Samuel. I was supposed to kill you."

Naomi groaned and laid her face in her hands.

Samuel pointed a finger at Cush. "You? Why?"

"Your father asked me to."

Samuel nodded. "He was ashamed of me. I remember."

"What happened Cush? With Jabal and Sam, in the woods?" Noah put his hand gently on her firstborn's shoulder.

Cush cleared his throat again. "The ark relics I sold to Jabal. He found out they weren't authentic, threatened to tell everyone. Threatened to shame the lineage of Ham. He agreed to trade his silence for a favor."

"Killing Samuel. He expected you to take the boy's life to keep your shame from exposure."

"Yes. My shame. My father's shame." Cush turned to Sam. "He took you hunting. I met up with you in the woods. Your father distracted you and I, I hit you over the back of the head. I told Jabal you were dead. I knew you weren't. I told him you were so he would leave."

"Did he check? Did my father search me for life?"

Cush choked out his words. "No, Samuel. He didn't. I took you away, to a cave I found once. I gave you that knife."

Samuel picked up the weapon and rubbed his thumb over the contours. "Thank you, then. Thank you for not killing me. Thank you for the fine knife."

Cush buried his face in his hands.

Her child needed comfort.

She didn't move. Naomi had nothing to offer the man she carried once in her own womb. Nothing for the child who sustained her joy through the early years of unknowns. Cush was to be their hope, the next generation to live for their God. She shuddered. She couldn't be his shoulder of strength any longer.

Ham was still. His eyes looked toward Cush without registering. She could see his mind putting broken fragments into a whole piece.

"The last time you went out alone, out gathering herbs," he said. "You hated that adventure. You never went again. Because you really went to kill a child. You carried the guilt."

Cush nodded.

Eliamah pushed away from the table and stood, guiding Samuel to her side. "We'll be in the stable," she said.

Samuel set the knife on the table. His fingertips glided over the surface as he slowly lifted his hand.

"You can keep it, Samuel," Noah said.

Samuel didn't respond as he considered it. "No," he said. "It belongs to Cush."

Cush grabbed the knife and collapsed on the floor in heaving sobs. Naomi bolted from the room. Away from her husband. Away from her firstborn. Away from the threat of any more sorrow.

Chapter Thirty-five

Naomi left the house without a word. Ham watched her leave, exerting no effort to stop her. She wouldn't want company, he knew. She would seek a place of solitude to absorb the disturbing facts just laid bare before them.

Sam and the girl slipped out of the home behind Naomi, leaving Ham with his father and the blubbery lump on the floor. He wanted to leave the whole wretched mess where it was thrown, too, but he couldn't. He couldn't escape. It had to be dealt with.

It. Cush. Cush had to be dealt with, and delaying the discussion wouldn't make it easier to clean up.

His son was no longer sobbing, no longer heaving his weak flesh in spasms of regret. He sat dry-eyed, staring at nothing but memories. Had that man really come from his own blood? Was he so stupid to believe Jabal would jeopardize his own livelihood to expose a few baubles sold in deceit? All Cush had to do was deny the accusations if they arose. No one would believe Jabal over the son of Ham, the father of Nimrod. Cush allowed a mere man to manipulate him. His vulnerability was sickening.

As was his intention to murder a child rather than face his shame. Or shame his father. Ham shuddered and felt the rise of foulness in his throat. He leaned against the wall and stared at the timbers overhead. Cush should have come to him. He would have dealt with the matter somehow. It didn't have to come to the rift of derision that would now follow his name. If Cush had any sense, if Cush had been anything like him…Ham forced his gaze back to his firstborn. If there had been men upon the ark other than his own brothers, he would have reason to suspect this boy was never from his seed.

Ham broke the stillness with the snap of his fingers, awakening his son from the images scrolling through his mind. "What were you and Jabal bargaining for this morning?"

Noah walked away from the window where he had been standing with his back to them both. Pink crescents underlined each eye. He eased himself onto a cushion at the table, but allowed his son to continue without interruption.

"The knives. I offered him the knives for his silence regarding the issue with Samuel." Cush didn't hedge. Ham willed his shoulders to release their taut and ready position. Dragging truth from his son wouldn't have been a mere mental exercise if Cush attempted to be elusive. The disappointment in Ham's soul would seek judgment, fists to flesh, before he permitted one more lie to fall. He didn't want it to come to that. There would be no lasting fulfillment, and in the end, no real victor.

"Did you really think he was going to admit he hired you to kill his son?"

"No, I suppose not. But I owed him. I owed him something for not fulfilling my end of the bargain."

Ham didn't try to hide his disbelief. "You thought you owed Jabal restitution? For not taking the life of his son?"

Cush shrugged. "He kept his silence assuming I did what he asked. I knew he'd be angry that the boy lived. I wanted to appease him."

Ham pushed away from the wall. He took his turn standing at the window, staring without seeing as he suppressed renewed desire to plant a blow on his son's pasty face. He had given Cush credit for trying to bargain with Jabal, Nimrod for Samuel. The credit wasn't warranted. Cush merely bargained for himself. Ham ran his hands through his hair, yanking through the tangled portions, ignoring the sting on his scalp. He thought he interrupted a reasonable deal between the two, one that pointed blame at the boy, vindicating Nimrod. Ham blamed himself for the trial outcome because he intervened.

Now he knew the truth. He wasn't to blame. He also realized how intensely he disliked his own child.

The thought startled him. He started to shove it away, then stopped himself. He allowed it to return and gave it purchase. Yes, it was true. If he was going to stare his own feelings in the face, he would admit he didn't like his firstborn. Had he ever? Ham gripped the window ledge and thought through the years. There were times when he was pleased with him. As a tiny new life, especially. Holding the screaming bundle in his arms, he liked the sound of life the boy emitted. Naomi was quick to satisfy Cush's demands, hush the cries, but they never bothered him. A man had to learn how to control his environment and his little Cush did just that, at least with his mother.

He couldn't honestly say he disliked Cush as a child. He was annoyed by his need for Naomi, perhaps, and his lack of interest in the activities that would have bonded them as father and son. There was disappointment, of course, and frustration. But dislike? No, he wouldn't go that far. Not until now.

He never imagined Cush had a vein of evil running through his good natured front. What else was hidden from his perception? Ham rewound his mind back to the night in the cave, after they left the home of Eli. One of the boys got up. He assumed it was to relieve himself so he paid no attention and fell asleep. But one of them got up. One of them left the cave and returned to that homestead.

He naturally thought it was Nimrod.

Could it have been Cush?

When the murder accusations first fell into their hands, the thought of Cush rising in the night in secrecy passed through his mind, quickly, leaving no tracks. That wasn't the Cush he thought he knew. Now Ham had to reconsider the possibility that his firstborn had still more shame hidden in the darkness of his heart.

The events of that day played through his mind again. Ham searched for motive. Why would Cush kill Eli? He found nothing. Why would Nimrod kill the man? There was no obvious answer to that question either, but Ham hadn't dwelt on the matter. Watching this boy grow into manhood, he understood Nimrod's need to maintain control, whether by controlling himself or controlling those around him, and he exerted far more self control than anyone realized. He had inner fire, readily kindled into flames when he allowed it to be uncovered.

Ham had seen him flare a few times, he had see the inner struggle released. He could be destructive. The murder accusation stunned the community, his own family even. It was a surprise to Ham, yes, but not because he believed in the gentle spirit of his grandson. Nimrod could kill a man. He would kill a man, if he had reason.

A trickle of salt dripped from his forehead into his eye and Ham realized his heart was thumping aggressively. He inhaled deeply and exhaled, then again.

Was Nimrod actually innocent?

▲

"Ham, Son," Noah said. "Let's sit again."

Ham didn't have to be asked twice. The tension he was able to muster to wrestle an angry tiger was completely gone, and his legs were in danger of melting where he stood. He dropped on the cushion and gave Noah his attention.

Cush spoke first. "What now? Will I stand before the Council?"

"You took items from your own mother, and from your grandmother. You stole from your family. For that, your father will determine punishment."

Cush glanced at Ham before looking back at the table.

"You lied to Jabal about their origins," Noah continued, "but I don't believe he was deceived. Your involvement with the taking and selling of relics is also up to Ham."

The family line of judgment then. Jabal would have to face his father and Japheth for punishment. His brother would set the precedent for Jabal's offenses. There would be a penalty for lying about his wares, but a much greater one would be issued for lying about the death of his child, and for seeking Samuel's death in the first place. Ham knew his brother well enough to know it would not go well for Jabal.

The fact that Cush took worthless items from family members and sold them at a profit was hardly a concern. Ham was eager to punish his son for allowing someone like Jabal to get the upper hand over him. His son's lazy ways were at fault. If he worked like a man to build his wealth, he wouldn't be making dark alley deals. He would work his son without mercy until Cush rippled in the strength of a man that labored, not cheated.

"For your involvement with Samuel," Noah said. "You didn't kill him and that's fortunate. I would not relish casting stones at you. I would have done so, if you had committed the act, Cush. Don't misjudge my duty to God before my duty to you."

Cush simply nodded in agreement.

"Samuel's chances alone were slim, though. You left him as dead in that sense. You gave him a knife, but you left him. You didn't lie outright to the community about how he died. No one asked you. No one had any reason to ask you. Jabal will answer to that offense. But you lied by omission. At the end of the line of figures we have a sum that says you grievously wronged a member of your Uncle Japheth's kin. That is an offense that must be presented before the Triune Council."

Cush sighed heavily, as did Ham. Noah wouldn't let the matter disappear in the night, though he could. Cush's involvement could be hidden if his father wanted it to be. No one would question his decisions. Sam and the girl would return to the wilds and never speak of it if Noah asked them not to. Naomi knew of course. He could keep her silenced. Cush was her beloved boy child, after all. She doted on him and protected him since the day he arrived. She wouldn't see him broken and exposed before all men. She wouldn't allow the name of Ham to be shamed.

Ham groaned. No, he couldn't assume that. He really didn't know that about his wife anymore.

"Ham?" His father and Cush both watched him. "Your thoughts?"

Ham brought himself back to the matter on the table. "He can't stand before the Council and be a member at the same time."

"No. He can never represent the Council again."

The finality of his father's words sent daggers through Ham's mind. "What? Never?"

"How can one who lies, and steals, and cheats be trusted to make righteous decisions?" Noah said. "He can't lead any longer."

"Then who will take his place?"

Noah thought for a moment. "If you repeal Cush's firstborn status, the right falls on Mizraim, your second born. That's your decision, Ham. If you leave your firstborn in place, his position on the Council will remain vacant, or perhaps I will choose a replacement. I don't know. I haven't had time to call to God for answers yet."

"We must decide. For Nimrod's trial," Ham said. "Unless you intend to sit out, Father. We can't have an uneven number."

Noah nodded slowly, his focus on Ham's eyes. Ham knew when his father made the decision in his mind. He could see the whirling process beneath the graying curls. The choices spun and churned as his father tossed them one by one into piles for discard until the one decision remained.

"You're correct Son," Noah said. "The decision must be absolute, no tied votes. You will sit out as well, Ham."

"ME?!" Ham was on his feet.

"For Nimrod's meeting, yes. You'll be there but you will not vote. That's my decision."

Cush slammed a fist onto the table. "So no one will speak for my son? You have determined his guilt and now it will be assured."

Noah's face turned crimson and he too stood. His finger stopped just short of Cush's nose. "You. Do not accuse me of injustice. Neither of you." Noah's eyes pierced through Ham before returning to Cush. "I can't trust either of you to be fair in this matter. My sons Japheth and Shem and their boys will listen with ears that hear. They will not be guided by rebellious hearts."

If his father continued speaking it was to an empty room. Cush followed Ham from the house and headed for his own. Ham started toward the stable then remembered who was in there and chose to go to the river instead. He had to get away. Away from Cush. Away from Noah. Away from the men that sought to destroy him.

Chapter Thirty-six

Three toothy grins laced with foul breathed slurped his face in greeting. Ham absorbed their adoration, given eagerly, without expectations. Their companionship was so much simpler than those with his family. He returned the affection, lavishing the dogs with praise, roughing up their fur and wrestling them to the ground. When he got back to his feet, the dogs danced around his legs, yapping enthusiastically as he led them to an isolated cove. They knew nothing of ark relics and shameful sons, dishonoring wives, or vengeful fathers.

At the bank, the animals waited for their master's command, anticipating the orderly progression into the water. They were eager to please him, tails in full swing, muscles poised to act promptly to the whistle. Why couldn't children do the same? Why did it have to be so difficult to live simply? Ham changed his mind about catching fish and allowed the dogs to jump into the water and make as much ruckus as they wanted. He stripped off all his clothing and strode out behind them, finding a place where he could stand chest deep.

The current had minimal force where he stood but the rocks beneath his feet were slippery. He had to concentrate on his balance. It would be easy to relax into the buoyant flow, allowing the gentle motion to pull him out of the calm waters. Beyond the safe zone of the cove, the Euphrates heaved viciously over boulders, forcing herself to hurry toward the great sea, longing to immerse herself in its depths, becoming one with it and the waters of the Tigris. How far could he travel in her arms, Ham wondered. How far could he go before the river dashed him onto a rock hidden beneath her churning skirts? He couldn't deny the temptation to free his limbs and simply let the river take him away.

But the dogs would follow, and that would be a horrible end to his devoted beasts. Ham leaned into the water and swam the length of the semi-circled area back and forth until he felt the burn in his chest from the effort. The exertion felt good. Both fatiguing and stimulating, the effort only made him stronger. He liked feeling strong. He liked being strong. The position of weakness he found himself in now tormented his very core.

When he emerged from the water, he planted himself on a rock facing the sun, the dogs collapsing around him. They were content, free of guilt. Free of worry. If only his own life could be so uncomplicated. It was far from it, and harmony seemed to be spiraling further and further from his grasp. He needed a plan, a set of directions to restore what he could of the disastrous route his life was taking.

Nimrod had to be vindicated. He couldn't allow mankind's hope to perish. To what extent would he have to sacrifice himself to see that it occurred?

Ham leaned back on his elbows and lifted his face into the warming rays that speared the earth. He couldn't stop picturing his blubbering firstborn. He couldn't squelch the disgust. No one pointed a finger at Cush for the attack on Eli. He couldn't envision it either. But that didn't mean he was innocent. Or that suspicion against him couldn't be aroused.

One of the boys left the cave. Evidence he should've disclosed in Council. He didn't, of course. It only complicated matters. He was protecting his heirs, protecting Nimrod, he thought. He could bring it up in the trial, though. He could speak as a witness and slant his words to point to whomever he wanted. He could implicate his own son.

Ham jerked himself into a sitting position, the weight of his conscience suddenly heavy on his chest. No, he couldn't pour shame over himself by doing so.

Or could he?

Would he, to save the chosen heir? He would place himself in a precarious position if he did. He left the cave that night, too, and wasn't sure if either Cush or Nimrod realized he had. There might be more accusations to contend with if the issue was exposed. Was he willing to take that chance? Willing to shoulder the repercussions?

There was the issue of Eli and Iris's boy. He was the only witness, claiming he saw Nimrod. Ham would remind the Council again that he was just a child, awakened from sleep. It was dark and stormy. It could have been Cush he saw.

Or, himself. How many times had people said Ham and his grandson were poured from the same mold? If it came down to it, Ham could say it wasn't Nimrod the boy saw. It was him.

But would he?

The dogs simultaneously tensed and turned toward the path. Ham threw on his tunic just as two men came from the tree line into view. His brothers.

Shem and Japheth sat beside him and offered a plate of dried fruits and a loaf of bread.

"Thought we'd find you here, Ham," Japheth said.

"You've spoken with Father, then?"

They nodded without looking at him directly. Here to gloat? No. For all their differences, his bothers weren't men who thrived on the misfortune of others. Still, he had no desire to be in anyone's presence. He wasn't some woman needing to talk about her woes and cry out her miseries on any available warm shoulder. He didn't touch the food and leaned back on his elbows, turning his face to the sun, closing his eyes. He could sort this out himself.

"I'm sorry about Cush," Japheth said. "And about the unpleasant events that seem to grow rather than resolve." His brother ran his fingers across his head, through his loose curls. He thought about his own history, no doubt. Before, when his life was falling to bits. How had Ham felt then? At first it was amusing to see his oldest brother fall short. That hadn't lasted long. It was painful. The long hours when Japheth was tormented with the decision about Denah and her fate was excruciating. Ham didn't want to see her banished. Or killed. He had crossed the lines of righteousness himself and he wanted her to receive mercy. It cleared his own conscience somehow to see her restored, forgiven.

He stood by Japheth back then, offering his support, his loyalty. Japheth wasn't so quick to do the same for him. He didn't act as a true brother in support of Nimrod's freedom or Samuel's guilt. Shem stood on the same platform with Japheth. Two against one.

"Yes," Ham said. "It seems where matters can be resolved, we're choosing the alternate route instead." He intentionally kept his eyes closed. He felt his brothers suck in air.

"Are you blaming us for your troubles, Ham?" Shem kept his voice even but Ham could hear the vise on his brother's windpipe tightening. "I stand before God with a clear conscience as to my decisions of late. You can say the same?"

"I'm not struck down by the God Who Sees, am I?"

"Nor are you blessed."

Ham raised himself to a full sitting position and peered at Shem. It wasn't like him to provoke a fight. He was the peacemaker among the brothers. "God punishes me with the shame of my offspring? Is that what you're saying, Shem?"

Shem shrugged. "Who's to say what God is doing? I'm just saying that I, and my firstborn, put God's ways before our own. We seek truth and justice over family bonds."

Ham felt the tension solidify in his limbs, ready to strike out and smack his brother. He gripped his knees tightly instead. "I am well aware that family bonds mean nothing to you."

Japheth released an exasperated sigh. "Stop it. This gets us no where. We came to support you, Ham. To be brothers, united."

"By lining up my descendants for execution? You would like to wipe the name of Ham from the new earth, just like our father?"

Shem jumped to his feet and stood over him, aiming a finger at Ham's face. "You brought this evil among us. Your children and your children's children shame you because of their upbringing."

Ham gathered the saliva in his mouth and shot it between his brother's feet. He stood slowly and faced Shem, hands clenching at his side.

Japheth placed himself between the two of them, taut, ready to deflect the blows that were hovering beneath the ripples of muscle. "Please, Brothers. Not this. Not now."

Shem's face was red and he held the accusing finger at Ham's chest. Whatever else lingered in his brother's mind needed to come spilling out. Ham crossed his arms over his chest and waited for the rest of Shem's tirade.

"You tolerate sin among your sons and it infects us all. Nephil blood will destroy more than the name of Ham." Shem spat out the words.

Ham flinched at the remark. He hadn't heard the foul term used in decades. They were gone, destroyed with the rest of humanity. What did the nephilim have to do with his own kin? "What are you talking about?"

His brother's countenance shifted. The narrow slit of eyes opened fully as he became aware of his words. He stepped back and turned away. Japheth looked between the two of them, puzzlement on his face.

"Oh, Ham," Shem said.

"What?' Ham pushed Japheth out of his way. He clamped his hand on Shem's shoulder and spun him around. "What are you talking about?"

Shem shook his head and looked at the earth. "You don't know. I was wrong to speak."

Ham pinched his brother's chin and lifted it, forcing him to look squarely, eye to eye.

Shem inhaled a large volume of air. "It's your wife. Naomi carries the blood of the nephilim. Your seed is tainted."

▲

It was the stillness in the air that made her skin prickle, Naomi decided. The leaves hung on the trees like linens on the line after a sound scrubbing, limp and shapeless. Not a one twitched. Birds vacated the breezeless skies. Insects rested. Beasts were hidden. Instinctively Naomi turned to the skies to look for slate tinged clouds rolling into formation. There was an unbearable silence preceding most thunder storms, as the darkened sky began its descent, threatening to surround her. But there were no signs of a deluge on the horizon.

A gnarled stump at the edge of the olive grove hugged her spine. She sat on the ground between the roots, tentacles reaching toward the stream before digging into the earth. Naomi leaned her head back, wanting to hear from God. Her mind was too strewn to form words. She wanted the One God, the Creator, the God of First Man, to speak to her. She wanted the comfort of someone willing to take control and turn the last month inside out. It was beyond her ability to make her family right again.

Naomi drained her tears into her hands. Releasing the torment cleared the emotional surge that overwhelmed her mind and left her like the tree leaves, lifeless and spent.

Where had it all gone wrong? How had it all gone wrong? Her grandson was turning his face from God. Proud already, he stood in the wake of his own execution and would not seek the One who saves. Her firstborn entertained killing a child to cover his shameful behavior. He lied. He stole. He cheated.

And Ham. Her beloved husband. He would send an innocent man to his death to protect his own kin. Or himself.

Naomi regretted the thought, but there it was. Three of her family were in the vicinity of Eli and Iris's home. One of them killed Eli. She didn't know which one.

Her husband's name would never be the same.

Her family would never be the same.

And repairing the damage went far beyond the previous month.

The words of Ham's great-grandfather were suddenly pressed into her mind. "The iniquities of the wicked heap woe on the innocent," Methuselah often said. Samuel and Eli, Iris and Eliamah. They were innocent ones suffering under the hand of her own family. The line of Ham had fallen far from the righteous standards they knew in their hearts. It was a web spun from minuscule threads of discord, woven into an intricate net of destruction. But not an invincible one. It could be swept aside with one stroke of God's hand, one breath from his lungs.

Judgment took hold of her heart and Naomi found the words to say to her God. "Forgive them, please forgive them."

The tingle on her skin made her shiver despite the solemn attitude of the winds. Naomi looked around, almost expecting to see that she wasn't alone. Only the trees stood nearby, listening, watching. She rubbed her hands up and down her arms and tucked her clothing in tight around her shins before checking again for the storm she knew was close at hand.

Chapter Thirty-seven

The beans were black and tarry, adhering to the bottom of the cook pot in an unappealing glob. Naomi yanked the pot from over the low burning fire pit and set it in a sand pile to cool. She hated wasting food. Even her husband's dogs would stay clear of the mess she just created. Not that they were here. Not Ham or his dogs. She hadn't seen her husband since the confrontation with Cush. That was two days ago.

Shem and Japheth got a briefing from their father after the horrific family meeting. They left the house in search of Ham, returning close-lipped about the conversation. Naomi read tension in the furrows lining their foreheads. She didn't try to pry words from them as to where Ham might be, what his intentions were. She hadn't realized at the time he was going to disappear.

His brothers hadn't been back to the house since, nor anyone from their households. Not even Denah. Naomi felt a keen shunning, as if they were guarding themselves from the shame among her offspring. Guarding themselves from sin. Guarding themselves from her.

She couldn't stop the roll of questions in her mind. What had the men discussed? Did they discover the truth about Eli? Were they protecting their youngest brother? Did they encourage him to flee?

Was the lineage of Ham a pariah among the generations of Noah, and no more would she enjoy communion with those outside her blood line?

Deep inside her heart was a question of far greater concern: How far would the righteous hand of judgment reach? How long would God wait to see that the sins were accounted for?

It was no wonder the others stayed away, really. They had reason to fear, never knowing how and when God might strike. Naomi might be tempted to flee the house of Ham herself if she thought she could be spared punishment. She couldn't of course. She and her husband were one in the eyes of God.

Nimrod met with the Council tomorrow. Would Ham be there? Had he abandoned her in shame of his firstborn? Of himself? Would she lose him as well as Nimrod, and then Cush, too?

Naomi stabbed a thick wooden spoon into the beans and began scraping them from the bottom of the pot. The burned aroma turned her stomach.

Noah was the only one in her home to feed. Their meal time conversations were subdued, and often they didn't speak at all. It wasn't uncomfortable silence. Both seemed to prefer the lack of chatter. His presence alone brought comfort. He understood, held the same load on his shoulders, and fought as she did, to maintain a semblance of normalcy when the urge to scream and run sought to prevail. There were no words needed.

Naomi began preparing another batch of beans that she and her father-in-law would push around for a while as if they actually had an appetite. If she prepared nothing, he probably wouldn't mind, but the task gave her purpose as she waited for the day to end.

▲

The smell of charred food wafted through the doorway. Ham crinkled his nose. He was hungrier than he realized. He'd eaten little in the few days he was gone, preferring to ride without stopping until, for the sake of his mount and the dogs, he had to hole up in a cave and try to sleep. He'd found several new tar pits. Not that he was looking. He rode in search of answers. He rode in search of peace. Neither of which he found.

The dogs panted at his side and he shooed them off towards the stream. He stood watching them as they trotted away, side by side by side, until they were no longer in sight. Still, he hovered, unable to cross the threshold of his own sanctuary, unwilling to face his wife.

The thumping in his chest and tightening of his jaw returned. He failed to find Naomi's deception a place of rest as he sped through the unknown lands. It still stood, ugly and unthinkable in his mind. Like the smell from within, his woman was foul.

The vile flow of nephilim blood traversed within her soft brown wrap of flesh. He enjoyed that flesh, united with it to create the children of his own seed. His people, his line. His heritage in the new world.

They were all cursed.

His offspring held the cup of wickedness because of the woman he eagerly wed beneath the brown tent. He symbolically gave her his rib and they were made one. But he didn't know. He didn't know what she was.

He hated the nephilim.

He would've put a knife to the throat of every last one, if he'd had the opportunity.

Their evil presence drowned in the deluge, forever gone.

Or so he thought.

He was wrong.

The mother of his offspring carried their foul blood.

▲

She felt his eyes burning into her back before she noticed the unwashed man scent mingling with the pot of food. He said nothing, so she turned, expecting a broken man, one whose son was a disgrace and whose grandson was in peril. She found instead a man knotted together with cords of anger. Relief at the sight of him was replaced with pangs of apprehension. "Ham?"

Her husband leaned on the doorframe with his arms crossed. Darkness covered his face. "Ham," she said again. "I was worried about you. I've been scared, and-"

Ham pushed away from the door and strode toward her. In a flash he took hold of her wrists. "You never told me." He spat the words out from clenched teeth. "It's your fault. The shame that has befallen me is all because of you."

Naomi pulled away from her husband until her arms were fully stretched, locked in his grasp. The word 'you' came from his mouth in a snarl. Her mouth went dry as his tone revealed what he knew.

He knew.

"Ham, let go."

Her husband's nostrils flared as he kept her gaze and squeezed more tightly. Abruptly he dropped her wrists and turned away, breathing heavily.

"How could I? How could I tell you? Or anyone?"

"You have destroyed me."

"No. The blood was thinned. I thought it was gone. I hoped. I couldn't tell you. I couldn't tell anyone."

"You could have refused my smiles. You could have turned that pretty little pouty face toward another. You didn't. You used me."

"I wanted you."

"To destroy me?"

"No. No. Of course not. They're my children, too. My offspring. And they aren't nephil. Look at your daughters. Look at the grandbabies. They're normal. They aren't nephil."

Ham cinched her chin in a vise of thumb and forefinger. "Look at Cush, Naomi. Look at your firstborn. He carries the stench within. You gave him the rot of nephilim blood in his veins and look what he has become."

Naomi pulled away and rubbed her jaw. "He made his own choices. Your father said-"

"Leave my father out of it!" Ham slammed his fist on the table, then froze, staring wide-eyed at her. "He knows, doesn't he? About you?"

Naomi nodded.

"You told him, and not me?"

"I didn't tell him. He knew already."

Her husbands lips tightened and he closed his eyes for a moment. Naomi didn't move.

"My father knew. He married me to you. And he knew."

She understood the torment in her husband's mind. Ham never measured up to Noah's standards like the other two. Even after Japheth's disgrace. It was Ham who fought for blessings that seemed to spread in every direction but his. "It isn't what you think Ham. He didn't bind us to punish you. I was a, a gift to you. He knew we were interested in one another and when you asked for me he gave his blessing. He said there is no evil in my blood from my ancestors. He said it would not carry to my children and my children's children."

"He's wrong."

"Ham, please."

"You told my brothers, Naomi? Or did my dear father have

that pleasure?"

"No, I didn't. But..."

"But what, Naomi?"

"Eran and Denah. They know." One of them betrayed her? Eran, of course. She had been overwhelmed by the news. And there were no secrets between her and Shem.

Ham paced in tight lines, running his hand over his dark stubbled chin. He was determining a course and Naomi needed to do something, anything, to pull the fury from his eyes. She picked up the spoon she dropped when she first saw his face in the doorway. "I'll have something for you to eat shortly." Her voice pitched up and down as she spoke.

Ham stopped. "No. You can't remain here. I don't want you in my home." It was the even keel of his words that struck her. His mind was made up.

Naomi stared into his eyes. His cold, unrelenting eyes. The spoon clattered on the floor again. "I'll, I'll grab a few things and go to Denah's then." She turned away quickly to escape the animosity steeping from her husband's pores.

Ham grabbed her arm, nearly wrenching it free of her shoulder. "No. I'll show you where you'll stay."

Her forearm was trapped in his grip, and when he yanked on it, she had no choice but to follow him out the door. He drug her down the path, past the fire pit and through the shards of dried dragon bone toward his workshop. The sharp slivers bit into her bare feet. Naomi winced. Ham didn't stop. When his dogs greeted him with tails wagging, he stomped and shooed them away.

Ham's lips were closed tight, saying nothing to her until they reached the brick building, nothing until he shoved her through the door.

"Sleep well," he said.

▲

Naomi landed on the stone floor with a thud as the door slammed and latched in place. Outside, heavy objects were dragged in front of the door, then the windows. Ham sealed her inside. She wanted to stand and scream at him. She didn't. She wanted to bury her head in her lap and scream at herself. She didn't do that either. She remained where she fell for a long while, until a shiver ran up her arm and she realized day was slipping into night.

Light still found its way into the interior from vents near the roof line. It would soon be gone. Naomi made herself get up and test the door, finding it immobile as she had imagined. The two windows covered by wooden shutters were blockaded, too. She was here for the night.

A quick check of the room was all that was necessary. Most of the room was lined with tables and shelves. They were covered in tools and wood carvings, gadgets made of bone or clay, bits of this and parts of that. The projects in her husband's mind were displayed in various stages of development.

There was still the stack of new bricks in one corner, the ones her husband made soon after the fateful tar hunting expedition. He had never even found them a place in the sun to fully harden. The tumultuous events since then had far out weighed all of his other concerns.

Her hand found a bedroll tucked under a bench. She unrolled the woven mat and the thick blanket and was immersed in the odor of Ham's dogs. Ham's wet dogs to be precise. The blanket hadn't seen a tub of water in some time and she knew it was covered in hairs. It was Ham's though, and his scent lingered in the dank weave, too. It was oddly comforting, as if she could cling to a part of her husband that didn't despise her.

Naomi pulled the blanket beneath her chin and tucked her hands beneath her head. There was no star filled sky above, no clouds puffing out into shapes of lumpy bread rolls. Just the darkness of the air above her head. There was nothing to occupy her mind except her thoughts, and they wanted to remember Before.

She was in the market, shopping with Jael and her sisters-in-law. The mocking was especially vicious that day and Ham wasn't there to buffer the blows. It was that ark, that insane project of Noah's that riled the crowds. That, and her father-in-law's insistence that his God would destroy any who denied he was the One God, the Creator. He had been correct of course, but that day she was so tired of it all. The years of ridicule were wearing increasingly thin, and her womb was an empty cavern. One uneventful day of shopping seemed hardly too much to hope for.

It was anything but uneventful. As they were leaving, a loud commotion caught her attention. A young nephil had been captured and was about to be executed. Even now she could see his expression. Fear and pain blended into a mask of hatred. She couldn't peel her gaze away. It sickened her very core, yet her eyes stayed on the man, but not to witness his horrific torture. It was his hair. It had a reddish tinge to it, like strands of pounded copper. Just like her grandmother's.

It was the moment she fully realized that the blood she carried had powers to spread tentacles of nephilim into her own children.

Traits did travel from kin to kin, there was no denying. Samuel and Jabal had the same hooked nose. Japheth sprouted the same curly mass of hair on his head as his father, and Nimrod bore the stance of Ham. If she saw a woman with hair the color of ripened wheat, more often than not, the woman's daughters did, too, and Eran's slim hips were abundant in her generations.

These were outside traits. Harmless ones. None spoke of nephilim ties. Canaan was tall, of course, and his sons were taller than most of their cousins. It had frightened her when her youngest son outgrew his older brothers, but the growth stopped in time. Canaan's blood was never questioned. And the new baby, perhaps he wouldn't be so different from his cousins either. On the outside.

Naomi prayed Noah was correct, that men held the same chance to choose good over evil. That the rebellion among them wasn't her fault. That God didn't hold her responsible. They all carried sin in their blood. First Man Adam passed it to everyone. Some stirred theirs into action and others chose to keep it suppressed, following in obedience. She had done both in her lifetime.

So had Ham.

Naomi rewound images in her mind, returning to Nimrod and Ham, side by side after the dragon was slain. A little boy looking out his window in the dark night could easily mistake one for the other.

▲

The full moon was obscured by clouds. Ham made himself step away from the window and lie back down on the bed. He was fully awake. On hunting expeditions, he could sleep readily on beds made of stone, or sand, or just the wild grasses and nothing on top but a blanket of stars. He'd slept in caves, and trees, and rafts made of reeds. Once, he fell asleep on his horse and woke up miles from home, his fingers still wrapped in its mane.

In his own bed, he couldn't drift away without Naomi. When she was out tending new babies in the night, he could find only snippets of rest. It wasn't until she lay in a crescent against him that he dreamed in the bold colors of contented slumber.

He stared at the blackness above him. The last few days had been a series of tests, one revealing incident on the heels of another. He'd handled them the best he could. He yelled at his son, of course. He yelled at his brothers. He yelled at his wife. When his father asked where Naomi was, he yelled at him, too. Now he yelled at himself for trusting, loving, protecting those he called family. They intended to eradicate his generations. He could see it now. Tomorrow they could begin picking off the best of his offspring.

They had the ability to stop Nimrod's execution. It was their votes alone. Even Cush had the power to prevent his son's death. He could take the blame onto himself. He wouldn't, though. His firstborn wasn't man enough to see beyond his own comforts.

It was up to Ham. He could stop the slaughter of his own flesh and blood, or select which one of them was placed upon the altar. With the right words, he could change the course of the day.

But would he? Would he allow deceit to pour from his lips in order to save the future of his name, and of all the sons of the earth?

Chapter Thirty-eight

The sky was a strip of pale amber framed by the air vents. It was morning.

The day of the Triune Council.

Naomi eased herself into a sitting position and rubbed her neck. It stiffened in the night and now resisted straightening. Her hip was tender as she pushed back the cover and her arm, too, where Ham held his grip. As she rose to her feet, she winced, stabs of pain traveling up her shins. A table ledge lent support as she coaxed her limbs to hold weight. Minor injuries only, scrapes and aches that would pass.

She tried the door again in case Ham had come and removed the barriers as she slept in an exhausted heap, but it remained solid. Her stomach growled and she had no choice but to relieve herself in a corner of the room. How long would he hold her here? No one would be alarmed if she wasn't at the meeting. That precedent had already been set. At least no one would be stoned without her presence. She was required to participate and Noah would make sure she was found.

The thought gave no comfort.

It was too early for the trial. Ham was awake though, she knew. She doubted he slept at all. His mind could not have allowed him a moment's peace. He had no control of the day before him and he would face it alone. Her husband was certainly in a position that would break most men. Did he seek his God for strength? For wisdom? She didn't know anymore. The God he claimed to serve seemed distant in the daily struggles. How far he had fallen since the days on the ark. How far they had fallen together.

Naomi ran fingers through her hair and secured the long strands behind her head with a piece of string. She wondered if Ham thought about her at all as he paced the vacant floors of their home. Or was it only Nimrod on his mind. Or just himself. He was wrapped in a darkened cloud from all sides.

A dog woofed outside and rustled in the grass. Naomi caught her breath and listened for footsteps. None came. The dog moved on. No one had reason to go to Ham's workshop, especially on this day. The well was her only hope. She might be able to attract attention from the vent if Noah came for water. It was unlikely. The pots were filled yesterday, but waiting without trying something was unbearable.

Ham's bricks were perfect for stacking, forming a secure platform against the wall. From the top, she could see out the vent facing the well. The dogs clustered there, one mass of fur and legs catching a moments rest. As she shifted her weight to see the house, the brick beneath her heel crumbled. Naomi fell against the wall with the unexpected jar to her spine. She shifted her weight again to find a stable location for her foot and sank with another collapsing brick. She jumped off the tower before they all became rubble beneath her.

Naomi grunted with disgust and picked up a broken chunk. The almond sized inclusion surprised her. It was no wonder the brick was unstable. Even she knew the inclusions had to be small and thoroughly blended with the clay in order to make the brick a similar consistency throughout. Pockets of foreign material were weak points. Another of the bricks had a similar lump of material, as did the next few she examined.

Naomi dug into a gritty brick and pulled a piece of the foreign material out. She gave it a spit polish then held it up to the light. The color made her heart stop.

Gold.

▲

Ham killed Eli.

Ham killed.

The thought teased her mind previously, like a moth fluttering on the brim of a petal. It held no firm purchase, easily blown away with a puff of reasoning. Confronted with the hidden treasure, it latched onto her senses.

Beni, Eli's little son, said it. Someone took his pretty rocks. No one paid attention because a man had been killed. Rocks were of no concern. But it was gold. Ham killed Eli and stole the child's hoard.

Naomi pounded each brick on the stone floor to release the misshapen lumps of evidence hidden among the fragile clay. The gold filled a bucket. A small fortune once, before the flood. Not now. Noah wanted it forgotten, so men wouldn't return to the worship of the mere rock over the God who formed it.

Ham remembered. He remembered the worth of these nuggets of glistening sun.

Naomi slumped on the floor with the damning bucket encircled by her legs, content now with her imprisonment in the workshop. How could she speak against Ham and bring his execution? She had his rib, they were one. Yet how could she not speak the truth? How could she permit Nimrod to be killed in his place? She would stay here and die alone rather than cast stones at either one.

Tears came, spilling onto her feet beneath her bowed head, leaving trails in the dusty coating. "God Who Hears," she prayed. "Help me."

▲

There was no new information for the Council. Noah brought up the springbone that killed the dog but Shem and Japheth said they taught the method of weaponry to their own boys. It pointed at no one in particular.

Iris was asked to repeat her story. Again. Ham let his eyes travel around the room as she spoke. The divisions between the family lines were blurred today, and the expressions less expectant. There was a solemn finality to the air, as if they all knew the outcome. Everyone knew what was ahead after the votes were tallied.

No one was anxious for a stoning. Even Iris spoke without venom, presenting her lines as if memorized and rehearsed. Noah permitted her to sit outside the circle, with kin, and not in the position of the accuser. Only the boy, Beni, latched onto her arm today. His mother's eyes held the empty gaze of a beast, shot through with an arrow but whose life blood had not yet fully drained. Life, yes, but living, no. Washed out skin sagged around her mouth. She looked worn. The robust woman he met on the homestead was gone, leaving this shell to function as Eli's voice.

She deserved to see justice. As much as he wanted this whole business to be resolved, his family walking away unscathed, Ham couldn't deny it. Her husband was killed and someone needed to be held responsible.

Who?

He sat in his usual place in the circle at Noah's insistence, Cush's position notably vacant. No one outside the family knew about the shame his firstborn brought on the name of Ham. His father didn't want it known. Not yet. One incident at a time. No one would hear about Cush striking Samuel on the back of his head. No one could connect that incident with Eli's own death blow.

No one was aware Ham had no vote either. He could sit as if he still belonged.

Cush hadn't been told to stay away from the meeting. It was his choice. He refused to stuff his selfishness away long enough to stand by his son during this trial. Was it because he knew Nimrod was guilty, or innocent? Ham didn't know. When his absence was questioned, Noah simply stated that Cush wouldn't be present. Ham picked up the nuance of the whispers among the crowd. Cush didn't have the stomach to be present for Nimrod's guilty verdict, they said.

Let them think what they wanted. The truth would come soon enough.

There was still information the council had not heard. One of the two boys left the cave. At this point, the information would only damn Nimrod. No one would believe Cush had the motivation to strike down another man. The fact he wasn't here proved to them how weak Cush was. Sharing this tidbit wouldn't cast blame on Cush, or help his grandson.

Ham monitored his breathing and forced himself to regulate the intake and outflow so that it was slow and steady. He still had the ability to save Nimrod.

He could confess.

He could speak the truth about the night of Eli's death.

He could shift the blame away from Nimrod.

His grandson sat next to Noah. He could be mistaken for a bodyguard to someone just entering the room. He moved little from his tensed position yet remained keen to the subtle shifts in his surroundings. Ham could see it in his eyes. Nimrod was skilled as a hunter for this reason, knowing when to be still and when to strike. He could read the movements of his prey with uncanny instinct and wouldn't reveal his full power until the moment he knew with certainty he held control. Once he moved, there was little hope for the target of his choosing.

For this hunt, Nimrod was the prey. He had shown no emotion as the evidence was unrolled before them again. He wore composure like his own skin. As the inevitability of his death rose like the mountains of Ararat, he didn't allow fear to pull sweat to his brow or to mold his face into a mask of concern. The strength flowed from him to Semiras, who sat behind her husband in the tranquility of a carved goddess. Loyal builders of the tower formed rows behind them, chests puffed and chins high in a berm of support.

Could anyone deny his greatness?

Nimrod was destined to lead.

If he survived the day.

Beni pointed a shaky finger at Nimrod before falling into his mothers arms and hiding his face. There was nothing left but the vote.

Ham needed to choose. His life or Nimrod's.

▲

Sunlight streamed through the slats by the time Naomi's heart was dry again. She took a scrap of cloth rag and scrubbed her feet where the dirt and tears mingled, cleaning the scrapes as best she could and eliminating the crimson roads of dried blood. With tweezers she extracted tiny bits of bone from the cuts. Her soles were tender, emphasizing wounds easily healed, unlike the gash in her soul.

Ham used to tend both. He rubbed scented oil into her weary

feet at night, after the long hours of feeding and cleaning on the ark. Then he fell asleep beside her, cradling her in arms of safety, whispering words of comfort. They had truly been one then, she and Ham. As horrific as those days had been, their relationship walked off the ark tighter than when it when in.

Eli and Iris were one, too. It wasn't fair to Iris to have Eli taken like he was. Naomi pictured the bereaved woman at the feet of her Eli, kissing the soles that connected him to the land he farmed, to the earth from which he was created. Iris would never walk beside her man again with his babe in her arms or in her belly.

Someone needed to pay the price for the crime against them.

But Ham? Naomi exhaled and looked at the gold, hidden by her husband's hand. A bucket full of evidence. Would he kill a man for it? Naomi tried to reconcile the ugliness in her mind. Even with the pail of treasure, her heart wouldn't rest on the thought. It was the same intuition she had about Nimrod, and even Cush. These men in her life had many faults but none of the three were murderers. Devotion blinded her eyes to their true nature at times, she realized. Not every time. There was another explanation. There had to be.

The rag in her hand was filthy, her feet clean. For the moment. They would be covered in grime again when she stood, and she'd have to soak them in salts for a few days to get them to heal properly. Barefoot or in sandals, they would-

Naomi's thought stopped on the thought of her sandals. In the house.

Sandals in the house.

Like Eli's. He didn't take time to put them on. He was more concerned with protecting his family than his feet.

His feet.

Naomi's heart thumped against her ribs, images one after another exploding in her head. Eli's sandals by the door.

His feet on the altar.

His clean feet. Feet that contrasted with the bloody wound matting his hair and tunic.

The deluge of rain the night he died.

The mud packed land by the stream where Iris found him. At least said she found him there. Had she really?

Eli's feet should have been covered with mud. They weren't. His clothing should have been stained with the red soil of the earth if he had indeed been laid low where Iris claimed. It wasn't. He had only blood stains. There was no evidence of wet ground touching his body.

Naomi jumped to her feet, ignoring the stabs. Iris said she gathered Eli from the ground and brought him to the city. Had she cleaned him first? She hadn't said that she did. One of them may have scrubbed his limbs of dirt, leaving the gaping mess of a wound on his head as evidence. His tunic hadn't been changed, though. His life fluid saturated the fibers. But there was no mud on it. His hair was matted with blood, dark crimson, without the hues of the earth mixed in.

Eli's feet were clean because he wasn't outside with bare feet.

He wasn't outside when he died.

Iris was lying.

Naomi pounded on the door and yelled at the blue strip of sky. "Hello! Can anyone hear me!"

She didn't know what it all meant, other than Iris told the Council a tale she knew wasn't true. And like ticks on a dog, when one lie was spotted there were countless more to be uncovered.

She had to get to that trial.

Chapter Thirty-nine

Naomi heaved the axe overhead then allowed it to drop. The blade penetrated the wooden door, barely, just enough to grab hold while the handle fell off in her hands, as it had the previous three times. It was in the workshop for repairs, waiting for its return to the barn where the other big tools were stored. She tossed the handle to the floor and scoured the tables again. Drills and hammers and files could get her out, in time. Not soon enough. Ham built his structures with resilience.

Finding nothing on the tables, she searched the shelves again. Her eyes flowed over the array of bone handles, the carving in progress. They stopped on Ham's whistle. Was anyone around to hear it? Ham and Noah were gone, of course. Most of the family, she had to assume, were hovering around the meeting place. Unless one was sick. Or Samuel and Eliamah? She swept the items off a table and dragged it toward the wall, then climbed up and faced the vents. There was a chance the young couple remained in the barn. With a lung full of air she blew the three staccato beats she heard from Ham's lips many times before.

The barking of dogs hit her ears long before she could see them. They followed the summons of their master, gathering at the door and pacing in small circles, waiting for Ham to let them in and shower his affection on their smelly coats. Naomi could hear the clickety clickety of their toenails on the stones, then the whines as they were barred from entry. Naomi blew the three beats again and set the frenzied barking into the air.

By the fifth set of whistle calls the dogs were howling between the mournful whines. Naomi pressed her face to the opening and peered at the path again. It wasn't empty this time. Samuel and Eliamah stood there, side by side, looking at the commotion. They couldn't hear her over the dogs so Naomi crammed her arm out the vent and waved as best she could.

"Hello?" Samuel's voice was close, and tentative.

Naomi withdrew her arm and peered out. "It's me Samuel. Naomi. Please help me get out of here."

"The door's blocked," he said. "There's a tree log against it. I can move it though."

Naomi jumped off the table and stood by the door. Samuel placated the dogs with his attention then turned his efforts to the obstacle, grunting as he pushed on the log. She could hear it scrape an inch, then another.

"Why are you in there?" Eliamah asked. She answered herself. "Your husband did this."

"Yes. He'll be angry if you help me, but I must get out."

"The meeting. I thought you were there."

"I need to be there, Eliamah. You understand, don't you? I have to get there. I have to save my grandson." As soon as the words left her mouth, Naomi gasped.

The scraping stopped.

"Eliamah, Samuel, Please." Naomi pressed her forehead against the door. "Please don't leave me in here. I don't know who killed your father, but it wasn't Nimrod, was it? He shouldn't die for a sin he didn't commit. Please. I'll give you whatever you ask. But please,

please, let me out."

A pause, then the grunts and scrapes resumed outside the door. Naomi exhaled.

"God wants truth," the girl said.

"Yes, it's time, time for this to be finished." Whatever the answers, whomever the guilty party, it was time for resolution. If there was a stoning among her kin even, it had to be completed.

The log crashed and Samuel unbarred the door. Naomi wrapped her arms around him and planted a kiss on his sweaty cheek. He grinned and turned away as color crept up his neck.

Naomi held out her hand to Eliamah. "Will you come? Will you speak the words of truth?"

The girls shook her head slowly without taking her eyes from Naomi. "I can't."

Naomi dropped her hand. The girl's eyes glimmered. The answers were there, just behind her quivering lips. She didn't stuff them away behind lies and deceit, to a place not easily found. She had been hidden away so the words wouldn't be discovered. "You were given to Samuel, to keep you away from your home. Away from people asking questions. Away from me, weren't you?"

Samuel stepped up to his wife and put a protective arm around her waist. She sighed and looked at the ground before glancing at him and providing a reassuring smile. With a tender finger she wiped a smudge of grime from his cheek. She looked back to Naomi and just perceptibly, she nodded.

"Will you tell me, then? Tell me who you protect, Eliamah?"

"My mother," she whispered.

▲

The horse responded to Naomi's commands and bolted from

the barn. Eliamah held the answers to her father's death but let no more escape from her lips. Naomi didn't try to coax any more from her. Two of the horses were theirs to take if they chose to leave, along with grain and supplies. Noah wouldn't mind, she told them. He wanted them to take the provisions they needed, and there was no possible way for him to bring all the donated supplies back to his village. As she galloped toward the meeting, she knew it was the last she would see of Samuel and Eliamah.

▲

"Is there other evidence?" His father was dragging the meeting out, delaying the inevitable vote. The weariness in his eyes made the lines branching from the corners deep and swollen. His hand shook a little when he tried to lift a mug of water, a mug that he held briefly then set back down a few times, waiting for someone, anyone, to speak. The rich curls circling his face were drained of color. His father looked old.

Ham couldn't take his eyes from the man who gave him life. Noah wasn't intent on destroying Nimrod. He could see it. He knew it. He could try to convince himself otherwise but Noah was only seeking justice. Ham could not despise his father for that. Noah's heart writhed in agony with the decision looming before him.

Noah looked at Ham with eyes reflecting his own inner turmoil. There was only one way to save Nimrod.

"Yes," Ham said. He swallowed hard. "I killed Eli."

There was no motion in the room. If eyelids peeling back and jaws dropping were audible, the sound would have been deafening. Ham pulled his trunk erect and cleared his throat, looking squarely into his grandson's eyes. "I'm the guilty one," he said.

"No. You aren't." The breathless voice came from the doorway.

Ham, and every other person in the room, jerked toward the pronouncement.

His wife stood there with her hands on her hips, crumpled, determined.

"Naomi, don't interfere," he said.

"I have evidence for the Council," she said. Her voice started high and fast then leveled as she strove for composure. They locked eyes and he anticipated venom swirling in the pools of deep green. What he saw instead was defiance.

What evidence? What could she possibly unearth in the confines of the shed? Who would she now finger in blame? Cush or Nimrod? He started to protest again, then shut his lips as the nature of the dust on her clothing caught his attention.

She knew. Ham rubbed his temples and sighed. "Naomi-"

Noah held up his hand. "Let her speak, Ham."

Shem handed Naomi a drink that she swallowed in one long gulp. He hadn't provided her water in the shop. He sighed again, determined to keep his lips sealed. Let her speak then. Let the answers fall where they belonged.

Noah scooted to allow Naomi room to sit in the circle. She squeezed Nimrod's hand and gave him a look that spoke of assurance. For the first time, Ham could see a glimmer of hope in his grandson's expression. Cush, then? She had evidence against Cush? Or she would seal the fate of her own husband by producing the gold?

Naomi inhaled a deep breath. "I don't have all the answers about Eli," she said. "There are inconsistencies, though, that need sorting." Naomi looked over her shoulder and searched until her gaze landed on Iris. She held the woman's focus for a moment before turning back to the circle.

Iris pinched her lips together and dropped her head.

"I had time to think," Naomi started, looking to Ham briefly. "And it occurred to me that Eli's feet were clean."

Ham listened as she reported her thoughts. Guilt twisted around his gut. It never occurred to him that Nimrod was actually innocent, not until Cush's behavior came to light. Even then, if he were to place a wager, the choice in temperaments spoke clearly. Searching for evidence seemed counter-productive. He didn't want to condemn his grandson any further.

Noah nodded as she finished, his hands tented beneath his chin, eyes closed, processing. Naomi didn't come right out and accuse Iris of lying about where she found her husband. And what happened to her husband. She didn't need to. It was clear there was more to the story of Eli's fate.

Iris was asked to come forward and sit among them in the circle. Beni refused to be left behind, clinging to her garments. Erin made room for them both to sit in front of her, between Shem and Elam. Iris sank to the cushions looking as if she wanted to continue sinking into the floor, disappearing before having to answer Noah's intent expression.

"What do you have to say, Iris?" Noah's voice was controlled. Clearing the name of one descendant meant another was at fault. He didn't gain either way.

Iris wrung her hands together, on the verge of tears. Eran placed her hand on the woman's arm and began an easy pat, like a child comforted in its mother's arms. Iris sucked back the tears and lifted her chin. "It was never meant to come to this."

"Tell us from the beginning," Noah said. "Tell us what happened to your Eli. The truth, Iris, speak the truth."

Iris lifted her moist eyes to the ceiling. "I didn't mean to. I didn't mean to hurt him. It was dark and I was scared." Her voice cracked. "I didn't know it was him when I swung the cook pot."

Ham felt a flood of emotion pouring through his mind. Iris was confessing.

Nimrod was innocent.

Erin wedged herself into the circle and pulled Iris into her shoulder. The woman wailed in Eran's arms while everyone sat stone still.

When the sobs were contained, Iris started again. "It was night, the night after those three were at our place. The dog was outside making an awful sound. I laid there and listened until it stopped. It was pitiful because he was dying, only I didn't know that then. I just heard him, like he was gone mad. It set my nerves on alert. That, and all the talk earlier of invaders and how I should be scared..." Iris blew her nose forcefully on a rag and inhaled a deep breath. "I had a hard time sleeping. I gave up after a while, and got up, all quiet like, so I wouldn't wake the others. I didn't know my Eli was up, too. The little ones were sleeping on either side of me." She closed her eyes and cupped her hands over the sides of her face. "I didn't know it was Eli. All I saw was a dark shape hunkered by the door and I hit it. Hard." Her eyes opened and her gaze found Noah's. "He was just putting his shoes on."

Naomi groaned and covered her mouth with her hands.

Iris licked her lips. "Eli works hard and sleeps hard, so I never expected him to be awake. Maybe he heard something, or someone. Someone woke him. Maybe he saw someone. My boy did. That's not a lie. Or maybe he worried over the dog, was going to check on it. I don't know."

Beni stared at his mother with wide eyes. She tried to pull him into her lap but he pulled away and crawled into Eran's instead. "It was an accident," she said to him. "I didn't mean to hurt your father."

"It was an accident. Yet, you accused Nimrod. Why? Why did

you do that?" Noah asked, a tinge of frustration crawling in around the edges.

Iris fixed a hard stare on Nimrod. "He shunned my girl. I wanted him punished for making her feel bad. I never meant for him to be stoned."

"But you were going to allow it to happen," Ham could not control the words.

Iris refused to respond.

A low rumbling around the room grew. Noah was forced to stand in order to regain control of the volume. Ham fought to control his relief. He wanted to hoot and scream and dance in triumph. He tried to catch Naomi's eye. She refused to grant him the favor. He couldn't blame her for her anger. His was gone, at least for the moment. She saved Nimrod. She saved the name of Ham. She saved him, too, whether or not that was her intention.

A hush fell over the room again as Noah tried to speak, all except the sobbing of the little boy. Eran gathered him against her chest and attempted to console him. Beni pointed a grubby finger at his mother. "Did she kill my dog, too? Did she take my pretty rocks?"

Ham turned to Naomi, now looking him squarely in the eye. She knew where the rocks were. She knew he took them. She knew what they were.

He waited. She said nothing.

The burn of someone else's stare forced his attention away from Naomi. To Nimrod. The glint in his grandson's eyes burrowed through his skin and Ham unwillingly shuddered. Nimrod hadn't moved except for the tensing around his eyes, but the lack of external motion didn't hide the emotion contained within. He was a solid dam of resilience with the power of the elements pressing to be released. Ham caught his breath.

Nimrod figured it out.

He knew about the gold, too.

Chapter Forty

Naomi checked her father-in-law's expression. Iris's boy asked about the gold and she could see a flicker of question on Noah's face. He started to speak then held his tongue, choosing not to hinder the momentum of enthusiasm rising among the crowd. There had been no murder. It was an accident. Eli's death wasn't planned. The realization gave buoyancy to the deadened room. Not only was Nimrod cleared, but so were they all. They had not plummeted so far in the ways of God to be murderers of their own kind.

Noah didn't realize it was gold that Ham stole from the little boy.

Naomi allowed herself to be drawn into a stream of hugs. The lightened air carried the sounds of restoration for the children of Noah. Nimrod would live. Ham and Cush, too. No one would face the punishment of death. No one would be required to cast the first stone.

She wanted joy to overflow her heart. It didn't. It was dammed by the truth left unspoken. Her husband was willing to confess to a grievous sin, one he didn't commit. He would have been stoned, to spare Nimrod. She wanted to be filled with admiration. It wouldn't come. Ham's confession was just another lie.

Iris lied and would have her tongue cut out. Shem had set that precedent once before and she knew he wouldn't be lenient now, despite the circumstances. The woman's actions almost led to the death of an innocent man. Shem would be sure the consequences were severe, and remembered.

What of Ham? There would be consequences for his theft, when Noah found out. It wasn't time to put the ugliness away completely and start again. The eyes of her God never closed. He knew. There was more truth needing exposure.

Noah's laughter filled her ears and Naomi let out a pent up sigh. There had been enough grief. Let the rejoicing take it rightful place. The rest could be dealt with later.

▲

The crowd milling in the streets learned the truth and like a wave in the great sea, it ripped across the town. A trickle turned to a flow of humanity, all come to rejoice in Nimrod's redemption. Naomi stood in the shadows as the merriment grew. The celebratory attitude was contagious and her grandson was soon on the shoulders of a few men, paraded around in circles to a cheering and adoring throng. Shem's kin stood with Japheth's, alongside her own. The divisions dissolved.

The same throng would have hurled stones at Nimrod had the verdict been different. Lines of brothers would stand against lines of brothers. Man was fickle, easily swayed by emotion. Had any sought their God? Naomi leaned against the trunk of an oak tree. The outcome of the day could have been so entirely different. She might have gone home a widow.

Ham's bellowing laughter rose from among the crowd. She couldn't see him among the dancing bodies. He'd been saved, and

Nimrod. Cush and Samuel, too. Naomi paused to lift her prayers to heaven. "Thank you, God of truth," she said. "Thank you."

A light hand on her shoulder interrupted the prayer. It belonged to Eran. "Don't hate me, Naomi," she said. Her eyes were moist. "I'm so sorry. Shem told Ham. I didn't mean for him to. I am so sorry."

Eran reminded her of a child about to be scolded for breaking a pot. Naomi exhaled. It was difficult to be angry. Eran wouldn't intentionally hurt anyone. "I don't hate you," she said. "I was hurt mostly, I needed you to stand by me. I still need you to stand by me."

Her sister-in-law's shoulders relaxed. "I know, I let you down. What you said was such a shock and, I reacted horribly. It isn't your fault there's sin again on earth. I know it isn't true."

"And if Nimrod was found guilty, instead of Iris? What would you feel then? Would it be my fault? Would it be my fault if Nimrod had killed Eli, because of my family blood?" She didn't mean her words to be so pointed.

Eran looked at her with wide eyes and shook her head. "I know rebellion exists in my family. We've tried, Shem and I, to keep our children in the ways of God. That's why Eli had to be sent away. His thoughts were straying and we feared he would infect the entire family. Then see, see what happened. Eli's death was an accident but Iris had evil on her heart. Maybe we shouldn't have sent them out. I don't know. I do know I was wrong to put blame on your head. I was wrong to hurt you."

Naomi wrapped her arms around Eran's shoulders. "What's done is done. I'm not angry with you. Ham deserved to know the truth about me. And I'm sorry for what will become of Iris. Maybe Samuel and Eliamah will help her tend the young ones until she heals."

Eran nodded. "And I rejoice with you that Nimrod was spared. And Ham."

Another loud cheer invaded their conversation. Naomi leaned back against the tree. The magnitude of the celebration surprised her. Flutes and drums now mingled in the laughter. She was glad for the outcome, of course, but a man was still dead, a woman convicted of harboring ill will and fostering lies. A family would suffer. This information was already forgotten it seemed, in light of Nimrod's restoration. She surveyed the faces and found herself smiling. Perhaps this is what they all needed, a reason to rejoice. A reason to celebrate in unity as one family, pleasing their One God.

Nimrod rode above the heads of the town on strong shoulders, washed in triumph. Naomi and Eran trailed the mob as they took him to his tower and placed him on a step so he stood above them. He allowed the cheers to continue, absorbing the praise with a satisfied countenance, standing tall and proud.

Naomi felt her own tensions of the past weeks falling away. There were issues with Cush to be dealt with, and Ham. She would have to fight to restore her marriage and face the consequences of her tainted blood. Her future was heavy, riddled with burdens she did not look forward to carrying. But for now, no one among her own kin was to be stoned. And God had no reason to strike a blow of fury against her children. The fiery wrath of Enoch's prophesy had been averted.

Nimrod lifted his hands to quiet the crowd. "It's good to celebrate," Nimrod said. "It's a time to rejoice."

Applause broke out and whistles came from every direction. Nimrod waited until the chaos diminished. "Tonight," he said. "As the full moon rises, let's make a sacrifice. Here, on the tower."

Naomi felt Eran stiffen beside her. It wasn't Nimrod's position to call for a sacrifice.

"We'll celebrate," he continued. "Celebrate my deliverance and the honor of my name!"

Eran and Naomi gasped in unison as approval flooded the streets around them. She grabbed her sister-in-law's arm and led her away on trembling limbs. The sacrifice would not be to God. Nimrod called for a sacrifice to honor himself.

▲

The atmosphere at Nimrod's home was buoyant. Family and friends, neighbors and workmen, men and women he barely knew, all celebrating with hastily prepared food and skins of wine. The light mood reached only so far into Ham's soul, the weight of his own involvement in the death of Eli anchoring the rest. He tried to push it aside, to enjoy the event, but he couldn't. He slipped away as soon as he could, preferring the solitude of his own home.

Nimrod was waiting.

Ham stepped through the door into the presence of his grandson. He stiffened, startled. He hadn't expected anyone to be here, especially not Nimrod. He didn't anticipate facing him. Not yet.

"Grandfather," Nimrod said. "You left my party. Somehow I knew you would." He stood with his arms crossed over his chest.

Ham knew better than to sit down. He could read the fire in Nimrod's eyes. He eased his way to a wall and leaned against it, looping his thumbs over his belt.

"You wanted to be the hero," Nimrod said. "I'm sorry that didn't happen as you planned."

Ham shifted his weight, trying to let the tone of Nimrod's voice slide past his nerves. "Confessing to the killing of Eli, you mean?"

"Of course. Apparently you had no faith that I would be exonerated. Says much for the all-powerful Triune Council, don't you think? You thought it was your place to save me. Willing to let anyone fall but me, the pride of your name. How very noble."

"And this makes you angry? You wanted your own mother to throw stones at your head? You should be grateful I was willing to take your place."

One side of Nimrod's lip curled up. "Did you really believe I would be stoned?"

"Noah would have seen to it. You know that."

"He would not have been allowed to toss a single pebble."

"Not allow-" Even as he started to ask, Ham understood. His grandson had followers. Men, loyal to him. Men willing to fight for him. Men who would do whatever it took to ensure Nimrod's safety if he asked them to. And he had asked them. How many? How large was his grandson's army? Ham swallowed the bile rising in his throat.

"You never assumed my innocence, did you, Grandfather? You never once asked me if I had actually committed that murder."

Ham stood erect and took a stance mirroring his grandson's. "You killed the dog. Cush never concerned himself with weapons. It wasn't his springbone, and it wasn't mine."

"It was mine. I knew the creature would be a problem later."

"Later? When you left the cave. You went back. The boy did see you, then. Why? Why did you go back to that property?"

Nimrod uncrossed his arms and put them on his hips. He began pacing, watching his feet as he moved. The tension in his muscles made his strength ripple beneath his sun drenched skin. Veins traversed the taut bulges, purple channels of life, engorged like a well fed serpent. They disappeared beneath a tunic made of pale linen.

Ham ran his eyes over the garment. Crimson stitching around the hemmed border hugged his shoulders and connected to intricate work around the neckline. It was not the work of anyone in their family. He guessed it was gift from someone, an expensive gift. The sandals on his feet, too, Ham noticed. The laces new, the leather unscarred, unsoiled.

"The same reason you did, apparently."

Nimrod stopped and locked his eyes in a cold stare. Ham caught his breath. "You wanted the gold."

Nimrod laughed. "Of course I wanted the gold. You taught me its worth, whether you ever meant to or not. You couldn't even say the word without drooling. And your little stash wasn't kept hidden for no reason, was it? There isn't much left, by the way. I've helped myself, enjoyed experimenting with it. Like you taught me. Thanks for the lessons, Grandfather."

Ham clenched his hands into fists, then made himself relax them again.

"I thought the boy's bucket of nuggets would be adequate for gilding the carved sun on my tower. Don't you think that would be spectacular?" Nimrod's voice held mocking tones.

Ham ignored the suggestion. "You fed the dog the springbone while I talked to Eli. You killed the dog so it wouldn't interfere when you went back for the bucket."

Nimrod raised his eyebrows. "Ahh, yes. The missing rocks. For some reason, I couldn't find them. Now I know why."

"Eli heard you. He got up and Iris killed him."

Nimrod held up a finger and wagged it back and forth. "Or Eli heard you. The boy saw you outside. The boy saw me outside. Eli heard you. Eli heard me. Who's to say? The man's death is not on my head alone."

Ham leaned back against the wall and ran his fingers over his head. It had surprised him that Eli's dog didn't bark and protest his presence. He brought rabbit bone to buy its silence but the animal was no where to be seen. He took the bucket, still sitting by the stream, and left without concern over the dog's whereabouts. It was dying somewhere, or already dead. As Nimrod planned.

"So where is it? You didn't put the new stash with the old. Where's the treasure you would let me die for rather than give up?"

The edge to his grandson's voice was sharpening. Ham felt his irritation rise as Nimrod tested his subordination. "It isn't yours to own, Nimrod. It isn't going to the tower."

His grandson nodded slowly and the arms resumed the position across his chest. "You weren't sure if it was me or you that was going to die today, were you?" Nimrod shook his head and laughed. "You were willing to confess to murder, but not to stealing. Killing a man is worthy of your name, but petty theft from a little boy? No, not by the son of the great Noah. You disgust me."

He would not be mocked by a grandchild. "Leave my house, Nimrod," he said.

Nimrod stepped toward him. "No. I don't think so, Grandfather. You owe me."

"Owe you?" Ham didn't move. His heart thumped powerfully in his chest as Nimrod moved again toward him. "Stand down, Son. Get out of here before you do something you regret."

Nimrod's lips smiled. His eyes did not. "Regret? Oh, I won't regret anything."

The blow landed on Ham's jaw and spun him against the wall. The crack sent piercing pain through his head and the briny taste of blood covered his lips. His own arms automatically turned to stone, weapons he would wield to defend himself and annihilate his foe. Except it wasn't a foe. It was his grandson. A man after his own spirit. A man of his own blood. Ham intentionally dropped his shoulders and put one hand gingerly to his jaw. Nimrod's anger was to be expected. Even so, the ferocity of the punch surprised him. His jaw was broken and-

The next blow bore the full impact of Nimrod's strength, the swing of his arm connecting with Ham's gut.

Ham dropped to his knees. A sour taste filled his mouth and his abdominal muscles clenched around searing jabs of fire. From the corner of his eye he saw Nimrod's foot lifting. Ham latched a hand around the other ankle and pulled him off balance. Both men lay on the floor heaving, their eyes never leaving one another.

"Where is it? Where's my gold, Grandfather?" Nimrod was rising again.

Ham tried to follow but his gut screamed in torment and he recoiled. It was just long enough for Nimrod to ram his foot against Ham's shoulder and send him crashing back against the cool stone. He tried to move again to clear Nimrod's foot. This time it smashed onto his throat. He was on his back, staring up his beloved grandson's shin into a face red with fury, but in full control. The hunter and his prey.

Ham forced himself to relax against the pressure. The aroma of new leather filled his nose as he sucked in air and tried not to swallow the blood and bile filling his mouth.

"Very well, son of Noah. Keep your gold. All I have to do is ask and there are countless men who will search the earth then throw it at my feet."

Nimrod stepped back and withdrew a dagger from its sheath. He smiled. "You tried to determine my outcome. I'll determine yours. I'm your council and I find you guilty of theft."

The blade connected with Ham's right wrist before he could roll away.

Chapter Forty-one

Ham arched his spine and yanked the belt from his waist. He rolled to his right side and put the fabric strip on the floor. With his left hand, he eased it under his right wrist then wrapped it around and around until the wound was secured in the linen bundle. His blood made a pool on the floor and it soaked into the bandage so that it was saturated already, new flow mixing with the blood already drained.

Returning to his back, Ham held the injured limb to his chest and waited for the throbbing to diminish. It didn't, so he dug his heels into the floor and pushed himself toward the door. Daggers of fire shot though his arm and abdomen. The exertion pushed more life preserving liquid from the wound so he collapsed his legs on the floor and propped the injured arm against a stool. He forced himself to remain still and to breathe. In. Out. In. Out. In. Out.

A cold sweat covered his brow. He had been willing to die for Nimrod. Not like this. The madness in Nimrod's expression burned in his mind. He could have ended Ham's life. He was in control. He didn't. The cut was not to Ham's throat.

Ham took inventory of his injuries: The jaw, broken. Not a threat to his life. The blow to his gut, severe. Men died from hard punches like the one he received. His muscles were strong enough to protect his insides from exploding, but only when they were tensed. Had he been ready for the blow, it would have bounced off his gut. He hadn't seen it coming. A mistake, the shock of the first punch still registering, he hadn't been ready for the second. The fact he was still alive, and thinking, was good. His insides still fought to preserve his life.

The slice on his wrist was the immediate concern. The cut wasn't clear through all the tissues, one side to the other. It was just deep enough to sever vessels and finger cords. His hand was attached, and alive, for now. He rolled his head to the side and examined his arm. The wound leaked steadily. Tiny rivulets streaked toward the floor from the saturated bandage. They would ease his life from his body unless someone came quickly.

Ham tried to get up. He needed to get to the door. As soon as he lifted his head a dark veil began descending over his vision. He put his head back down.

This was it, then.

What came next?

His father believed men went beyond the cloud-filled skies when their mortal life was complete, past the starry second heaven to the third heaven, where God himself dwelled. Not every man though. Just those who believed in the words of God, those who believed in God himself, and who strove to walk in the ways that the Creator ordained. Men like his grandfather Lamech, and great-grandfather Methuselah. Like Enoch and Abel, and Adam. Men whose grasp on the One God was stronger than his.

It wasn't that he doubted. He knew the truth and the power of the God who spoke to his father. There was no room to question the Omnipotence who lived without visual image, without audible words, without a tangible touch, yet lived among them all the same.

It was the walk where Ham faltered. He knew it. He had always chosen a slim line between defiance and obedience. His ways took preference over God's many times. It never mattered before. There was always time to apologize or to make a right wrong. There was always a buffer, someone to ease the tensions, repair his damage. He never seriously hurt anyone. His actions bore little weight beyond the pleasures or pain of the moment. He always knew it could be fixed later. He would do better later.

Now it was later, and there wasn't time to make it right.

He couldn't fix the mess he was in. Naomi would come home and find him dead.

Breathe. In. Out. In. Out.

He didn't wish that upon her. It wasn't suffering he would place on her shoulders. He had burdened her enough, unfairly. Now they would part on battle fields, ripe with hostility. Ham groaned and eased his hand into a different position, noting the blue cast to his fingertips.

He was wrong to be so angry about her nephilim blood. It wasn't her fault she had it. She should have told him but the sins of his children were not hers to carry. The sins of his children were their own.

And his. He pushed those notions from his head for long enough. Lying on the cold floor with his last remnants of life, Ham allowed himself to see with open eyes. It was time, time to draw his mistakes in and accept them as his own. His offspring chose a path of rebellion or compliance of their own accord. But he was their guide. His children and their children followed his example. His example. What had he taught them? Where had he led them?

Deceit. Greed. Pride.

Vengeance.

Ham closed his eyes and squeezed the tears out of the corners. He knew he deserved to die.

But not like this. Not now.

His strength had been an asset, his congeniality a tool to gain control. His power, his reason, his actions. Ham relied on himself. There was no helping himself now. He needed his God.

In. Out. In. Out.

The One God, the Creator, the God of Adam, and Noah. He alone was to be worshipped.

In. Out.

"Help me," he whispered.

▲

Her grandson was freshly bathed, his hair slicked with lavender oil and tied away from his face. His eyes danced with the peaceful rhythm of a contented soul. Naomi set another bowl of fruit in front of him. He smiled and helped himself to a large chunk of dried mango.

Freshening up again, that's where he'd been. Ham had disappeared, too, and she hoped the two were together, that they talked about the events of the day. The good and the bad. She hoped Ham made him realize that it was God they needed to honor, that the sacrifice couldn't occur as planned.

At some point, this would all be history and her family could press forward, keeping their God first. There were issues to contend with, of course. She scanned the crowd for her firstborn, wanting him to rejoice with his son. He was no where to be seen. He sat on the perimeter of the gathering for a while, his face flat, revealing nothing of his own turmoil. She knew he wouldn't remain with the jubilant crowd for long. He would retreat to his own home to sort his mind. Once Ham wasn't monitoring his firstborn any longer, Cush disappeared, too.

At least Nimrod was back to enjoy the gathering and take on the well-wishers. She wanted to find her own quiet space, but that wouldn't be for hours yet if the appetites of the men were any indication.

Noah was already asleep in a hammock, voices kept low to allow him to rest in the cool shadow of a terebinth tree. His exhaustion was palpable. None of his heirs murdered another, and for that, he slept with an easy heart. So would she, eventually.

All her kin would live to see another sunrise.

▲

"Where's Ham?" Denah asked her this time and Naomi responded the same way she had for the past hour. "I don't know." It was nothing really, for him to be absent, considering the tumult of the previous weeks. Still, this was his family and in sorrow or jubilation, he needed to be present. He understood that. He always sought refuge for brief moments when there were crowds. He never disappeared completely. Never for this length of time.

"I'm going to run home and see if he's there," she said. "He may be asleep on his own hammock. I won't be long."

As soon as she stepped away from the gathering, Naomi felt the need to run. It was a short distance to her home and she could see it standing as it always had. Nothing was amiss. Dread poured from her pores anyhow.

She looked in the barn as she passed. Eliamah and Samuel were gone.

The door to the house stood open and she hesitated before entering. "Ham?" she spoke into the still air, waiting for her vision to adjust to the change in light.

A low groan rose from the floor. It was Ham, and he was

covered in blood.

Chapter Forty-two

Naomi dropped beside her husband and gripped his shoulders, screaming his name. Ham winced, then his eyes fluttered open. She put her hands to his face then recoiled, her stomach knotting at the position of his jaw, offset and swollen. Dried blood coated his lips and streaked down his neck, merging on his tunic with blood from his arm. He forced his eyes to focus on her face, then they drifted closed again.

Her husband's skin was clammy and shivers followed one after another in an endless chain. He was breathing, for now. The blood loss was heavy and she knew he could slip away from her and never return. "No, God. No." she cried.

Gritting her teeth, she examined his arm. The fingers were faded blue in color and felt like cold stones from the river bottom. They were bent back at the base knuckles, then bent forward at the other joints, his hand positioned like a claw. Ham didn't flinch when she touched them or when she applied pressure to see if the color changed. It didn't. The tissues would be difficult to save.

The fabric around his wrist was drenched in blood. It hadn't been able to contain all of it, spilling liquid life down her husband's arm. The streaks were dry. Naomi placed the arm on Ham's chest, lowering it from the upright position to one that allowed more blood flow, then grabbed the kit of supplies she took when delivering babies and tending to the mothers. Her hands were shaking as she laid out a clean cloth and several basins of water with the tools.

When the bandage was removed, she could see the cut along his wrist. It was a sharp, clean cut, partially into the tissues beneath, not through the bones. She exhaled in relief. Any deeper and she would have had no choice. She would have to remove the hand to prevent the deadened tissues from sending poison through her husband's body, poison that would kill him slowly and with much agony. There was still a chance to save it.

With a steady rhythm she wiped the blood from the arm around the open, oozing gash. Ham lay still but his eyes came to life when she poured vinegar and salt into the area to cleanse it. "I'm sorry. I'm sorry," she said. "It has to be clean."

Ham nodded and pinched his eyes shut again.

The biggest vessel had not sealed itself so Naomi tied a tiny length of flax around the end. The finger cords were gone, drawn up into Ham's arm. She couldn't retrieve them without cutting him open further and he was in no shape to withstand the loss of more blood.

The hand tissues might live. The use of it was gone. Restoring finger control was beyond her ability. There was nothing she could do but pray for them to heal on their own or by the touch of God himself.

Naomi withdrew a bone needle from her supplies. In one swift motion she pierced Ham's intact skin above his wrist and threaded a length of flax through the opening. Ham groaned and his spine arched. Then he was quiet. He passed out. Naomi quickly inserted the needle again and again, sealing the wound closed with tiny even stitches.

When the skin was reunited, she laid his arm bedside his chest on the floor. She waited for the color to change. Ham groaned and shifted the arm as the deathly pallor was replaced by pale pink in his palm. Naomi placed a wooden dowel along the back of his arm, hand to elbow, and secured it with a fresh bandage. If the hand lived, it would freeze straight at the wrist rather than cocked awkwardly. If it lived.

If Ham lived.

Naomi wiped the sweat from her face and exhaled loudly. Ham opened his eyes again and stared into hers. "Thank you," he whispered, only it came out "Ang oo."

She squeezed his left hand into her chest. "Don't you leave me, Ham," she said. "Don't you leave me."

Ham turned his head side to side in small increments. "Un-uh," he said. "Arry. O' arry."

Sorry, so sorry, he was trying to say. Naomi wiped tears from her face before they fell onto his. "Hush," she said. "Rest."

Who did this to Ham? Naomi's mind reeled. Samuel was gone. Could he? No. Not he or Eliamah. Even if they knew about Ham stealing the rocks, it wasn't in their nature. Her mind flittered on the face of her firstborn. Cush? No. He wasn't a fighter, either. And he could never get the best of Ham.

Naomi's heart stopped. Nimrod.

Both he and Ham left the celebration.

There were few men who could pummel her husband, few who would even consider such action against the son of Noah. Only one could be so bold and yet walk away unscathed. Ham wouldn't be willing return blow for blow, not against Nimrod. He would die, with or without stoning, for the heir of his lineage. Naomi put her hands to her mouth. "Oh," was all she could say.

Ham's eyes were open and intense on hers. He groaned again and tried to roll to his side and sit but the effort was too great and he collapsed back to the floor. The youthful fire in his eyes dimmed. He looked old beyond his years. Perhaps she was wrong. Perhaps he fought back. And lost. Ham's breathing was sharp as he tried to inhale through his nose rather than his mouth. "Aff oo op im. Aff oo op im."

"Have to stop who? Who did this, Ham?" She didn't want to hear the name. She had to. No more covering for the sins that rose from the seed of their union.

Ham winced as he deliberately set his jaw to form the words. "Sacrifice. Stop Nimrod."

▲

Noah, Japheth, Shem and Canaan lifted the corners of the tarp and carried Ham to the soft stack of cushions. He fought off sleep, striving to speak his thoughts to them, trying to make them understand where his mind had traveled as he lay on the floor with no one but God to whisper in his ear. Death had not prevailed. Not yet anyhow. Eran and Denah were gone to town for the medicinal herbs that would fight the poisoned blood that was destined to come with the injuries he sustained. The words he needed to say had to be released while his mind could still form coherent thoughts.

Nimrod was gone, they said. He disappeared from the party shortly after Naomi left. Noah organized a search team and put Elam and Gomer in charge. They were simply to find him and bring him to Ham's house. They wouldn't. They wouldn't find him if he didn't want to be found. He was a hunter, his grandson. He knew how to become invisible in plain sight. The men wouldn't find Nimrod unless he chose to make his presence known.

But he would be at his tower later. That was no gamble.

"Why would he do this? I don't understand. Ham was prepared

to take his place at the stoning." Shem paced the floor with his hands pressed together palm to palm for a moment then both hands went to his neck. He reached for the comfort of the black stone but it wasn't there. It was around his throat at the Council meeting, he said. He didn't notice it was missing until he was awakened beneath a tree by Naomi's screams for help. It wasn't on the ground beneath him.

Ham had no doubt whose hands held the stone representing spiritual leadership of the men of earth. No doubt at all.

Naomi looked up from the tea remedy she was preparing and caught his eye. He knew the look. She sought permission to speak. To speak the truth. Ham tipped his chin enough to say yes. Too many lies for too long.

"Ham took the boy's rocks. It was gold. A bucket full of gold."

The room grew silent. Ham watched his father's expression deepen.

"I think Nimrod figured that out and blamed Ham for all the trouble." Naomi continued. She looked at him in question. He nodded again. "If Ham had confessed his theft when the accusations were first made against Nimrod, the blame for Eli's death would have fallen on him."

"I'm so sorry." Ham garbled the words several times until he was understood.

Shem walked over and knelt by Ham's side, his eyes on the right arm, now wrapped in clean linens. "Punishment for theft," he said. He was partially correct. The hand would have been cut off completely if Nimrod sought pure punishment for the crime. He didn't. The useless hand was worse than no hand. A stump could be used as a tool and fitted with a hook. A dead hand had no purpose.

A knife slashed vertically up his arm would've led to profuse blood loss in short order. Nimrod knew this. Ham would not have survived. Death wasn't his grandson's intention, either. He wanted to maim. He chose the injury, specifically. He knew how deep he wanted the cut and that's how deep he made it. The incision was calculated. His grandson, the great hunter. Some lessons he learned well.

Noah eased down beside him and dragged a cool towel over his forehead. A crisp curl of hair fell over his father's eye. It was white, turning so in the last month. Ham reached up and brushed it back, his palm resting briefly on his father's cheek as he looked in the man's eyes. There was no judgment. There was sorrow and the deepening creases that come with pain, but no contention welled up. For all the grievances, all the sin, all the unheeded advice, Noah always forgave his rebellious ways.

Ham stopped his father's arm with his left hand. "I'm sorry," he said. He wanted to say why he was sorry. For not listening. Not trying to follow a straight path in line with God's ways. For leading by example. Bad example. But he could not get the words to come out.

Noah placed his leathered finger across Ham's lips. "I know, Son," he said. "I know."

Chapter Forty-three

Orange flames flickered against the deepening indigo backdrop, the tower itself wearing the glow from torches lining the stairs and perimeters of each level. Nimrod's tower was outlined in fire, a stepped pyramid pointing to the heavens, to the God who saves. But the masses hovering over its surface weren't voicing praises to the Creator. They were shouting the name of Nimrod.

Noah groaned and put a hand over his heart as the sight unfolded before them. The entire town appeared to be assembled on or near the structure. Children were on the shoulders of their fathers. The infirm were carried on mats. Newborn babies were bundled and strapped against their mothers. No one wanted to miss the inauguration of the tower.

Shem and Japheth grabbed Noah's elbows to keep him from collapsing. "Where is he? Where's Nimrod?" he asked. His eyes didn't linger on the crowd in search of his great-grandson. They didn't travel up the tower either. They went immediately to the top.

Naomi swallowed hard and focused her gaze to the same location, the seventh level. Nimrod's ornate sacrificial altar wasn't yet complete. It wouldn't stop him. There were men up there, scurrying about, preparing a temporary one from brick and stone. Nimrod was there somewhere, she knew. This was his moment. He was on the pinnacle with no one above him.

Except God.

Chill bumps prickled down Naomi's arms. She shivered and wrapped them over her chest, protecting her heart. "No, God, no," she prayed.

"This can't happen," Noah said. "He means to honor himself with this sacrifice. He's leading the people to dishonor God."

"They need to hear you speak, Father," Japheth said. "The father of us all. You have to speak."

Noah nodded and immediately began weaving through the sea of his descendants, his two sons creating a path. Naomi followed closely behind them.

The crowd parted reluctantly. No one wanted to give up their position. Once they saw that it was Noah trying to access the tower, they stepped aside. Noah was followed with words of congratulations and excitement. They didn't know he was here to stop the celebration. They didn't know what Nimrod did to his grandfather. They didn't know the rebellion that dwelled in Nimrod's heart, disguised and kept dormant until it was time to strike.

They didn't know. Or did they?

A hand gripped her arm and Naomi turned to find Eran and Denah behind her, following the family toward the base of the steps. "Thank God you are here," Eran said. "We need to be one against this. We must stand together and not let God be angered against us."

A wall of men blocked the bottom step. "Let us pass," Japheth said.

The men glanced at one another, unmoving. Abed stepped to the front. "We were told not to allow you to step onto the holy temple."

Japheth drew in a sharp breath and his hands clenched into

fists. Noah put a gentle hand on his arm. "By whom?" he asked.

"Nimrod," Abed said. He looked down at his feet as he spoke. The other guards were shifting uncomfortably as well, the presence of their patriarch putting a waver in their resolve.

Noah smiled. "And does he have a voice higher than my own?"

Abed pinched his lips together and looked again to the others. They avoided his gaze. He looked back at Noah and shook his head. "No, Father Noah. He does not."

Noah took another step. Abed didn't move aside. He hesitated. Naomi's stomach churned. Standing face to face with God's chosen, the guard wavered in his loyalty. Noah's light among his descendants dimmed visibly in the shadow of their new, self-proclaimed leader.

Noah placed a hand on Abed's arm. He didn't speak, allowing his eyes to carry words to the man's heart. The guard nodded and moved out of his way.

Once Noah started up the tower, he didn't look back. He kept a steady rhythm, climbing toward his great-grandson. Naomi's heart pounded as they ascended. It was supposed to be her God at the top, waiting for them to fall before him in honor and repentance, praise and worship.

It would not be God. It would be Nimrod. She didn't know where God would be.

Or what God would do.

Noah breathed hard at the top of the tower. All of them did, and their clothes stuck to their wet bodies from the pace. Naomi pushed strands of hair off her forehead and waited for her father-in-law to catch his wind and speak. He would stand on the steps and appeal to the crowds below with the fervor of his God. Before the flood, before the first gopher tree was leveled and planed into timbers, before the first nail was driven into the hull of the dry land vessel, Noah preached righteousness. He would do so again. He would draw them back from the cliff.

But Noah didn't turn around to face the masses.

He stood still, facing the altar, waiting.

Nimrod emerged from the shadows. A fine linen drape fell from his waist to his ankles. It was deep grape in color, richly embroidered around the hem and waist band. It was not the garment of a hunter. It was not a garment prepared in haste. His bare chest was shaved and oiled, his skin reflecting the fire light. Around his neck was a thick gold chain with one black stone. The Blood of Adam.

Nimrod was claiming leadership.

Naomi shuddered at the truth before her. Nimrod had been planning his rise to leadership for a long time. And he had not been alone in his efforts. Semiras followed behind her husband, dressed in extravagance as he was, in purples that draped along her curves and billowed in the light breeze. Her hair was braided and coiled with beads and both wrists were ringed with bracelets. Gold bracelets.

All the men on the seventh tier, several dozen of them, had a drape of linen around their waists, falling to their knees beneath new leather belts. Belts holding weapons. Naomi grabbed Eran's hand. Many of the men were of Shem's kin.

Naomi shook away the black spots fogging her vision, threatening to claim the moment and take her to a dark hollow of unawareness. She made herself focus on filling her lungs with air, then letting it go slowly, slower than the pounding rhythm in her chest.

"Well, there they are. My family, come to celebrate my exoneration." Nimrod lifted his hand at the men, permitting their attention to return to the completion of the altar.

"Son," Noah said. "It is only God we honor with the sacrifices. You must stop."

Nimrod crossed gold covered arms over his chest and laughed. "You have had your reign. The people are eager for a new start. They want me. And I shall do as I please."

"Nimrod, do not anger God."

"I will unite all people. No power will prevail against us when we stand as one. Your God can only look on and see that we don't need him anymore. We are strong without him."

'Your God,' Nimrod said. Not 'my God.' Naomi ran to her grandson and fell at his feet, hugging his legs. They smelled of fragrant oils. "He is your God, Nimrod. He saved you from death."

Nimrod leaned over and lifted her up by the arms. He brushed a tear from her cheek. "No, Grandmother. It was you who saved me. Now it's my turn. I'll save our people. I'll lead them honorably. We'll never fear the God of vengeance again. In our strength, he will become weak. You won't quake at the storm clouds any longer."

Nimrod's handsome face smiled at her and he took her hands in his. His right knuckles were puffy and discolored. Naomi pushed away from him. "You nearly killed your grandfather."

"He nearly killed me." Nimrod's expression turned cold. "It's time for my fathers and grandfathers to step aside. Let the past be done with."

Japheth and Shem bolted toward Nimrod. Six men stopped them, their knives drawn. Noah was surrounded by four others.

Nimrod walked to the edge of the tier and looked down over the people in the dappled firelight. When he raised his arms over his head they cheered and the 'Nimrod' chant began again. Nimrod basked in the glory.

"Men of earth," he said in a loud voice that brought an immediate hush. "Tonight we celebrate!" The din rose from the ground and swirled around her. With a nod of his head, Nimrod sent the order to light the altar. The piles of kindling and wood took rapidly and the crackle blended with a woodsy scent with an almost lemon-like overtone. It took a moment for Naomi to identify the frankincense burning among the wooden pieces. The dried resin filled the ark once, after it had been desecrated for idol worship. In one voice, Noah, Shem, Japheth, Eran, Denah and Naomi screamed. "NO!"

Nimrod laughed, the echo from a hard heart penetrating the air. He took his place on a platform near the burning altar. There was no beast nearby for the sacrifice.

Then she heard the whimper of a baby.

A human baby.

Denah and Eran heard it as she did and the three clutched one another. A man stepped from the shadows with a small wrapped bundle. Naomi gasped. She recognized the young father. He stopped in front of her, holding the tiny girl that Naomi delivered from the womb of his wife, the twin of his first born son. The infant was wrapped in the same fine purple swaddling that covered Nimrod.

The man scowled. "She was allowed to live. When she was spared, Nimrod was cursed." Naomi grabbed at the baby but was pushed back with a knife to her throat.

The father took the baby to Nimrod, who lifted her in his arms gently, like the moment he was handed his own firstborn. He looked in the infant's face as he cradled the bundle against his chest, his thumb stroking the pink puff of cheek. He was the image of a father with new born child. Until he raised his eyes. There was no love for this innocent one in the black expression.

"NO!" Naomi screamed again and fell to her knees.

Nimrod ignored the desperation grasping for his compassion.

The stench of incense swirled around her. Nimrod was the presentation of what they had done right on the new earth. Wasn't he? He was good. He was honorable. He was their future.

It was all a mask. Her beloved grandson, child of her child, was drenched in evil. Pride sprang from his dark eye sockets and pierced into the heavens. He stared God in the face. He did not cower.

The baby was lifted to the heavens on Nimrod's hands. The crowd started to cheer, then a blanket of silence swallowed the noise.

Only one sound rose from the tower toward God.

One voice of innocence called for deliverance.

The baby's cries pierced the heavens.

Naomi scanned the faces of the men on the platform and read the surprise, then the horror, as they finally realized what was about to occur. But no one moved. No one tried to stop Nimrod.

She collapsed to her face.

That's when she felt the first tremor.

Chapter Forty-four

Shem clamped Naomi's arm in his hand and pulled her to her feet. "We have to leave," he said. "Now."

None of the men holding them at knife point seemed aware that the platform beneath their feet had moved. They had their eyes transfixed on Nimrod and the crying baby. Shem had urgency in his voice as he turned to Noah, Japheth, Denah and Eran in turn. "Go," he said. "Get down. We have to get off this tower."

The next tremor was accompanied by a low rumble that stirred from the belly of the tower itself. It vibrated through Naomi's feet and crawled up her spine. She dug her fingertips into Shem's arm. Nimrod's men looked at one another and though their weapons were still drawn, none of them stopped Noah and the others from turning toward the steps.

Nimrod raised his voice and began the words of a sacrifice. Naomi froze despite the blood boiling in her gut. She could not leave yet. She spun around and ran to the base of the platform where Nimrod stood and grabbed his ankles. "Give her to me!"

Her grandson stopped mid-sentence. He scowled at her, then at his men, who stood unmoving, as if their legs were planted in place. He tried to shake Naomi's hand from his ankle as the next vibration shot through the tower. Nimrod was caught off guard. He lost his balance, freeing his arms to break his fall. Naomi tipped against the platform and reached for the falling bundle but Japheth's arms got there first. He tucked the babe to his chest while Shem hauled her back to her feet and pushed her to the steps.

The guards remained where they were.

Denah and Eran flanked Noah on the descent, each supporting one side to help him move more quickly than his old knees wanted to go. The guards allowed them to pass through. Men and women on the steps did the same. The expressions were confused. They came for a great sacrifice, a magnificent celebration. Only there was no beast, just a baby, and it was being hauled away. Questioning eyes and Nimrod's vehement shouts were the only things following Naomi and the others as they made their way down, down, down, away from the altar.

She heard the next grumble from the tower's belly before she felt the edge of step beneath her foot crumble to bits and cascade down the slope in front of her. She scrambled for footing, bracing herself for a mass exodus from the tower.

Still, no one moved. Men and women stood to either side of the steps, the path to safety left clear. What was wrong with them? Someone caught her sleeve and pulled her to a halt. It was Mara, Abed's wife, asking her something. There was confusion in the tone of her voice but her words were garbled.

"Keep moving!" Shem pulled her from the other arm.

Naomi shook Mara off and continued her descent. Why weren't the people frightened? Why weren't they leaving? Couldn't they feel the tower quiver?

Noah's knees gave out as they neared the bottom. He collapsed back onto the stone and was unable to rise. Japheth thrust the child into her arms and picked his father up in his arms, carrying him down the final length. As soon as his feet left the bottom step and struck the earth, a rumble descended from the heavens. It combined with screeching bricks, groaning stones, in an angry roar.

The people screamed as God lifted the veil protecting his chosen one, Noah. Now they felt. And heard. And understood. The air was suddenly a cacophony of fear.

Naomi pushed through the crowd, forcing her way to the outskirts. Her chest heaved as she collapsed on the ground beside Eran and Denah, comforting the baby as best she could amid the chaos.

Those on the tower were now in a mad rush to descend. It was visible, the shaking of the tower upon its base, and with each motion men and women were tossed off balance and crashed against the people in front of them, tumbling down the tiers. It was if the tower couldn't rid itself of them fast enough, shaking itself to free the vermin crawling on its skin.

Dust puffed in clouds, blending with the smoke of torches that fell and were extinguished against bricks. Bricks that were disintegrating. As people emerged from the haze and stepped free of the structure, they ran in the opposite direction. Naomi scanned the fleeing faces for Nimrod as they darted this way and that, but could not find him among them. "Forgive him, O' God!" she cried. "And save him. Please save him."

The hand of God shook the tower until the last of mankind ran from its presence. Then it stopped. The air grew calm. Too calm. It was an unnatural stillness. The stillness of the earth before the sky turned black for the first time. Before the earth itself heaved and broke apart.

Before God sent his judgment.

The hair on Naomi's neck stood up and her heart beat furiously, wanting to flee the confines of her chest and escape the wrath to come. Noah put his hands over his face and began to weep.

Japheth wrapped his arm around Denah on one side and Naomi on the other. He called out to God, his voice blending with Shem's. They cried for mercy. They felt the air, too. God's hand was not yet finished.

Naomi cradled the tiny girl in her arms, and waited. Her heart ached for Ham.

What would God do? He would not send flood waters again. But the consuming fire? First man Adam was warned of destruction to come, destruction by the flames of the Almighty. Was it to be now?

The air around her began to vibrate with an unseen tension. Naomi rocked back and forth with the bundle secured to her chest. Her eyes were drawn back to the tower. It hummed.

The top level quivered first, then collapsed on itself. The sixth level followed. Then the fifth. One by one the tower levels crumbled as if built from flour by the hands of a child. Dust plumed toward the sky.

Naomi wrapped her garment over the baby to shield her and tucked her own face into Japheth's shoulder. It should have been loud. A falling tower of stone and brick should crash and rumble and cause the ground to reverberate.

It didn't. There was only a repeated whoosh as the formidable elements turned to powder and fell in a heap.

▲

Nimrod's tower was gone.

"God has judged." Her father-in-law's voice was solemn, and was the only voice to be heard. The silence around them was heavy, settling into the ground like the dust, yet she knew God had not destroyed mankind again. They were there, in the shadows, in the homes and shops, watching. Waiting. And calling out to their God? She hoped it was so. Mercy needed to rain down upon them all.

Naomi rose to her feet and walked to the mound where the great tower stood in its defiance, only to be leveled into a pile of bits, and blown away with the breeze. Not even a piece the size of a robin's egg remained. No rubble or remnants. Just dust.

From nearby she heard the footsteps of someone running towards her. Nimrod. Her heart wrenched at the sight of him and she instinctively wrapped the babe in her arms, closer to her heart.

She was right, that he wasn't a killer. At first. He didn't murder the man Eli. But he would murder the child in her arms. And he would claim the praises to God for himself.

Nimrod fell to his knees at the site of his tower. He raised his arms over his head and screamed. Not the cries of a man full of remorse, seeking the mercies of his God. His was an angry lament. Nimrod was angry with God.

She loved this boy. He played at her feet and grew to manhood under her eye. Inquisitive, demanding of wisdom and knowledge. God favored him with a keen mind and a strong body. He had intuition and charm. Nimrod could have been a great leader. He should have been a great leader.

The blood coursing through his veins was the same as hers, and every child of Adam. Full of blackness. But choices could be made, choices to do right in the eyes of God. Nimrod chose himself instead.

She despised what Nimrod had allowed himself to become. She could only stand and stare at him, covered in the dust of his creation. God had not destroyed him, again, and he showed no gratitude. Before Nimrod's eyes, God revealed himself as judge, and the boy spat in his face. If the ark was standing beneath the clear blue expanse of sky today, Nimrod would be among the mockers. He wouldn't believe the words of Noah. God would lift the mighty door and seal her inside, leaving Nimrod outside as the rains fell from the sky.

Her grandson pulled himself to his feet and stumbled toward her. His elegant garment was torn, his face streaked with tears. His eyes had the burn of one who was wronged, one who wouldn't be humbled and even as a dead man, would seek revenge if he could. He gestured fiercely as he spoke, the tone hard, not defeated.

But Naomi couldn't understand a word of what he said.

▲

Ham tried to sit but the fog in his head was too thick and he was forced to lie still again. The black swirling ceased after a minute and he was able to open his eyes. His gut was broiling and he had to fight not to gag. Not that there was anything left to bring up. He didn't want the force on his jaw. It would knock him out cold again, and he wanted time to think clearly.

It was dark in the house. And quiet. His groans didn't alert anyone, didn't send Naomi or one of his daughters to his side. He was alone, and the realization made his temples throb. Had they left him? No. No, they went to the tower. To stop Nimrod. Some of them anyway. Most went to worship him.

Ham put a hand to his face and felt the wrap crossing over his head and lifting his chin into position. He didn't remember it being secured. Another bandage bound his right arm against his chest. Peeling back the end, he could see his fingers. He couldn't feel them. He couldn't move them. He squelched another wave of nausea, his guilt riding the torrents. How could he provide for his family now? How could he face them? Or anyone. He was supposed to be a leader, and he led them into sin. He deserved what happened to him.

He deserved worse. "God of the heavens, is there any forgiveness left for me?"

▲

The insistent chirp of a cricket brought consciousness back into Ham's grasp. Still no one home. He forced himself into sitting, bathed in the light of the full moon streaming through the window. How long had the family been gone? Was it so difficult to put an end to the sacrifice?

His grandson's calm assurance of survival burned on Ham's mind. He had protection. He had followers already, men in place willing to prevent his judgment, eager to elevate him. What else were they willing to do? Would Nimrod hold his grandmother and the others against their will? He looked at his arm. Or worse? Would-

The door burst open and slammed against the wall. Ham startled then winced as the pains from the motion shot through his body. It was Cush. Ham felt his heart quicken. He tensed and could do nothing about the daggers ripping through his flesh. His firstborn recoiled, his eyes growing wide when they landed on Ham.

So, he didn't know. Cush didn't know what his son had done.

His firstborn choked back a sob when their eyes met. He looked Ham up and down then collapsed on the floor by his knees. Ham laid a gentle hand on Cush's head. His boy was due an apology. For the years of neglect. The years of indifference. The years of resentment. Cush's sins were his own, but Ham had done little to guide his steps. Perhaps they could start again. Perhaps they could form a relationship. They could end their years as more than father and son. They could be friends.

"My Son," he tried to say. "Forgive me."

Cush lifted his head and looked at Ham. His eyebrows were

raised in question.

Ham put his hand on his jaw to steady it, to form the words more clearly. "Forgive me," he said again.

Cush cocked his head and spoke.

It was Ham's turn to misunderstand. His son's words were fast and garbled. They rose in tone at the end like he asked a question. "I didn't understand," Ham said. He shook his head back and forth to clarify his own distorted words.

Cush spoke again. Ham couldn't identify one word in the line of peculiar sounds. He shook his head, his eyes not veering from his son's.

His firstborn drew in a deep breath, then spoke. Another string of nonsense. Then another.

Ham didn't respond. He pressed his eyes closed for a moment, then opened them again, as if it would clear his mind.

Cush spoke three words, slowly, loudly, distinctly.

Ham didn't know what any of them meant.

Cush rose to his feet abruptly and stared down at him, his hands covering his lips. He stepped back as tears formed in his eyes. Or he was pushed by fear.

He wanted to comfort his son. Assure him that all would be well. The words he managed to spit out flew beyond Cush's understanding. His boy let tears run freely down his cheeks, whispering more of the odd sounds, more to himself, or the air, or the floor.

Ham smacked the wall, jolting his senses with a new rush of agony. Was he so confused he couldn't interpret his son's words? Men hit in the head became confused easily. They lost their senses. Only he wasn't hit in the head. He was dizzy. He was weak. He was in pain and nauseated. He was not confused. What-

A wave of judgment washed through his pores. Ham gripped

the edge of the bed and groaned as a shroud of sorrow descended over him. He knew then. He knew what was wrong. He had been found guilty. The hand of God had moved, separating him from his firstborn.

Ham patted the bed beside him and motioned for his boy to sit. With his left arm, he gathered Cush against his chest and held him there, allowing his son's tears to saturate his clothing. For once, there was understanding. Sobs wrenched his jaw but he could not stop the torrent.

Chapter Forty-five

It was more than dust rising from the streets of Shinar. It was frustration.

Impatience.

Confusion.

As people emerged from hiding, their voices grew louder. Hand gestures were animated and tones were less than cordial. Naomi could hear it now. The strange words, the unknown sounds shooting from the lips of mothers to their children. The children replying with their own garbled noise. Sisters not understanding sisters. Brothers confused at the words of brothers.

God did not twist the tongue of Nimrod alone.

Naomi held the baby into her chest and ran back to her in-laws. She pushed to get through the ring of people surrounding them. Noah stood on a rock in the center, reaching for the heavens with both arms, and eyes, his heart and his soul rising above the barrage of words spoken in fear and distress. Denah and Eran, Shem and Japheth huddled protectively around him. Could they understand each other? Could Noah decipher their words?

A weeping woman grabbed her arm and hurled a mournful cry in her face. She was pleading, desperate. Naomi shook her head. "I don't understand you. I'm sorry. I don't understand." The woman screeched her words again, as if it were the volume that mattered.

Japheth parted the innermost rows of people and pulled her inside. He gripped her shoulders and looked intently into her eyes. "Can you understand me, Naomi?" His voice held the same desperation as the woman's.

"Yes! Yes. I understand." Noah, Eran, Denah and Shem sighed collectively. "All of us then? We all understand each other?"

Shem nodded, pushing a frantic man away from Noah. "Yes. God has sheltered us from this judgment. He has shown mercy. Again."

A familiar face appeared above the throng. Naomi turned and embraced her youngest son as he roughly pushed his way into her arms, his cheek pressing into the top of her head. Canaan held her tightly, breathing deeply. His heart thumped rapidly. When he pulled back, he tenderly took her face in hands. There was fear in his eyes. He spoke softly, his eyes locked into hers.

Naomi's storehouse of tears burst open. His words were meaningless.

▲

The stab of fire in his gut didn't diminish so Ham stopped trying to stand. He leaned back against the wall and wrapped his left arm over his abdomen, waiting for the intensity to subside. He was alone again. Alone in the big house that once held his brood. There were days he would have done anything to escape the noise and the fuss of meeting needs not his own. Now he couldn't stand the silence.

Cush left in a torrent of words beyond his comprehension. It occurred to Ham then that he didn't know which of their ears God's hand had scrambled. Was Cush marked like Cain, with an unalterable mark that forever labeled his guilt? Would he run to his wife for comfort and not understand her words, either?

Or was he the one, forever stained?

It had to be him. He was the father of Cush, the mentor of Nimrod. They followed his lead, listened to his words. God made certain he could do so no more. He was the one who would seek his wife for comfort and find only garbled sounds. And coldness. How could she love a man she could not understand? A man with a useless right arm? A man who grieved his God and by all right should have been struck down dead?

He was alone.

He would always be alone, even in a home full of family. "God, my Savior, forgive me," his heart cried.

▲

The lump on the bed raised and lowered to the sound of ragged breathing. Naomi collapsed against the door frame. Ham was alive. She didn't know as she ran if that would be the case. He could die from the blow to his belly. He could die at the hand of God.

The rebellion generated among her kin wasn't her husband's alone to claim. She prayed as she ran further and further from the dusty tower that God would take them both or spare them both. He did. Only by God's mercy, both still breathed.

Ham opened his eyes. They were red rimmed and his cheek was swollen and deformed despite the bandaging. He didn't attempt to speak.

Naomi sat down beside him and took his hand. Her own breathing was harsh and frantic. How could she even begin to explain? "The tower. It's gone," she said. "And-"

Ham's eyes grew wide.

Naomi couldn't stifle the moan that rose from her heart. He didn't understand. She buried her face in his shoulder.

His arm pulled her in tightly against his chest. "Omi."

Garbled.

"A-omi."

Naomi lifted her eyes to Ham's face. It sounded like her name. "Can you understand me?" she whispered.

Ham nodded.

Naomi fell to her knees and lifted her face to heaven. "Mighty God. How much mercy can you pour out on me? How deep must your forgiveness dwell?"

Chapter Forty-six

The stream was no more than ankle deep and she could jump clear over it with a running start. Naomi stepped onto the rock where Mara and Abed's boy stood with his arsenal of pebbles, mesmerized by the dragon standing in the shadows of the opposite shore. The rock was surrounded by dry land now. The tributaries off the mighty Euphrates always began a gradual slowing as summer progressed. This was different. The river itself turned its course, easing away from the city on the plain of Shinar and taking the life giving flow with it.

In the year since the tower disintegrated, the city itself showed signs of decay. As the water disappeared, so did bands of people. Family groups understanding the strange sounds of one another packed up their belongings and dispersed, following paths that they themselves created. In some, fathers and sons remained united. In others, children and parents were separated. Wives were moving in opposite directions from their sisters, grandparents saying farewell to grandchildren for the last time. Where words were not understood, the language of tears intervened.

Nimrod held fast, yet separated himself beyond the bounds of language. He wouldn't depart from the place of his birth, and he wouldn't acknowledge the family who gave him life. He disowned his grandparents, his uncles, and even Noah himself now fell beneath Nimrod's feet. Those who worshipped the One God were his downfall, in his eyes.

He wasn't alone, however. There were men still clinging to his torn majesty, learning to understand his words. Loyalty sprang from Shem's kin for the most part, men refusing to pull their roots from familiar soil. Under Nimrod's direction, new bricks were again stacking up in open fields and homes were rising along the river's new course.

The old city, called Shinar for the plain in which it dwelled, had never been officially named. It was now. Babylon. The City of Confusion. Nimrod would rebuild it, she was sure. And he wouldn't rest until it was his to rule.

"Fill the earth," God told them as they knelt beneath the rainbow. 'Fill it', not settle in one place and gradually add territory. The birds and beasts obeyed, multiplying and dispersing as their Creator commanded. Those in the image of God had not obeyed. Now their sons spoke different tongues, and they followed the beasts to new lands.

Their desire to be strong in unity was disrupted with the sweeping breath of God.

He was to be their strength. Their hope was to be in him, not in man.

Naomi hopped off the stone into the warm trickle and tipped her jar sideways to catch the water. Their own well was dry and Ham had no way to dig a new one. She would take him to his father's home soon, to live. They had no reason to remain in the city. Other than Nimrod, her sons and daughters, grandchildren and great-grandchildren, were all gone. Seeking the riches of the earth beyond the plain, beyond the sea of sand, beyond the reach of the Tigris and Euphrates, they would live in caves and tents, traveling until they found the place to call home. They would be safe, if they listened, if they followed God's lead.

Naomi was anxious to leave, to live among those who understood her words and worshipped her God. It would be like the early days, the Eight in one place. Japheth and Denah had been beneath the roof of Noah and Jael several months now. Most of their children were gone as well, only small pockets remaining around Shinar. It wouldn't be long until they would break Denah's heart and following the trail of the ones before.

By God's mercy, she wouldn't have to live without the laughter of children, without the gift of new life birthed among them. Shem's third born, Arphaxad, kept the mother tongue. Three of Arphaxad's children did as well, with all their wives and children. Eber's son was born the day the tower fell, giving Shem a great-great-grandchild. Peleg, he was called, Division, for on the day of his birth the generations of Noah became many peoples. Even in God's wrath, he sent them hope, secured in a bundle of swaddling cloths.

A young woman stepped into the stream beside Naomi, carrying the baby girl spared from Nimrod's flames. The baby's aunt had been crying, her face red and streaked with tear stains. She held the golden haired child to her chest, kissing the rose colored cheeks. Her words were tender and loving, but not of a language Naomi understood.

The young woman waited for Naomi to set her pot aside, then placed the baby in her arms. She stepped back, wrapping her arms around her waist.

Naomi gathered the sleeping child into her heart, grateful to see this precious life once more before the family moved away. They were packed already, heading north, towards the mountains and the lands beyond the rocky peaks, the bitterness of the elements, the harshness of the terrain not deterring their resolve.

With a kiss of farewell she held the baby out for the aunt.

The woman shook her head. Tears resumed a course down her pale cheeks.

Naomi looked at her in question.

The woman took another step back, arms still around herself, not the child she adored.

Naomi swallowed against the lump in her throat and nodded, hugging the child in close again, her own tears overflowing. The baby was hers now. The aunt would leave her in safety rather than take her on the dangerous journey. Her actions spoke words of devotion beyond any words they may have shared.

The woman turned and fled without looking back.

"God, protect her," Naomi prayed. "Protect us."

▲

Ham leaned against a tree stump on the edge of Noah's vineyard. Naomi listened as he practiced the words of the sacrifice with Shem. His jaw still moved at an awkward angle and Ham wouldn't admit it, but she could read the grinding pain in his expression. His right arm lay on his lap, the clawed hand stiff, frozen in place. Always clever, he had developed various tools to fit into it, to make what use of it he could. Among them were garden implements, and beyond her wildest expectations, cooking tools. With Cush gone, he took it upon himself to master cooking skills and it showed in the girth around his midsection.

She couldn't help but smile. His battered body held a new heart. A heart that finally grasped the nature of the God he served and wanted obedience above all else. No more would he overlook the bones of rebellion emerging from the men of earth. Neither would she. They would be broken and buried beneath the eyes of heaven.

The seeds were planted, however. The children of Noah were now seventy-some peoples, all with sin sewn among them. As they moved towards the ends of the earth, the rebellion would take root when the soil was fertile. She could only pray the generations of Noah remembered their God and put him above all else, destroying their sins along the way.

Obedience was the path of hope, one she would walk with Ham, side by side, hand in hand. In the storms of judgment, the trials of living, they would trust in God's mercy. Again. And again. And again.

Naomi made her way to her husband's side. He smelled like wood shavings, reminiscent of a time long before, when he planed wood for the ark. They lived by faith, then, believing that what God promised would come true. They lived by faith now, day by day, moment by moment.

Ham leaned over and kissed the top of her head, pouring his love over her. "For always," he said.

Thunder rumbled in the dark clouds filling the heavens above them. Ham wrapped her in his protective arms. Naomi smiled as she snuggled against him. What was a little rain? Her God held the door to the storehouse of hail, and the key to the storehouse of grace. Mercy was hers for the asking.

For always.

Rachel S. Neal - 334

A Note from the Author

There are so many fascinating concepts in this book that I'd love to explain: Linguistics and the formation of nations, the beginnings of the Ice Age, the reality of dragons, even the concept of cavemen. I'd need another 300 pages to cover it all. Since that isn't practical, I'll do my best to include these topics on my blog site, gracebythegallon.com. AnswersinGenesis.org is a great source for information regarding these topics, and many others.

As in Blood of Adam, I used the Bible as my primary resource for facts, but otherwise took creative liberty with the family of Noah. The eight survivors of the flood were human with all the faults and failures we have today. They found discipline when they strayed from God's commands, but grace was there waiting, willing to forgive. It is the same for us today. Through Jesus, our rebellious bones can be buried forever.

I hope this novel sparks a flame of curiosity in your soul, one that needs to research and understand the Bible and the history recorded for us there. I pray you find your own gateway to God always open.

Thank you for reading this novel.

About the Author

Rachel S. Neal lives under the Big Sky of Missoula, Montana with her husband, cat and as many daylilies as she can fit into her garden. She believes in the accuracy of God's Word and writes to share those truths in fictional format. When her hands aren't typing, they are transforming discarded remnants into her version of art. You can find out more and visit her at gracebythegallon.com.

32660550R00217

Made in the USA
Middletown, DE
12 June 2016